Praise for *Bitter River*

"Julia Keller is a beautiful writer and *Bitter River* has an elegiac force to it that is powerful and gripping. Bell Elkins is one of the most fully realized characters in fiction today." —Michael Connelly

"Once again, Keller combines masterful storytelling, a vivid sense of place—the beauty and poverty of Appalachia—a complex cast of characters, and a suspenseful, superbly executed plot that displays a depth rarely seen in mystery fiction." —*Booklist* (starred review)

"A literate, gritty, character-driven tale with another surprise ending." —*Kirkus Reviews* (starred review)

"Outstanding . . . the eerie setting of a dying West Virginia town and its struggling inhabitants lends a haunting air to the story." —*RT Book Reviews* (4 ½ stars)

"Julia Keller's lyrical and evocative prose propels the novel until all you can do is hang on until the final page. Her sense of place is spot-on and bittersweet." —C. J. Box

Praise for *A Killing in the Hills*

"*A Killing in the Hills* is a remarkably written and remarkably tense debut. I loved it." —Dennis Lehane

"A gripping, beautifully crafted murder mystery that shows that small-town West Virginia is no longer Mayberry. Great reading." —Scott Turow

"Be careful opening this book because once you do you won't be able to close it. Instead, clear the weekend, silence the phone, and settle into Acker's Gap, a place as fascinating and fraught with violence and beauty as Daniel Woodrell's Ozarks or William Gay's Tennessee. A killer novel."   —Tom Franklin

"Julia Keller is that rare talent who combines gripping suspense, a fabulous sense of place, and nuanced characters you can't wait to come back to. A must-read."   —Karin Slaughter

"A terrific debut—atmospheric, suspenseful, assured. I hope there's more to come in the story of Bell Elkins and Acker's Gap."
                                                            —Laura Lippman

"A twisty plot—and a soulful depiction of a beautiful, besieged 'afterthought of a town'—propels this debut mystery."
                                                            —*People* magazine

"Outstanding . . . Keller does a superb job showing both the natural beauty of Appalachia and the hopeless anger of the people trapped there in poverty . . . Unforgettable."
                          —*Publishers Weekly* (starred review, Pick of the Week)

"A page-turner with substance and depth, this is as suspenseful and entertaining as it is accomplished."   —*Booklist* (starred review)

"A fictional debut for a Pulitzer Prize–winning journalist, born and raised in West Virginia, whose love for the state, filled with natural beauty and deep poverty, pervades a mystery that has plenty of twists and turns and a shocking conclusion."
                                          —*Kirkus Reviews* (starred review)

"A superbly detailed and suspense-drenched mystery."
                          —*Library Journal* (starred review, Debut of the Month)

Also by Julia Keller

A Killing in the Hills

BITTER RIVER

JULIA KELLER

MINOTAUR BOOKS ⚘ NEW YORK

BITTER RIVER. Copyright © 2013 by Julia Keller. All rights reserved. Printed in the United States of America. For information address St. Martin's Press, 175 Fifth Avenue, New York, N.Y. 10010.

www.minotaurbooks.com

The Library of Congress has cataloged the hardcover edition as follows:

Keller, Julia.
   Bitter River / Julia Keller. — First Edition.
      p. cm.
   ISBN 978-1-250-00349-2 (hardcover)
   ISBN 978-1-250-02245-5 (e-book)
   1. Murder—Fiction. 2. Teenage girls—Fiction. 3. West Virginia—Fiction. I. Title.
   PS3611.E4245B58 2013
   813'.6—dc23

                                                              2013013927

ISBN 978-1-250-04896-7 (trade paperback)

Minotaur books may be purchased for educational, business, or promotional use. For information on bulk purchases, please contact Macmillan Corporate and Premium Sales Department at 1-800-221-7945, extension 5442, or write specialmarkets@macmillan.com.

10   9   8   7   6

To the ghosts of home

Acknowledgments

It is a great pleasure to thank Lisa Gallagher, whose wisdom and acumen—and friendship and unflagging good cheer—have been fundamental. And I am indebted, once again, to Susan Phillips. Dr. Holly Bryant kindly provided salient medical details. The music of Kathy Mattea and the poetry of the late Irene McKinney continue to be inspiring and revelatory.

Thanks are due as well to Kelley Ragland and Andy Martin at Minotaur, and at Headline, to Imogen Taylor and Vicki Mellor.

To my fellow West Virginian Ruth Ann Hendrickson, who shares my complicated love for a complicated place, I will be forever grateful, just as I am for the efforts of two professors at Marshall University who took an unruly Appalachian girl and taught her how very much books and ideas matter: Leonard Deutsch and the late Warren Wooden.

There is nothing in the world, neither man nor Devil nor any thing, that I hold as suspect as love, for it penetrates the soul more than any other thing. Nothing exists that so fills and binds the heart as love does. Therefore, unless you have those weapons that subdue it, the soul plunges through love into an immense abyss.

—Umberto Eco, *The Name of the Rose*

PART ONE

Chapter One

Three people stood on the south bank of the Bitter River. Two of them, a petite woman and a stocky man, had stationed themselves near the water but the third, an older and even bigger man in a long black overcoat and a brown flat-brimmed sheriff's hat, was positioned halfway up the steep slope, a spot that granted him a more generous perspective. All three looked anxious, uncomfortable, as if they weren't quite certain what to do or how to be. Motion was their preferred state, action was how they defined themselves, and this interval—this standing and waiting—was unusual. It made them feel clumsy, pointless. Their arms flared out slightly from the sides of their bodies, hands retracted into fists that they held next to their thighs. Each wore a pair of dusty black boots. Their feet were spread a little wider apart than normal, to help them keep their balance on the riverbank.

It was a cold, dry Thursday morning in early March. The occasional cloud sliding by was difficult to distinguish from the sky surrounding it; both were flat and gray and featureless. Here on the ground, though, there was a sharp-edged clarity to things, as if the shapes had been carefully traced and then cut out with a new pair of scissors and arranged for maximum dramatic effect.

The call had come in just after sunrise, when a passerby spotted what would prove to be the roof of a car in the river. As she moved closer, the caller said, she had noticed the rhyming ruts leading to the water's edge. It wasn't unusual to glimpse junk dumped in the river— tires, old washing machines, and beer cans led all categories—but when the object was big, as big, possibly, as a car, people liked to have the law check it out. The investigation had been delayed until Leroy Perkins could get here with his rig.

Right now, Leroy was up to his biceps in the greenish-black water, cursing in a low continuous mutter—his mutter seemed to mimic the river's steady rustle—as he tried to attach the big rusty hook under any part of the car. The hook bounced and joggled at the end of a greasy black cable. The cable stretched its way to a winch on Leroy's truck, which he had backed down the riverbank as far as he could safely go. The truck was pale blue and on the driver's-side door, in flaking white letters, were painted the words LP TOWING HAULING & SALVAGE, and on the next line ACKER'S GAP WV.

The river wasn't forbiddingly deep here. The current was more of a frisky scallop than the thunderous wallop that would come later, after the water had twisted around the mountain and picked up speed on its way to the mighty Ohio. There was no real danger. But retrieving the vehicle was proving to be a tedious and cumbersome task, and Leroy was ticked off.

"Damnation," he sputtered. He was a big-nosed, medium-sized man, compact and balding, with a horseshoe of curly gray hair that looked as if it had been perched on his ears like a commemorative wreath. His denim coveralls were permanently stained with grease and muck, and his thigh-high rubber wading boots—not currently visible, submerged as they were beneath the viscous liquid constituting the Bitter River—were dark green, with a thin line of yellow piping around the tops.

"Damnation," he repeated, grabbing at the hook, having missed the back bumper yet again. He had meaty, callused hands that clearly had done this sort of thing many times before. "I'm tellin' you, Nick," he complained, "this ain't as easy as it looks."

Sheriff Nick Fogelsong, the big man in the long black coat standing higher on the riverbank, nodded. "I hear you, Leroy," he said.

Greg Greenough, one of the two deputies, turned and looked up at the sheriff. His expression spoke for itself: *Maybe give him a hand?*

Fogelsong shook his head. *No.* Leroy was the professional. The sheriff didn't want his personnel interfering. One slip of that winch, one errant swing of that big hook, and Deputy Greenough's head would open up like a melon dropped on a sidewalk. The sheriff had seen it happen before. Twenty years ago, as a young deputy loaned out temporarily to another county, Fogelsong had investigated a felonious assault allegedly perpetrated on a coal barge, and while he was ambling around the deck, kicking at coils of rope and kneeling down to run a thumb across motley stains on the pitted wood, he watched a six-year-old kid—the son of the barge owner—get his scalp ripped off when he blundered into the path of a swinging hook. Everybody was sorry, everybody felt terrible about it, but those torrents of emotion and regret couldn't bring back Chauncey Simms, who had bled out in minutes, his small body twitching on the deck like a caught fish.

That was the kid's name. The sheriff hadn't realized until now that he still remembered the name, all these years later. Seeing the big hook had jarred it loose from his memory.

Chauncey Simms.

He wondered what the boy's father had done with his grief and his guilt—and his love for his boy. Where had he put them? Had he carted them around with him, all these years, like extra cargo on the barge? Or had he been able to unload them somewhere along the way?

"Hold up, hold up," Leroy called out. Groping under the water, he'd come to the open window on the driver's side, and that was when his probing fingers had encountered something. Something that didn't feel like part of a car.

Fogelsong shoved his memories aside and bucked forward, almost toppling on the sharp-angled bank; he'd momentarily forgotten where he was. He righted himself and kept going. Greenough and the other deputy, Pam Harrison, let him pass and enter the water first, then followed right behind.

"Just a sec," Leroy said. "Lemme get this out of the way," he added, meaning the big hook. He backpedaled, securing the hook

JULIA KELLER

between his hands for safekeeping, and gave the sheriff a clear lane to that side of the car.

"Shoulda brought your hip waders," Leroy lectured amiably, watching the water fill in around Fogelsong's churning knees and then his hips and his waist and his chest as the sheriff moved forward, his big black coat spreading out around him like a water lily.

Fogelsong didn't answer. He was reaching under the river's surface, feeling for whatever had caught Leroy's attention. He couldn't see his own hands—the water was alarmingly cold and dark, the start of the massive spring runoff from the mountains—and he was aware of the spongy river bottom below, sucking at his boots.

He located the window frame. Let his fingers inch hurriedly around the curve, like a blind man trying to read a face. He reached in.

And then he found it. He waited a second or so, to let the human being part of him register the shock before the sheriff part of him—the professional part—kicked in.

Instantly, he knew what it was.

A body.

And he wished like hell that he had access to something more profound in his inventory of verbal responses. A poem, maybe. Or a line from a hymn. Something dignified. Something commensurate with the enormity of what he'd now be forced to reckon with.

As it was, he said the first word that came to mind.

"Shit."

Chapter Two

Bell Elkins grimaced. She was still a good eighty-five miles from Acker's Gap, and she'd made the mistake of stopping for coffee at a place she didn't know. She'd slammed down the liquid and now it burned and it roiled, punishing her stomach.

Might as well have scraped up some road tar and mixed it with a little hot water, Bell thought. *Same difference.*

Hell of it was, she knew better. All coffee was not created equal.

She crushed the empty cardboard cup and flipped it over her shoulder without looking. It landed on the backseat of the Explorer, joining the newspapers, file folders, and briefcase that she'd slung there yesterday afternoon when she left Acker's Gap in a hurry, and it rode the rest of the way snagged in a crinkly nest of Little Debbie Oatmeal Creme Pie wrappers.

She'd needed the caffeine. Desperately. Leaving a motel on the outskirts of Alexandria, Virginia, at 4 A.M. made sense if you wanted to get home before the start of the business day, but after the first hour or so on the road, Bell's focus had begun to drift and blur. The cockpit of her vehicle quickly succumbed to the stale, sullen, boxed-in feel of the predawn road trip, a taint that not even the abrupt rolling-down of all four windows in succession could eliminate, so she'd rolled them right back up again, flicking her finger restlessly on the buttons that controlled the motion. Her head throbbed. Her eyes were clouding over. If she didn't have some coffee soon, she knew, she'd be getting intimate with one of the chunky gray coal trucks thumping along in the opposite direction, the kind that bumped and quivered over these roads, taking the dirty treasure of West Virginia away from its birthplace, load by lurching load.

So she'd stopped. The place was called Lively's Market, and the sign said it sold gas, cold beer, live bait, and hunting and fishing licenses. Bell hoped that list might include coffee, too.

It did. With the jerk of a dirty thumb, the woman behind the front counter—slit-eyed, sallow-faced, wide-hipped, and big-stomached, with badly dyed hair and a misshapen nose that suggested a savage accident and so-so repair job—indicated a cloudy coffeepot and a short stack of dusty cardboard cups in the far corner. Bell helped herself, forked over a dollar and a quarter, and left.

Back on the road, she'd taken a hasty gulp. Instinct told her to spit it right back into the cup, but she was on a narrow section of the highway, hemmed in on three sides by coal trucks, and she couldn't take her attention away from the windshield. So she swallowed. And then, because the degree of her fatigue had started to worry her even more, she took another drink and swallowed that, too, and another, until she'd finished the whole damned thing.

Wicked, wicked stuff.

Bell's impulse—impractical, but delicious to contemplate—was to whip the Explorer right back around again and flame down the road and march into Lively's Market and demand her money back, while hollering at the woman about all the laws that prohibit the mixing of old motor oil, battery acid, and cleaning fluid and selling it as coffee.

She would've done so, too, if she'd been able to spare the time.

Bell Elkins had a temper. She could be calm and reasonable, but she also had a razor-edged aggressiveness that could leap out at any moment, like a box with a booby-trapped lid, the kind that could open fifty times without incident but on the fifty-first, might explode right in your face. She had a good excuse for that—her childhood had been a rough one, and fierceness was required for survival—but the fact that it was justified didn't make it any easier to live with. Not for the people around her, and not for herself, either. *The anger thing.* That's what her ex-husband called it, giving it its own category years ago, for handy reference in future disputes. *Gotta get that anger thing under control, Belfa. Gonna get you in real trouble one of these days.*

Yeah, well. She'd managed to deal with it so far. Hell with him, anyway.

She would turn forty in less than a month. Her shoulder-length hair, which looked brown in some lights and faintly red in others, still didn't have any gray invading the temples or edging the left-side part. But Bell knew it was coming. She had counted the lines she'd been seeing around her eyes for the past few months, lines that winked in and out of sight, depending on her expression, on the severity of a grin or a grimace. *Tick tock,* Bell always thought when she noted the total. *Tick tock.*

What bothered her wasn't just the fact that she was getting older. Hell, who wasn't? What bothered her was the fact that she was getting older in Acker's Gap, West Virginia, where time seemed to keep a different rhythm than it did anywhere else, like a counting system tied to something other than base ten. Time moved slower, but people aged faster. Which made no sense, but there you were. *This place,* her daughter, Carla, had once said, shivering with disdain, *is where time goes to die.* Bell had given her resistance on that point, had made a show of arguing back, but she knew what Carla meant: If time didn't exactly perish in Acker's Gap, it surely slowed down so much that it seemed to be playing dead. And yet, in the way-too-well-lit mirror in the small bathroom in the Hampton Inn that morning, Bell had discovered a new line on her face. Deep-set, already. *Damn.*

The driver of a coal truck going in the opposite direction honked at her, a long, sustained complaint. Her left front tire had drifted over the center line. Just a little bit, but a little bit was all it took to initiate disaster in these parts. Bell yanked the wheel.

"Screw you, buddy," she muttered at the now-long-gone truck driver, which was really just a gruff thanks for reminding her to focus.

She needed to be more careful. The mind-drift, she knew, had gotten to be a habit. Sometimes a dangerous one. It happened even when she wasn't wildly sleep deprived. Since late last fall, whenever she drove anywhere—down the street or through the county or across the state—she perpetually scanned both sides of the road. Just a quick, tidy sweep of a glance, up and down, over and back, every now and then. But it was enough to distract her momentarily.

She was looking for her sister.

Come on, Bell scolded herself, not for the first time. *Don't be a dumb-ass.* There was no chance—surely less than a 1 percent chance, if you wanted to get all statistical about it—that she'd actually find her sister here, along this particular stretch of highway. *I mean,* Bell went on scornfully, her thoughts as black and bitter as the coffee she'd just downed against her better judgment, *how would that work, exactly?*

How many wild coincidences would have to line up just so, in order to create a situation in which Shirley Dolan suddenly would happen to be walking along the very road down which her little sister, Belfa, happened to be driving? At precisely this moment in time?

You really are *a dumb-ass.*

Still, she looked. On casual drives, on work-related trips, no matter where she was or how many other things were on her mind, she always looked. She'd been looking since last November, when Shirley was paroled after almost thirty years in prison and, instead of waiting for Bell to pick her up on the day of her release, instead of starting a new life with Bell's help, had disappeared. She'd left Lakin Correctional Center an hour before Bell arrived to take her home with her.

Naturally, Bell had checked with Shirley's parole officer, and he was maddeningly—but lawfully—curt: *I can give her your phone number, Mrs. Elkins,* he'd said, *and I can deliver a message, but I can't divulge her whereabouts. It's policy.*

So Bell looked. Knowing the odds were ridiculous, absurd, she looked. It was a habit now. She looked in Raythune County, and she looked in Washington, D.C., and she looked in all points in between. She'd even let her eyes do a quick frisk of Lively's Market that morning, wondering what the hell she would've done if—probabilities be damned—she'd spotted a thin woman with a worn face and grit-gray hair standing near the stack of cardboard cups, hunched, furtive, watching the world out of eyes that were the color of Bell's eyes but different, too, so very different, because they had seen things Bell didn't know about and couldn't imagine.

Or could imagine, but didn't choose to.

Her cell phone, wedged in the crease of the seat beside her, suddenly came alive and played a jaunty little tune. Carla had rigged the new ringtone, canceling the standard one and selecting the ubiquitous jazz riff. *Now you're cool, Mom,* Carla said. The four of them—Bell, Carla, Sam, and Sam's girlfriend—had been sitting in the restaurant in Georgetown last night, waiting for Sam's friend to show up. Bell's reply—*So that's all it took?*—as she slid the phone back in her purse had made her daughter and her ex-husband laugh.

Bell retrieved it without taking her eyes off the road.

"Elkins."

"Back yet?"

It was Sheriff Fogelsong. He knew about her trip to D.C. to have dinner with Carla. Since Christmas, Carla had lived there with Sam.

Fogelsong had to know Bell's general whereabouts at all times because she was prosecuting attorney of Raythune County. If there was trouble—and it seemed like there was always some kind of trouble—Bell was the first person he notified.

"Close," she said. "An hour. Maybe less." Wishful thinking, but he understood that and would, she knew, automatically add some time to her estimate. "Actually," Bell went on, "I was getting ready to call you myself. Got some news. At dinner last night I found out that—"

"Hold on," he said, interrupting her. "Mind if I tell you my news first?"

Bell listened as he sucked in a deep breath and then let it back out again, taking twice as long to get rid of the air as he'd taken to acquire it. She waited for him to speak; when he didn't, she took up the slack.

"Nick?"

"Hell of a homecoming for you."

"Do tell."

"Found a body this morning."

"Where?"

"Bitter River."

She felt a flicker of fear and mild panic. Just a small spiked tendril of apprehension, opening and closing in the interval of an eyeblink. It was a feeling that had lived in her since November. Since her sister had slipped away.

Each time Sheriff Fogelsong came across a body—and it happened more often than most people probably realized, even in a small county, although it was usually an elderly person who'd died of natural causes or the young victim of a single-car accident out on some godforsaken stretch of twisty road in the middle of the night—Bell felt the little plantlike thing in her gut, felt it unfurling and then curling right back up again.

Always, she half-expected to hear that it was her sister.

"Drowning victim?" she said.

"Probably. Body was in a submerged car."

"ID?"

"No official announcement yet." Fogelsong paused. "But it's Lucinda Trimble."

Bell rooted around in her memory. She knew the name. Not well, but she knew it. Acker's Gap was a small town.

A cloudy image swam up from the depths. The face of a young woman, a year younger than Carla. Maybe two years younger. Brown hair? Yes. Brown hair. Long, strong legs. An athlete. And a good one.

"We're waiting on preliminary autopsy results," Fogelsong went on. "Could be accident or suicide, but if it gets complicated, I wanted you to be up to speed."

Bell pressed the phone a little more snugly against her ear. She wasn't the least bit tempted to utter a platitude about everything happening for a reason or about God's mysterious but ultimately loving ways. Words wouldn't do a damned thing for Lucinda Trimble now. She deserved their rigor, not their sentimentality.

"Who reported it?"

"Deputy Harrison on the overnight. Took a call from Marylou Ferguson just before sunrise. Marylou jogs down that road 'bout every morning, she told us, trying to get back in shape after her sixth child. When Harrison got to the riverbank, she saw the top of a car. Called Deputy Greenough, and Greenough called me. By the time Leroy Perkins met us there, it'd started to look like Grand Central Station on the goddamned riverbank at six A.M., I'm telling you." He paused.

Here it comes, Bell thought. Everybody else gets to go through a terrible moment and then move on, she had realized shortly after being elected; everybody else in the world is encouraged to put depressing information behind them as quickly as possible. Not sheriffs and prosecutors. They were required to tell the story over and over again, to hold the tragedy up to every conceivable light and to consider it from every possible angle, while compiling an official record. To live with it forever, as if it were a small ghostly scar, albeit the kind of scar visible, at long last, only to a loved one who knows every square inch of you.

"Leroy was hauling out the vehicle," Fogelsong said, "and that's when we found the body."

"She was alone in the car."

"Yep."

Bell started to ask another question, but he interrupted her.

"Hang on," he said. "Buster Crutchfield calling in." Buster Crutchfield was the Raythune County coroner.

After a short assault of static and then a click, Fogelsong returned to the line. "Got an update."

She waited.

He took another long breath. She could hear the inhalation plainly, as plainly as if she were sitting across from him in his courthouse office and not ripping along Route 234, exceeding the speed limit by a good thirty miles per hour, just as she'd been doing from the moment they first began to speak.

"Lucinda Trimble was dead before she hit the river," the sheriff said. His voice didn't change, but Bell had known him so long that she didn't need to hear his voice change to know what was going on inside him. "Strangulation, looks like. This was no accident, Bell. What we've got ourselves here is a murder. And."

"And?" Her stomach gave another little twist. Bad coffee and bad news: What a combo.

"And she was pregnant, Buster says. Three months."

Chapter Three

Madeline Trimble was always called Maddie, and it was not just a handy shortening of her first name. A lot of people in Acker's Gap considered her certifiably insane.

She lived in a small, seen-better-days cottage along Route 4, about twelve miles southeast of the city limits. Except on mornings when rain was in the forecast, her front yard looked like a crowded aisle at the Dollar Store. It was covered by the things Maddie sold in order to keep her and her daughter, Lucinda, fed and clothed: twine-and-feather concoctions called dream-catchers; watercolor paintings of rivers and mountain ranges; brightly trimmed ceramic dishes, mugs, and ashtrays; crocheted throws and baby blankets and quilts; and life-sized, white-plastic statues of high-stepping deer, rearing stallions, bald eagles, and a mildly smiling Jesus with his head tilted and his hands spread to either side, palms up, as if he were stumped for the question to match an answer on *Jeopardy!*

Maddie had personally created every item except the plastic statues; those, she'd picked up at the permanent flea market over in Swanville and added a 20 percent markup for her trouble.

But it wasn't the blankets draped across her bushes or the kind-eyed Jesus blessing her flower bed that had persuaded people in Acker's Gap that Maddie Trimble was nuts. If anything, those items were regarded as the final tattered shreds of her good sense, hanging on for dear life against the storm of peculiarity that her very presence seemed to whip up wherever she went.

What rattled the good citizens of Raythune County was the sinister implication of the two bumper stickers she'd procured at a comic book convention some years ago and proudly fist-ironed across her front door. I BRAKE FOR WITCHES AND ELVES. TROLLS CAN TAKE THEIR CHANCES, said one, while the other one read: WITCHES TRAINING ACADEMY.

Maddie liked to play with the townspeople's expectations of her, to "mess with their heads," as she often put it to Nick Fogelsong. At her request, he'd stopped by one afternoon last year, because somebody had stuffed firecrackers in her mailbox, blowing the black metal cylinder clean off its wooden pedestal and leaving curling bits of shrapnel in the yard.

Nick, standing on her porch that day, rubbing the back of his neck, had been honest with her: There was virtually no chance they'd ever find out who did it.

Then he had looked around her yard, his gaze moving fitfully amid the colorful legions of junk stacked on a succession of card tables—she actually did a fairly brisk trade by virtue of the occasional passing tourist or trucker, at least enough to meet the mortgage—before finally coming to rest again on the stickers.

"Why?" he'd asked her, waving a stray hand at her front door so she'd know what he meant. "Why do you make life so dadburned hard on yourself, Maddie? Folks around here—they don't like the witch stuff. Don't like it at all. Some of 'em keep telling me that you've got a big black pot out back and you make your potions there. Every time we go a few weeks without rain, they say you put a curse on the county because your property taxes went up and you're pissed about it. Some of 'em claim you've got a Satan-worshipping thing going on in your toolshed." He shook his head. "Why egg 'em on? Why, Maddie?"

The look she gave him in return was proud and defiant. She had long gray hair that she refused to subdue in a braid or a ponytail, like other women her age did in these parts, and startlingly intense green eyes. Her face had hard angles and prominent bones yet the skin that stretched across it was soft, with a peach-hued glow that some of those same women deeply envied. Her fifty-four-year-old body was strong and lithe, another source of jealousy and exasperation from those of a similar age who were far less limber.

"You know what, Nick?" Maddie had said. She was standing right next to him on the porch, hands on her hips. "I live where I live—out here in the sticks—so that I can do exactly what I want to do, exactly when I want to do it. And if that includes a little devil-worship now and then, whose business is it?"

To the look of alarm that made his face twitch and crinkle, she'd laughed a deep, smoky, luxurious laugh.

"Nick Fogelsong, for heaven's sake!" Maddie had said. "All these years we've known each other—and you still can't tell when I'm pulling your leg."

He had smiled, but it was a minor smile. A polite one. Nothing more. "Okay, Maddie," he said. "Make your jokes. But when the folks start getting mad enough to destroy your property—" He looked out at the shattered post, formerly home to her mailbox. "—then maybe it's time to straighten up. Not just for your own safety. You've got to think of Lucinda, too."

"I do," she'd declared, serious now. "I think of her all the time. That's why I have to be my own person, Nick. What kind of example would I be setting otherwise?"

She had a point. She was the single mother of a sixteen-year-old daughter, and whatever else anybody could say about Maddie Trimble, they had to admit she was a good parent. Lucinda played basketball and was president of the chess club and the computer club. She wrote poetry, too, and one of her poems had won a national student writing contest. She'd already been contacted by Duke and Stanford about full scholarships, although, as she had told her mother confidentially, her heart belonged to Virginia Tech, home of her favorite poet, Nikki Giovanni. Last the sheriff had heard—he kept a close eye on the young people in his county, and when people tried to pat him on the back for it, he pointed out that it was really just blatant self-interest, because when kids strayed and raised hell, it was Nick Fogelsong who had to clean up the mess—Lucinda was on track to becoming valedictorian of her class at Acker's Gap High School.

"Tell you what," Fogelsong had said. Much as Maddie Trimble might have brought her troubles on herself, he didn't like the idea of just walking away, of telling her to put up with the vandalism. Petty as it was, it was still against the law. "Deputy Greenough lives out this way. I'll ask him to swing by here now and again. Take a look around. Keep an eye out."

She'd nodded. "Appreciate it, Nick. Lucinda will, too. Lots of nights, she's up pretty late studying, and she hears things. Gets a little scared." A smile, sudden and warm, had instantly softened Maddie's features. "Not that it slows her down. She's quite a kid, I'm telling you. My baby girl is going to do great things in the world. Smart as a whip. Knows exactly what she wants and works hard till she gets it."

The sheriff had nodded. When a young person in his county radiated the kind of potential that Lucinda Trimble did, there was a part of him that felt as if he had a stake in it, too, as if all their fates were somehow tied together, and if one succeeded, if one rose up, then everyone else would be lifted, too. Just a bit—but enough. He kept that idea to himself, worried that it might sound silly if he said it out loud, but still he carried it around with him on his long drives through the night-washed back roads of Raythune County.

And now here he was just a year later, carrying the worst news in the world.

The sheriff felt an ache of remembrance as the Blazer drew up in front of Maddie Trimble's small tattered house. In his mind's eye, he could see Lucinda's face the way it had looked the previous spring, just after the Acker's Gap Lady Tigers won the state semifinals. They'd ended up being crushed in the finals, but to get as far as they did—with the smallest gym and one of the skimpiest athletic budgets in the state—was very close to a church-certified miracle. Right after the semifinal win, enabled in large part by Lucinda's twenty-nine points and seven steals, the whole town went crazy. It was almost enough to make people forgive Maddie her eccentricities. Lucinda, the starting point guard, was jubilant that night, standing at center court right after the foghorn bellow of the final buzzer, face glowing with sweat and accomplishment, brown bangs plastered across her forehead.

Nick moved the memory out of his line of sight. Work to do.

He switched off his engine.

It was just past 9 A.M. Maddie's wares were already spread across the lawn in motley waves of hopeful plentitude, the doodads and knickknacks and whatnots and whatchamacallits, the trinkets and keepsakes and tchotchkes you surely couldn't live without for a minute longer—although as Maddie's perky little signs implied, even if you *could* live without 'em, why on earth would you want to? She'd added, Nick noted, a flock of wooden bird feeders that hung on short lengths of twine from a clothesline strung along her front porch. Each bird feeder had been carefully painted a bright appealing shade: pineapple yellow or pumpkin orange or apple red. She'd done a nice job with them. Maddie was handy with a hammer and saw.

Nick climbed out of his vehicle. His clothes were still wet from the river, and they clung to his body in clumps and rumples, making odd little slapping sounds as he trudged up the walk. He hadn't wanted to take the time to go home and change. He never hoarded bad news. Once he knew a tragic fact, he felt an obligation to share it right away with the people to whom it mattered most. Wasn't fair not to. If you hesitated, you did it to protect yourself, not them.

Any other day, wet as he was, he'd have been chilled to the bone. But with the news he had to deliver right now, he was numb. His boots felt as if they weighed a hundred pounds apiece, and not just because they were waterlogged. He had served in law enforcement for more than thirty years and he'd notified the next of kin many, many times. But today felt like the worst day of his life.

Maybe he'd been doing this job too long. Because a lot of days lately felt like the worst day of his life. The bar kept drifting.

As he angled himself sideways between the dozen-plus card tables on Maddie's front lawn, many of which overlapped onto the walk, as he stepped slowly and carefully so as not to bump or jostle those tables and thereby dislodge the pottery sets and glass globes and long diaphanous scarves and bright knitted caps and framed portraits depicting sunset over the mountains, Nick was putting words together in his head, then pulling them apart and starting all over again. He'd been going through the excruciating mental exercise the whole way over here, wondering how he would tell Maddie Trimble about the call he'd received early that morning from Deputy Greenough, and about how, as he'd yanked on his trousers and fumbled for his boots in the dark, careful not to wake his wife, he had had a foreboding, like a hawk's wing brushing the top of his thoughts—but that even with the ominous feeling, he was still unprepared, he still wasn't ready, he still staggered under the ghastly burden of what he now knew. And was obliged to share.

He was trying to figure out how he would tell Maddie that her daughter was dead, that they'd found her that morning in the Bitter River.

And that her death wasn't an accident.

Chapter Four

God. Small towns, is what Bell was thinking.

"I didn't know about that," is what she said out loud.

"Well, it was a long time ago," Nick countered, sounding more defensive than he meant to. Long-ago love affairs—especially the kind that were ill-advised from the get-go—could do that to a person. Make you snappish, short-tempered, when you recollected the mistake. "I was twenty-five years old, okay?"

He pushed a french fry in his mouth and proceeded to chew it with unnecessary vigor and thoroughness. He started to pick up another one from the small cardboard boat in which the fries had just been served up to him, the side dish to the grilled ham-and-cheese sandwich that would be coming along shortly, but instead he shoved the container in her direction. He and Bell had started the day so early that it felt like lunchtime to them and they'd ordered accordingly, despite arriving at Ike's at the tail end of the breakfast rush.

"There. Help yourself," he muttered.

She did. She was still tired, she still felt like a piece of old rope that was slowly unraveling, but food would help keep fatigue at bay for a little while longer. When the sheriff had suggested, at the end of his call, that they meet here instead of the Raythune County Courthouse, Bell had agreed instantly. Because once they showed their faces at the courthouse, they'd be swamped by people wanting information about the body found that morning in the Bitter River. The news was already on the move, already racing down the hollows and sweeping across the scrubby fields, poking into the rusty trailers and the fragile-looking shacks propped against the hillsides, scampering up the mountain and then back down again. Bell had felt it as soon as she hit the county line; she could swear that she'd actually been able to sense the news of the death, spreading through the area like a chemical spill after a train derailment.

People didn't know the particulars yet, but when they did, the fact that the victim was a promising young woman—and that her death was violent and mysterious—would engulf the region. News like this had a texture, a heat, a shape, a destiny. Bell was half-convinced it would move the numbers on a bathroom scale.

The moment Nick had told her the victim's name, she began to wonder: Which threads would link the young woman to someone she knew? Because it never failed. Living in a small town in West Virginia meant that just about every time she approached a case, Bell discovered a connection.

And here it was.

A thousand years ago—really only twenty-seven, but it felt, Nick had just told her, more like a thousand—he'd dated Madeline Trimble. *No biggie,* he'd added as soon as they took their seats in a booth in Ike's. *Strictly casual.* He insisted on this point, which was the tip-off to Bell that it meant a lot more to him than he was willing to say.

A couple of trips to the drive-in over in Blythesburg. A few dinners. A picnic or two. Then it was over, he said. No drama, no torment, no fevered phone calls, no regret on either side. No look-backs or if-onlys. Nothing like that. A year later, Nick had met Mary Sue Ross, a third-grade teacher at Acker's Gap Elementary, and married her. Maddie, too, moved on. She hooked up with Eddie Geyer, Lucinda's father, until that good-for-nothing sonofabitch—the description was Maddie's, and she always offered it matter-of-factly, not angrily, certain that no one who knew Eddie was likely to disagree—hit the road when Lucinda was still an infant, leaving Maddie to raise her daughter alone. Which she did, and did brilliantly.

End of story.

Except that in these parts, the story never ended. No matter how long ago it was, Nick Fogelsong had a link to Maddie Trimble, a tie. When he talked to her these days, Bell thought, he probably had to raise his voice a little bit to be heard over a soft confusion of echoes.

This morning, he tried to deny it. *Christ,* he told Bell. *Only seen Maddie Trimble once or twice a year since the late 1980s. Always by accident.* And when the paramedics had first pulled the body out of the car, he went on, he hadn't even been sure it was Lucinda. Deputy Greenough, whose daughter, Kendra, was on the basketball team with Lucinda, had made the preliminary ID. Not Nick.

But still.

He was connected.

Hell. As both Bell and the sheriff knew, *everything* was connected around here, including—no, especially—the past and the present.

She reached for another one of his fries. She was ravenous, and her own order—a Cobb salad and a glass of unsweetened iced tea—was stalled somewhere behind the counter, perhaps a victim of its novelty. Ike's was known for biscuits and sausage gravy, eggs and bacon, burgers and fries. Not salads. Bell knew she was taking a chance when she ordered it. But she craved something green and grease-free.

She looked across the table at the sheriff. In the crisp glare of the diner's fluorescent lights, he could be mistaken for an old man. His face wasn't fat, but the flesh was breaking through his chin line in new places. Clearly, he'd bolted out of his house that morning without taking the time to shave; the gray stubble crawled up his cheeks and lapped around his neck like an old poultice.

Bell still had her own news to report, too, but realized it would have to keep. Homicides took precedence over everything else. Everything, that is, except hunger.

She hooked the Heinz bottle in a curved hand and drew it across the table. Upending it, she smacked the glass bottom while offering a repetitive muttered command—"Come *on*"—to encourage a coy drop to roll from the rim onto the shiny pile of fries.

"So how soon," she said, eyes on the ketchup bottle, "till Buster Crutchfield has anything for us?"

"You sure you don't want to go home before we crank this thing up?" the sheriff replied. "You look like hell."

"Well, thanks. Good to see you, too." Which might have been sarcastic but at least was more polite than saying what she was really thinking: *Passed any mirrors lately, Nick?*

"You know what I mean. We can wait a little while on this. You got on the road—when? Five A.M.?"

"Four."

"Four, then. How's Carla?"

Bell paused. Just after Christmas, her seventeen-year-old daughter had gone to live with Bell's ex-husband in his condo in Alexandria. Bell had promised Carla that once she turned sixteen, it was her decision: She could stay in West Virginia with her mom or move in with her dad. Bell had never seriously expected Carla to leave. But after the events of last fall—Carla had been kidnapped and almost killed—it made sense that Carla might want to take a breather from Acker's Gap.

At least twice a month, then, sometimes more often, Bell made the five-hour round trip to D.C. to spend time with Carla, even if work commitments usually decreed that she had to turn right back around and head home again after only a few hours. Phone calls just didn't satisfy Bell. She needed to see her daughter. To touch her. To look in her eyes.

"She's okay," Bell said. "Loves her new school. Fancy private place. And get this, Nick—they have archery classes. Carla's in a tournament next weekend."

The sheriff took a swig of coffee to hide his grin. "You know," he said, "we got that sorta thing in these parts, too. We call it bow-hunting."

Bell swatted his wrist. "Point is, she's happy. So I'm happy."

"Dinner at some swanky place?"

"Oh, yeah. Sam and his brainless bimbo of a girlfriend love to show off." Bell rolled her eyes. Every time she visited D.C, her ex-husband insisted that they head toward a fantastically expensive restaurant—for the sole purpose, she suspected, of enabling Sam to spend a good twenty minutes frowning knowledgeably over the wine list. "He brought along a buddy this time. I used to know him, too, back when I lived in D.C."

"Maybe he's trying to fix you up." Nick waggled his eyebrows suggestively. He got a kick out of teasing her; he'd been doing it since she was ten years old, and it was still a bright spot in his day.

Now that he'd stopped by his house to change into dry clothes—although he still hadn't taken the time to shave, knowing that Bell was waiting at Ike's—he was feeling marginally better. He felt capable of a little whimsy.

She groaned. "Give me a break. And let's get back to the case. I mean, if it's okay with you if we do the job for which we're being so handsomely compensated by the good people of Raythune County."

Their conversation was stunted by the sudden appearance of Georgette Akers, who'd popped up alongside their booth with a platter in each hand.

"Hey there, Georgette," Bell said.

"You need some extra dressing, honey?" the waitress asked. She was a heavyset woman with piled-up hair dyed bright blond and bobby-pinned into submission. A slab of sparkly green shadow weighed down each eyelid.

Bell nodded at the salad as Georgette slid it onto the table in front of her. "No, this looks great."

"Saltines? Slice of bread?"

"Nope. All set." Bell picked up her fork to illustrate her intentions. Georgette nodded. "Okay, then. Sheriff? How 'bout you?"

He waved vaguely toward the sandwich on his plate. "I'm satisfied as well, Georgette."

"Lemme know if that changes."

From anyone else, it might have sounded like an innuendo, but

Bell had known Georgette Akers long enough to seriously doubt it. Georgette Akers didn't do innuendo. At least not with Sheriff Fogelsong. The rumor was that Georgette and the owner of Ike's diner, Joyce LeFevre, were a couple; they were discreet about it, because the conservative-minded churchgoers of Acker's Gap were not likely to approve, but they'd shared the apartment above the restaurant ever since Joyce's husband had taken off with another woman ten years ago, leaving Joyce to run the place as best she could.

Together, the two of them had done what seemed impossible: kept the small diner in business even as the town's population steadily dwindled. Even as more and more fast-food chains set up shop along the interstate, drawing away the younger citizens of Acker's Gap the way a sugar spill does a conga line of ants. "I'd say we're operating on a shoestring," Joyce liked to crack, when anybody asked her about it, "but that would imply we had shoes. Truth is, I hocked those last month to pay the gas bill." She was kidding, but just barely. The two-story, gray-brick box housing Ike's was one of the oldest structures still standing in Acker's Gap; in its century and a half of life, it had been tinkered with, added to, subtracted from, built up, broken down, and otherwise manhandled and manipulated each time the current owner came up with some extra cash to shift a chimney or relocate a bearing wall.

Bell had long rooted for Ike's to survive. It was just up the street from the courthouse, making it a handy place for off-the-record meetings with her two assistant prosecutors and for conferences with the sheriff. No matter how dark and troubling the matter under discussion—murders, robberies, assaults, another round of bone-deep budget cuts—the fact that you were discussing it in the presence of a plate of food and a hot cup of coffee tended, Bell knew, to make it bearable.

Today's grim topic was putting her theory to the test.

Before Georgette abandoned their booth, she looked meaningfully at the sheriff. "Heard you found something in the river," she said.

"We did."

Georgette waited.

"Somebody local?" she asked. She'd wanted him to break the stale-mate, but gave up.

"Can't release the ID yet," he said.

The waitress pondered this. "But somebody we know, right?"

"Georgette."

She shook her head, exasperated, but it wouldn't last. She'd forgive him. Bell watched her hustle over to a table in the corner, where Abner McEvoy, a white-haired and feisty eighty-seven-year-old, was waggling his empty coffee mug at her as a grumpy summons.

"Hell," Nick muttered. "In fifteen minutes, she'll have more information about this case than we do. Maybe ten."

"Way of the world," Bell said.

"Way of *this* world."

Bell was ready to get back to work and so didn't bother with a clever segue. "How long had the car been in the water?"

He reached toward the seat beside him. Fetched up a notebook. It was the kind with a cardboard cover and a short coil of wire across the top. For each new case, Sheriff Fogelsong procured a fresh note-book. He flipped it open but didn't need to look at the pages to answer her question.

"Can't say for sure until the state crew gives it a good going-over, but it had to have been less than six hours."

She nodded. Communities such as Acker's Gap relied on the West Virginia State Police Forensic Laboratory to gather evidence at crime scenes and run the relevant tests.

"Based on what?"

"Based on the preliminary word from Buster, and on the fact that Maddie says she checked on Lucinda last night before she went to bed herself, and she was asleep in bed at midnight."

Bell nodded again. She had finally unearthed the sliced-up hard-boiled egg in her salad, and was arranging it on her fork along with a hunk of ham. After her first few bites, she was wishing she'd said yes to the extra dressing; the salad was dry and tasteless. *Serves me right,* Bell thought. *No grease, no glory.*

"Was her purse in the car?" she said.

"Nope. Found it on the riverbank. Contents dumped out all over the place."

"Robbery, maybe? A holdup that got out of hand?"

"Could be."

"Sexual assault?"

"No sign of that, Crutchfield says."

"So let me get this straight: Sometime between midnight and six A.M.—when your jogger comes along and calls 911—a sixteen-year-old girl sneaks out of her house, drives away, gets herself murdered by somebody. And then she and her car end up in the Bitter River."

"Except for one thing."

"What's that?"

"It wasn't Lucinda's car. She didn't have one."

Bell chewed and swallowed, assuming the sheriff would use her downtime to elaborate. He did.

"The car had dealer's plates," he said. "It was registered to Doggett Motors."

Alton Doggett was the biggest car dealer in three counties. Bell had bought her own vehicle from Doggett when she first moved back here. The lot out on Riley Pike covered almost an acre, a mammoth and motley expanse of cars, trucks, and RVs parked in earnest, perfect rows, their headlights lined up like shiny-eyed soldiers at reveille.

"Turns out," Fogelsong went on, "the car was checked out to Shawn Doggett, Alton's son. He's sixteen. Goes to the high school with Lucinda. They'd been dating for the past year or so. Father of the baby."

"Everybody's got an alibi, no doubt."

"I sent Deputy Harrison over to the Doggett house this morning to find out. Just heard back, on my way over here. Shawn was home all last night. At least that's what Wendy Doggett says."

"Alton's wife."

"Yep." Fogelsong paused to take the first bite out of his sandwich. Wiped both ends of his mouth with a napkin, then tucked the napkin back under his plate. "Her story's verified by Ketchum Doggett, their other son. He's fourteen. After supper, nobody left the premises." He shook his head. "Deputy Harrison said that when she gave them the news, they all seemed truly shocked. Shawn, especially. Cared a lot for the Trimble girl, seems like."

Holding her fork like an excavating tool, Bell poked at her salad. "And the parents?"

"Real upset, both of 'em. Said they thought the world of Lucinda. Weren't thrilled about the baby at first—they admitted it readily—but had finally come around to the idea. Accepted the fact that their son wanted to marry her."

"And Lucinda's ambitions? What would've happened to those? College, grad school?"

He repeated his shrug. This time, a twitch of impatience showed up in his big shoulders. "You're moving rapidly past my field of expertise here, Bell. I just don't know."

She looked down at her salad. She'd managed to spill bacon bits and blue cheese crumbles around the front edge of her plate during her doomed search for more chunks of ham, while listening to his replies. Georgette was bound to comment on the carnage when she came to retrieve their plates, which she'd be doing soon, just in time to ask if they wanted pie. Pie was a specialty at Ike's. Joyce made it from scratch.

"How about Maddie Trimble?" Bell said. "Alibi-wise, I mean."

"Home all night, too."

"Can she prove it?"

"She gave me her word."

"Anybody else able to back that up?"

"Her word's good enough for me."

Bell looked him squarely in the eye. "We can't just go by your instincts," she said. "You've got a history with this woman."

"It was twenty-seven years ago, Bell."

"Doesn't matter. You know that."

The sheriff moved his jaw back and forth a few times. He did so, she knew, when he was miffed but wanted to tamp down his aggravation before speaking. Get it under control again. She was accusing him of poor professional judgment, which, she further knew, was about as low as you could go with Nick Fogelsong.

It was, she sensed, high time to change the subject.

"Did you recover the victim's cell?" Bell asked.

"Nope. Checked the car. Also the stuff on the riverbank from her purse." He turned a notebook page. Bell could tell by the suddenness of his gesture that he was grateful for the shift of topic. "We got the record of her calls about an hour ago," he went on. "Last ones she made were early in the evening. We contacted those folks—friends from school—and they all said that everything was normal. Routine. Lucinda didn't say a word to anybody about going back out that night. She'd texted some with her best friend, Marcy Hillman. Nothing out of the ordinary there, either. Marcy showed us the texts."

"Marcy Hillman. Any relation to Bert Hillman?"

"That's her daddy."

Bell frowned. Bert Hillman was a handful; he was the kind of perennial annoyance that every prosecutor's office had to find a way to put up with, like a gravity-related drainage problem in the public lavatory. He was forever filing complaints against his neighbors for petty infringements upon his dignity, waving his shotgun at people who mistakenly wandered onto his property, leaving snarled messages on Bell's voice mail that always began with the phrase, *I know my rights, lady, and so you better . . .*

The endings were various: *You better arrest that sumbitch who cut me off the other day up on Route 3, him and his big-assed Suburban, thinkin' he owns the whole damned road* or *You better get one of them assistants of yours to check out them deputies who spend too much time sittin' in their patrol cars on their fat assess doin' nothin' instead of protectin' us taxpayers* or *You better watch yourself, lady, I got your number and you ain't no saint, let me tell you. . . .*

"So what happened to Lucinda's cell?" Bell said, meaning it rhetorically, but she'd take a literal answer, too. Back to the case. The world was full of Bert Hillmans, and any time spent fretting over their nonsense was, in a sense, a victory for them. "A teenager leaves her house without it? Not buying that one, Nick. You tried tracking it?"

"No signal. Maybe it's at the bottom of the river. We just don't know yet."

"What did her mother say? Any sign of it in the girl's room?"

Fogelsong blinked twice before replying. "I'll have to go back. Didn't ask her about the cell. Didn't think of it."

Because you have a personal tie. Because you were distracted. And that, Bell said with her expression, even though nothing came out of her mouth, *is why we don't interview suspects with whom we have an emotional history. Because it makes us sloppy and inefficient.*

The sheriff read the lecture right off her face. He didn't need words. And any other day, perhaps, it would've ended right there: They would finish their meals, and Nick, duly chastised, would hand over his interview notes with Maddie Trimble to Deputy Greenough or Harrison or Mathers, and one of them would commandeer that aspect of the investigation, and then the sheriff and Bell would move on to another corner of the case, another angle.

Bell, though, was still feeling out of sorts, with a frustration that was doing a number on her gut—worse, even, than the plot cooked up by the coffee from Lively's Market. Frustration, she'd always thought, was anger in the larva stage, anger before it grew up and left home to practice its havoc. The bitterness had started to stack up in her last night, and today's news had only hastened the accumulation. She was sorrowful over the death of another young person in Acker's Gap—a girl who reminded her, naturally and uncomfortably, of her own daughter—and she was irritated at Fogelsong for potentially making the case a lot more difficult for her. He'd conducted the first official interview with someone guaranteed to be a suspect, and he was tainted by an old association. Thus the interview was tainted. Any decent defense attorney for the person they ended up arresting for the crime would, Bell knew, make hay with the sheriff's blunder.

A deeper realization hit her all at once, as if a biscuit had been hurled at her head from a corner of the diner: She was tired. Tired

JULIA KELLER

from her drive, and more than that, too: She was tired of living in a place where everybody was tangled up with everybody else—always had been, always would be. Tired of Acker's Gap and its troubles. Tired of wondering if she'd made the right decision, returning to a run-down town in the middle of Appalachia, after working so hard to get out from under the shadow of these mountains. Tired of driving back and forth to see Carla, when by all rights, Carla ought to still be living with her in the big house on Shelton Avenue. Tired of colleagues—people who ought to know better—disappointing her with their mistakes.

Tired of this damned tasteless salad.

With a push from the heel of her hand so hard that she almost sent it skidding off the table edge, Bell rejected the red plastic bowl. "Thought I could depend on you, Nick," she snapped. "No matter what else was going on, I thought at least I could depend on you to do your damned job right."

That one, as Carla and her friends would've put it, left a mark. Seeing the sheriff's face, she was instantly regretful, but it was too late. An odd pause seemed to engulf the room, a moment during which Bell could've sworn that ordinary noises—crisscrossing voices, dropped flatware, rattling coughs, the loose music of scooting chairs—slacked off and slowed down, and then everything resumed again at normal speed, as if nothing at all had happened.

Abruptly, in one continuous motion, Fogelsong slid out of the booth and stood up.

"Gotta go," he said. "Lots of details to attend to." He reached over for his hat, which he'd placed on the bench seat beside him when he first joined her, and he used both hands to settle it on his head. He wore his gray-black hair short enough to please a marine, and the hat sat snug and level. "Can you settle up here? Next one's on me."

Okay, maybe she'd been a bit too harsh. She wasn't wrong—but she could've been more diplomatic. "Listen," Bell said, looking up at him. "I know this is a tough one. Maddie Trimble's a friend of yours. Her child is dead and you had to tell her about it. Hardest thing we ever have to do."

32

Four months ago, they'd solved a homicide case involving a six-year-old boy murdered in his basement. Bell still remembered the haunted expression that set up shop in the mother's face during the trial, the way the grief chased all the light from her eyes. Nick, she was sure, remembered it, too.

"Maddie's in a lot of pain," he said. His voice was low. He didn't want the other customers to hear him. "When I told her, I thought she was going to collapse."

"Best thing we can do for her now," Bell reminded him, "is to find out who killed her daughter and her grandchild."

"Even though you think it might be Maddie herself."

"Never said that."

"Didn't have to."

He wouldn't meet her eyes. Her attempt to patch things up had failed. Their conversation had lost its easy rhythm, that natural cadence of long camaraderie that typically characterized their interactions.

He shrugged and walked away. Without breaking his stride he nodded at Georgette, and he waved at a woman and two children sitting in a booth in the corner after one of the children called out, "Hey there, Sheriff!" But he didn't look back at Bell.

Just before he reached the front door, his cell rang. He answered it, but then kept right on going. He'd deal with the call outside.

Chapter Five

Maddie Trimble hadn't moved from her seat. Nick Fogelsong had told her the news about Lucinda a good hour ago and then left; he needed to meet Bell Elkins, he'd said. At Ike's. He had to go.

Maddie, though, had stayed exactly where she was. She hadn't even changed her position in the chair: legs crossed at the ankles, hands clasped in the lap of her leaf green corduroy jumper, eyes fixed on a spot on the wall of her living room. It wasn't that the spot had any particular significance. She just didn't have the energy or the will to move her head.

Hell. She didn't have the energy or the will to blink. Breathing, thank God, was out of her hands.

Lucinda.

Baby girl.

Her child. Found dead in a car in the Bitter River.

Lucinda. Dead. The two words didn't fit together in the same sentence. *Lucinda* was bright and light and free, a feather hitching a ride on a wind current, flying and turning through the spring air. That was why Maddie had chosen the name sixteen years ago, when she'd first held the breathtakingly tiny newborn in her arms.

Dead was heavy and blunt and ugly. Never left the ground.

After he'd delivered his grim bulletin, Nick had offered to call someone for her. Anyone. He'd started to say, "From your church, maybe"—she'd been able to tell from the rhythm of his sentence just where his words were going, because it was a natural thing to say to almost anybody in Acker's Gap—before he stopped himself.

Church? Maddie Trimble didn't belong to any church. Despite the fact that she stocked ceramic angels and plaster busts of Jesus in her front-yard emporium, she was militant about her atheism. Which was, of course, another reason why certain people in Acker's Gap were convinced that she and Satan were in cahoots to swipe souls. *Atheist* was commensurate with *devil-worshipper.* Around here, there was no middle ground. If you didn't believe in God, you obviously cavorted regularly with his rival.

She'd turned the sheriff down flat.

"Don't need anybody. Just leave me alone, Nick," Maddie had said. Voice empty. "Go away. Now."

Hesitant, he had looked down at her. He was holding his sheriff's hat in his hands, turning the stiff brim around and around with his big fingers, as if he were checking for imperfections in the workmanship. He stood directly in front of her chair. His feet were spaced unnaturally far apart, as if he were bracing himself, expecting headwinds. At least he'd persuaded her to sit down before he gave her the news. At least he'd done that much.

Otherwise, Maddie thought, *I might've fallen down when he told me. And never gotten back up again. Ever.* She had lost all sense of her body as an entity that had any volition, any way to account for itself.

As stricken as she was, as confused and distraught, she had looked up at the man who stood in her living room, a man she'd known for a long, long time, even if not so well in recent years, and she'd thought, with mild surprise: *You're an old man, Nick Fogelsong. You got old. While I wasn't looking, you got old on me.*

"Will you please just go, Nick? Will you? Please?"

He had paused. Then, apology in his tone, he had proceeded to ask her about her whereabouts the night before. She sighed and looked down at the scuffed and warped hardwood floor, and then she answered: *Right here. I checked on Lucinda at midnight or so—I'd been out back in the shed, finishing up some birdhouses, and she comes and goes as she pleases, because she's never given me a lick of trouble—then I went to bed myself. Got up this morning. Assumed she was sleeping late. She's been real tired lately, what with the pregnancy and all. Until you knocked on my door, I thought she was still asleep. Safe in her bed.*

Nick had nodded. He would let her know, he'd mumbled—turning around at the door, big hand on the knob, so big, it seemed to swallow the knob whole—if they found out anything, if the clues led anywhere. He would keep her posted. And he'd let her know, too, when they were ready for her to come down to the coroner's office later today to identify the body. Then he'd given that knob an angry twist and yanked at the door—his gestures always became more emphatic, Maddie remembered, as the emotions thickened inside him—and lurched across the threshold.

The sudden stab of daylight from the open door had forced her to wince. He'd closed it behind him again, but it was too late. She had felt as if someone had flung acid in her eyes.

"Lucinda," Maddie murmured, her lips barely moving. "Baby girl."

With the sheriff gone, she could give full vent to her sorrow—to, at least, this early version of it, because she had no idea how it would evolve over the next several minutes or, for that matter, over the next several years, and where it might leave her. If she even lived through it.

If.

Lucinda Lucinda Lucinda Lucinda

Each time she softly intoned the three syllables of her child's name—she wasn't sure if she was really saying it out loud, because it seemed to exist somewhere between a thought and a sound—she felt starburst spasms of pain, as if she were repeatedly poking at her palm with a pearl-handled knife. But she couldn't stop.

Baby girl.

She couldn't stop whispering *Lucinda* and *baby girl* and she couldn't stop thinking about what she'd done. What she might have set into motion.

About what she hadn't told Nick Fogelsong.

About the argument. All the yelling. And the terrible thing she'd done. She, Maddie Trimble, who had preached her whole adult life about honesty and integrity, who'd once driven through a dark night to reach Washington, D.C., to join an early-morning march against the Iraq War, giving ten-year-old Lucinda a sign to hold: NO BLOOD FOR OIL.

Oh, she was supremely well stocked with slogans, wasn't she? She was Maddie Trimble, hippie, peacenik, tree-hugger, warrior for truth, so full of good intentions. So full of kindness for all the creatures of the earth.

So full of shit *is more like it,* Maddie thought bitterly. Recalling what she'd done to her daughter, she couldn't stand herself anymore. She was revolted. Sickened. She had to shuck off the foul burden of what she was, of what she hadn't shared with Nick Fogelsong—but should have.

Her cell was on the small table by the chair. With a clumsy lunge she had scrabbled at it, missing it and trying again, finally dragging it toward her, picking it up. Breathing was suddenly a labor-intensive activity. Choking out the words, she asked the operator for the sheriff's contact information; his number, she knew, was public. *Price of the job,* he had once explained to Maddie, right after he'd been elected sheriff for the first time, more than a quarter-century ago. *Public service is public service. Period.* Back then, it meant his home phone; now, it meant his cell.

She and Nick Fogelsong didn't talk regularly anymore, though; they hadn't been in each other's life like that for a very long time. So she didn't have his number.

"Nick," she said after the cell stopped in mid-ring, the tip-off that he'd answered the call. "This is Maddie Trimble."

"Hang on."

She heard heavy noises in the background, men's voices, women's laughter, the brief shrieks of pulled-out and pushed-back chairs, the *clink-clink* of silverware scraping plates, and then the sounds abruptly ceased. Nick had just left some busy, crowded place. Yes, he'd still been at Ike's. Everybody knew that Ike's was like an auxiliary office for the sheriff.

Through the phone line, she heard his hard breathing. He was walking fast. A door opened—it had to be his Chevy Blazer, the big black county vehicle he drove—because in another second she heard the *ding ding ding* that indicated a key had been placed in the ignition while the door was still ajar—and then she heard the door latch shut again. The dings stopped.

"Okay," he said.

"I have to tell you something."

He waited for her to elaborate.

"I did it," Maddie said. Matter-of-fact now. Her voice was cold, unadorned, a thin straight line. No emotion. She needed to be very, very clear. "It was me, Nick."

Chapter Six

Any other day, Bell would have left Ike's and gone straight to her office in the Raythune County Courthouse. That's what she had intended to do right now, in fact. Work was why she'd left the motel just outside Alexandria this morning long before dawn, when the highway was still a dark ribbon broken only by the sudden chaos of a car or a truck sizzling past, followed by a spate of eerie, end-of-the-world quiet. She needed to make it back to Acker's Gap by the start of the business day. Needed to head for her office. She was facing what seemed like a million cases—and now, thanks to Nick's news, a million and one. But she didn't do that.

It had taken her only a few seconds to make up her mind. *I can just call Lee Ann and ask her if there's anything going on,* Bell thought, and as she thought it, she pictured her secretary's lined face—Lee Ann was three months shy of her sixty-fifth birthday—and what was sure to be her secretary's slight, barely perceptible but definitely meaningful smile at the news that Bell was stopping by her house first.

She'll figure it out. Dammit.

You couldn't hide a thing from Lee Ann Frickie. She'd know why Bell might want to have a brief spell of privacy before plunging right back into her formidable caseload. A precious interlude of personal time before jumping into the messy, endless business of administering justice in Raythune County.

Lee Ann knew about Clayton Meckling. Hell, the whole damned town probably did.

Bell paused on the sidewalk just outside Ike's. Where was Nick? She'd expected to run into him out here, finishing up his phone call or readjusting his hat, before he fit his big body into the Blazer and drove the two blocks back to the courthouse. He was required to take his vehicle along, no matter how close his business was to the sheriff's office; he had to have it handy for emergencies.

She wanted to say, "We're okay, right?" To clear away the awkwardness of that last ragged minute and a half in the booth in Ike's. They'd known each other too long to let any bad feelings fester. Almost thirty years, in fact. Sure, they'd disagreed before; they'd snapped at each other, and they'd argued, and there'd even been some daylong episodes of frosty cordiality, when a stiffly executed hat tip from Nick as he passed her in the courthouse corridor had to substitute for a hello—until they were able to resolve whatever it was that had derailed them in the first place. A quarrel over strategy or tactics. A disagreement over what charge to file against a particular defendant. She and Nick were both headstrong. Both stubborn. Both knew what it felt like to be called a bully and a hard-ass, and neither one gave a damn about it. Standoffs were common. *We're like two drivers in a hurry who pull up to a four-way stop,* Bell had once pointed out to him. *And each of us thinks we got there first.* Always, though, they'd eventually been able to patch it up.

But he was gone. And so was the Blazer.

Bell stepped a little to the left of the diner doorway, to let an old man go in. A tired-looking sun was doing what it could to brighten up the morning, but it had a fight on its hands; a yellowish smear of cloud cover reduced its efforts to a wan haze. She put a fist on her hip and looked around.

Acker's Gap was a small town, and even in the middle of a weekday morning, there was not much to look at, not much action to capture the eye. A red pickup truck rolled by, sending forth little powder puffs of smelly exhaust from its over-the-hill muffler. It was followed by a tan Chevette with a black garbage bag duct-taped to the rectangular area that ought to have framed the passenger-side window. Even at low speeds, the bag snapped and clattered. Across the street and two doors down, Bell noticed an old lady coming out of the low-slung, pink-brick storefront that housed the Raythune County Public Library. She moved slowly, almost torturously so, but with a determined forward momentum. Bell recognized her right away. It was Edna Hankins, gray-haired, sore-hipped, planting her walker firmly ahead of her before embarking on each carefully premeditated step in her bright white New Balance sneakers. In the wire basket hooked to the front of the walker was a stack of books, a stack that shifted in rhythm with her lurching progress.

Edna lifted a hand from the walker and waved. The old woman's fingers, Bell noted as she waved back, were so twisted and corkscrewed with arthritis that they very nearly curled into her palm.

"Belfa Elkins!"

"Morning, Edna."

Old cars. Old brick. Old people. Acker's Gap was an old town. There were times when its antiquity and all the problems that went along with it—a dwindling tax base, a sense of steady decline that lived in the crumbling public buildings and the cracked sidewalks—got to Bell, darkening her mood. Cynicism, though, seemed too easy, too simple. Anybody could get depressed in a place like Acker's Gap; that came with the territory. What required real creativity was optimism—the kind of optimism that had brought Bell Elkins back home in the first place, five years ago, after residing in the Washington, D.C., area for most of her adult life.

A belief that things could change.

Which was why, after all, she'd run for prosecuting attorney. Despite her lack of courtroom experience, she had won handily, which said more about the generally unappealing nature of the office—she'd faced only one serious opponent, and even he seemed a bit ambivalent about the prospect of doing the job—than it did about Bell's political skills.

She made another circuit with her eyes, surprised all over again that the sheriff had made such a quick getaway. She was struck, as always, by how small everything looked here, how colorless and used up, when she compared it with D.C., or even with Charleston, the state capital. She had grown up in Acker's Gap. She knew these streets well. Knew the businesses lined up along them, and knew the businesses that had been here before, too, the ones that had closed, the ghosts of what the town had once been. She knew the people who struggled to make a go of it here. Knew, too, the mountains piled up in the near distance, the jagged slabs of solid rock that always threatened—or so it had seemed to Bell, when she was a little girl—to gradually close over the top of the town, like a lid on a soup pot. Those mountains were majestic and beautiful, yes, but they could also be stultifying.

She'd tried to describe it once to a big-city friend, tried to put into words the singular feeling of living in a place presided over by a watchful mass of black rock, by a permanence you couldn't push back against. Well, you could try—but it wouldn't matter. You could spend your entire life trying and, in the end, the mountains would remain right where they were.

In Acker's Gap, Bell had told her friend, *the only way out is up.*

Her eyes fell to earth again. She was resigned to it now: no sign of the sheriff. A prickly defensiveness flared in her thoughts. *Screw you, Nick Fogelsong.* Let him stew in his own juices for a little while. He knew she was right. This was the start of a major investigation. A young woman had been murdered. They had a difficult job ahead of them, and the sheriff was well aware that the culprit most likely would come from the small pool of people who had known the victim: family members or friends. Bell and the sheriff could be kind to the bereaved, they could be sympathetic, but they had to be firm. And they had to do their jobs, no matter whom it hurt, insulted, or inconvenienced. Alibis had to be checked and double-checked. Possible motives must be explored, poked at, mulled over.

Twelve minutes later, Bell was pulling into the driveway just to the left of the big stone house on Shelton Avenue, the first house she'd ever bought on her own. She had commissioned the crucial improvements—replacing the tiles on the slate roof that had gone AWOL, reglazing the windows, tuck-pointing the blue-veined river stone on the broad flanks, staining the wooden fence that squared off the front and back yards—the way most folks in Acker's Gap bought big-ticket items at a discount store: on the layaway plan. Doing a little bit at a time. Doing what they could, when they could.

Before getting out of the Explorer, she sent two texts. The first one went to Lee Ann Frickie, who, after long resisting Bell's entreaties, had finally succumbed to the purchase of a cell that could send and receive texts:

Back n town. Call if u need me.

The second went to Clayton Meckling:

U free?

Chapter Seven

He was younger than she was. Fifteen years younger, to be precise about it. She'd thought at first that the age difference would bother her, and she'd girded herself for an onslaught of "robbing the cradle" wisecracks, but soon it didn't seem to matter. Not to the two of them, at least. And if her constituents cared—*Well,* Bell had shot back at Nick Fogelsong, the first time he told her of a crude remark he'd overheard about her romance with Clay Meckling, *that's why we have elections, isn't it? Free damned country. They can vote for somebody else next time around. Somebody,* she'd added, piling on the sarcasm so thick that her voice quivered under the load, *who lives up to their high moral standards.*

She and Clay had weathered the initial reactions of mild surprise, the slight lift of an eyebrow or dirty-minded smile or half turn of a head when they met for coffee at Ike's. They had dated since just after Christmas—*dated* struck Bell as a ludicrous word, silly and juvenile, but she couldn't find a better one. At Clay's suggestion, Bell had fought off the impulse to reply to early questions about their relationship with her default fury—*And just what the hell business is it of yours?* It was sound advice. He was a good influence. A calming one.

From her seat at the kitchen table she watched his back as he made coffee at the counter, letting her eyes rise with slow-blooming pleasure from the scuffed-up heels of his steel-toed boots to his stove-pipe legs—encased in a well-worn but clean pair of navy blue Dickies work pants—to the shoulder-spanning square of his brown Carhartt jacket to the wavy reddish-blond hair that just touched the turned-up collar of that jacket. He was plainly overdue for a haircut. The length of his hair, she knew, was always a reliable measure of how busy he'd been, because he liked to keep it cut short. *What's the deal with the men in my life?* Bell wondered idly, picturing Fogelsong's brutal-looking crew cut. *Would it kill 'em, every now and again, to go a week without putting their backsides in a barber chair?*

The kitchen was small, with warped, dingy wooden cabinets that had instantly gone on the list—a long, long list—to be replaced once she could afford it, and a brief series of gray plastic-laminate counter-tops linked by scallop-edged seams that appeared to be spreading a little farther apart by the day, creating dark narrow troughs into which crumbs invariably tumbled and stuck. There was a tiny square window over the sink. The dishwasher worked only when it wanted to, and most of the time, didn't want to; the old house's jury-rigged plumbing lacked the requisite water pressure to support it. The refrig-erator was new, but the old gas stove—as soot-black and squat and gnarled as a tree stump in a burnt-out forest—looked as if it might require one of Leroy Perkins's big salvage hooks to ever remove it, and even then, it would surely take along with it a significant hunk of the floor when finally pried loose, accompanied by creaking and shrieking and Chewbacca-like howls of inanimate outrage. Bell was half-convinced the stove had actually taken root, right where it was.

Still, this was her home. *It's mine. I live here.* Five years on, the thought could still make her proud. When Bell had moved back to Acker's Gap, she'd deliberately picked a house with a history, reject-ing one of the tidy one-story rectangles wrapped in pastel aluminum siding that were available in a subdivision across the Bitter River, houses that sometimes looked, in the right light, like overgrown Kleenex boxes with detached two-car garages. They featured all the modern conveniences. *And no backstory*, she'd said to Nick Fogel-song, explaining her choice to him on the day of the closing at the

48

Mountaineer Community Bank. *No personality. No mystery.* His arch reply: *Yeah, damned shame about those brand-spanking-new appliances and maintenance-free siding and state-of-the-art security systems and finished basements and ceramic-tile foyers and—*

Got it, Nick, she'd said, cutting him off. *Got it.* Sometimes he could sound an awful lot like her ex-husband.

Right now, though, she wasn't thinking about the sheriff or Sam Elkins. She was thinking about Clay Meckling. He had immediately texted her back—*U bet. On my way*—and a few minutes after Bell had unloaded her gear on the hall table, piling up her purse and coat and scarf and briefcase and car keys, she'd heard his truck arriving in the driveway.

"I guess you prefer the usual nuclear-strength blend," Clay said.

He turned around to look at her. His grin had its usual effect: Bell felt a small flip of arousal, the slightly fizzy feeling in her stomach that would've embarrassed her if she thought anybody else could detect it. *For God's sake,* she scolded herself, like always, *I'm a forty-year-old woman. Not some horny teenager.*

"Well?" he prodded her.

"Stronger the better."

"Thought so." He turned back and attended to the coffeemaker, adding twice the recommended dosage of freshly ground beans and a little over three-quarters the water. "I believe," he said, sending the words over his left shoulder, "this pretty much explains your ability to function on two hours of sleep a night."

"Could be."

A few minutes later he'd taken a seat at the small round table, too, and they faced each over a couple of steaming mugs. The living room would have been more comfortable, but by this time, she knew, Clay Meckling had figured out one thing for sure about Bell Elkins: She didn't always want to be comfortable. When she needed to talk to him about something serious, when she'd just returned from a car trip or a courtroom or a crime scene, she liked to do so at the table. Back straight, feet on the floor. She didn't want to relax.

Not yet, anyway.

"This," Bell said, setting down the mug after her first swallow, "is possibly the best cup of coffee I've ever had in my life."

"You always say that."

"And it's always true. You keep upping your game, Meckling."

"Been hanging around my daddy's job sites since I was five years old. My line of work, you either learn to make good coffee or the guys take a nail gun and pin your shoes to the floor." His father, Walter Meckling, ran a construction company. Clay had worked as project supervisor for nine months, ever since his graduation from the University of Virginia. His degree was in urban planning and his dream was to design public transportation systems in large cities, but his father had asked him to postpone grad school and help him out for a year or so.

Walter Meckling, Bell guessed, probably hadn't foreseen that his son would spend it keeping company with a forty-year-old woman. *Well,* she'd console herself, when feeling a pinch of guilt, *I didn't exactly see this coming down the road, either. Life packs a truckload of surprises*—that's *for damned sure.*

"You're kidding, right? About the nail gun, I mean?"

"If my coffee didn't make the grade," Clay said, offering a *whatcha gonna do?* shrug, "I'd be missing a couple of toes. Guaranteed. Those guys don't much care about their aim."

She laughed. "You're making this up."

He reached over and touched the back of her hand, which she had wrapped up into a fist. She hesitated before loosening her fingers, enabling him to slide his hand into hers.

When they came together again after a separation of any length, things could be awkward at first. This originated mainly in Bell—she had dated infrequently after her divorce, and her feelings for Clay had taken her by surprise and still could ambush her with their intensity—but sometimes he, too, seemed unsure of things, seemed ready for her to say to him out of the blue, *This is a mistake, right? Don't we both know that?* It kept him on edge. But he didn't seem to mind that. An edge, he'd explained to her, is the secret to doing a good job. He'd shown her his chisels, pointed out their exactingly sharp edges, and then demonstrated how he sharpened his tools. Was Clay too young for her? Hell if she knew. She only knew that she liked herself a little bit better when she was around him; his habit was to look forward, not back, and that was a rare quality in Acker's Gap.

By this point in their relationship they had made love multiple times, with increasing degrees of pleasure and an escalating ability to read each other's unspoken desires, like a couple of nifty jazz musicians in a midnight jam session. In daylight, though, the awkwardness could sweep in, along with the hesitation, the formality, like a cold breeze taking advantage of a poorly latched door.

He leaned over and kissed her. Then, sensing her preoccupation, he squeezed her hand and let it go. Sat back in his chair.

"The body in the river," Clay said. "Want to talk about it?"

Trusting his discretion, she'd given him an outline of the case when he first arrived. *I'm a real pro when it comes to small talk,* Bell had thought ruefully as she described the salvage operation and the tragic surprise. *Really know how to set a romantic mood, don't I?*

"Not much to say." She looked down at his hand, the one he'd just withdrawn from hers. It was tanned, with blunt, squared-off fingernails, and big. The calluses on it—irrefutable evidence that the boss's son knew how to frame a house and shingle a roof—had a look of permanence. Bell didn't like men with smooth hands. Didn't trust them. Smooth hands reminded her too much of her ex-husband, who had parlayed his law degree from West Virginia University into a career as a dazzlingly successful lobbyist in Washington, D.C. The only way Sam Elkins could get a callus these days would be from breaking in a new nine-iron or shaking too many hands at a cocktail party.

"You know Maddie Trimble, right?" Bell went on. "Runs a little roadside stand at her house out on Route 4? Bunch of homemade crap?"

Clay thought about it. "Yeah. Okay."

"It was her daughter, Lucinda. Sixteen years old. And pregnant." As she said the words, Bell felt Clay's hand close on top of hers again, an acknowledgment of the gravity of the news. "Sad as hell," she added. "Still waiting for the full autopsy report. But it wasn't an accident. Somebody killed her."

"Jesus."

"We don't know who or why. But we'll find out."

"Friend of Carla's?"

"Don't think so. At least not a close one. Carla's a year older. At that age, a year makes a hell of a difference. Whole different social group. But I'm sure she knew her. Not a call I want to make." Bell paused. "Kids here grow up differently from kids in other places, don't you think? I mean, they know the hard things too early. Violence. Pain. How brief a thing life can be. Comes from living so close to the land, I guess. And close to the bone."

She could have been talking about her own history. She'd told Clay about it a month or so earlier, when their relationship showed signs that it might go on for a good little while. Told him about her father, Donnie Dolan, who'd sexually molested her sister, Shirley, for many years, until the night he finally came after ten-year-old Bell—at which point Shirley cut his throat and burned down the ratty trailer they called home. The first time she and Clay had spent the night together, he'd been nervous with her, halting, almost passive. When she asked him why, he'd looked away, wanting to say something but not quite able to. *Clay,* she'd whispered. *Is there—?* He turned back, voice husky with fury: *That goddamned sonofabitch. After what that bastard did to you, I thought maybe—maybe it's hard for you to— you know.* In response, she had kissed him. A long, slow, languid kiss, with an unmistakable subtext. *Clay,* she said. And that was all she'd needed to say.

Six months ago, Shirley had been paroled after spending more than half her life in Lakin Correctional Center for the murder of their father. And now Shirley was out there somewhere, carrying the other half of Bell's memories, the matching half of her childhood. Until Shirley was ready to come home, there was nothing Bell could do.

Neither she nor Clay spoke for a moment. They let the silence settle in around them. It was, Bell thought, a kind of makeshift tribute to the victims. The passing of Lucinda Trimble and her unborn child wasn't just an item on a list. Wasn't just a piece of news to be conveyed and then brushed aside, superseded by another bulletin.

"Your trip," Clay finally said. He knew when to let silences be. And when to interfere with them. It was one of the things that Bell had appreciated about him right away. He didn't have to fill every space with the sound of his own voice, with the bite and drive of his own opinion. He talked when he had a reason to—and not when he didn't.

"My trip."

"Yeah," he said. "Your trip."

There was, she realized, a note of impatience in his tone.

"How was it?" he went on. "You usually have a million things to say about Carla and Sam right off the bat. Not this time."

It was true. After one of her overnights to see Carla in D.C., Bell relished giving Clay a full rundown of Sam's outrageous braggadocio and chronic name-dropping, behavior that generally commenced before her ex-husband had even cleared the front door. She'd provide an inventory of his pathetic show-off moves, from the way he'd frown pretentiously at the wine list to his habit of sweeping off his suit jacket like a matador's cape and flamboyantly fitting it across the back of the restaurant chair. Lately she had a new addition to the show: her hilarious—to herself, at least—imitation of Glenna St. Pierre, Sam's skanky live-in girlfriend, whose faux-British accent made her sound like a cheap knockoff of Harry Potter's pal Hermione.

"Is it the new case?" Clay continued. "Probably got a lot on your mind. It's gotta be tough—finding a sixteen-year-old girl like that. God, Bell, I don't know how you and Fogelsong do it sometimes. Really don't."

"No." She couldn't lie to him. Never had, and wouldn't start now. "It's not about the case." Truth was, she didn't want to fill him in on what had transpired at the restaurant in D.C. the night before.

"Bell?" he said.

Casually, as if she wanted only to pick up her mug for another drink, she drew her hand out of his grasp. But it was a strategic withdrawal: She'd rather not be touching him when she told him her news. Because if he didn't like what she had to say, if he disapproved, he might pull his hand away first—and Bell didn't want to feel that. Better to be the one who severed the contact. Better to break it off yourself. Better to initiate than be forced to react.

She had been raised in a dismal series of foster homes, most of them mediocre and some criminally abusive, and she'd perfected the dark art of emotional survival. It was part of her now. She could feel it moving in her blood, and she surmised that Shirley must hear the soft hum of it, too, which was why, most likely, her sister had fled last fall just before her reunion with Bell. Because the song in the blood was composed of only one word, repeated over and over and over again:

Run. Run. Run.

Bell wanted things to work out with Clay—didn't she?—and so she fought back against her instincts, against the impulse to shut down. To protect herself.

"Okay," she said. She looked away from his face, knowing how searching those gray eyes of his could be. "Happy to fill you in, Clay. Hell, it'll be nice to talk about something other than a homicide. But hear me out before you pass judgment. Deal?"

"Judgment about what? What's going on?"

"Just listen, okay?"

"Bell, what the—?"

A finger placed against his lips finally silenced him. Now she did seek out his eyes, and as she looked into them, she let her finger drift lower, to the cleft in his hard chin, a crease that she'd kissed and she'd licked, an especially tender and delicious part of their foreplay. The fizzy-stomach feeling started up again, the feeling that made her blush with recollection and desire. *God,* she thought. *Wish I could solve everything that way. Wish it could all be that simple.* And then she told him the story.

Chapter Eight

Shortly after Bell had arrived at the restaurant the night before, Sam announced that they were expecting one more person for dinner. *Three guesses,* he said. *But you'll never get it. Not in a million years.*

"Who?" Bell asked. She hooked her purse strap around the back of her chair with savage impatience. She was irritated, and had reason to be. She had an early day tomorrow. A long road home. To hell with Sam and his little games.

Carla was sitting to her right; across the table were Sam and Glenna St. Pierre. A waiter circled them with an unctuous and fluttering solicitude that Bell found highly annoying. This, she knew, was the price she had to pay; if she wanted to see her daughter, she was routinely blackmailed into having dinner with Sam and Glenna, too. *It's called being* civilized, *Belfa,* was how Sam had put it, when he first instituted the silly ritual. *You can't just drive here, have your time with Carla, and then rush right back to Acker's Gap. Let's slow down, okay? Savor life a little bit?*

"Who?" Bell repeated. "Who's coming?"

Sam smiled mysteriously.

Screw you, Bell thought, knowing that her ex-husband would figure out the gist of her response without her having to say anything out loud. She settled back in her chair. *Fine.* Let him enjoy his big moment. She did, however, have to keep track of the time.

She looked around. That might be tough to do in a place like this, a place that seemed elegantly sealed off from the whole concept of chronology, hovering as it did just above the rackety mess of the world. It was a place that seemed lit from within by a sumptuous glow. The stemware on the tables, each table draped with a thick cloth bleached to an arctic whiteness, reflected the light from the six ornate chandeliers dangling languidly from the coffered ceiling. Soft jazz oozed eel-like through the room, insinuating itself below the warm burr of discreet conversation. The perfection was entirely contrived and utterly artificial, Bell reminded herself, but damned if it wasn't still delectable.

Finishing his Glenlivet in a single swallow, Sam ordered a second round for the table. Golden margarita for Glenna St. Pierre, whose hair looked as if it had been dyed to match her drink. Diet Coke for Carla. Coffee for Bell.

"Is this decaf?" she'd asked the waiter just after he had placed another glass mug in front of her. Bell hated glass mugs. She had found herself longing for one of the big, heavy mugs served at Ike's, bulbous and off-white and squatty-looking, with a chip on its rim. Which, she always thought, matched the chip on her shoulder, the one that never really went away.

"Of course. As you *requested,* madam," the waiter murmured. His umbrage at the insulting notion that he might have botched an order was apparent only in the extra crispness of his nod.

"Okay. Just checking." She needed to get at least a few hours of sleep before heading back to Acker's Gap.

A snicker from Sam, delivered from the side of his mouth. "Decaf coffee," he said. "You're not the wild young thing I knew back in high school, Belfa, I'll tell you that."

Bell carefully set down the mug. She'd taken a brief polite sip. She looked at the mug, not at Sam, so that he wouldn't have the satisfaction of seeing the irritation in her eyes. He'd used her given name on purpose. Probably to piss her off.

Always worked.

"I'm not the only one at this table," she said with malicious politeness, "who isn't the person she used to be." In the years since their divorce Bell had discovered the exquisite pleasure of the oblique put-down, the subtle slam. Sam couldn't get mad about the insult without revealing that he had, indeed, been insulted.

She looked over at Carla. Her daughter was preoccupied with her napkin ring, a loop of burnished metal decorated with intricate scrollwork. Having drawn out the thick linen napkin, she now balanced the ring on its side, then flipped it over and scooted it idly around the pedestal of her water glass.

Bell tried to catch her eye. No dice.

Ever since Carla decided to go live with her father—away from her mother, away from West Virginia—the separation had been almost unbearable for Bell. Phone calls and e-mail and Skype appointments were frustratingly inadequate substitutes for what they'd had before, for conversations over the breakfast table or late-night talks on the wide front porch, while the crickets and the tree frogs and the spring peepers doggedly offered up the background music. Even when those conversations devolved into arguments—and they had done so, Bell readily conceded to herself, with increasing regularity as Carla plunged headlong into adolescence—the face-to-face interactions still were a rich and vital part of Bell's day. Missing her daughter, she had found, was an ache that never went away; it would rise and fall in intensity, depending upon the workload in the prosecutor's office, but it was always there. It was like a severed limb: The phantom pain was a permanent presence.

Looking across the table at her little girl's short dark hair and thin face, a face that softly echoed her own to an extent that still brought a lump to Bell's throat, she wondered how Carla was doing. *Really* doing. Not just the polite boilerplate replies that Carla gave when Sam and Glenna were present: *Everything's fine, Mom. Totally, totally fine. Okay?*

On this trip, there'd been no time for a private conversation between mother and daughter. No chance to talk about the letter Bell had received the day before from their friend Ruthie Cox. Ruthie and her husband, Tom, had been their neighbors back in Acker's Gap, until a harrowing series of events last fall. Ruthie had moved to North Carolina to live with her sister, Ann. She corresponded regularly with Bell—not through e-mail, but the old-fashioned way, sending pale blue notes slipped into pale blue envelopes.

Because of Carla's school schedule, and because of her own heavy caseload, Bell's visits this spring had become swift and widely spaced. Yet they were all she had now, take it or leave it—and Bell would take it. Always.

And while there might have been a part of Bell Elkins—an ugly, shallow part, she conceded—that secretly hoped her daughter hated it here with Sam and Glenna, and longed for her mom and for their life in West Virginia, there was a larger, saner, and more wholesome part of Bell that knew it couldn't be a competition. The point was Carla's happiness.

Christ, Bell thought. *I hate being reasonable and mature. Screw the high road, anyway.*

"He's here," said Sam, whose seat faced the front door.

Bell turned.

"My God," she said. "Matt Harless. I didn't know—"

She tried to rise to greet him, but he motioned for her to keep her seat. Then he leaned over and kissed Bell's cheek.

"Try that in West Virginia with the wrong woman," she said as he sat down next to her, "and you'll be picking lead out of your backside for a month. Got to watch out for those jealous husbands and their shotguns."

Matt laughed. Sam didn't. Her ex-husband hated it when Bell brought up their home state; he had worked very hard to scrape off any trace of it, the way you'd hastily rake your shoe against a rock to dislodge a yellow smear of dog manure. She knew that, hence brought it up as often as possible.

"Matt Harless," Bell repeated. Shook her head with unabashed pleasure. "Jesus, Matt. What a surprise. Damned good to see you."

He looked older—hell, so did she, right?—but still fit, with a lean frame and a supple, self-assured way of moving. Same firm jaw, squaring off the bottom of his face. The hair she remembered as almost golden blond had faded to a sort of whitish-yellow, and there was definitely less of it these days. Matt had glasses now, too, delicate silver wire-rims, behind which lived the same slate-gray, intelligent, almost unnervingly observant eyes that she recalled from a decade ago. He was dressed in what looked like a deliberate echo of Sam's outfit: dark suit, white shirt, light blue tie. The D.C. executive uniform. Only the tie shade ever altered over the years, Bell thought; red and yellow were out, pastel was in.

Matt and Sam had been colleagues at Sam's first job out of law school, at a firm in Dupont Circle, but it was Matt and Bell who really hit it off. Their ritual was to meet three or four mornings a week for predawn runs, decked out in sweatpants and hoodies, keeping steady pace with each other through Rock Creek Park. There was very little conversation, just the camaraderie of motion and effort, just the twin rhythms of rising knees and clenched fists and, on frosty mornings, identical small blossoms of rapidly expelled breath. Matt Harless had left the firm at roughly the same time that Sam did, only instead of joining a company like Strong, Weatherly & Wycombe, where Sam now enriched himself and his clients as a devastatingly effective lobbyist, Matt, Bell recalled, had gone into some kind of government work. She'd lost track of him.

"Sorry I'm late," Matt said, addressing his apology to the table at large. "Hey, nice to see you again, Sammy. Long time." Matt gave a nod to his old colleague, and then added another toward the woman who had scooted her chair so close to Sam's that she was, for all practical purposes, in his lap. "You're—Glenna, right? Good to meet you, Glenna." Then Matt regarded Carla. "And this," he said, "has got to be Carla—although the last time I saw you, you were about two feet shorter and hauling around a purple stuffed animal. A giraffe, right? Bet you don't remember me. Used to work with your dad when your folks first moved here. Came over to your house for dinner a few times."

"Nope. Sorry." Carla, shrugging, scooted the napkin ring in a circle around her plate.

Bell took over. "It's just so great to see you, Matt. What've you been doing with yourself? We said we'd keep in touch, didn't we? Never works out that way. Hell with the good intentions."

He smiled. She remembered that smile: It changed everything. There had always been a severity about Matt Harless, a tense reserve, but when he smiled, his whole body seemed to relax and prepare to kick up its heels, like an accountant whose plane has just touched down in Vegas.

"Spent a lot of years overseas," he said. "Damn near ran out of pages in my passport."

"Marriage? Kids?"

He shook his head. "Too many moves. Couldn't drag a family through that. Not fair."

She remembered—it seemed like a lifetime ago—trying to fix him up with Samantha McGreevy, one of her friends at Georgetown Law School. Nothing ever came of it. Bell had wondered at one point if he was gay, but never got that vibe. Never had the nerve to ask him about it, either. *Besides,* Sam had said back then, and Bell had agreed, *if Matt Harless is gay, he'll say so. He's not the kind of guy who lives by somebody else's rules. You know what I mean?* She did. She did know what he meant. *So maybe,* Bell had said during that same conversation with Sam, *he's just picky. Like me.* And then she'd leaned over and kissed Sam, because this was before her marriage had come undone, and she was still working at it, still hoping, still hanging in there, still yearning to keep her family—the only real family she'd ever known—intact.

She had failed. Tried, but failed. And then Bell, all those years ago, had arrived at a decision that her friends had tended to call brave and momentous—but that Bell herself referred to exclusively as "scary as hell." She had divorced Sam and scooped up her daughter and moved back to Acker's Gap.

And now, once again, here was Matt Harless. Seeing him tonight had kicked up a small cascade of memories, which merged into one large memory: the time in her life when she'd known him well, the time when Sam was her husband, when an apartment on Capitol Hill was her home. When West Virginia was her past, not her present.

While they ordered dinner, Bell sneaked a closer look at her old friend. Same sleek watchfulness. Same intensity. Matt Harless, she thought, had always reminded her a lot of herself. She was glad to see him. But why was he here?

"So—it goes like this. Matt calls me up," Sam declared, "and says he'd like to join us tonight. Make it a little reunion. So I say, 'Sure, why not?' "

At the table next to theirs, now empty, a waiter bent gravely from the waist, gathering up the silverware and soiled dishes. Occasionally there were faint, musical sounds as a lifted fork bumped a water glass, a procured plate grazed a bowl.

"Hated to hear that you two split up," Matt said, "but looks like it's worked out okay. You both look great. Anyway, it's just terrific to be with you guys again."

Sam raised his glass. "To old friends," he said.

A murmur went around the table: *old friends.*

"Thanks, Sam," Matt said. "Truth is, I'm at loose ends these days. Had a pretty high-stress job. I can talk about it now, although for a while there, I couldn't. Would've been breaking about a dozen national security regulations." He smiled. "I was a CIA analyst. Based— for the past eight years or so—in Iraq and Afghanistan."

"Jesus, Matt," Bell said. Carla, she noticed, had stopped playing with her napkin ring and was listening intently. "CIA?"

"Well, yeah." He shook his head. Looked down at his glass, a bit embarrassed. "Sounds a lot more glamorous than it was. No secret meetings with double agents. And definitely no midnight hostage rescues. I'm a lawyer, remember? Didn't even get to carry a gun—just a briefcase. Believe it or not, there are boring bureaucratic jobs in the CIA, just like anyplace else." Hearing his clarification, Carla had shifted her attention back to her napkin ring.

"Still," Bell said. "CIA. Jesus."

"Wore a suit and tie every day, just like I did back here. Mainly sat around analyzing data. Translations of articles in foreign journals, TV newscasts, that kind of thing. But I'm out now," Matt went on. "End of the line. Taking early retirement. I'll be thoroughly debriefed at Langley, starting in a week or two. Until then, I just need to chill out. You know? In some place that's not D.C. A place where I can clear my head. I remembered how you guys used to talk about that little town in West Virginia where you're from. How quiet it is. How peaceful. Couldn't remember what you called it—so I tracked down Sammy here. And he reminded me. Acker's Gap." Matt loosened his tie, as if even the name of the place had a calming effect. He turned to Bell. "And then he tells me that you actually *live* there now. The more I thought about your hometown—way up there in the mountains—the better it sounded. Good place to hang out until the agency's finished with me and I can get on with the rest of my life. If it's okay with you. I mean, I don't want to get in your way. I know you've got a hell of a job. Sam's told me all about it. So maybe you can just point me to-ward a decent short-term rental—and tell me where the fishing's good—and I'll stay out of your hair. What do you say?"

"I say it sounds great," Bell declared. She felt a small flutter in her stomach and she realized, to her surprise, that it was excitement. You could go a long time in Acker's Gap without seeing a different face, a face you hadn't seen every morning for as far back as you could remember. Was there something else, too? Another kind of excite-ment? Back when her marriage was on its last legs, back when Sam had stopped bothering to hide his affairs, she'd thought about Matt. And sensed that he'd been thinking about her, too—as more than just a running buddy. What had stopped her? *Anything I start right now,* Bell remembered telling herself, all those years ago, *I'm doing to get back at Sam. No other reason.* Wasn't fair to Matt. So she'd never brought it up. Neither had he.

"Really great," she added. "Starting when?"

"Soon as I can get there," he said.

"Terrific."

"Only one catch."

She waited.

Matt smiled. The effect was like the sudden raising of the blinds in an attic room. The sun rushed in, changing everything. "I remember—this was right after I'd first met you two—asking why it was called Acker's Gap," he said. "Thought maybe there was a mountain man with a rifle and a corncob pipe and a long white beard way back there somewhere—an Ebenezer Acker, maybe. Or Zachariah Acker. But you were pretty cagey about it. Said if I wanted to know, I had to visit. Well, now I'm coming. So you can tell me."

Bell shook her head. "No way. Not till you cross the city limits." She looked over at her ex-husband. "And no fair telling him ahead of time, Sam."

"No worries," he said. "Not sure I even remember anymore." Sam was lying. Bell knew; he was hoping to persuade the world—or was it just himself?—that he'd eliminated all trace of West Virginia from his mind and his life. Left his past behind him. A clean break. This was his world now: here in D.C., where he drove a Range Rover, got himself called *sir* by waiters on a regular basis. *You're a damned fool, Sam Elkins,* she thought, and hoped he still knew her well enough to read her mind. *The past? The present? All the same thing, Sam. All the same damned thing.*

Bell was the first one to leave the restaurant. She had to be on the road in about four hours, she pointed out, smiling her good-byes, hugging Carla, accepting a kiss from Matt, offering Sam and Glenna a joint nod. Cordial one, but just barely.

It was twenty-three minutes past midnight. Only four cars, including Bell's Explorer, remained in the parking lot. In the sky, it was another story; there were so many stars that it looked as if someone had taken a hole punch to it. Through each tiny cutout, light seemed to leak through from the other side. The wind was stronger now and packed a nasty chill, like a boxing glove with an iron bar secretly sewn in the lining.

Bell had just unlocked the door when she saw Carla, her lithe figure unmistakable as she hurried across the blacktop. The lot was illuminated by a series of bulbs strung on wires draped between tall metal poles; on this night, windy as it was, the lights bounced and swung on the line. They reminded Bell of trouble lights, the kind with a hook on the top of the aluminum cup housing the bulb. When a poor West Virginia family had its electrical service disconnected because of nonpayment, sometimes they'd hook a trouble light to a generator and use it at the dinner table. There was a nickname for that kind of light, Bell recalled: a West Virginia chandelier.

"Hey," Bell called out. "Where's your coat? You've got to be freezing out here." She took off her jacket and spread it across her daughter's shoulders. Pulled the collar up and around her pale thin neck.

"Oh, Mom," Carla said with a sigh. But she didn't give back the jacket. "I told them I wanted to say good-bye again. Since you're leaving so early in the morning and all. But the truth is, I need to talk to you."

"What is it, sweetie? Is everything okay?"

"Yeah. Yeah." Carla looked away. Beyond the bright lot, darkness waited. When she looked back, her face had changed. The aloofness was gone, the bored disdain, and a kind of troubled earnestness had set in. She captured her lower lip beneath her front teeth and held it there.

"Are they treating you all right?" Bell said quietly. "You've got to be honest with me. You won't get in any trouble. Promise."

"They treat me fine. Just fine. And I love my school. There's a ton of stuff to do. And I've got some good friends already. That's not it, Mom. Really."

Bell waited. She knew better than to push Carla, to hurry her. That never worked.

"So," her daughter finally said, "the thing is—oh, it's nothing. Really. I don't know why I came out here. I know you've got to get going."

Bell rubbed her daughter's shoulder. "Sweetheart, I'll stand out here all night if you want me to. Just take your time."

"Okay," Carla said. "Yeah. Well, everything's fine. I mean it. Seriously. You don't have to worry about me. Swear. So, good night, then." She turned away from Bell, took a step, then whirled back around. "Oh, wait. Your jacket."

"Keep it, honey. I'll get it the next time."

Carla paused. The words, when they came, came in a rush. "You know what, Mom? It's great living here now—it's really, really great—but I miss West Virginia, too. I think I always will. I wanted you to know that."

Bell nodded. She was still touching her daughter's hand, not so much holding it—Carla would have shrugged her off right away if she'd tried to hold it—but maintaining contact. "What happened last fall—well, it was scary," Bell said. "For all of us. I know you needed a change. If you want to live here with your dad, then that's what I want, too. Really. I just miss you so much, honey. I just—" She closed her eyes. By the time she opened them again, she had fought back the wave of emotion that threatened to upend her. She didn't want to make Carla feel guilty about her decision. "Look, you've got a lot of bad memories back there. I don't blame you for wanting to leave."

"So do you, Mom. You have bad memories back there, too. But you stay."

They had talked about Bell's childhood only a few times, and even then, just briefly. Carla had never met Shirley. At this point, Bell didn't know if she ever would.

"Yeah," Bell said. "I do."

For a moment, neither spoke, but not because there was nothing to say. There was too much to say.

Yes, Bell stayed. She stayed because she believed that she was doing some real good as Raythune County prosecutor. Fighting back against the prescription drug abuse now ravaging the state, busting up the rings of dealers and trying her damnedest to save the next generation of Appalachians from an easy surrender to pain pills. But that wasn't the only reason. Stubbornness was a big part of it, too. Sheer cussed stubbornness, a stubbornness that Nick Foglesong had likened to an old fence post stuck in the ground, one that outlasts storms and lightning and flood and drought and just stays planted there, leaning a little more to one side or the other, maybe, after so many hits, but still there. *Appreciate it, Nick,* Bell had said ruefully, first time he pulled out the analogy. *Just what every woman wants to be compared to. An old fence post. Lord.* He'd laughed and said, *You know what I mean.* And she did. Acker's Gap was full of ghosts for her. Always would be. But she was too pigheaded to let them win. She wanted to tell those ghosts—the ones that followed her around, trying to get a rise out of her—that they could kiss her ass. She'd show them she wasn't afraid.

"I know you and Dad were really worried about me after—after what happened," Carla said. In addition to her own ordeal at the hands of a killer, she had witnessed the shooting deaths of four people. Sam had found an excellent therapist for Carla in the D.C. area; she was a great help. Bell was deeply grateful to her ex-husband for that, and had told him so.

"I'm okay, though," Carla said. "Really." She took a deep breath. Watching the rise and fall of her daughter's petite shoulders, Bell felt a small piercing ache. The ache was like a stitch in her side, the kind of stitch she'd sometimes experienced when she ran too far, too fast, on those vivid, chilly mornings with Matt in Rock Creek Park, or earlier in her life, too, when she'd run track in high school and college. Stopping didn't help. You couldn't get rid of the ache by resting. You just had to wait it out—and keep moving.

She was the world's worst mother. Wasn't she? Yes, she was. She'd driven away her daughter. Again and again, she'd picked her job over her family—and for what? To end up in a cold parking lot in the middle of the night, suddenly smitten by the realization that everything she'd tried to do in Acker's Gap didn't matter a damn compared to the young woman who stood before her, arms crossed and shoulders hunched against the wind, small face tilted forward, grave with concern.

"Mom?" Carla said. She'd been unnerved by Bell's silence. "Are you okay?"

The tables had turned. Now Carla was the solicitous one, the one giving aid and comfort.

"Getting there," Bell said.

* * *

She'd not said a word to Carla—she'd not said a word to anyone, not even Nick Fogelsong—but lately Bell had been considering a return to D.C. For keeps.

Ever since Christmas, when Carla had left to live with Sam, Bell let certain thoughts linger longer than they ought to: *I could go back. I could live in D.C. again. Get a job with a big law firm. See Carla more often. Sam and I could trade off weeks.* But it wasn't that simple. Hell, nothing ever was.

If she went back, she might never find Shirley.

One day, Bell believed—believed against all logic and reason—she'd see her sister walking along some lonesome West Virginia back road. Head down. Pack on her back. Worn-out shoes and patched-together jacket, stained with mud and sweat and bad memories.

And so Bell had stayed in Acker's Gap, which—along with the ex-cruciating fact that it kept her separated from Carla—was so damned small. And isolated. And dingy. And predictable. Bell had lived in a big city and she knew a city's pulse and energy, its ceaseless sweep and vigor and vibe. Sometimes—hell, most of the time—she longed for that: the energy. The colors. The diversity. The chaos. God, sometimes she even missed the traffic. *I miss the world,* Bell had mused a week or so ago, when spring began to bust through the gray winter crust, knocking at the door, right on time. She'd startled herself by the stark hunger of the phrase: *I miss the world.*

Turning in her motel bed that night, trying to rack up a few hours of sleep before she headed back to West Virginia, she thought about Matt Harless and all the places he'd lived, the stories he could tell, and again she felt that flip of excitement in her belly. *Maybe I don't have to miss the world, after all,* she thought. *Maybe the world's coming to Acker's Gap.*

Chapter Nine

"Dammit."

Clay's voice had a heat building up inside it. During Bell's description of the dinner, the two of them had stayed in their seats at the kitchen table, the coffee cooling in their mugs, the kitchen clock ticking with its slightly obnoxious relentlessness. Now, though, Clay stood up.

"Jesus, Bell," he said, petulance growing in his tone. "You already work fourteen hours a day. And a lot of weekends, you're on the road to D.C. The last thing you need is a babysitting job for some Austin Powers wannabe while he waits for his pension to kick in."

She knew this side of Clay Meckling. She'd seen him this way before, but his ire was usually aimed at the slipshod workmanship of somebody on the crew he supervised. Or was generated in response to news accounts of some hypocritical politician who'd screwed over West Virginia yet again. Clay's passion for fair play was one of the things she liked best about him. It meant that he still cared, that he still thought the world could be saved—and was worth saving.

He stormed back and forth across the linoleum floor, hands knifing deep in his back pockets, shaking his head. When he reached the countertop at one end, he had to pivot and head back in the other direction until he was stymied by the refrigerator and had to turn again.

She remained quietly in her seat, watching him. The wall clock continued to tick away smugly, its mechanical pulse amplified by the lack of human voices to offset it.

"It's only for a few days," she said. "What's the big deal?"

He stopped pacing. Shrugged. Sat back down in his chair. She sensed what he wanted to say but didn't—out of shyness, out of a fear of looking foolish: *Because I want more of you than you're giving me, dammit, and this is just one more thing to get in the way.* He wasn't really angry. Just disappointed.

"What did Nick say?" Clay asked.

"Haven't told him yet. With the murder of the Trimble girl, we've been too busy."

"Can't imagine he'll be thrilled. Doesn't like surprises any more than I do. Or outsiders, for that matter."

"He'll get over it."

Clay moved his big boots restlessly under the table. "And just what're you supposed to do with this guy?" he said. "Show him the sights? Take him hiking?"

"Help him get settled. Find him a place to stay."

"Okay, fine. Great. Terrific." He said it gruffly. "As long as it's not here. That's where I draw the line."

Bell leaned over and kissed him. "You know the rules. No overnight guests. And if I ever do make an exception—well, there's only one name on that list, mister, and it's yours." She kissed him again, this time letting it linger.

Given her position in town, and given the religious sensibilities of a great many of her constituents in Raythune County, Bell had never let Clay spend the night in her home. Reluctantly, he'd agreed with her caution. If they wanted to be together, they would drive separately to Charleston and stay in a hotel there, or meet at the lodge in Hawks Nest State Park. The point, she'd explained to Clay in response to his inevitable *So you're ashamed of me* jab, delivered with stinging belligerence and hot pride, was not to hide anything, but to make life a little bit easier for everybody. To save people from having to react, pro or con, to their relationship. And to save herself and him, too, from having to react to their reaction. Easier by far, she'd argued, to be a little discreet.

"I'm just concerned," Clay went on, "about how much time this Harless guy's going be taking up." In a flash, he'd opted for honesty. What the hell. "I mean—Christ, Bell, I don't see you enough as it is. You go in a hundred different directions every day from the time the sun comes up. And with a new murder case—" He broke off his sentence, letting his exasperation finish it for him.

Bell stroked his cheek. The skin on his face was tanned and taut; each time she touched him, the softness took her by surprise. She remembered their first kiss. Cold night in early December. They were just coming out of Ike's. It was their second date, although to call it a "date" was a bit of a stretch; she'd met him at the diner after work. The special was fish and chips. Talking, laughing, they'd lost track of the time. Barely made a dent in their food. Following him out the door, turning around to pull the heavy door shut behind her, marveling at how easy it was to be with him, she'd turned back around to face forward—and there he was. He kissed her, after which she forgot about the fact that they were blocking the entrance to Ike's or that they were in plain sight under a flickering streetlight on Thornapple Avenue in the middle of town. She forgot about the cold, forgot everything else.

Bell looked at the man who sat next to her at the kitchen table. They had let the silence rise up all around them, like the soft gray fog that filled the mountain valleys on cold spring mornings. She was nervous about the time, but didn't want to break the spell.

"He's an old friend," Clay finally said. "I get that. Look, I know it's hard for you, Bell. This place—well, if I didn't have grad school on the horizon, I think I'd go crazy. Be a bitter old fart in no time. Sorry I got so pissed off."

"But you're okay with it, right?"

"Guess I'd better be."

"Good." She stirred in her seat. "Look, I'd like to stick around awhile longer, but there's a homicide investigation under way, and so—"

"I know," he said. "You've got to go."

Chapter Ten

Nick Fogelsong was well aware of the fact that he should've called Bell right away. He should have asked her to accompany him back to Maddie Trimble's house. And if Bell was unavailable—she had, after all, at least a dozen cases on hand at any given moment, with only two assistant prosecutors to help her, and lately, she even had a personal life—then he should have radioed for a deputy to meet him there. Pam Harrison, maybe. Or Charlie Mathers or Greg Greenough. Somebody.

Point was, he shouldn't be heading there alone, and he knew it.

But that's just what he was doing.

"Stay put," he'd said to Maddie on the phone. Harsh and definitive. "Don't move. And for God's sake, don't call anybody else until I get there." He'd slapped his cell shut and started the engine.

He didn't know what she meant by her words. Her confession. Was she being literal? Had she actually murdered her child? Or was it just Maddie being Maddie—the Maddie he remembered from all those years ago?

She'd been a drama queen extraordinaire, a woman who milked every situation for its last wacky drop of emotional excess. He didn't remember much from the days when they were romantically involved—he couldn't tell you, for instance, any of the gifts they'd bought for each other, or how many evenings they'd driven down the shadow-wrapped back roads of Raythune County, listening to Willie Nelson plaintively insist *You were always on my mind* courtesy of Nick's second-rate car stereo—but one thing did remain clear in his memory: the grand operatic heights to which Maddie Trimble could rise on a moment's notice. A casual disagreement could blow up in his face, prompting a weeklong brooding silence. At the flicker of a misunderstanding, an outing with her could instantly escalate into Gettysburg.

That was why, after a few months of the constant tumult, Nick had broken off the relationship. He had enough drama in his job. He didn't need it in his private life. Later he'd met and married Mary Sue Ross, a third-grade teacher at Acker's Gap Elementary. Twelve years younger than him, but just what he wanted.

Calm, stable, reliable Mary Sue.

Yeah, Nick thought as he pointed the Blazer away from the downtown area and headed toward Route 4. *Joke's on me, right?* After several years of ominous symptoms, the diagnosis for Mary Sue had been confirmed a year and a half ago: depression with psychotic features. Probably schizophrenia.

Almost nobody in Raythune County knew the extent of what their sheriff had to deal with at home—her mood swings, her plunging, soul-scouring sadnesses and the even scarier manic episodes, and the delusions, the paranoia. Bell Elkins knew, but few others. He'd chosen to keep it quiet. Never had cause to revisit his decision.

Nick rearranged his grip on the big steering wheel. He hoped like hell that Maddie's confession had been overheated hyperbole. But he didn't know for sure.

People on the street waved at him as he drove by: Clint Jessup; Junior Atkins; a kid he didn't recognize; Sarah Ann Ewarts; the seventy-year-old Dabney twins, Betty and Arlene, who'd been dressing in identical pantsuits since they were six. When he passed cars going in the opposite direction, a lot of the drivers waved, too, and added friendly horn honks. Nick's Blazer, with its massive silver grille that looked like complicated orthodontics and with the white county seal painted on both its shiny black sides, was unmistakable.

It was a burly, tanklike vehicle that was surely more than Nick really needed for the job—he was always looking for ways to trim the budget, and he'd done the math, calculating the manner of usage and average daily cost of gas and upkeep—but when he proposed swapping it out for a smaller car that didn't chug petroleum like a backsliding AA member at the bar at Applebee's out on the turnpike, his constituents rebelled. They wouldn't hear of it. He'd suggested the change at a meeting of the county commissioners, and the response was swift, passionate, even outraged: *Keep the Blazer.* Even in a county like Raythune, where public funds were chronically depleted by an economic downturn that hung around like a low-grade fever, the citizens didn't want their sheriff driving around in something more economical but less impressive. Less sheriff-like. They liked the look of the Blazer. Its size seemed to give them confidence.

Big car. Big man. Big job.

Nick returned a few of the salutes, but mostly he focused on the road. And on the pestering voice in his head: *Call Bell Elkins. Do it now.*

Bell was right about everything she'd said. The fact that he'd once dated Maddie Trimble—no matter how long ago it was, and regardless of how many seasons had passed since they'd exchanged anything more than a casual hello—meant that he shouldn't be interviewing her alone. Especially if she might be about to implicate herself in a crime. Their ancient-history romance was bound to come out during any trial. Acker's Gap was a small town, and Nick adhered to the old slogan: *The smaller the town, the longer the memories.* It would make Bell's job harder, and it could work against Maddie. It could work against him, too.

He really should notify Bell. Right now. But he kept on driving. And he didn't make any calls.

Chapter Eleven

Maddie was sitting in the same chair he'd left her in.

She hadn't answered his knock—he rapped five times in succession, firm and fast. When there was still no response, Nick gripped the knob and entered.

Had she moved at all since he left her earlier that morning? He couldn't tell.

Of course she'd moved. She'd called him, hadn't she?

The cell rested in the lap of her dress. It looked as if it had just slipped out of her hand after she'd used it, as if she didn't much care if it stayed there or ended up on the floor. Her eyes looked glazed-over, faraway. He wasn't sure if she was even aware that he'd come in.

Nick crossed the room. Two long strides did the job; it was a very small house. Small and fantastically cluttered. Items upon which Maddie was still working—half-crocheted scarves wrapped around chair backs and lampshades and a hat rack, portraits-in-progress propped up on dinette chairs, soon-to-be dream-catchers that were still just soft piles of feathers and webbed riggings of colorful thread—were spread out everywhere, from floor to table to couch to windowsills. She'd lived here a long time. This house knew addition, never subtraction. Nick had to step with care.

He had a wild flash of memory: hurriedly zipping up his trousers on his way out the door on a late-summer morning twenty-seven years ago—long before Nick had met Mary Sue, long before Lucinda was born, long before lots of things—and he was rushing through this room, blinking and preoccupied, stumbling, stupidly late for work, and suddenly he tripped over the cracked pedestal of a concrete birdbath Maddie had nabbed at a yard sale and taken apart the night before, planning to repair it. Nick went flying. *Ass over teakettle,* as his father, Big Jim Fogelsong, would've described it. Nick yelped *Dammit!* which brought Maddie running out of the bedroom, naked except for her pink slippers. Instead of helping him up—stunned and flustered, he was sprawled on his butt in a heap of quilts, feathers, paintbrushes, ribbons, and bows, his legs sticking up like a showgirl's—she laughed and plopped right down beside him, and he had to laugh, too. *Mister Dignified Deputy Sheriff,* she'd managed to gasp between cascading giggles, grabbing hold of him and kissing his neck, kissing him on the top of his head, *are you aware, sir, that you've got feathers in your hair?*

"Maddie," Nick said.

She lifted her face to look at him. She hadn't been crying, which surprised him. Her eyes looked dry, as if the entire concept of tears would be utterly foreign to them, strange and exotic. She stood up with an abruptness that startled him, almost as much as did the lack of tears. The cell slipped off her lap and hit the wooden floor and skidded a short distance. She paid no attention to it.

"Come on," she said. Flat voice. Her eyes didn't match up with his.

"Listen, Maddie, I'm here because you called, and I know you're probably still in shock, but if you're going to make some kind of statement, I need you to come down to the courthouse right now so I can read you your rights and—"

"I said *come on,*" she interrupted him, shaking her head. It was more like a shudder, moving down through her body in a single solemn pulse.

She turned her back on him and walked toward the small hallway, the one that led to the two minuscule bedrooms at the back of the house. In the time that Nick had known her, the second bedroom served as what Maddie called a junk room; the designation always made him laugh because, as he often pointed out to her, playful in his umbrage, kidding her, relishing her faux-outrage, *Your whole damned house is a junk room, lady; it's not like you keep the godawful mess confined to one little ole room, you know?*

Now it must be Lucinda's room, he guessed. He had to guess; he hadn't been here in decades.

Maddie opened the door to the room. She stepped back and turned sideways, flattening herself against the threshold, motioning impatiently for Nick to go in first, ahead of her.

He took a step forward.

He saw a single bed, neatly made up. One pillow. The bedspread was maroon with a white pinstripe. Next to the bed was a small wooden desk. Arranged carefully on top of it was a green metal gooseneck lamp, a closed laptop, a stack of textbooks of assorted sizes with the bottom edges squared up. A straight-backed wooden chair was pushed in under the desk. The room was ringed by bookshelves, flimsy-looking ones made out of pressed particleboard, little more than snapped-together sticks, available in cheap kits sold at discount stores. *A couple of hard sneezes in here,* Nick thought, *and those'll buckle and collapse.*

There were two posters stickpinned to the wall over the bed—the only wall space unblocked by bookshelves. One showed a thin, pretty young woman in a shimmery white gown, holding a guitar and flinging her curly blond hair so vigorously that it projected almost horizontally from the side of her head, like a flag in a strong wind. The words TAYLOR SWIFT bounced across the bottom of the poster in round pink letters. Nick knew the name. Liked the songs. The other poster was Albert Einstein, the famous shot in which he was sticking out his tongue. Hair wild, in that electric scribble.

Nick was uncomfortable. He knew he shouldn't be here. The formal investigation of Lucinda Trimble's death would include this space. He was breaking about half a dozen points of protocol. But he was conscious of Maddie Trimble right behind him, breathing hard, blocking him, willing him to take it all in. To understand.

Understand what? Nick wanted to ask her. Wanted to demand from her, really, if he'd had the nerve to take her by the shoulders and to look long and hard in those glassy green eyes, without worrying that it might be misconstrued. Touching her in such a way, that is.

What did she want him to get from this? To see in this room? He could have turned around at any moment, he could've pushed right past her and left the house, and he knew that—but he didn't. He stayed put. He avoided sudden movements, because he was apprehensive around grief. Respectful of it, yes, but also a little bit leery of it. Grief unleashed something primitive in people. Something elemental and unpredictable and uncontrollable. If nothing ever happened to knock it loose, if they never—thank God—experienced the sudden loss of someone they loved with a passion past all reckoning, then the grief might stay safely tucked up inside them forever. But if released, it packed vast power, a power that Nick Fogelsong had witnessed many times in his career when he notified people of the calamities that had befallen their loved ones, a power he marveled at. And secretly feared. And definitely kept his distance from, as much as he reasonably could.

His gaze roved over the objects that had defined a young woman's life. Tilting his head, he read the words on the spines of the books on the desk. *Organic Chemistry II* and *Calculus with Analytic Geometry* and *Modern British Poets*. And topping the stack, a well-worn yellow paperback: *The Awakening.* By somebody named Kate Chopin. He read a great deal, but he'd never heard of it.

A muddy, half-deflated basketball was wedged under the bed. A wooden baseball bat—its business end riven by a long black crack that testified to a hard pitch and a fierce swing—was propped in the corner.

He needed to leave. *Now.*

He stood there.

What the hell was he doing?

"Maddie," Nick said. "I know you're hurting, but as sheriff of Raythune County, I need to advise you to—"

"You have to see this—to *know*—to realize—," Maddie said, cutting him off. "I want you to see my girl, my baby girl—you didn't really know her, nobody did, you have *no idea*—" She broke off. She was still behind him. He could hear her swallowing, could practically hear the crackle as a few drops of saliva made their way down that dry throat. "This is where my baby girl lived, where she dreamed her dreams. She was *special*. You have to see this, Nick, you have to feel it. You have to *know*. So you can truly understand what a terrible thing I did. Terrible and unforgivable."

Now he turned around to face her. "Maddie," he said. "Listen to me. Did you hurt Lucinda? Is that what you're trying to tell me?"

The initial reaction to his words came from her eyes. They widened in horror. "*Hurt* her? Good God, you actually think I'd be capable of—?" She interrupted herself with a hard bark of a laugh, a laugh that had nothing to do with amusement. "So that's what you think. You think I'd harm my own child. You're just like everybody else in this rotten little stink-ass town, aren't you? You think I'm some kind of monster. Some kind of sick, twisted monster. I know we've lost touch over the years—I know we haven't exactly kept up with each other, but surely you know I'd never—"

"You called me—you said—" He was confused. "You said that you'd—"

"Yeah, Nick. Yeah, yeah." An exaggerated sarcasm veined her voice, spreading to every edge of it. "You got me. That's right. You're goddamned Sherlock Holmes and you dragged the truth out of me. Just ripped it right out. Oh, yeah. I'm a witch, remember? I did a magic trick and got rid of her. That was it. Couple waves of the wand, a little bit of chanting, maybe some incense—" She shuddered. Recovered herself. But the anger stayed. "No, Nick. Not why I called. Not what I meant." Deep breath. "Thing is, I never appreciated her. Not like I should have. You see how special she was. You see this room. You see what she was like—so bright. Such a hard worker. Lucinda was going to do great things in this world, Nick. You can see that."

He sensed that there was something more, that she wasn't telling him everything, but he was too exhausted to push her. He hadn't realized how tiring it was, holding his body so tensely. Fearing a confession. Knowing he should've brought along another witness, one of his deputies or the prosecutor. To do things by the book.

And then, after all that, after all he was risking by being here, by coming when she'd called him, by trying to help her, she still wasn't telling him the whole truth. She was holding something back.

"Maddie," he prodded her, "a few minutes ago, you said, 'I did it.'"

She was thinking. He could sense how fast her mind was going. She had summoned him here for a particular reason, but now—he was speculating, but he could usually read a face as easily as other people read the morning paper—now she'd changed her mind about divulging whatever it was that was eating at her.

Here he stood, though. Right in front of her. So she had to come up with something.

"Yeah," she said. "Well." Her mind was still going; he could practically hear the sizzle and pop as the synapses fired. "Okay. Here's the thing. I yelled at her. I said horrible things. Told her how much she'd disappointed me." Maddie shook her head. She put the heel of a hand in each eye socket and pressed hard, as if hoping to crush the memory so that it couldn't torment her anymore. "She was pregnant, Nick. I was so disappointed in her. I'd warned her. I did. And so I said things no mother should ever say to her child."

"Last night? You said those things last night?"

She lowered her hands and looked at him. Blinked in confusion. "Last night? No," she said. "We didn't talk last night. I barely saw her."

"But you saw what time she went to bed."

"Yes." Too quickly. "She must've left the house after that. Unbeknownst to me. And then maybe somebody followed her. And killed her."

"So did you see any strange cars last night? Hanging around the house?"

"No. Everything was normal. Same as always." Maddie took another deep breath. "Our fight was before. A week or so ago. Worst one we've ever had. She was going to have the baby and marry Shawn Doggett and I—I screamed at her. I said terrible things. Because I wanted something *different* for her, Nick. Something better. I wanted her to get the hell out of Acker's Gap."

Maybe so, Nick thought. *Maybe that's true. But there's more, Maddie. There's something you're not telling me.*

He'd been a law enforcement officer for a long time, long enough to know when people were cutting and pasting as they went along.

Now Nick understood why she'd insisted on showing him this room. Why she wanted him to behold these things: books, posters, basketball, bedspread. Personal things. Revelatory things. An array of them. If people wanted to persuade you they had nothing to hide, this is what they did. *Here. My daughter's life. Every last detail. Right here. Look.* The only people who insisted they were putting everything out in front of you, Nick knew, were the people who were keeping something back.

"Okay," he said. Pointless to call her on it now. Not here, anyway. They were standing in the dead girl's room.

No, he corrected himself: *He* was standing in the dead girl's room. Maddie was still in the doorway. He, Nick Fogelsong, was the one who'd gone in deeper. Too deep.

She'd wanted him to. She'd practically pushed him in. But he knew that didn't matter. He was the professional; she was the grieving mother. He was the one with the obligation to do the right thing. Which meant, at the moment, *getting the hell out of here.*

The dimensions of the room, and the house in which it was tucked, suddenly were unbearable to him. He felt like a clumsy, bumbling giant who was going to bust through the roof at any second, him with his wide shoulders and thick feet and heavy load of responsibility. The air felt stale and insufficient. He knew he needed to get out of here and send over a deputy to take the rest of her statement, just as Bell had advised him to do. He was compromised in all kinds of ways.

Before he could squeeze past her, though, and head back down the short corridor, she'd grabbed his coat sleeve. Her grip was intense, so hard that Fogelsong felt as if the fabric were caught under a rock ledge.

He wanted to tear his coat away. To escape. He wanted to say, *I spared you. I didn't tell you what it was* really *like out there today, finding your daughter's body— Have you ever seen a dead body, Maddie? Have you? Bet not. Well, I have, I've seen it lots of times, and I spared you, I haven't described it to you. Her eyes were open. People die with their eyes open, Maddie, did you know that? So it's like they're looking at you, and they're asking* Why? Why'd this happen to me? Why didn't you help me? Why weren't you there? *It's like they're asking for justice, Maddie, for justice and truth, and they're asking it with their eyes because there's no other way for them to ask it now. Their eyes are all they've got. Those open eyes.*

Why aren't you telling me the truth, Maddie? Why? What the hell are you hiding?

He didn't say anything like that.

Instead he looked down at his sleeve, the one that Maddie Trimble still clutched. Panic in her grip. Her hand trembled. It was paler than usual, from the exertion of holding on to him so fiercely.

"Nick," she said. Something hard in her voice, behind the sadness. Hard and flinty. She was pleading, desperate, but she was also angry and resolute. "You'll find the killer, right? Whoever did this? You'll find the fucking bastard who took my baby girl and her child and you'll make 'em pay, right?"

And then he did the thing he never did, the thing he'd told his deputies never to do, because there were no guarantees in a murder investigation. There couldn't be. There was always more doubt and murk than certainty. Promises just gave false hope. Promises were kind in the short run but brutal and cruel in the long.

Why did he break his number one rule? He wasn't still in love with her, he could read his own heart well enough to dismiss that theory out of hand; moreover, he knew she was withholding something from him, something that might be essential. So why did he make the promise? The past seemed to have him in its clutches, in a grip even tighter than Maddie's.

"Yeah," he said. "Absolutely. We will. Word of honor."

Chapter Twelve

There was no such thing as too much information.

"Thanks for coming by, Deputy," Bell said. She stood up at her desk. Greg Greenough was frozen in the doorway, as if cognizant of an invisible force field prohibiting entrance without specific invitation. Recognizing his hesitation, she nodded impatiently, a means of summoning him on into her office.

She'd reached Greenough on his cell an hour ago, after an abrupt and preoccupied good-bye to Clay Meckling. Asked the deputy to stop by the courthouse as soon as he could. His patrol shift, he'd informed her, was almost over. So here he was, filling up most of the threshold that separated Bell's private office from the outer one where Lee Ann Frickie worked, dragging his brown hat off his big head and pressing that hat against his chest, as if he were a church usher and the hat a collection plate he'd just retrieved at the end of the pew. An empty collection plate, that is—which was increasingly the case at churches throughout the county, as hard times had hit and showed little willingness to move on.

Deputy Greenough was fifteen years older than Bell, but his daughter, Kendra, was roughly Carla's age. And Kendra had been a friend of Lucinda Trimble's, which meant that Greenough might have some insight into the victim.

"Sit for a minute?" she said.

"All the same to you, ma'am, I'd rather stand. Got to get over to the jail real soon to spell Charlie Mathers."

Bell nodded. That was better, actually; she liked to do interviews on the fly, without the tedious niceties of sitting down and trading banal greetings before you could start your business. The day was already getting away from her. A meeting with assistant prosecutors Hickey Leonard and Rhonda Lovejoy was set to convene in three minutes. First, though, she wanted a word with Greenough, to help fill out her picture of Lucinda.

When townsfolk grew worried in the wake of a violent act, Bell always tried to press home to them a salient fact: Random violence perpetrated by strangers was exceedingly rare. No matter what people saw on TV shows, a serial killer likely wasn't lurking under your front porch. Most homicides arose directly out of the ordinary circumstances of daily life. Out of the sticky web of people, passions, prejudices, entanglements. Which meant there was no such thing as too much information. The more facts she had about Lucinda, the closer she'd be getting to a possible motive for her murder. And from there, to the identity of her killer.

Greg Greenough was a square-built, big-faced, heavy-limbed man, given to repeatedly dipping his head in the manner of many overweight men, silently and persistently apologizing for his inconvenient bulk. When he was younger, his curly hair had been a vivid, tawny red; it had faded to a bland salmon pink shade. He had taken his time to marry and start a family. Lola Greenough—formerly Lola Toles—had been the dispatcher for the Raythune County sheriff's department when she and the deputy met. Bell had seen the three of them—Greg, Lola, and Kendra—at the annual summer picnic for courthouse employees, strolling around with their corn dogs and with their Styrofoam bowls of the homemade peach ice cream that Charlie Mathers concocted in his grandpa's hand-cranked churn, year after blister-making year. The Greenoughs were a close family; Greg and Lola would know their daughter's friends. Would keep an eye on them, for Kendra's sake.

"Thing is, Deputy," Bell said, "I just want to get a better sense of Lucinda. She and your daughter were good friends, I take it?"

"Yep. I mean, not *best* friends—you couldn't say that. Lucinda's best friend was Marcy Hillman. That's what Kendra told me."

"But Kendra and the Trimble girl were teammates on the basketball team, isn't that right? Makes a difference. A special kind of relationship."

"Yes, ma'am," he said. "Lotsa nights, they'd go running together."

"Does Kendra have any idea who she was meeting at the river? Even just a guess?"

Greenough squinted, as if recollection involved long-distance eyesight as well as an expenditure of brainpower. "Well, ma'am, she said that more'n likely it was Shawn Doggett. If he says he wasn't there, well then—" He shook his head. "Lucinda's not the kind to go off like that, Kendra told me. Not unless a friend needed her. Needed to talk something over."

"I gather that Lucinda and Shawn were pretty serious."

"Yes, ma'am, I believe that's so."

"Did she confide much in Kendra about the relationship?"

Greenough doubled down on his squint. Scratched his cheek. "Well, ma'am, even if she did, Kendra wouldn't have turned around and told me about it. Teenagers—well, they're pretty loyal to each other. You know about that."

It was a polite reference to Carla, but Bell was too busy to react, too focused to return a rueful *Tell me about it* or other commiserating platitude. Instead, she moved forward:

"Any indication that things were rocky between Lucinda and Shawn? Any reason for Kendra to think they weren't getting along? Maybe—with a baby coming—things had gotten tense?"

"Could be," Greenough said. "I know that Kendra and her friends were kind of worried about Lucinda. About how she'd cope and all."

"Thanks, Deputy." She needed to go. She was late for the meeting with her assistant prosecutors. Without looking at him—she leaned over to gather files on her desk, and her attention was absorbed by the assortment of printouts and manila folders and loose sheets—she waved vaguely in his direction. "Appreciate it. My best to your family."

"So what do we have?" Bell said. "Who'd want to kill a sixteen-year-old girl and then shove her car in the river?"

She was sitting in the tiny office in the basement of the courthouse. The assistant prosecutors' lair was a pinched-looking, windowless place whose slimy stone walls and musty smell—pungent with fungus and dust and other things, too, things nobody wanted to think about for any length of time—surely violated at least a dozen OSHA standards for workplace safety, Bell had often surmised. Rhonda had recently counted seventeen decaying spider carcasses in her desk drawer. That was a new record, although it was an excellent bet that the record would be shattered with the subsequent opening of the next drawer down.

Bell preferred to meet with Hick and Rhonda in their digs rather than in her office on the first floor. On the main level of the courthouse, townspeople were always bumbling in to ask if this was where they could pay their parking tickets—*No, that office is down the hall to your right, room 127*—and ringing phones always seemed to interrupt some crucial point in their deliberations. Here, however, the very unsavoriness of the dingy niche adjacent to the boiler room guaranteed a perverse sort of privacy: Nobody in her right mind ever wandered down here. Nobody who didn't have to, that is.

Earlier that afternoon, as Bell's kitchen-table conversation with Clay was winding down, she had texted Rhonda and Hick: *Yr office 4:15.* Most trials were recessed by that time each day. She knew they would be free. And she needed them.

There had been no opening pleasantries. No small talk. No tall tales. Not even from Hick, who typically started out their meetings with a brief off-color joke—just last week, he'd told the story of the psychiatrist whose male patient had shown up encased in Saran Wrap, leading the doctor to note, *Clearly, I can see you're nuts*—solely for the pleasure of witnessing Bell's wince and hearing Rhonda's groan. With the investigation still in its crucial opening stage, the mood at the moment was unrelievedly serious.

Bell hitched up her chair closer to the shoved-together desks. Spread across the top were multiple mugs holding various levels of old cold coffee, a half-eaten ham biscuit marooned on a grease-weakened napkin, a pile of used-up yellow legal pads, two laptops with scratched lids and power cords dribbling out of their backsides like rats' tails, a massive black rotary dial phone and—Hick's most cherished possession—a bobblehead doll of Jerry West, the pride of Cabin Creek, West Virginia, the NBA star who, as Hick was happy to remind people, had once shaken hands with his father, Wendell Leonard, when Wen was an undergraduate at West Virginia University in the 1950s and made a habit of crowding in at courtside so that West would have to trot right past him on his way to the Mountaineer locker room at halftime.

"Okay," Bell said. "Here's what we've got."

She summarized the contents of the sheriff's preliminary report. Deputies Harrison and Greenough had interviewed Lucinda's friends and teachers. They'd put together a tentative picture of the young woman's final hours—as much as they could find out from their initial inquiries.

Lucinda had left Acker's Gap High School at 4 P.M. yesterday afternoon. She'd met her best friend, Marcy Hillman, for a Diet Pepsi at the Taco Bell out by the mall. Despite her pregnancy, Lucinda was still on the track team, but the after-school practice had been canceled that day because the running track—it circled the football field, a red-pebbled loop with thin white lines designating the lanes—had flooded earlier in the week, on account of the copious early-spring rains, and still hadn't dried out. Asked what they had talked about at the Taco Bell, Marcy told the deputies: *You know. Stuff.* Lucinda, she had added, said nothing about going out again that night.

Hick held up his iPhone and waggled it. "Harrison e-mailed me her notes an hour ago," he said, naming Sheriff Fogelsong's youngest and most efficient deputy. "Early list of potential suspects. Just her opinion, but a place to start."

He was perched backwards on a spindly armless wooden chair that he'd pulled out from under his desk and flipped around when

Bell walked in. He'd stationed his elbows on the top of the chair back, a position that made his shiny brown suit coat bind and pinch across his back and tug unbecomingly at the armholes. He was fifty-seven, heavyset, with a round face and broad hands and the rumpled, amiable air of a man exceedingly comfortable in his own skin.

Five years ago, he had opposed Bell during her initial run for prosecutor. The day after her victory, she called to offer him the job of assistant prosecutor. Since then, not an hour had passed during which Hick didn't wonder how the hell he'd ever thought he could handle the top spot. He'd observed the toll it took on Bell: long hours, lean budgets, hard choices. What looked like power was really just crushing responsibility. You could dress up the word "prosecutor" all you wanted, you could make it sound special and important, but in the end, it just meant that you were the one who got the 3 A.M. phone call. You were the one who never had a vacation that wasn't cut short by a crisis. You were the one who got the threats and the curse-laden vows of vengeance, usually screamed by enraged relatives as their pride and joy was led away by the deputies after a no-brainer conviction, the sweaty face of the vow-slinger twisted up like a dishrag left to soak overnight in a scum-crusted bucket.

Next to Hick sat Rhonda Lovejoy, looking almost edible in a bright red taffeta dress with a complicated ruffle across the bottom and a coyly daring neckline. She was a plump, personable young woman whose family was related to four-fifths of the population of Raythune County, a fact that gave her a measurable edge when it came to seeking information the old-fashioned way—in other words, being expertly attuned to local gossip, which, according to Rhonda's informal algorithm, ended up being accurate at least 99.7 percent of the time.

"Let's hear the list," Bell said.

When she first arrived at their office this afternoon, she'd grabbed the only other available seat in the place, a dusty pink plastic lawn chair that Hick had dragged in from his backyard shed three years ago, once it became clear that the county commissioners weren't going to authorize the purchase of an additional chair. As Sammy Burdette, the longest-serving commissioner, had put it back then, pointing with his toothpick: *You got two people who work regular in that office, right? Two people means two butts. Two butts means two chairs. Not three. You ever meet anybody with a second butt on 'em? Didn't think so. And if you do meet such a person, by God you'd better call the* National Enquirer. *And take a picture while you're at it. Bound to make us a million bucks.* Then Burdette had returned the toothpick to its accustomed spot on his fleshy bottom lip, a decisive gesture with only one meaning: *Debate's over.*

Hick went back to his iPhone. He touched an icon with a chubby thumb. Scrolled down. "Here we go. Deputy Harrison says that if we're thinking it's somebody who knew the girl—always a good bet—then in addition to Marcy Hillman, there's her mother, Madeline Trimble. There's Lucinda's boyfriend, Shawn Doggett, and after that, there's the rest of the Doggett family. Alton and his wife, Wendy, and their other son, Ketchum. Harrison spoke with the family this morning. And she said that—"

"Alton and Wendy Doggett," Rhonda broke in, "weren't exactly thrilled about their son's relationship with Lucinda Trimble."

Hick, not exactly thrilled himself about being interrupted, used the top edge of his iPhone to scratch under his chin. "And just how," he said with appreciable testiness, "do we know that? You good buddies with the Doggetts, is that it?"

"I know that," Rhonda replied smugly, "because Wendy Doggett was recently heard discussing the relationship during a luncheon at the Rainey Hollow Resort and Country Club. My cousin Dorothea's been a member out there forever. And she said that Wendy Doggett said, and I quote—because Dorothea quoted, and she's got a great memory—'That worthless piece of white trash has got my boy's head all turned around, but if there's a god in heaven, my Shawn will come to his senses pretty soon and kick her to the curb. We'll pay the child support if we have to, but that's it.' Everybody around the table got real quiet after that."

Bell nodded. Rhonda's information, she knew, was gold. In a big-city prosecutor's office, Rhonda's associates would be known as confidential informants; in a small town, they were just folks. Folks whom Rhonda Lovejoy had been greeting on the streets of Acker's Gap ever since she started talking—*which was about ten seconds outta the womb, my mama claims!* Rhonda had once said to Bell with a cackle, making fun of her affinity to send and receive gossip—and who had been greeting Rhonda right back, usually appending a tidbit of news to the howdy.

For a time last year, Bell had considered firing Rhonda Lovejoy. The assistant prosecutor struggled with routine tasks such as showing up for work on time or dressing with a modesty appropriate to a solemn public office; her sartorial tastes leaned more toward Dolly Parton than Ruth Bader Ginsburg. But Rhonda's network of sources was too vast, and too valuable, to lose. Bell had been forced to put her on probation twice in the past three years, once for chronic tardiness and once, more seriously, for forgetting about an arraignment—a lapse that very nearly put a rapist back out on the street—but Bell, after an intercession by Hickey Leonard, had sighed and agreed to keep Rhonda, despite the young woman's flamboyant flaws.

"How long had they been dating?"

" 'Bout a year," Rhonda replied. "Real *Romeo and Juliet* stuff. The Doggetts are rich as all get-out. Lucinda's poor as dirt—I mean, you've seen where she and Maddie live, right? Not sure how Maddie makes ends meet. Can't be that much money in running a permanent garage sale on your front lawn, now, can there?"

Bell watched a daddy longlegs high-step across the chipped wooden floor, exhibiting its delicate scramble of balletic grace and tensile toughness. It reached the corner and started up the water-stained plaster wall. "What did Shawn's parents say in the interview this morning?" she asked. "Did they express any reservations about the relationship? Or was it all sweetness and light once the tape was rolling?"

Hickey's thumb had already resumed its scroll down the small bright screen. "Got it right here. According to Harrison, they were pretty candid. Alton said—and this is a quote—'We're just all broke up about this. She was so dear to our son and she was the mother of our grandchild. But we'll be honest. We were hoping this was just puppy love. Hoping that they'd decide to put the baby up for adoption and then move on.' Wendy Doggett, it says here, added something then. She said: 'We have high hopes for our son Shawn.' Hang on. Harrison has put in a parenthetical note here."

Hick squinted at the screen. "Right about then, Ketchum Doggett came into the room. He'd been doing some exercises when the deputies first got there. In his home gym. The one his folks installed after his accident. State-of-the-art equipment. Lord knows, Alton Doggett can afford it. He must have a couple of million bucks' worth of inventory out on that car lot of his."

"Ketchum's accident," Bell said. "Tell me about it."

Rhonda wanted to answer, and waved off Hickey as if they were two outfielders tracking the same fly ball. First, though, she had to finish a mammoth swallow of Diet Coke from the can on her desk.

"A real tragedy," she said. Hand pressed flat against her mouth, she suppressed a belch resulting from her rapid intake of the carbonated beverage. "It was about six years ago, Bell. Before you came back to town. Ketchum and Shawn and some of their friends were swimming in the Bitter River. In the part over by Louie Sizemore's farm, where it's real shallow. Way too shallow for diving. Ketchum went in headfirst—right off a tree branch hanging over the water— and broke his neck. Been in a wheelchair ever since. Paraplegic.

"You wanna know what I think?" Rhonda went on. "I think Wendy Doggett's just a little bit ashamed of Ketchum. Wants to keep him at home, so nobody can see him. Or feel sorry for him." She made a sour face. "Never could stand Wendy Doggett. Nose in the air. And you know what's funny? Her people are from out back of Coon Path Road. No matter how fancy and la-di-da she acts these days, her family's about as trashy and no-'count as families can be in these parts. If she hadn't married Alton Doggett, him with that car dealership and all the money, she'd be scrubbing toilets out at the Highway Haven," Rhonda said, naming the gargantuan truck stop out on the interstate, the one with twelve pumps, three-quarters of them diesel.

"Anything else?" Bell said.

It was Hick's turn. "Just that the Doggetts were home the whole night. That's what they say, anyway. They received several phone calls throughout the evening, and Greenough is checking with phone company records to verify time and length of the calls."

"Won't prove a thing," Bell said. "Anybody could've taken those calls. A housekeeper, for instance. Anything else?"

He shrugged. "Coroner's expecting you and the sheriff later on today. He's going to have the state crime lab folks double-check his results, but he's ready to rule it death by strangulation. Here's the hinky part, though. If you're planning to strangle somebody—why do it in a car on the riverbank? Pretty complicated. Why not just dump the body in a field somewhere?"

"Maybe it wasn't planned," Bell said. "And once she was dead, the river was right there. Handy. Perfect way to wash away the evidence."

"But who'd want her dead in the first place?" Rhonda interjected. "Listen, guys," she went on. "I knew Lucinda Trimble a little bit. Couldn't find a sweeter kid. So you've got to ask yourself—who stood to gain if she was gone?"

Rhonda sucked in a deep breath and then roared forward, answering her own question. "Lucinda and Shawn Doggett were in love. But his rich daddy and his prissy mama didn't want 'em to stay together—which is kind of nervy and hypocritical when you think about it, because things aren't so all-fired great between Mr. Moneybags and his stuck-up little wife. He's taken his fist to her a few times. No police reports—remember, Alton Doggett's got more money than God and that means he can buy enough brooms to sweep *anything* under the rug—but the Doggetts aren't this perfect little family. Lord, no."

"And Lucinda," Hick put in, "was ruining all their plans for the golden boy. And then she turns up dead. A little too convenient, don't you think?"

"Granted," Bell said, "but doesn't it also stand to reason that—"

Her words were suddenly drowned out by a heavy-duty trilling from the big black phone on the desk; it had a thick, clotted reverberation, like a gong struck repeatedly underwater.

Bell picked it up. "Yes."

"Bell, it's Lee Ann. You've got a visitor up here. A Matt Harless. Says you're expecting him."

"Okay. Be up in a bit. Get him some coffee, will you?"

She dropped the clunky receiver back in its slot. Frowned. "Dammit," Bell muttered to the universe at large. She had clean forgotten he was coming. Much as she'd been looking forward to his visit, she resented the hell out of the interruption.

"Bad news?" Hick said.

"Good news. The only thing bad about it is the timing. Just a friend. Somebody I used to—"

All at once a shrill mechanical scream invaded the stone cavity. From over their heads came the frantic pounding of heavy steps. The massive vibrations unloosed a shimmery rain of ancient yellow dirt; it dropped from the crooked seams in the old ceiling onto their hair, onto the desks and the floor.

They knew very well what the sound was. They knew it from the emergency drills that Sheriff Fogelsong had run at least once a year, ever since 9/11. It was the courthouse panic button. And the small red activation switch was rigged to a side panel under Lee Ann Frickie's desk.

Chapter Thirteen

He heard the crazed shriek of a siren in the distance and wondered what was going on. The commotion came from Acker's Gap, whose slowly rotting rooftops he couldn't quite make out through the solid weave of trees surrounding the small cabin, trees that sealed off this section of the woods like a lid screwed down tight on a canning jar.

Even though the town was out of sight, he knew precisely where it was and could imagine just what it looked like, down to the last broken-off curb and row of closed-down businesses, their empty windows so covered with grime that you couldn't even see your reflection in them anymore. It was the kind of place you never forgot—that clung to you, in fact, like kudzu—even if you'd been away from it for more than fifteen years, which he had. *Hate small towns,* he'd told somebody once. But it wasn't true: He didn't hate all small towns.

Just this one. Just Acker's Gap.

The siren's roller-coaster moan—up and down and up again, in undulating waves—moved out from the Raythune County seat, riding the air in wobbly concentric rings. He lifted his head, wondering if he'd be able to pick up anything through the trees, a flash of color or shudder of motion, but he didn't rise. He remained sitting on the torn-up steps of the ramshackle cabin, arms extended across his knees, hands dangling languidly from his wrists. He'd been here for at least an hour now. Waiting. He turned his head, scratching the bottom of his chin against his right shoulder.

Behind him, the battered front door hung open; the door had rotted off its hinges a long time ago and been quickly and indifferently fixed. Didn't close right. Never would again, without an intervention by somebody with tools and know-how. Somebody who gave a damn. He was grateful that spring was almost here. Had this still been the middle of winter, a broken door would've been a bitch and a half.

He wondered when the siren would die down. Car accident? Maybe. No telling. Nick Fogelsong, he thought, would probably be overseeing the response, whatever the emergency might be. He could see Fogelsong in his mind's eye: setting flares, waving his big fat hands over his head, directing cars to avoid the jackknifed semi, marching back and forth in his big boots and big hat, ordering folks around, trying to show how goddamned important he was.

Then again, he reminded himself, Fogelsong might look different now, after all these years. Last time he'd seen Nick Fogelsong was . . . what, 1983? '84? He'd been surprised, frankly, when Maddie told him that Fogelsong was still sheriff. Hell, how long could you work at the same damned job without going crazy? Doing the same thing over and over again—that was his idea of hell on earth. And Fogelsong had always struck him as more ambitious than that. He didn't like the man—his history with Maddie was enough to guarantee that—yet still and all, Fogelsong seemed plenty bright enough to have gotten the hell out of Acker's Gap.

But here he was. According to Maddie.

He shook his head. *People.* You never really knew a damned thing about them. About what was going on in their heads. Or what they were capable of, if you pushed them hard enough.

The siren still hadn't quit. That surprised him. Continuing that way, it sounded now like some kind of air raid. Like an emergency drill. Had somebody spotted a tornado, maybe? Or was there a jailbreak? He wished he had a phone or a computer or even a goddamned portable radio. Some way to get the news. But he was broke. Dependent on her for everything—food, coffee, Camels, this crummy cabin with the door that wouldn't close right, with its piece-of-shit porch steps—and so what could he say? Buy me a damned radio, lady, or handle things by yourself?

He heard another sound, not nearly so loud as the siren, but growing closer. A muted snarl, like something clearing its throat to signal bad intentions. He didn't move, didn't shift his position, but he was alert.

The car seemed to squeeze through the wall of the woods, rocking and bouncing across the dirt road that wasn't really a road at all, just a couple of parallel gouges in the ground in which the tires could slot themselves as the vehicle made its way toward the cabin.

He stood up. Squinted, to make sure of the visitor's identity. Squinting like that made his face hurt; he was still feeling the effects of that bar fight last month over in Covington, Kentucky. The sonofabitch had come after him with a knife. Took a hunk out of his cheek.

Good. It's her.

He stayed right there on the top porch step. He'd be damned if he'd go running at her, like they were in some shitty movie. Some chick flick. Like they were long-lost lovers, crying and kissing when they reunited. *Yeah. Right.*

The car—it was a rusted-out mound of crap, and he wondered why that cheap bastard Alton Doggett couldn't have given her a deal on a better one, being as how they'd almost been family and all, and being as how he'd loaned Lucinda a nice one—bounced to a halt. The engine trembled before it quit.

The car door flapped open. She didn't bother closing it behind her. She charged straight at him, long green dress clustering around her ankles, hands formed into little fists, and he thought again what he'd thought two weeks ago, the first time he'd seen her after all that time:

Damn. She looks good.

Her hair was gray—it streamed out behind her—but she still had her figure. She hadn't let herself go, like so many women did. Hell, she looked better than he did. He had a gut on him now. It was the beer. And not only that: His hair was turning on him. Creeping backwards.

Disappearing a little more every day. Wasn't a damned thing he could do about it. His daddy'd been as bald as a baby by the time he was fifty-five. Ran in the family.

"Hey," he said. "What the hell's going on in that town of yours? That siren liked to scare the shit outta me. What in the world is happenin' out—"

He was startled. She'd run up the three broken steps and grabbed him. She was pulling at his neck, and she was wrapping herself around him, and while she could be this way when she wanted to, usually he had a little advance notice. She'd called him a month ago, having tracked him down through Randy Bostwick—that loudmouth prick, he'd pay him back one day, Randy'd better keep an eye out for him— and at first she'd been cool. Kept her distance. Delivered her news, said her piece, made her proposition, that was that.

And now, this.

"Eddie," she said, and he had to hug her back, despite himself, because she had tucked herself into him, attaching herself. He put his arms around her and felt the heat in her, a heat that came off her body in waves. A familiar feeling, that heat. Despite her distress, despite the tears, he felt his body responding. God, she had a way about her.

"Eddie, Eddie," she said, voice thick from the weeping.

"The noise—what the hell's with the siren?"

Confused, she shook her head. She hadn't been aware of any siren. She was too deep in her grief and pain. "I came as quick as I could, Eddie," she said. "'Fraid they'd be watching me. Had to wait. Bide my time." A great gust of sorrow washed over her, causing her to quiver like the uppermost leaves of a tree in a wild wind. "She's dead. Our baby girl is dead."

Chapter Fourteen

With a gloved index finger, Nick Fogelsong touched the tiny *O* in the window above Lee Ann Frickie's desk. He could reach it easily, without stretching or straining. That meant the entry point was at a height chillingly commensurate with the back of Lee Ann's head as she sat in her chair, working at her computer, which is precisely where she'd been and what she'd been doing at the moment the bullet arrived.

"Bert Hillman," Bell said. Her voice, to her irritation, was shaky; she didn't know if anyone else noticed it, but she did, and that was enough. She blamed the close call. "Had to be him, Nick. Had to be. Just the kind of stunt that crazy sonofabitch would pull."

The sheriff, without looking at her, acknowledged the comment with a nod. He continued his work at the window. "Lee Ann agrees with you," he said. "Already following that angle. We'll find him right away and question him. Check his weapon."

He probed the circle's crisp little edge gingerly, respectfully—as if, Bell thought, he half suspected the glass might sue the county if he didn't show it the proper deference. She knew he was informally gauging the size and shape of the point at which the round had hit the window, moving through it far too fast to shatter it, matching it against a mental inventory of bullet holes he'd encountered in his long career. Deputy Harrison was outside on the street, using her hastily calculated angle of trajectory to figure out from where it might have been fired. Harrison had already called Fogelsong to report that the shooter had vanished. A ballistics team from the West Virginia State Police Forensic Lab was on its way.

Arriving within seconds of the start of the alarm—his office was in an annex right down the hall—the sheriff had assessed the situation, shut off the siren's infernal wail, put the courthouse on lockdown, sealed the perimeter, and asked Lee Ann for the first name that popped into her head when she heard the phrase *vengeful gun-toting fool.*

Bert Hillman, she'd said. No hesitation.

"Need a doctor?" Nick had continued. "That's my second question. Should've been my first. Apologies."

"Not a scratch on me."

"Not what I asked."

"I'm fine, Nick. Fine." Lee Ann's slightly embarrassed manner told the story: She hadn't been injured, and so thought perhaps she'd overreacted. "Figured we might be under some kind of assault," she explained. "Wish I hadn't had to scare the bejesus out of everybody by pushing the button."

"You did the right thing," the sheriff said.

Lee Ann stood in the middle of the small office, breathing in and out carefully, deliberately, as if newly appreciative of the simple miracle of being able to do so. The old woman wasn't panicky or distraught but only quiet, thoughtful, like someone long resigned to such near-misses and could-have-beens, such narrow escapes. She was the calm center point of a bobbing carousel of people, a nervous circle that included Bell; Hick; Rhonda; Deputy Charlie Mathers; County Clerk Polly Vinson; Vinson's assistant, Tina Sheets; and Janet Leftwich, the courthouse custodian—many of whom were visibly agitated, reaching out to touch Lee Ann's arm, shaking their heads.

Bell and her staff had hustled up the twisting stone staircase leading out of the basement to find, on the first floor of the courthouse, a murmuring herd of confused people. The corridors in the old building were oppressively narrow, like arteries fatally cushioned with plaque, and the thronging presence of courthouse employees and people who'd been working or shopping in town when they heard the siren and flocked here made the place feel like the first night of the Raythune County Fair, when people wedged themselves into every available inch of the fairgrounds at the town's edge. *Back to back and belly to belly,* was how Bell's friend Dot Burdette liked to describe the crowds on those August nights, when the air was spiced with the overlapping smells of sweat, fried dough, and livestock excrement. Nick Fogelsong always topped Dot's description with his own favorite line about the smushed-together multitude: *People're butt to nut out there.*

"I'd just bent over to get a file out of the bottom drawer," Lee Ann said, "when it happened." She swallowed. "If I'd had my head up, looking at my computer screen, like I'd been doing just a second before, that bullet would have—"

She couldn't finish. She didn't flinch, but nor could she finish her sentence. She simply stopped talking. Tina Sheets reached out to stroke her arm. "Oh, sweetie," Tina said.

When Bell had first charged in, her eyes made a swift but thorough accounting of the people crammed in the room. She'd spotted Matt Harless right away. He was in the far corner, down on one knee, head bent over like a preacher in prayer, but the focus of his attention wasn't some inscrutable deity; he was frowning at the starburst gouge in the pale yellow plaster wall near the baseboard that marked the spot where the bullet had lodged. After checking on Lee Ann, Bell had moved over to him.

"Matt," she said. "Are you okay?"

"Unscathed." He stood up. "Your secretary here is amazing. She's one cool customer."

Bell put a hand on his forearm and nodded, her meaning clear: *If you're okay, I've got work to do.* Then she parted the crowd with a motion like a swimmer doing the breaststroke, heading toward the sheriff, seething with her certainty. She didn't bother with a greeting or an expression of relief that nobody was hurt. No time for empty platitudes.

"Bert Hillman," Bell said, well aware that she was repeating herself and fully intending to. "That troublemaking bastard just has to be behind this."

"Okay," Fogelsong said. He still faced the window, his broad back to the room. Thoughtfully, he traced the circumference of the bullet hole over and over with a slow-moving finger. When he finally did turn around, he looked past Bell, having eyes only for Lee Ann. "I mean it," he said to her. "You did exactly the right thing. Setting off the alarm. Good thinking. Not sure I would've had the presence of mind. Under the circumstances."

This wasn't the first time, Bell knew, that Lee Ann had had a close call. She'd been born and raised in Sawyer Fork, a corner of Raythune County subject to clockwork spasms of violence, home to a poverty-sparked despair that seemed to soak the ground at regular intervals like a solemn gray rain. Lee Ann had witnessed men and women being killed or badly harmed by knives, by guns, by dogs, by fists. *Hard to say,* she'd once remarked to Bell, *which is worse.* When she was twelve, she'd seen her own mother beaten into a coma by her father, who had served four years in the West Virginia state prison in Moundsville for aggravated assault before dying of liver cancer. Through all those traumas, Lee Ann Frickie had remained steadfast and stoic.

This, though, might affect her more than she realized it would. Because, Bell thought, it had happened in the courthouse. This wasn't Sawyer Fork. This was a safe place.

Or at least it was supposed to be.

"Sending my staff home for the rest of the day," declared Polly Vinson. She was a short, heavy woman in her late fifties who kept her raspberry-colored hair cut in complicated layers and her ears busy with pendulous earrings, all with the intention of distracting the eye from her burly body. She'd been county clerk for more than two decades. "Everybody's way too shook up to work, anyhow," she announced.

"Scared the pee out of me," admitted her assistant, Tina, with a dramatic shudder followed by a nervous giggle. "Siren goin' off like that. And then all the screamin'." Tina was thirty-two, the mother of seven of her own children and stepmother to her husband's four. The head count sometimes made Bell dizzy when she thought about it too long, particularly after she'd glimpsed the small trailer in which the family resided. Tina's husband was distantly related to Lori and Deanna Sheets, the mother and daughter whom Bell had prosecuted last year in connection with a homicide.

"Deputies are checking the rest of the courthouse," Fogelsong said. He aimed his gaze once again at Lee Ann. "Anything out of the ordinary happen just before the gunshot?"

The old woman thought about it. A strand of gray had broken loose from the tight bun that corralled her hair, and now trailed across her shoulder.

"Well," Lee Ann said. "Bell was meeting with Hick and Rhonda downstairs and I'd just called her and told her about her visitor and—"

"Visitor?" the sheriff said. "What visitor?"

"Right here," said Harless, voice rising from the back of the crowd. He slid sideways to facilitate his trek forward.

Fogelsong looked him over. Not noticing a stranger in his midst was a measure, Bell knew, of the sheriff's distress and preoccupation. Usually he'd know right away when a new face was on the premises; she'd once accused him of possessing a secret antenna that picked up a signal when someone crossed the county line without his fore-knowledge.

"Matt Harless," Harless said. "Friend of Bell's."

From Fogelsong there was no welcoming smile. No automatic proffer of a handshake. Bell had seen that before—his slow molten stare at a newcomer—and had called him on it, whereupon the sheriff had retorted, *Never met the lawman yet who takes to strangers. Ninety-nine times out of a hundred, strangers mean trouble.* Where-upon Bell was always tempted to reply: *Yes—and they also mean revenue for local businesses and diversity and fresh ideas, but by all means, let's chase 'em out. Soon as possible.*

Fogelsong switched his glare from Harless to Bell.

"He's from D.C.," she said. "Going to be around for a week or two." She'd give Nick the lowdown once they were alone.

The sheriff grunted. "D.C.," he said.

Harless nodded.

"Well, you sure picked a hell of a day to show up." Fogelsong turned back to Lee Ann. "Soon as we're through here, I'm going to have Deputy Greenough take you home."

"No need."

"I didn't say there was a need. I said I was going to do it." Nick took Lee Ann's elbow and led her back to her chair. Guided her into it. "I know you're fine. You're as tough as they come. But it might get to you later—just the thought. Don't want you driving when it does."

He took a step back—he didn't want to crowd her—and then he said, "Tell me what happened after that. After you called Bell."

Lee Ann touched the front edge of her desk, as if to make sure that it was still real, that things were just as they'd been before. "Well," she said, "I leaned over to put away the file—the one I'd been using—and before Mr. Harless had even gotten a chance to sit down—" She moistened her lips. "—the shot came through that window."

"No doubt in your mind about what it was," Nick said.

"No doubt in my mind." Lee Ann looked up at him. He knew Sawyer Fork as well as she did. She'd heard plenty of gunfire in her life. "I jumped up." She put a hand on her forehead. "Instead of hitting the deck. Like a damned fool, I jumped up."

"Reflexes," Nick said. "You having a beef with anybody other than Bert Hillman? Anybody you know who might think this kind of thing is funny?"

"No." Her hand stayed on her forehead, as if she needed it there to keep her thoughts in line.

"Other than Bert, any threats lately to this office?" the sheriff went on. "No defendants that maybe seemed a little more pissed off than usual?"

A faint smile. "Nick Fogelsong," Lee Ann said, "you and I both know that the day a defendant doesn't threaten to take you, me, Bell, and all of our kinfolk and household pets and dump the whole load of us out on Route 6 and run over the lump again and again with an eighteen-wheeler—after first prying out our eyeballs and smashing our kneecaps with a ballpeen hammer—well, that's the day we know we've gone too easy on the sonofabitch. You know what I mean?"

Nick looked a little startled at the incongruity of such language coming out of Lee Ann Frickie. She'd taught Sunday school at the Rising Souls Baptist Church for the past thirty-eight years and had been known to fine Nick and his deputies—and Bell, too—a nickel each time they resorted to profanity in her presence, donating the proceeds to the church's overseas mission fund. Her point, however, was a valid one. Threats were a regular part of the job in a criminal justice system in a place like Raythune County, where people lived as close to their emotions as they did to the mountains. Feelings were packed in tight, with no space in between, and could easily rub a raw mark.

"Point taken," Fogelsong said. "Still and all, though, I'd appreciate it if you could think about it and see if anything occurs to you."

Lee Ann waited thirty seconds. "I still agree with Bell," she said. "Bert Hillman. He's been calling here every day for three weeks. Getting madder and madder. Kind of becomes like background noise around here. Hardly notice it anymore."

"What's got him riled up now?"

"That new road the county's putting in," Lee Ann said. "Claims the rain runoff's bound to end up in his front yard. Also says he has a clear line of sight from his porch to the road crew and—this is a quote, Nick—he's going to 'blow their gol-durned heads off.' "

The sheriff nodded. "Got it." And then, as if he'd just remembered him, Fogelsong looked over at Matt Harless again. Gave him a truculent glare.

"Bet you think this is par for the course, don't you, mister? Just what you'd expect in West Virginia. People taking potshots at each another, just for the hell of it."

"You have a beautiful county here, Sheriff," Matt said evenly. "That was my only expectation. Looking forward to seeing it for myself. And I'm just happy that nobody got hurt here today."

Bell stepped forward. "I'll call you later, Matt. Help you get settled."

"Sure." He took her meaning and edged toward the door, sliding between the people jammed in the room.

The sheriff was talking again. "Until we figure this out," he said, addressing everyone now, "I'm hereby requiring all courthouse employees to keep their blinds closed and their drapes pulled. I'd close the place down if I could while we're investigating, but that's just not practical." His gaze whipped back to the window above Lee Ann Frickie's desk, as if to let it know he hadn't forgotten what had started this mess. "We'll know more when the state boys give us the ballistics report. They ought to be getting here within the hour. Now, come on, Lee Ann. I'll walk you out. Greenough should have the Blazer around front by now."

"Got a ton of work to do," she said. "I'll have to come back later today."

"We'll see," the sheriff said. As he helped her up, he spoke to Bell. "Got a call just before all hell broke loose. Coroner's ready for us."

Bell's mind made a quick, complicated turn back to its original setting, like a truck with a wide wheelbase forced to maneuver on the fly.

The Trimble girl's murder. The body in a car in the Bitter River. Work to do.

"Lee Ann?" Bell said, making a final check before she switched her focus. "You need anything, you call me. You decide you want some time off—that's no problem. No problem at all."

"See you in a couple of hours," Lee Ann said.

Chapter Fifteen

They took separate vehicles. It made sense, Bell knew; if Nick received an emergency call, he'd have to leave right away, with no time to drop her back by the courthouse. Still, there was an odd feeling to being part of a somber two-car parade that wove slowly up Main and around Donnelly and finally over to Route 6, stopping in the gravel lot next to the cinder-block box with the gray awning that housed the county coroner's office.

Buster Crutchfield, an elderly physician whose XXL lab coat was no longer even close to fitting around his middle, met them in the reception area and led them to the room in the back. The room that civilians never saw. There were times when Bell wished she'd never seen it, either.

This was one of those times.

The body of Lucinda Trimble was faceup on the stainless steel table, white sheet pulled to her shoulders and tucked around her torso, slender arms straight at her sides. The body had not been in the water long enough to swell. The areas where that tended to happen first—the face and tips of the fingers—were slightly puffy, but otherwise, the corpse looked largely unmarked by its ordeal.

Staring at it, Bell found herself wishing—perversely, she knew—to have to endure the familiar grotesquerie of the typical victim of a river drowning, undiscovered for many days: the ghastly color, the balloonlike limbs and beach-ball belly, and the natural slashes where the skin had split as the gases pushed out and breached the body's perimeter. *At least then we'd know it was too late,* Bell told herself. At least then she wouldn't have the strange and harrowing compulsion to touch Lucinda's perfect shoulder and say, *Wake up, wake up, it's time to go home. You don't belong here, sweetheart. It's all a mistake. Your mother's waiting for you at home. She's worried sick.* The terrible beauty of Lucinda's face was a kind of curse.

The only sign that anything about the young woman was out of the ordinary—aside from the bizarre fact that she was lying on a table under the bright lights of a laboratory and the prying eyes of three people, and that she was partially covered by a sheet to hide the preliminary work done by Buster Crutchfield—were the small bruises on her neck and the scattering of tiny red dots across parts of her face.

Other than that, Bell thought, *she's lovely. And dead.*

It was part of her job as a prosecutor to know the particulars about the violent deaths that occurred on her watch—and to behold those particulars prior to the careful, clue-destroying cleanup perpetrated by Floyd Fontaine and his sons over at Fontaine's Funeral Home. In previous visits to the coroner's office, Bell had seen victims of car accidents, victims of shootings, victims of attacks by fighting dogs. She'd seen people who had slipped while climbing and ended up at the bottom of the mountain, after hitting dozens of sharp rocks on the way down. She'd seen faces torn apart, faces smashed and burned and mutilated. She'd seen decapitated bodies. Bodies sliced in half by trucks and by trains.

But this was always the worst: a body with a face that looked just fine. That looked as if you could gently tap an arm and whisper a name, *Lucinda, Lucinda,* and this young woman might very well open her eyes, cough, blink, sit up, and look around at the trio of people gathered alongside the table—Bell Elkins, Nick Fogelsong, and Buster Crutchfield—and then look down at herself and realize she was covered only by a sheet, but instead of being shocked or embarrassed by it, would just politely ask for her clothes, and then ask what time it was, and when she heard the answer, would ask somebody to call her mother for her. *She'll be so worried about me! Wow—I'll be in big trouble if I don't get home pretty soon.*

Buster Crutchfield broke Bell's reverie by clearing his throat. It was the gentleman's way of saying, *Let's get on with this, okeydokey?* Crutchfield had a broad doughy body and a mushy face, and what bits of hair he had left on his head were as white and soft and randomly distributed as the effluvia shed by cottonwood trees. He had been a general practitioner in Acker's Gap for more than fifty years and coroner as well for the last thirty of them. He spoke in a courtly voice that still shivered with the delicate rhythms of his southern Virginia upbringing. The flounce and swoop of his accent reminded Bell of a dust ruffle on a bedspread: "As I told Nick earlier, darlin', she wasn't in the water very long. No more'n four or five hours."

Bell gave a single nod of acknowledgment. She moved closer to the table, to indicate to Buster that she was ready for the briefing. Madeline Trimble, she knew, would be showing up soon to make the formal identification for the record. Bell didn't especially want to be here then. She wanted to finish what she had to do and leave. She'd seen grief in all its varieties—the wild kind that made people scream and claw the air and drop to their knees and curse God, and the quiet staring kind that was like the awful pause right before the dynamite blows at the base of a mountain that's in the way of a new road—and she didn't need to see it again. There was nothing more she could learn from anybody's grief.

"Move in close here, darlin', can you do that?" Buster said to her.

Bell obliged. He leaned in over the body, too, and jabbed a fat, crooked finger in the air just above Lucinda's neck. "See the marks? Somebody pressed a couple of thumbs against this li'l gal's windpipe. We've got all the classic signs. Tongue and larynx? Enlarged. Hyoid bone? Fractured. And see these itty-bitty red dots on her face? I think you folks know this already, but that's what we call petechiae—little breaks in the veins, caused by the pressure. If you looked at the insides of her eyelids, which I did and which you're both welcome to do for yourselves if you've a mind to, assuming you put on gloves first, you'd see the same thing." He stood upright again. Winced from the effort. "No water in the lungs. This gal was dead before she hit the water, and that death came from strangulation."

From anybody else, "gal" would have caused Bell to add to the local death toll by murdering the purveyor of such blatantly sexist language, just as would the constant iteration of "darlin'." But Crutchfield was an old man. *Pick your battles,* Fogelsong had advised her, during their very first homicide investigation. *Don't waste your outrage on Buster Crutchfield. Or any other good ole boy around these parts. You'll never change 'em. So just wait 'em out.*

"Any evidence that she struggled? Fought off her attacker?" Bell asked.

Crutchfield shook his big head back and forth. The jowls on his face waggled when he did so, and the skin on his neck quavered and then settled back down again. "I think it was too quick, Miss Belfa. Nothing under her fingernails to indicate that she scratched or dug up any skin. Looks like she didn't know what was coming."

Bell turned to Fogelsong. "So somebody killed her in the car—or somewhere else, and then put her in the car. And then the car rolled in the river."

"Looks that way."

"But she didn't fight off her assailant, apparently. So she didn't think she was in any danger."

"Until she was," the sheriff said.

"Does that make sense?"

"Making sense has got nothing to do with it."

She granted him the point. How many homicides had they investigated in which the perpetrators were sloppy or impetuous or illogical or just plain dumb? Her job—and the sheriff's job—wasn't to outwit some criminal mastermind. Wasn't to follow the logic of an elegantly diabolical act by some backwoods Hannibal Lecter. It was to figure out what happened and who did it, and then to figure out how to prove all of that in a courtroom.

"No ring?" Bell said.

"What?"

"She's not wearing a ring—or any jewelry, for that matter," Bell said. "Most teenage girls do." She was thinking about Carla, who tended to switch out her accessories hourly—but always wore, at any given time, at least three rings, a necklace, a braided wristband, and multiple earrings, the kind that traveled up the rim of her ear like a curved line of braille. "Did your deputies take it off?"

"My deputies," Nick said, voice icy with umbrage, "don't remove anything from a body recovered in a homicide investigation unless specifically authorized to do so. And they weren't. So—no. No, they didn't. If you don't see a ring, then she wasn't wearing one." He moved his jaw back and forth. "But I'll check with Maddie Trimble, just to be sure. Get back to you on that."

Fogelsong still hadn't really looked at Bell yet. He was looking at Lucinda's body. Without taking his eyes away from it, he addressed Crutchfield. "Can we cover up her face now? If you're done here, I mean."

So it's bothering him, too, Bell thought. *The awful perfection. The fact that she's whole. Her excruciating beauty.*

"Christ Almighty, Nick," the coroner said. "This gal's mama is on her way. She'll want to see her girl. Make sure it's really her and that she's not coming back. Hard to understand, maybe, but it brings a kind of solace. A certainty. I believe you know that. And have for some time."

"I do," the sheriff said. Apology in his tone.

They had been doing it the same way for decades. Family members who arrived to identify the bodies of their loved ones were escorted into a small room that accessed this space from a separate entrance. Then slowly, almost reverently, the drape on a narrow eye-level window was cranked open. The victim was arranged on what looked to be a padded table, with only the head showing. A blanket was tucked discreetly over the rest of the body. No other bodies were visible. The public didn't see the stainless steel table, or any of the tools of the coroner's trade. A polite fiction was allowed to live in the air: the sweet lie that the deceased had come in just this way, looking for all the world to be simply asleep, at peace, and that no havoc was wrought upon the body during the infliction of mortal injury or, after that, in the service of science.

"I'm just a little jumpy on this one," Nick went on. "A little extra-sensitive. Knew the mother pretty well."

"I do believe I remember that," Crutchfield said. He didn't say anything else about it, which was another way of saying a great deal.

The coroner wasn't quite finished with his comments on the body, however. "One thing's kind of peculiar about our poor young friend here, based on my preliminary observation," Crutchfield added. He joined his hands together at the putative waist of his white coat, the knuckles of one hand fitting neatly into the curved palm of the other.

Bell and the sheriff waited for him to elaborate, which, after a meditative pause, he did.

"Human body's a strong thing. Resilient as all get-out. Puts up with all kinds of abuse and neglect, day after day, year after year. But you know what? If you want to shut the dang thing down for keeps, all you have to do is to put a little pressure right here—"

Crutchfield uncoupled his hands in order to lift his right index finger to his throat. He tapped it twice.

"—for not very long, and that's it. Lights out. Loss of consciousness and then death. It all comes down to this li'l ole strip of flesh right here. Doesn't matter how big you are or how powerful you are. Doesn't matter how fast you can run or how many push-ups you can do. Whole dadburned show can come to a screeching halt right here. In no time flat."

"Meaning what, Doc?" the sheriff said.

"Meaning that the marks on her neck don't indicate that a great deal of sustained force was used to kill this little lady. This wasn't some kind of wild, prolonged rampage. You've got to keep in mind that killing somebody by choking them to death can happen pretty fast, especially if your victim is not expecting it. I'd almost be willing to speculate that whoever did this might've been just as surprised as the victim was when the action took her life."

"So we're looking at an accident?" said a skeptical Bell, frowning.

"Not saying that," Crutchfield replied. "Not saying that at all. What I'm trying to suggest, though, is that your killer might've had something else in mind when he or she grabbed this sweet young lady around the throat."

"Like what?" Bell asked.

Fogelsong, whose mind had leapt ahead of Crutchfield's slow-moving speech, answered before the coroner could:

"Like shutting her up."

Outside, the night air was cool. During the time they'd been meeting with Buster Crutchfield, the sun had gone down, vanishing behind the mountain with such absolute finality that—as Bell remembered from her childhood—you sometimes wondered if it ever intended to return. A bleak feeling.

The sheriff was still back in the coroner's office. Bell had paused to see if he would leave when she did, but he'd waved her on. "Catch you later," Nick said without looking at her. "Got some business to talk over with Buster." She didn't believe him. She thought he was still sore at her, still nursing his wounded pride, and he was making her pay. Depriving her of his company at the end of a godawful day.

Well, screw you, Bell thought, but the thought was sparked by loneliness, not animosity. Things were still strained between them, awkward, and while they did their jobs, same as always, she missed their easy companionship. The effortless give-and-take.

Back in the Explorer, she turned on her cell. She always switched it off in the coroner's office.

The only message was from Carla. Bell hadn't found a moment yet to call and tell her about Lucinda Trimble. And now it was too late to be the one to break the news.

"Mom—oh my God." Carla's voice was soft, wobbly. "I got about a million texts from my friends back there. Oh God—Lucinda." She coughed. Took several deep breaths. "I didn't know her super well, Mom, but—oh God, I just can't believe it—Mom. Mom, what hap-pened? Can you—? I just don't—" There was another short pause, and then the snuffling sounds of tears. And the fact that Bell was listening to a digitally recorded message instead of talking to her child face-to-face, stroking her hair, comforting her—made her feel ragged and empty, as if, during the hour that she'd been in the coroner's office, she'd lost a lot more than just the sun.

Chapter Sixteen

A few minutes later, while guiding the Explorer down a dark road whose edges seemed to slope away from her headlights, Bell called Clay. "Hell of a day," she said. "You busy?"

He hesitated. Muttered something about how late it was. And— what about the neighbors?

"News flash," she replied. "I'm fresh out of give-a-damn." She'd made a decision: Tonight, she'd break her rule about overnight stays.

First, though, she had to stop by the courthouse to pick up some documents that needed her review. If he got to the house ahead of her, she said, he should wait for her upstairs.

She arrived home twenty minutes later. No lights were visible. She saw his truck parked in her driveway; the sight made her smile. When she went inside, she didn't touch any switches. She climbed the stairs, undressed, slipped into bed next to him. Put a hand on his bare chest. He kissed her, and then he kissed her again, and she could feel the solid length of him, fitting himself next to her, making sure the quilt covered her body so that she wouldn't be cold.

Her fingers found the long jagged scar on his right shoulder. He'd been injured in a hunting accident when he was a boy, hit by a stray bullet fired by his dad's hunting buddy, Judge Foster Crimmins. Crimmins rarely hunted sober. Everybody knew it, but until Walter

Meckling's nine-year-old son saw his own small shoulder explode and heard a bourbon-laced mumble—*Sorry 'bout that, kid*—the judge's problem was conveniently ignored. After the accident, Walter never spoke to the judge again. His about-face seemed to give tacit permission to the community to do what it had long wanted to do. Crimmins was impeached for drunkenness on the bench. He died a year later, and when he did, the coroner had remarked to Walter Meckling that he'd seen tree bark with more give in it than Foster Crimmins's liver.

Now Bell ran a gentle finger along the thick scar, which stretched from Clay's collarbone all the way down to his elbow. The scar felt rough and ugly, as if there were a heavy rope buried under the skin, making the crusty upraised area on the surface pucker and twist.

"Any leads on the courthouse shooting?" he murmured.

"No."

"Want to talk about it?"

"No."

She'd reached out to Clay because the sight of Lucinda's body, coupled with the chilling business of Lee Ann Frickie's close call, had been deeply, profoundly troubling. She knew she needed help tonight. The dead young woman seemed so much like Carla—same slender body, same dark hair, same dreams.

She relaxed in Clay's arms, letting the day's heaviness lift from her little by little, bit by bit. Bell knew it wouldn't go away all at once. She didn't want it to.

Detaching from a difficult day was like rising after a deep dive, she believed. You couldn't do it too quickly. You'd get the bends. You had to be gradual about it, careful, measured, or you'd pay the price, on account of the pressure differential. The weight of the terrible crushing sadness had to be broken down slowly into smaller increments, so that it could be balanced against normal life.

So that she could sleep.

So that she could live.

She'd seen what happened to people who tried to get rid of it all at once. Who rushed things. Who didn't let the day's summary of ugliness depart from them gradually, in its own good time. Cops, docs,

EMTs, combat vets—anybody who, like Bell, was forced on a regular basis to stare down some of the worst things in the world. Homicide, rape, drug addiction, child abuse. She'd seen what happened when people tried to shed the day's grimness too fast. Frantic, desperate, suffering under the load, they'd use alcohol, drugs, food, sex, rampant risk-taking—or a combination of all that and more—to free themselves. To get themselves past the pictures in their heads. Pictures of the dead. Or pictures of the living, of people who were gray and grieving, stripped raw.

Go slow, Bell reminded herself. She had learned that. Learned to go slow when, at the end of a hard day, she tried to separate herself from the sorrow or the frustration of the job. She couldn't shuck it all off too fast. It would leave—but not if it was pushed. Not if it was forced.

Go slow.

Bell felt Clay's breath on her face and then on her neck. Felt his sturdy, capable hands moving slowly down and across her skin. Felt the length of him, his body seeming to touch her everywhere, all at once. Felt herself dissolving into the rhythms he created and maintained, rhythms that rhymed with her own desires. And as she felt all that, she sensed the day's grave essence breaking into smaller and smaller fragments, and then into smaller particles still, after which they softly floated away from her, dark truth by dark truth, like frail flakes of ash from a dying fire.

Chapter Seventeen

Sheriff Fogelsong sat in the Blazer, now parked beside his house after the drive home from the coroner's office. He'd shut off the engine two minutes ago. The engine ticked on for a spell, keeping his thoughts company.

Darkness had risen up all around him, the benign nightly ambush. The sun had gone down while he was still at the coroner's with Bell, which meant that his trip home had been the kind he liked: fast motion through a shadow-blackened landscape, as if he were a bullet shot straight up into the night air. He liked being, for blessed intervals, the only motion he had to be concerned about.

He'd passed two cars and a coal truck on his way home, but it was too dark to see the drivers. That pleased him. No need to wave or nod or honk. Most of the time he didn't mind acknowledging people he knew; some nights, though, it got on his nerves. The waves, the nods. The goddamned honks. Or, if the encounters were in person, the *Hey-howya-doin'* followed in lockstep by the *Can't-rightly-complain-how-'bout-you.*

Repeat.

There were times when he craved anonymity. Not a bucketful. Just a little taste of it. A sip, every now and again.

Bell had left the coroner's office twenty minutes before he did.

Fogelsong had stayed until Maddie Trimble arrived. Why was she late? What could've been more important than making the formal identification, for the record, of her child's body? He hadn't asked her for an explanation when she finally showed up, and a few minutes later—when the drape was slowly inched back on the rectangular window, revealing the mortal remains of Lucinda Abigail Trimble, supine on the padded table, white sheet covering all but her face and neck—it didn't matter, because Maddie had become hysterical again, screaming and sobbing and flinging herself around the room, and Nick had his hands full just keeping her from doing physical harm to herself.

Buster Crutchfield had helped him get Maddie into a chair. Brought her a glass of water. They stood on either side of her, the sheriff and the coroner, while she shivered and wailed with her grief, bending over and beating her knees with her fists. Buster stroked her hair, murmuring, "I know, darlin', I know. I know." Nick didn't say anything.

Now he peered through the Blazer's big side window at his house. It was built against the back of a mountain, in the shadow of a shelf-like projection known as Smithson's Rock. Nick had bought the house from a mine foreman who'd been transferred to Wyoming, where the mining company was concentrating most of its efforts. Leaving West Virginia behind to fend for itself.

No lights on.

Didn't surprise him. He and Mary Sue had lived here a long time, since a year after they were married. She could move through the house easily without light. She seemed to prefer it, in fact. Several times, in the middle of the night, he'd discovered her fingering her way down the dark upstairs hall, sliding along the wallpaper like a spider, turning this way and that, brushing back shadows.

Don't turn on the light! Don't want any lights! This way, I can't see 'em. And they can't see me.

Who, honey?

Them.

Them?

The ones who're after me.

Fogelsong was bone-tired. There was an ache across his shoulders. A forking jab in his lower back when he twisted his torso, even slightly. Questions flitted around the inside of his skull like stupid clumsy moths, tumbling, fluttering, bumping the rounded sides of their cage. Annoying him.

He didn't know who had killed Lucinda Trimble. He didn't know why somebody had taken a shot at the prosecutor's office in broad daylight, an act so brazen as to be unthinkable in years past—but not now. Not now.

Nick arched his back. Stretched out his fingers.

It was time to go inside. He knew that.

He didn't move from the Blazer.

Normally, after a meeting like that with the coroner, Nick and Bell had a ritual. He'd nod at her across the room, a nod that meant: *Let's go.* It was time for them to discuss the case privately. They'd head back to the sheriff's office in the courthouse, and he'd sit behind the flimsy black metal desk and he'd open the spiral-bound notebook upon which he'd recorded his preliminary thoughts on the case. Then he'd look up at the prosecuting attorney, who'd be sitting in the wooden straight-backed chair that faced his desk, and they'd compare theories.

If they didn't want to go back to his office, they'd sit in the Blazer, talking and strategizing. If they didn't want to sit in the Blazer, they'd go to Ike's. Toss ideas back and forth while the coffee in their cups got cold and the pie on their plates was forgotten.

But things were unsettled now between him and Bell, and they'd been that way ever since she'd questioned his objectivity on the Trimble case. Their relationship felt like a limb that had abruptly lost its flexibility, that had stiffened up on account of an unexpected cold snap.

So tonight, he hadn't asked her to stick around and work on the case with him. He was still angry that she'd told him to recuse himself in the questioning of Maddie Trimble—even though, he'd acknowledged to himself almost immediately thereafter, she was right.

And there was something else. He'd sensed her restlessness. Her pre-occupation.

Nick knew its origin.

He was well aware of the fact that Bell was dating Clayton Meckling. The sheriff liked Clay—he'd known the young man since he was a kid, when Walter Meckling would bring him along to county meetings—but he wasn't sure if Clay was good enough for Belfa Elkins. Hell, he wasn't sure if anyone was.

He'd been looking out for Bell since she was ten years old, and sometimes it was hard to remember that she was all grown up now. Possessor of a law degree. Mother of a teenager. She didn't need him to hold her hand anymore and tell her things were going to be okay.

Moreover, the one who needed help these days, it seemed, the one who was struggling, was Nick Fogelsong. Not Bell.

He wasn't following protocol with the Trimble case, which wasn't like him. He'd done things that surprised himself: handling the initial interrogation with Maddie Trimble when he had a personal tie, then going back to Maddie's house later that morning after she'd called him. No matter who was ultimately charged with the crime, any good defense lawyer would pounce on those irregularities. What was he doing? Was he losing his grip?

Hell and damnation.

His father's favorite curse.

Where had *that* come from? He'd not thought about Big Jim Fogelsong, dead for two decades now, in quite some time.

Nicholas Fogelsong, came his father's voice, rearing up in Nick's memory, *get your butt inside this house. Now. What're these boots of yours doing here in the hall? You think your mama's some kinda maid or something? Well, she ain't. Hell and damnation, son, you're as lazy as a barn cat sneakin' into the chicken feed.*

Big Jim, though, had said those things with a smile on his face. Big Jim was a good man. Firm, set in his ways, but kind. And fair. Would've been a fine sheriff, Nick thought, if he'd been so inclined. Instead, Big Jim had watched his son take the oath. And was busting-out proud of his boy, for the few short years that remained to him after Nick was elected to the post, until the cancer that was gnawing away at Big Jim's insides finally finished the job.

Nick pushed open the Blazer's heavy door. Swiveled his hips and swung his big boots down onto the driveway. Smithson's Rock loomed off to his left, a jagged promontory that blocked the heavier weather from this property, made it a little island off to itself.

If the past was going to come chasing after him—that was how Bell saw it, he knew, sometimes describing the past as a mean dog with a good scent in the nose, yapping and snarling and always trying to run you up a tree—the least he could do was to give the mutt a moving target.

"Mary Sue?"

He took a few steps into the living room. He hated to turn on a light, knowing it would startle and alarm her.

"Mary Sue?" he repeated.

He thought he heard a shuffling sound in the corner, so he headed that way. He'd made as much noise as he could as he had entered the house, not wanting to surprise her; he'd tromped across the porch with brick-heavy strides and he'd let the wide front door rattle shut behind him. The house still seemed to be shuddering from the blow.

"Hey, Mary Sue."

No response.

Working steadily toward the corner of the living room, Nick called out again. "Mary Sue?"

He hit something with his thigh. Didn't hurt himself. Just bumped it, running into it. It was, he realized, the small table next to his reading chair. He kept his books there: history books, mainly. Biographies of military leaders were a special passion. He never talked about how much he read. Easier, really, to play the bumpkin sheriff. The small-town hick. Once, he'd picked up some smart-ass punk who worked for the governor—Nick was supposed to drive him around Raythune County to look at flood damage—and the punk picked up the thick crinkled paperback on the passenger seat of the Blazer, the book Nick had been reading while he waited for him to show up. With a smirk, the kid had read from the cover: *The Coming Fury*. It was one of Nick's favorites, the first volume in Bruce Catton's Civil War trilogy; he'd read it three times and was now happily embarked on a fourth. But when the kid said the title, he'd put a little barb of a question mark in his voice, as if to scoff, *You? A book? Really?*

Nick could've slapped that arrogant asshole. Sometimes wished he had.

"Mary Sue? Honey?"

He reached out a hand, thinking she might be crouched behind the recliner, down where he couldn't see her. He'd found her there before. Squeezed into a ball, chin on her knees, arms wrapped around her folded legs, shoulders shivering. Flesh tipped up into goose bumps. Wearing only her nightgown, a flimsy cotton thing whose frilly hem barely brushed the tops of her feet. Middle of winter it was, when he'd found her that way. He'd had to reach down and pull her up slowly, slowly, talking gently to her the whole time. If he spooked her, he knew, she was liable to get hysterical. Scream for the rest of the night.

"Mary Sue? You down there?"

She wasn't. His eyes had adjusted to the darkness by now and he could see that the area behind the recliner was empty.

Where could she be?

Nick checked the kitchen, the pantry, the first-floor bathroom. With every repetition, his call of "Mary Sue? Sweetie?" gradually became less gentle and soothing and more annoyed. *Dammit.* He was tired. He'd had a long day. Playing hide-and-seek with his crazy wife wasn't at the top of his to-do list tonight. Or any night.

The moment the phrase "crazy wife" dropped into his thoughts, Nick Fogelsong felt a heavy cringing shame. It almost knocked him down with its strenuous force. He knew it wasn't her fault. This wasn't Mary Sue's doing. The woman he'd married—the pretty little third-grade teacher, second cousin of his childhood friend Joe Pete Hamby, and it was Joe Pete, in fact, who'd introduced them, all those years ago, at a church picnic, at which point Nick had felt a tickle in his gut that told him she was special, she was somebody he wanted to rescue from a burning building or change a tire for, do something, do anything that would showcase his skills—that woman, that pretty young thing, hadn't planned on being diagnosed with schizophrenia when she was twenty-six years old. Hadn't planned on being chained to a regimen of medication for the rest of her life, pills that made her sleepy and fat. That forced her to resign from Acker's Gap Elementary School and spend her days at home, waiting for him to arrive from the courthouse each night, listening as he called her name in dark room after dark room.

He heard a scream.

Mary Sue.

Then came the sound of the back door slamming shut.

Nick still hadn't taken off his heavy black coat, which cut down on his speed as he ran through the house.

He charged across the back porch and onto the lawn. The yard was tucked under the jagged shadow of Smithson's Rock. He couldn't see a damned thing—a year and a half ago, she'd made him unplug the big security light out here because she hated the harshness of it, the glare, the way it made the porch furniture and the shed beyond it look vivid and menacing, garishly bright—and he almost tripped over a coiled hose and then a shovel. Caught himself just in time.

"Mary Sue! Where the hell—?"

He found her beside the shed. She was hunched over, cowering, breathing hard, hands fluttering like nervous birds. Her nightgown was waterlogged with sweat.

"Nick," she said. "Nick, Nick, Nick."

"Sweetheart." He lifted her up and he put his big arms around her and he held her that way, a way that would've been uncomfortably tight for most people but that would, he knew, help settle her down.

"There was somebody out here, Nick. I saw him. Just a minute ago. At the kitchen window. I came out and he ran away—but I *saw* him, Nick, I did. I saw him. He had on a cap. A black cap. Nick, I swear."

She smelled like sweat and like something else, too, something old and matted and closed up. Rusty. He put his face against her neck. He didn't care how she smelled. He loved her. He always would. And what Nick Fogelsong loved, he protected.

"Mary Sue, there was nobody at the window," he said. Soft voice. Soothing, or so he hoped.

"You don't *believe* me!"

She tore herself out of his arms. There was anger and outrage—not hysteria—in her voice. She backed away a step and stared at him.

"He was *there,*" she said. Matter-of-fact now. Not upset anymore. Merely irritated. She was, Nick thought, very like some of the witnesses he interviewed at crime scenes, the reliable ones, the ones who were calm and specific. And—if they weren't believed—pissed off.

"I *saw* him," Mary Sue went on. "I'm not hallucinating, Nick. Because all the lights were off, I bet he thought there was nobody home. I was in the kitchen, getting a glass of water to take my pills. I looked out the window over the sink and there he was."

He knew why she'd added the detail about taking her pills. That would've been his next question: *Have you taken your pills today?* And his meaning would have been clear: *Are you having delusions again? Is this some kind of paranoid fantasy?*

She reached up to grip his shoulder. "Nick," she said. "He was there. That's why I screamed. And then I ran out here to chase him down." She sighed, lifted her arms, let them flop back down again. "Lost him."

Nick looked around. Even on a starless night like this one, he could make out the mountain in the near distance, rising high above Smithson's Rock, its peaks looking soft as pencil smudges against the darker smudge of the sky. The mountain was his reference point. No matter what was going on in his life, no matter how many changes came along to knock him sideways, the mountain was always there. He got his bearings from it. A mountain, he had theorized long ago, was like a bookmark. It wouldn't let you lose your place.

He turned back to Mary Sue. "So you chased him out here," he said patiently. "But there's no trace of him now."

She reacted to the flatness in his voice. "You still don't believe me," she said. "You think it's just crazy old Mary Sue, making trouble again."

"I do believe you," Nick said.

But he didn't, and they both knew it.

"Come on," she said. "Let's go back inside." Resigned to his skepticism. She glanced down at her bare feet. Laughed. The laughter contained a slight shiver of hysteria, as if that hysteria had somehow crept back in while she was busy with other things. "Jesus, no wonder I'm cold!"

Nick laughed, too, to keep her company, as if it were a lark, a game, as if it were the most amusing thing in the world to run barefoot into the backyard after dark, chasing a man in a black cap.

A man who didn't exist.

He remembered another night like this one, a few years back, when the full extent of Mary Sue's illness had recently been made clear to him. The massive size of it. The endlessness.

We can control the symptoms, the doctor in Charleston had said. *But we can't cure the disease.* And Nick's reply—confused, distraught, groping—was: *Wait a minute. Wait just a gol-durned minute here. You said it was depression. That's what you told us, when we first started coming here.* The doctor nodded, as if he'd been expecting the question, as if there was nothing Nick could ask that would surprise him: *True. That's what we thought. It's a common misdiagnosis. Turns out that when people begin to manifest symptoms of schizophrenia, they become frightened. They withdraw. It looks like depression. But it's not. The depression is just another symptom—a symptom of the schizophrenia.*

On that other night, Nick had come home after dark, just like tonight. Heard a scream. Ran out to the backyard, wondering all the while if she'd harmed herself in some way. Envisioning all the tools available out here for her to do so. The tools in his shed. Knives and saws and axes. Things with sharp edges.

He'd found her huddled in the shed. Terrified, confused, but alive.

And he was relieved.

Or was there a part of him—a part he could never acknowledge, neither to himself nor anyone else, *ever*—that he was not relieved but . . . disappointed?

As they walked back through the yard, Nick fit his arm across the span of Mary Sue's shoulders. She let herself be drawn closer to him. They didn't speak, which allowed a new thought—a connection, a sliding-together of elements until there was an almost audible click—to enter his mind.

Earlier today, a gunshot through the courthouse window.

And now—if by some weird miracle Mary Sue *had* actually seen something real and not imagined, if this wasn't another one of her paranoid riffs—a face at his own kitchen window. But whose?

Chapter Eighteen

She woke before Clay did. When he finally appeared in her kitchen, shirtless, sock-footed, wearing yesterday's jeans and rubbing the reddish whiskers on his chin, she'd already finished off half a pot of coffee. She had a file open on the table in front of her, pages spaced out in three stacks, yellow highlighter in her grip. The moment she heard his step on the stairs, she'd pulled off her black reading glasses and stuffed them in the pocket of her robe.

"Lord," Clay said, wincing at the news delivered by the small clock on the stove. He pulled on the flannel shirt he'd draped across the back of a chair the night before and looked around the kitchen for his boots. "It's past seven. Should've gotten me up so I could make my escape before your neighbors take notice."

"Don't worry about it."

"Never have." He poured himself a cup of coffee. Left it on the counter so he could have both hands free when he looped around behind her chair. "Figured you do enough worrying for the both of us." He leaned down and put his hands on her shoulders. Kissed the top of her head. When he'd finished with the kiss, he peered at the papers on the table.

"Whatcha got there? Ever take a day off, sweetheart?"

JULIA KELLER

Bell snatched them up. Closed the file. "Official business. Has to stay confidential. You know that."

"I do." He retrieved his coffee cup. Pulled out the chair beside hers and sat down. "Just taking an interest in your work." A teasing tone danced in his voice. He was feeling good this morning, and no wonder. "Come on—I'll reciprocate. Go ahead and ask me about the Tolliver remodeling job. I'll tell you whatever you want to know. Custom-made cherry cabinets? Dimensional shingles for the new roof? I'm ready to spill the beans." Terry Tolliver was a county judge and a good friend of Bell's. He and his wife were adding two bedrooms and a glass-paneled conservatory to their house out on Jefferson Drive.

Still protective of the file, Bell pushed it to a far corner of the table. *Jesus Christ,* she thought. *Just hate the awkwardness that's hanging in the air this morning.* But she didn't know how to get past it. Couldn't think of a way to be smooth and funny and lighthearted with a man she'd recently had sex with, a man in whose presence she'd dropped her guard with such passionate abandon. There was a part of Bell that dearly wished he had sneaked out in the middle of the night—but not because of nosy neighbors.

Because then she wouldn't be enduring this moment.

Not all mornings with Clay made her feel so clumsy and stilted, so unable to react to him the way she'd reacted last night: hungrily, urgently, ready to please and to be pleased, as she felt his skin beneath her fingertips, as she rose to meet him with a shudder and a cry. In the past, some of their mornings together had seemed like natural extensions of the night before; they were electric and sexy.

But she'd gone too far last night. She'd needed him too much. She'd been so hollowed out from her harrowing day that she'd let him in too deep—Bell blushed at the thought, knowing how some people would interpret the words as a dirty joke, and wishing like hell that she *did* mean it in a naughty way, because the truth was that it was a profoundly disturbing issue for her, the defenses that she felt forced to maintain to protect herself, those inviolable shields—and now she was itching for distance from him.

From a man before whom she felt excruciatingly, unbearably vulnerable.

"Your friend from D.C.," he said. Opting for small talk. "When's he supposed to get here?"

Matt. She'd clean forgotten about him. There was too much going on—not just events, but emotions, too. Bell suddenly realized how much she craved solitude to reconnoiter, to think, to plan, to figure out how to meet her obligations—and to gather evidence to help find the killer of a sixteen-year-old girl.

"He's here."

"Do tell." Clay, trying to sound casual, concentrated on his efforts to button the cuff of a plaid sleeve.

"Showed up at the courthouse yesterday," she said. "Hardly had a chance to say hello, though—too much going on."

"No kidding."

Restless, Bell rose from the table. Headed to the coffeepot for a refill. She didn't offer to freshen up his cup. When she turned back around from the counter, their eyes met, and Clay nodded. He was a quick study. He didn't need words to hear what Belfa Elkins was saying.

"Got it." He stood up. "Good luck today. With everything."

There were, she knew, so many things she ought to be giving him at this moment—explanations, reassurances, promises to try harder, pledges to be more open and trusting during daylight hours—but she couldn't do it.

Not now.

Not ever, perhaps.

That was the poisonous legacy of Donnie Dolan, her father. That was the perverse gift he'd bestowed upon her, courtesy of his grotesque appetites. He'd made it hard for her to ever let herself be touched without flinching. Without running away. Without feeling a dangerous anger rise up inside her like a surfacing shark, all teeth and no reason.

There were times, of course, when she had been able to overcome it; she'd been married, and she'd had other romantic relationships before and after her marriage. But the anger and the panic were always waiting, just below the water line.

She and Clay had talked about her past, about her father and about the older sister who had finally freed Bell by killing him. Clay had pressed her for details during a late-night drive in February—they were coming back from a Shelby Lynne concert in Charleston—and Bell had obliged. Clay was sure he knew the story now.

But nobody knew the story. Because knowing the facts didn't mean that you knew the story. It only meant that you knew the facts.

Lee Ann Frickie had started the coffee. Bell could smell it in the courthouse hall before she reached her office.

"Couple of calls so far," Lee Ann said. "You want the list?"

"Sure." She stood in front of her secretary's desk, holding the handle of her briefcase with both fists, trying not to glance too frequently at the window now covered with cardboard and trimmed with duct tape. The state forensics team had removed the glass square and taken it back to the lab in Charleston for analysis.

"Here goes," Lee Ann said. "Sheriff Fogelsong wants you to know that his deputies tracked down Bert Hillman last night over in Spencer. Family funeral. Ton of witnesses can place him there. He wasn't even in town when the shot was fired, so he's in the clear." Lee Ann looked down at her notepad and continued. "Let's see. Your friend called. Matt Harless. Left his cell number. Says he's at the Red Roof Inn out on the interstate."

"That it?"

"That's the important stuff. Some media calls about the Trimble girl. Funeral's going to be Monday. I got that from Rhonda Lovejoy. Is there *anything* that goes on around here that she doesn't know? Bet not."

Bell grunted in agreement. "Sure to be a packed house," she said. The mysterious death of a pretty young girl would have them hanging from the rafters.

Before moving on to her desk, Bell said, as casually as she could, "How're you holding up?"

"Belfa Elkins." Lee Ann pushed back her chair, folded her arms across her chest, and tried not to scowl when she looked up at her boss. "If one more person asks me that, I swear I'll give 'em a good smack. I know people mean well, but—really, I'm fine. Okay?"

Lee Ann didn't want to be fussed over. She'd seen too much violence in her life to be distressed by it anymore—which, Bell thought, was both good and bad. It meant that her secretary could be right here this morning, doing her job. But the fact that almost being shot in the head was no big deal—well, it implied things about living in Acker's Gap that Bell didn't much like to think about. Before she could ask a follow-up question, however, Lee Ann had turned away, reaching for the ringing phone. The moment was lost. And the day was under way.

Chapter Nineteen

"A deal's a deal," he said.

Bell was driving on the interstate and so couldn't look over at him, but had she been able to, she knew what she'd see: She remembered Matt Harless's triangular grin when he was teasing her, the way it lifted the skin around his eyes. His face had the thin, bone-haunted look of a runner, and his smile took up a lot of the real estate on that face.

"Hold your horses, mister. We've got plenty of time. Two stops to make today."

It was Saturday morning, dry and chilly. Bell had picked him up at his motel just after eight, having first swept off the detritus—three books, six file folders, a ratty gray sweater generously ventilated by moth holes, a flyer announcing a tent revival on Sunday at the Hinton Hollow Church of the Savior that she'd found stuck under her windshield wiper, a receipt for a deposit at the Mountaineer Community Bank, two empty Diet Coke cans, and the clingy plastic wrapper peeled off a package of peanut butter crackers—from the passenger seat of her Explorer, dumping the load onto the floor of the backseat.

He settled back in the passenger seat, hands riding the knees of his corduroy trousers, navy canvas jacket zipped up to his chin, as if he might be expecting gale-force winds. His hiking boots, Bell noted, looked new enough to go right back in the box and be returned to the store for a full refund. A small compass dangled from his belt loop, courtesy of a green carabiner.

"Okay—but I mean it," he said. "Before I leave this place for good, I want to know why it's called Acker's Gap."

"Try Google."

"I did. Nothing."

"Ah," Bell said with satisfaction. "Finally, a Google-proof fact. You have to actually do some research. At the source."

"That's why I'm here. Kept up my end of the bargain."

Without taking her eyes off the road, she patted his arm. "All in good time, city boy."

Edna Hankins, legs crossed, open book propped on her lap, sat on a spindly plastic lawn chair on her front porch. At the sound of car wheels displacing the gravel in her driveway, Edna reluctantly raised her face from the page and glared meanly through her thick glasses; she was at a critical point in the story and resented interruptions. Seeing that it was Bell, however, her expression softened. She waved and retrieved the folded-over gum wrapper she was using as a bookmark.

"Morning," Edna called out.

Her hair was the color of a dirty Q-tip and cut extremely short— *Whatever you have to do, just keep it outta my face,* Edna routinely told Polly Purvis, the hairdresser whose shop over in Blythesburg she patronized, *so's I can get on with things,* and by "things" she meant her reading—and it bordered the top half of her face with the thinnest of lines, like the trim around a dinner plate. That face had receded long ago into a complicated nest of wrinkles and sunken flesh. Yet Edna's dark brown eyes were still startlingly bright; even behind sturdy glasses, they looked out at the world with an interest undiminished by having watched that world for eighty-two years now, day by fascinating day.

Edna and her husband, Roy, had bought this house sixty years ago, right after they were married. Bell had heard the story from Rhonda Lovejoy, the story about how Roy, a concrete contractor, had painted it pink as a surprise for his new bride, because he thought it was her favorite color, and when she saw it, she screamed in horror and ran away from him, and when he finally caught up to her and managed to grab her wrists so she couldn't keep punching at his chest and asked her what in tarnation was the matter, she said she hated pink. *Hated* it. Turned out—at this point in the story Rhonda poked Bell's shoulder, a signal that the big finish was imminent and thus extra attention ought to be paid—Roy Hankins hadn't actually *asked* his bride if pink was her favorite color. He'd just assumed it was. *Thought pink was* every *woman's favorite color,* he'd told her, genuinely mystified and honestly heartbroken at her reaction. *Thought likin' pink was part of the deal. Part of bein' born female.* Roy had grown up with eleven brothers and no mother; his daddy, Harlan Hankins, was a widower. Velma Hankins, people speculated, had probably just died of fatigue after giving birth to a dozen children in fourteen years, and while not verified by medical authorities, it was as plausible an explanation as any other. Roy was the youngest. He barely remembered her. His knowledge of women, therefore, came from rumor and hearsay.

After Edna's patient lecture that not all women liked pink—that, in fact, women were individuals and, as was the case with men, had separate opinions and unique inclinations—Roy had promptly repainted the house a simple shade of white, and he and Edna lived there for the next fifty-four years, until Roy's death from pancreatic cancer in 2007.

At which point Edna, who was not known as a sentimental person, but who had loved Roy Hankins with an intense and abiding love that still astonished her when she was able to let herself remember it without being toppled by her grief, had paid Grady Burgess to paint the house pink. *Because,* Edna told her friends, *the best way to remember somebody is by their loving mistakes.* Pink it had stayed, to the present day.

The same pink had been used on the garage, which Roy Hankins had converted into a rental unit to bring in a little extra cash during the recession of 1978.

"Kind of cold this morning for porch-sitting, don't you think?" Bell said.

"Oh, heavens. This is balmy." Edna didn't get up. Her hips were riddled by arthritis, and she had to carefully ration her movements. "Wish it was colder, matter of fact. Gets stuffy around here, once winter's vamoosed." She frowned, finding herself in the grip of a darker thought. "Heard about that poor Trimble girl. Any luck finding out who mighta done such a terrible, terrible thing?"

Bell shook her head. She and Matt now stood at the bottom of Edna's porch steps.

"And the courthouse shooting," Edna said. "That one solved?"

"Not yet."

"Well," the old woman said, "if there's a God in heaven, you'll catch 'em both." She perked up again. "This handsome young man here must be the one Rhonda told me about. Pleased to meetcha, sir."

Matt smiled, climbed the three steps in one silky move, and shook Edna's twisted hand.

"Matt Harless," he said.

It was Rhonda's idea, because Rhonda knew every vacancy in town. Edna's previous tenant had moved out of the garage apartment a month ago. Times being what they were, a line of people eager to rent it was not exactly zigzagging across her small front yard. Matt was her only nibble. Edna had said, "Sure," over the phone, before Rhonda had even had the chance to tell her the best part: He'd be paying cash.

Edna was happy to show them the place, and they waited patiently while she uprooted herself from her chair and—slowly, slowly, gripping the walker with quiet ferocity once she'd lurched down the front steps—led the way. Bell knew better than to offer her a hand, and Matt seemed to intuit the same unstated restriction: You had to let Edna handle her own locomotion. She had a prideful streak as wide as the sky.

The apartment consisted of a single windowless room. The furnishings were limited to a stained brown sofa that, after putting up an honorable fight, would sometimes let itself be wrestled into a pull-out

140

bed, a floor lamp with a red tasseled shade, a camp chair, a small round table, and a bathroom that was set off behind a green plastic curtain. The bathroom—the "room" part being purely aspirational— was roughly the size of an upright coffin and featured a gray sink and toilet and a plastic shower stall. In a far corner of the room, across the orange linoleum, a mini-fridge emitted a furious grinding noise, as if it had to bear down just to maintain a semblance of cooling. This would be Matt's home for as long as he wanted it to be.

"Towels're on that little shelf over there," Edna said. She stood behind Matt and Bell at the threshold of the room, one hand on the walker, the other one gesturing. "Put a new bar of soap in the shower for you. All I got's Ivory. You want something else, you let me know."

"It'll be fine, Mrs. Hankins," he said. "Just fine. I appreciate it. Got my gear in the back of Belfa's SUV. Already checked out of the motel. Left my car over there, though, in case you didn't like the look of me."

Edna chuckled. "You look just fine, Mr. Harless." She waggled her eyebrows in Bell's direction. Edna Hankins was a notorious matchmaker. "Don't you think so, Belfa?"

Bell dismissed the innuendo with a shrug. "We'll let you get back to your book, Edna. We've got a few more stops to make."

But Edna wasn't finished. She grinned at Matt. "Let me guess," she said. "Bet you never thought you'd be living in a pink house, now, did you, Mr. Harless?"

"Nope," he replied. "Can't say that I did."

Twenty minutes later, Bell and Matt had cleared the city limits and begun the climb on Riley Pike.

"So what's wrong with my Audi?" he said.

Bell gave him a sideways glance. "An Audi is not exactly commensurate with your stated wish to fade into the woodwork around here. Probably not a good idea to drive down Main Street in a vehicle that screams, 'Look at me! I'm driving a car that cost more than most of you'll make in three lifetimes!'"

The solution she proposed was a trip to Doggett Motors out on Riley Pike, to procure a temporary substitute. Something that would blend in. It didn't have to be a pickup truck—but it ought not be a spiffy black sports car with a D.C. license plate. Matt could park his Audi A6 in the alley behind Edna's house.

"So this dealer of yours," he said, "will have a car I can lease for a couple of weeks? A less conspicuous one?"

"Yep." Bell checked the left lane and then pulled into it, impatient with the speed of the driver in front of her. Riley Pike was one of the few four-lane roads in the area, and it was even four lanes only on the way up the mountain. The idea was to enable cars to whip around slow-moving coal trucks that were stymied by the steep grade. At the top of the mountain, the lanes slimmed back down to two again. If you didn't make your move on the way up, you didn't make your move.

They passed a wheezing coal truck, the smoke from its hopelessly overworked exhaust blowing in all directions, wrapping the hapless contraption in a gauzy black cocoon. After that, a rock-dinged red pickup. Then a lopsided purple sedan valiantly towing an old wood-sided trailer, upon which was stacked a washing machine, a blue sofa missing its cushions, and a mud-buttered dirt bike.

The gray-black mountain still wore its dour winter face, although a few stray spots of green had begun to appear here and there, the early flags signaling springtime. By summer this mountainside would be a single ravishing color, a green so intense and magnificent that it forced you to find another word altogether to describe lesser items formerly known as green.

"Any more trouble yesterday?" Matt asked. When Bell shook her head, he added, "Your secretary's still doing okay, right? The more I think about it, the more impressed I am. I've seen tough old combat vets go to pieces from sniper attacks that weren't half as close as that."

"Takes a lot to scare Lee Ann Frickie."

"So things'll settle down for you now?"

"Not likely." She filled him in on the murder of Lucinda Trimble, of which he'd surely already heard if he'd wandered even once through the lobby of the Red Roof Inn the night before. It was the kind of news that people couldn't help but talk about, with strangers as well as friends.

"Carla attending the funeral?" he asked.

"She wants to, but no. She's got three midterms on Monday." Bell leaned forward in her seat, trying to see past the dazzle. The sun had just emerged from behind a rolling gray tarp of cloud, and there came one of those brief, spangled moments of unexpected radiance that seemed to change everything. The light was beautiful, but it also made it hard to keep track of the road.

"There'll be a great turnout, though," Bell went on, slapping down the visor. "And not just local folks. Lucinda was young, and it was murder, not an accident—so you can expect a few TV stations to send a big fat van and their own Diane Sawyer wannabe. Tragic death. Lost potential. Curse of the mountains. Et cetera, et cetera. Then they'll all move on."

"You don't like TV news, I take it."

"Doesn't matter whether I like it or not. Way of the world. But no, I'm not crazy about the practice of dispatching some grinning fool with perfect hair and over-whitened teeth to stand in front of a trailer park and look all serious and concerned whenever there's a death in West Virginia—when the victim is good-looking and when the investigation is liable to be long and hard." She kneaded the steering wheel with her thumbs, pushing at it restlessly. "If they want to cover something, why don't they cover the real story around here? The fact that over half of the children in Raythune County go to bed hungry at night? Or the fact that a majority of our senior citizens can't afford to keep the heat on all winter long? Or that prescription drug abuse is killing us, little by little? I'll tell you why. Because it's not sexy. It's not titillating. It's just a damned shame. And nobody has any idea what the hell to do about it."

Matt paused a long time before he spoke. "I know you hate compliments, Bell. But I'm going to give you one, anyway. You haven't changed a bit. You're still the most honest person I know."

"Me. Honest."

"Yeah."

"Let me tell you, Matt, just how honest I am, okay? Before you go shopping for my halo? Sure, I think you need another car to drive, for as long as you stick around these parts. But that's not the only reason we're stopping by Doggett Motors this morning." She shifted into a lower gear to accommodate the steeper grade. "I want to talk to Alton Doggett on his own turf. Casual and friendly. I'd like to find out how he really felt about Lucinda. Is he all torn up about her death, like he says he is? Or did he think she'd ruined Shawn's life—and if that's the case, was he mad enough to kill her for it?"

Chapter Twenty

Trudy Baird, personal secretary to Alton Doggett, looked up at Bell and Matt and offered them—or possibly only Matt, being as how she'd been trained throughout her seventeen years of life thus far to aim her charms mostly at men—her brightest, widest, warmest, phoniest smile, a smile enhanced by shimmery red lip gloss that looked as if she'd just finished nibbling an overripe cherry and deliberately neglected to dab her mouth dry.

"Hey there, Mrs. Elkins," Trudy said. "You, too, sir." She batted her eyelashes at Matt exactly three times, slower each time. "How can I help y'all?"

"I'd like to speak with Alton," Bell said.

Bell and Matt had stepped up to the shoulder-high counter behind which Trudy sat, her chair pushed back from her desk, legs crossed at the knee, a pose that induced her short skirt to ride up beguilingly on her bare thigh. The high counter was designed, Bell surmised, to be a kind of security device. If you were coming after Trudy—or any of the financing specialists at Doggett Motors, whose offices spread out behind her in a dull row of cheap wooden doors—you'd have to be as fit as a circus performer to leap over this counter. The last door on the right was decorated with the words ALTON DOGGETT, PRES in peel-and-stick gold letters.

The phone endlessly trilled its two-note chime, but another woman—overweight, middle-aged, loaded into a lavender polyester pantsuit, her desk exiled far to the left of Trudy's—took care of it, answering, "It's a great day at Doggett Motors. How may I direct your call?" in a dreary voice, over and over again.

Throughout the glass-walled showroom that Bell and Matt had crossed to get to the counter, a half-dozen people milled about, stroking the shiny flanks of the new models that were arranged on the bright white tile. Windows rolled down, leather seats polished, dashboard gleaming, every car looked as inviting and arousing as the skirt that slid up Trudy's thigh. Country-pop music bounced overhead. *If I hear "Boot Scootin' Boogie" one more time,* Bell thought, *I'm going to put a boot up somebody's backside.*

In the lot outside, a jumbo square ringed by thin wires that bounced and spun in the wind, wires from which hung fluttering red, white, and blue plastic pennants, another crop of people moved slowly between the rows of cars, trucks, and SUVs. They stopped periodically to bend forward at the waist, hands in their jacket pockets, peering at the price stickers on the side windows. Most shuddered at the numbers, shook their heads, and then stepped to the next one. Big white signs were propped on easels at the end of every aisle: BAD CREDIT, NO CREDIT? NO PROBLEM! and LIKE IT? DRIVE IT HOME TODAY!

"I'm sorry to say," Trudy replied, in a frisky little voice that indicated she wasn't sorry at all, "Mr. Doggett is tied up at the moment. Could another one of our salespeople help you out?"

"No."

Trudy looked peeved. Usually the smile and the bashful flap of the eyelashes did the trick. Even if people came in to complain—and there was always somebody charging up to the counter to bellyache about something—the customers generally dropped their hostility the moment they saw Trudy's sweet smile. That smile often caused male customers to stammer and whisk the sweat-stained caps off their heads and apologize profusely to Trudy for interrupting her day. The activity they had interrupted was, more often than not, a long series of text exchanges with Brad Snavely, her boyfriend.

"Well," Trudy said. "I can check, but like I said, he's kinda busy."

"So am I." Bell's words came in low and sharp.

One side of Trudy's mouth twitched. This was a small community, and so she knew who Bell was, of course; even if she couldn't exactly drag Bell's specific job title out of her rarely overtaxed memory, Trudy equated Bell's face with a vague idea of law enforcement, courts, power. The ability to make trouble.

"Well," Trudy said. "I can check, I guess."

"You do that."

Trudy sighed at the momentous imposition this constituted—the walk to Alton Doggett's door was at least three steps, and besides, she'd been just about to respond to Brad Snavely's texted suggestion that they go see a movie tonight over in Blythesburg—and so, as she walked over to the boss's door, she gave a saucy little waggle of her ass.

On this occasion, it wasn't intended to be lascivious. Bell could translate easily:

Screw you, old lady.

Alton came right out. He was a big man, somewhere between fifty and sixty years old, with a belly that flopped over his silver belt buckle and an enormous bald head that seemed to pop up out of his shirt collar like something squeezed from a tube. Shiny blue sport coat, pale blue shirt, brown plaid wool tie.

"Mrs. Elkins." He made a wide loop around the side of the high counter. There was a faint *shush-whish, shush-whish* sound that accompanied him. Bell wondered what it was, until she noted his brown corduroy pants and the chubby thighs encased therein.

Bell shook his hand. "Alton, first let me say how sorry I am," she said. "This must be so hard for Shawn. I didn't really know Lucinda, but I understand she was a fine young lady."

"Oh my, yes. Yes, yes, indeed." Alton held on to Bell's hand, pumping it at random intervals. "Terrible news. Just terrible. We're all pretty upset, I can tell you. Nice girl. Real sweet. Can't believe somebody'd want to do her harm." He noticed Matt. "Don't believe I've had the pleasure."

"This is Matt Harless," Bell said. "Friend of mine. He's going to be in town for a couple of weeks. Thought you might have a vehicle for him on a short-term lease. Something to get him up and down these mountains. Without having to push it himself, that is." She finally was able to extricate her hand.

"We'll fix you right up," Alton said, and then he winked. Bell remembered that wink. He'd offered it to her just after she'd signed away her soul for her Ford Explorer five years ago, when she'd first moved back to Acker's Gap. She'd make the final payment later this year. The celebration was already planned.

"Hold on," Alton added. "Lemme get Jeff." He looked over at Trudy, who had resumed her seat. And her texting. "Honey," Alton said, voice lapsing into a kind of wheedle, "could you track down Jeff Hinerman for me? Last I saw, he was out on the lot somewheres."

Bell watched the way Trudy responded to the boss. She lifted her eyes from her cell. A frown of annoyance spoiled her red-rimmed mouth. She seemed to be considering whether or not she had to do what he said—and if she did, whether or not she had to do it right away, or if she could wait for a more convenient moment. Her eyes met Alton Doggett's for a single, revelatory second.

It was Alton, not Trudy Baird, who looked away first.

They're sleeping together, Bell realized. *Interesting.* She wasn't shocked. Alton was a notorious and proudly indiscreet philanderer, and this certainly wouldn't be the first time he had hired an employee for an attribute other than familiarity with a spreadsheet—although the word "spread" surely was applicable. Still, it made Bell just a little bit sad. Sad for Trudy.

Had Trudy been aware of Bell's pity, she would, of course, have told her exactly where she could stick it. Nonetheless, Bell felt sorry for Trudy Baird. For all the Trudy Bairds. These young women always thought they had the upper hand. They knew Alton Doggett wasn't going to leave his wife for them; Lord knows, that wasn't the plan. The plan was to trade their looks for a few nice things, for just a little while, and then to move on to their real lives, to the boyfriends who hung around in panting packs while they were young and pretty. Trouble was, though, before they knew it, a lot of years had gone by and those good looks of theirs had slid away. They didn't have their pick of boyfriends anymore. Their breasts sagged and their bellies weren't so flat and there was a circle of fat around their necks like a ruffled collar, and while Alton Doggett, once he'd tired of them, didn't fire them, didn't get rid of them, he did something worse: He put them out to pasture, as if they were broken-down horses or dried-up cows. Livestock.

Bell looked over at the heavy woman in the lavender pantsuit. Now she remembered where she'd seen her before. She'd been a few years ahead of Bell at Acker's Gap High School. And five years ago, Bell recalled, Lavender Pantsuit had been sitting in Trudy Baird's seat. Some other dumpy woman had been sitting where Lavender Pantsuit sat now. Funny: Alton Doggett could get old and fat and ugly—and it didn't seem to matter.

But did any of this mean he was capable of killing Lucinda Trimble? The leap from serial infidelity to murder was a large one.

Courtesy of Rhonda Lovejoy and her never-fail network of gossip, rumor, and innuendo, Bell knew a lot about Alton Doggett. She knew a lot more, most likely, than he was aware of. She knew that he didn't just cheat on Wendy Doggett. There were rumors that Alton, despite his Velcro handshake and easy grin, made a habit of knocking her around. And of doing it in a strategic, systematic manner that left ambiguous injuries in out-of-the-way places. No black eyes. No busted lips. No inconveniently broken bones. Yet in the absence of any police reports or witnesses, and most crucial of all, in the absence of Wendy's cooperation, all the whispers in the world couldn't help them build a case against him.

"Jeff Hinerman. Come to the showroom, please. Jeff Hinerman." Trudy's amplified voice crackled through the PA system, having first interrupted Kenny Rogers as he sang the sage if rather-too-obvious advice that one should know when to hold 'em and know when to fold 'em.

"Jeff'll fix you up," Alton said, winking at Matt. "Oh, yeah. He'll get you situated, sir, right quick. He's my top man. Knows everything we got on the lot."

"Appreciate it," Matt said. "Short lease not going to be a problem?"

Alton snorted. "Lemme put it this way. Business is so bad these days, I'd let you have it for an hour—even if you told me you were on your way to a demolition derby." He shook his head, offering an extra little grimace in Bell's direction, because she could confirm it. "Never seen it this bad before. Including that spell in the late '70s. I'm telling you. We're down twenty, thirty percent of our usual volume."

"Looks pretty busy to me," Matt said. He nodded toward the people in the showroom, the ones weaving slow, preoccupied circles around the bright new cars.

Alton snorted again. "Them's browsers, Mr. Harless. Not buyers. World of difference." The grimace bit deeper. "As Mrs. Elkins here can tell you, we've got ourselves some rocky times right now."

The glass double doors were yanked open, and in fast-walked a tall, skinny man with a fist-sized Adam's apple, a black goatee, and straight gray hair that flopped onto his forehead like fingers. Jeff Hinerman's suit was moss-green plaid. A brown tie fluttered across his narrow, slightly tubercular-looking chest as he hurried forward.

Bell didn't know Hinerman well, but she knew enough. She knew that his twenty-three-year-old daughter, Amanda, was serving a fifteen-year sentence at Lakin Correctional Center for robbery and aggravated assault. Desperate for cash to buy the prescription pain pills that had turned her from an even-tempered, hardworking nurse at the Raythune County Medical Center into a gaunt, curse-spewing panhandler at a truck stop out on the interstate, Amanda Hinerman had beaten a man nearly to death with a Louisville Slugger in a dispute over a drug deal. Jeff and his wife, Merilee, were raising Amanda's two little girls, Kaylee and Karmen.

"Howdy, there," Hinerman said. He couldn't figure out which one was the customer, so he shook hands with both Bell and Matt, eye contact functioning like flypaper, capturing every glance in his direction and holding on tight.

Alton Doggett explained. Hinerman nodded. He tapped a long bony index finger against his pursed lips—once, twice, three times—

like a philosopher pondering the finer points of free will versus pre-destination.

"Gotcha," he told Matt, wrinkling his nose and turning his body a few degrees, eliminating Bell from his audience. *Men's business,* the wrinkle insinuated. *This little lady you brought along? None of her lookout.* "Know just the thing," he continued. "Come on, buddy. Right this way."

And then Hinerman made his mistake.

He moved in closer and looped a long, friendly, rubbery arm across Matt's shoulders, preparatory to leading him to the outside lot for a look-see at the merchandise.

The instant Hinerman's arm brushed him, Matt's body exploded into action as if he were undergoing a grand mal seizure. He grabbed the salesman's wrist, twirled him like a dance partner, and pinned the skinny arm against his back at a grotesque and punishing angle. Hinerman's shocked round mouth gave forth a blurt of noise and air—*uhh-hhh*—that sounded like a cross between a moan and belch.

Then Matt—in a fluid motion, a motion so nimble that not a single molecule appeared to be displaced by it—hooked his other arm around Hinerman's throat in a vicious choke hold that made no accommodation for the historical purpose of the man's windpipe. Matt's feet were spread. His spine was straight, his body rigid as rebar. He had the perfect leverage to do, in the next second or so, whatever the hell he wanted to do. Eyes narrowed, mouth jammed against Hinerman's ear, spit visible on his lips, Matt rasped through clenched teeth, *"Don't—you—fucking—touch—me—you—"*

Chapter Twenty-One

It had happened so fast that customers were oblivious. The few who did glance over seemed to assume it was horseplay, all in good fun, the kind of frat-boy tomfoolery for which Alton's salesmen were famous. Trudy Baird still texted. Lavender Pantsuit still answered the phone: "It's a great day at Doggett Motors. How may I direct your call?" Rosanne Cash complained about a seven-year ache.

Only Bell seemed to recognize the imminent peril to Jeff Hinerman. She had to do something. But she couldn't risk touching Matt. He was in another place right now. In a trance of violence.

"Hey!" she called out sharply. "Matt! Matt, for God's sake." Her voice rose. "Matt!" she repeated. "Matt!"

A second passed.

Another.

And then he let go.

It was as if a black mist lifted from Matt's eyes, as if whatever lethal enchantment possessed him had abruptly lost its power. He pushed Hinerman away—Hinerman stumbled a few steps but didn't fall—and then Matt put a fist to his own temple, like a man with a migraine. He took several deep, head-clearing breaths.

Bell addressed Hinerman. "You okay?" she said.

The salesman was coughing, thin face as pink as a tutu, rickety

JULIA KELLER

shoulders heaving up and down and up and down again. When he was able to, he choked out, "Yeah." Gulped, swallowed. "Think so. Yeah." He winced when he moved his arm, testing it out, bending his elbow. A tremor ran through his skinny body, like a plucked guitar string. He risked a sidelong peek at Matt.

"Jesus Christ, mister," Hinerman muttered.

Alton Doggett—eyes wide, mouth open, as mesmerized as a kid at a kung fu movie—couldn't keep the awe out of his voice.

"Holy shit," he said. *"Holy shit."*

They had left Doggett Motors in a hurry. Now they rode in silence. The woods threaded past on either side of the Explorer, hectic flashes of black and white like a Rorschach test on fast-forward, a flickering panorama of branches and underbrush and, when the trees momentarily thinned, pale gray scraps of sky. The trip down the mountain always felt quicker than the trip up; that was gravity, and it was something else, too, Bell believed. The second half of anything—journeys, lives—tended to pass more swiftly, as the moments accelerated during the downhill ride. The end was in sight.

"What the hell, Matt?" she said. Her voice was a wondering murmur. "What the hell?"

He didn't answer. He was her friend—wasn't he?—but she didn't know him. Not really. *If you don't know what someone is ultimately capable of,* she thought, *do you really know him at all?* The Matt Harless she knew—or thought she knew—was a strong yet gentle man with a steady moral compass. A decent man. A man who kept himself fit and honed, yes—but not in order to be a better fighter, for God's sake. Like her, he ran because he liked the way he felt after he'd run: Balanced. Capable. Independent. In control. What happened to him today? Where did the good guy go? And who was this hothead, this bully, who'd taken his place?

The woods continued to tear by on both sides, dense tangles that screened off the road from the rest of the world. Bell found herself wishing it were later in the spring. She knew the green was on its way, pushing, pushing, but she could've used a little green right now,

154

something innocent and familiar. The silence in the car lengthened out. As they neared the turnoff from Riley Pike onto Sayman Street, Matt finally spoke.

"I guess," he said, "this means I can forget about a good deal on that lease, right?"

"Make all the jokes you want," Bell said coldly. "You're damned lucky that Hinerman's not pressing charges for assault. At least for now. He could change his mind. And if somebody mentions this to Nick Fogelsong—" She paused. "He loves this town, Matt. He's not going to let you stick around if you pull that kind of crap."

"Free country." Matt's voice had lost its levity. Defiant now. "He's a sheriff, not a goddamned king. He can't tell me where I can and can't be." He stared straight out the windshield, but he wasn't watching the scenery. "That guy *touched* me, Bell. He put his *hands* on me. Not acceptable."

"Oh, for Christ's sake, Matt. He's a salesman. He was being friendly. Salesmen do that. They shake your hand. They pat you on the back. If you're a woman, they pinch your cheek and smack you on the ass. It's not an attack."

She slowed down to let a car pass. She didn't like to go too fast on her way down the mountain. She'd had a close call on a mountain road last fall, and it was the kind of thing you don't forget. She guided the Explorer around a series of tight curves, and even though she was going at a careful rate of speed, the motion rocked them from side to side, and then from side to side again.

As they crossed the Acker's Gap city limits, Bell waited for Matt to say something else. To justify himself, perhaps. They'd be back at Edna's place in another five minutes. He was running out of time.

It wasn't the violence that had rattled her. Bell knew violence. Knew it inside out. She'd grown up with an abusive sonofabitch for a father, in a home where physical violence was a common occurrence. The older she got, the more she realized that Donnie Dolan had done her a favor, really. A savage and accidental one, but a favor nonetheless. Because she was never surprised by violence now, never shocked or cowed by it. Her father, in his own sick and selfish way, had made her fit for the world. Prepared her for what the world could do to you if you weren't strong, if you didn't stay alert.

No, what stunned her was Matt's agility. His cool professionalism. His quickness and his power. The grace of his rage.

"You were an analyst, Matt. Right? Isn't that what you said? You crunched numbers. Monitored transmissions. Read journals."

"Yeah."

"So where'd you get all the *Mission: Impossible* moves? What the hell's going on?"

"Everybody's trained. We all go through a program."

He wasn't going to tell her a damned thing. That much was clear.

"Appreciated your covering for me back there," Matt said after a spell of silence. "Good idea. The military angle. Hinting around about posttraumatic stress and all."

"Well, you really were in Iraq and Afghanistan. Drawing a government paycheck." She flipped on her blinker, preparatory to turning at the four-way stop.

"Yeah." He looked down at his hands, which rested in his lap. Palms up, as if he were trying to tell his own fortune. "Funny how people will cut a soldier all kinds of slack, but if you'd said 'CIA'— well, I have the feeling that I might be advised to get the hell out of Acker's Gap by sundown."

She shrugged. "The CIA has kind of lost the moral high ground lately. You have to admit."

"I admit nothing." He grinned. "I'm CIA, remember?"

"Retired."

He looked at her. "Right," he said. "Retired."

She pulled the Explorer into Edna's driveway. The old woman wasn't sitting on her front porch anymore, which surprised Bell; after a shaky start, the day had turned out fine, with the kind of mellow, amiable sunshine that made the mountains look like shy, misunderstood giants who had come out to play.

Bell's car window was open, and through it she heard a faint and sustained jingle in the distance, almost like choral singing. The sound, she knew, came from Paw Paw Creek, which curved along the north border of Edna's property before joining up with the Bitter River. It was one of several dozen small creeks and streams that ran persistently toward the river, like restless kids who might wander on their own across the countryside but, in the end, always come home again.

"Got a few more questions for you, Matt."

He didn't hesitate. "Come on in. Let's see if I can rustle us up a drink."

He found two mugs in a cupboard. One was clean; one wasn't. Matt handed her the clean one and then rubbed his shirttail inside the dirty one; he squinted at it, and then rubbed more. There was nothing on any of the shelves or in the tiny refrigerator, so he rummaged in his backpack. Pulled out a half-filled bottle of Wild Turkey and directed a splash into each mug.

"In case of snakebite," he said. "Never leave home without it."

She sat on the broken-down old couch. He took the small camp chair next to it, stretching out his long legs, resting the cup on his right thigh.

"Okay," he said. "Fire when ready."

"What did you really do in the CIA?"

"Not much I can tell you."

"So far you've told me nothing. So 'not much' will be an improvement."

"Fair enough." He drained his mug but still held on to it, running a thumb around the rim. "I was an interrogator. Not the kind of thing you brag about these days, you know? Last assignment was in Arbil. Northern Iraq. It's a major way station between Baghdad and Mosul. If a local was arrested on suspicion of terrorism or, say, spying for Iran—which is a sort of slow-motion terrorism, when you think about it—they were sent to me."

"To you."

"Yes."

"Why you?"

He shrugged. "I'm a lawyer, right? Guess I was pretty good at cross-examination. Plenty of practice, anyway."

"So what did you do?"

"I extracted information."

"You mean you tortured people."

A scowl. "No. No torture. Jesus, Bell. You *know* me."

"Thought I did." She could still picture Hinerman's terrified face. "So nobody died in your custody?"

"I didn't say that."

She waited. She would've liked another drink, but didn't want to ask, didn't want to give him an excuse to change the subject.

"I didn't say that," he went on, "because it wouldn't be true. Fact is, Bell, people do sometimes die during interrogations. And sometimes it's not the fault of the interrogator."

"Really." She shoehorned her skepticism into one word, like someone packing a parachute. Yards of flowing silk, folded into a small packet. "Really," she repeated.

"Yes. It can happen, for instance, because the detainee was ill to begin with. Asthma. Epilepsy. Heart disease. We don't always know the underlying conditions. During the autopsy, of course, we find out. But while we're doing our jobs—we're in the dark."

"That's not what I mean. I mean the kind of thing you read about. The torture. Abu Ghraib. The deaths of people in American custody."

He shook his head. "We don't kill people on purpose. We have a saying in the CIA, Bell. 'The skull is mute.' Just another way of reminding us that dead men tell no tales. It's information we're after— not revenge."

"So how many died on your watch?"

"One. One person."

"I want a name."

"Why?"

"If you remember his name, it means you're telling the truth. It means the death was accidental. That it still haunts you. If you enjoyed the killing—you wouldn't remember the name. If you didn't enjoy it—you'll never be able to forget it."

"Abdu Yusef." He seemed relieved at the chance to speak the words.

"Iraqi?"

"Yeah."

"What did he do?"

"He was a spy. That's all I can tell you."

"And he died during an interrogation?"

"Yeah."

"Which was not your plan."

"It's never your plan." Restless, Matt put the mug on the floor by his chair. He stood up. "I pushed. He pushed back. In the end—well, things happen. Things you wish didn't, but do." He rubbed his hands together. Sat back down. "Look, I was out of line with the car guy. Sometimes the old training just kicks in, you know? Won't happen again. So are we okay here?"

"One more question."

"You want *more* information? Good Lord. Did you train at Langley?"

She laughed. "This one's a snap. I understand what you did in Iraq. But why are you here now?"

"Been over this."

"I don't mind repetition," she said. "Tell me again."

He nodded. She remembered that nod of his; she would see it at the end of a long satisfying run in Rock Creek Park, when they were both exhausted, both bent over and grabbing the baggy knees of their gray sweats. She would look sideways at him and nod, and he would nod back, acknowledging how good this felt, this glorious fatigue, and how it reminded you of something you used to know. For people who lived mostly in their heads, as she did, and as he did, too, the fatigue was cleansing, restorative. Fundamental.

"Look," he said. "I've done a lot of things in my career that I'm not too thrilled about. Okay? Point is, though, it's over. Still got a few good years left in me. And I want to be someplace that's not Iraq, not D.C. Just want to be up in the hills for a bit. Clear my head. Do some fishing. Watch the hawks. I remember you telling me—a long time ago—about the hawks. They fly over these mountains like it's their morning commute, right? And it can take your breath away, seeing them up there. Well, that's what I want. I want to look up and see those hawks—because they don't give a damn about what's going on down here."

Driving home, Bell thought about another man who had once come to Acker's Gap, just as Matt had. A friend of Nick's. He and Nick had grown up together in rural Raythune County. They were hunting and fishing buddies. Then the man moved to Chicago and joined the police force there. She remembered his name, even though she hadn't ex-changed a single word with him: Emmett Hostettler. One day he just showed up back at the courthouse, looking old and battered and used up, despite being several years younger than Nick. Looking like he was seeing things other people didn't see. He'd slept on Nick's couch for a few weeks. Ate his meals at Ike's, sitting by himself. *Don't ask him any questions, Bell,* the sheriff told her. *Don't approach him. Don't try to make friends. Just let him be. He needs the mountains right now. Needs space and quiet. He's been through some things. A line-of-duty shooting on the South Side of Chicago. Killed a kid. Emmett thought the kid was holding a gun. Cell phone, it turned out. No charges filed—Emmett did what he had to do—but, well, you know.* Then Hostettler left, just as quickly and mysteriously as he'd arrived, and Nick never mentioned him again.

Bell knew the kind of solace that the mountains could provide. She'd felt it herself. That part of Matt's story, she didn't question.

Chapter Twenty-Two

Eddie Geyer looked at the necktie. The service was going to start in ten minutes—and now *this*?

It was long, thin, silky. Slick to the touch. Red background, with a pattern of tiny blue curlicues that might be—what? Commas? Seahorses? Fishhooks?

Maddie had driven up in her old car, met him on the porch of the falling-down cabin, and draped the tie across his forearm. Then she stepped back, as if half-afraid of his reaction. As if maybe she thought he'd fling it back in her face. Or wrap it around her neck, maybe.

No. He'd never been violent with her. Ever. Only cowards were violent with women. His mama had taught him that. He'd disappointed Henrietta Geyer in just about every way it was possible to disappoint a mother—he'd dropped out of high school, gotten himself arrested twice before he turned nineteen years old, once for possession of burglary tools and another time for drunk and disorderly—but he'd never, ever hit a woman. His mother was dead, she'd been in the ground for twelve years now, but wherever she was, whatever reward she was now enjoying in heaven as a consequence of a blameless life lived in the midst of many sorrows—Eddie, mean as dirt, was surprisingly sentimental about his theology, believing fervently in pearly gates and harp-soloing angels and the whole shebang—Henrietta Geyer had to know that no matter how mad Eddie got, or how drunk, or how nasty, he would never strike a woman.

"It'll look good, Eddie," Maddie said. "You gotta wear a tie. It's a funeral. Coat and tie. It's expected."

He continued to stare at the tie on his arm. Of course he was going to wear a tie. He wasn't an animal. He knew what you wore to a funeral. Especially when the deceased was your own child. Your own flesh and blood. Your baby girl.

Even if you'd laid eyes on her for the first time in almost sixteen years just the week before. Even then.

He looked up from the tie to take in Maddie's face. She'd aged at least a year in the past few days, or so it seemed to him. There were new lines around her eyes. Her hair was frizzy, wild, as if she'd given up and now just let it do whatever the hell it wanted to. The flesh on her face was slack and gray. The blue dress hung on her like an old sack, dropping in a free fall from her bony shoulders until the bottom hem brushed the floorboards of the crummy old porch on which they stood. And yet he was still wildly attracted to her. *Don't that beat all,* he thought.

"So you'll wear the tie," Maddie said.

"Sure. Looks real good."

She peered at him. He knew she was confused, because this amiability wasn't like him. This wasn't the Eddie Geyer she knew. He was far too calm. Three days ago, when she first told him about Lucinda's death, she had hugged him and then she'd stepped back—just as she'd done today, after the tie delivery—because she feared his reaction. She probably figured he'd go tearing off in search of the killer himself. Crazy, out-of-control Eddie Geyer.

But in the years he'd been away from Acker's Gap, he'd learned a thing or two.

Like the fact that the best revenge is a slow thing. Not a fast thing.

"Thought maybe it was too colorful for you," she said. "I know you don't like bright colors."

He grunted. "It'll work."

He didn't tell her that he already had a tie in his pocket, that he'd picked it up yesterday in Alesburg. She'd driven him over there to get some groceries. Dropped him off, then picked him back up again. She still didn't want them to be seen together. Ashamed of him, probably, although she didn't say so.

He'd gone to the Foodland, and he'd gotten some Ritz crackers and peanut butter, and a can of Chef Boyardee ravioli, and he'd tried to buy a six-pack of Miller Lite, but they wouldn't sell it to him— dammit, it was Sunday, he'd clean forgot—and then he went to the Goodwill store and bought a tie. It was black. Black seemed right. It was the color you wore when you were sad. *Well, it ain't a* color, *exactly,* he'd corrected himself. *More like no color at all. Which is the point, right?*

He already had a sport coat and decent dress shirt and polyester slacks. She'd brought him all those things the week before.

Before it had happened.

She had wanted him to look nice when he talked to Lucinda. When he finally met the little girl he'd abandoned so many years ago, when she was just a smelly blob with a mess of hair on top, yelling and squawling all the time—*Sweet Jesus, can't you keep that fuckin' brat quiet for one goddamned minute!* was what he'd hollered at Maddie back then, over and over again, sometimes throwing something, too, in no particular direction, to show how pissed he was—before she became a person.

Before she became Lucinda. A young woman. But still his baby girl.

The only thing he didn't have was a tie. So to surprise Maddie, he'd gotten one at the Goodwill. Picked it out of a big barrel of ties, all colors, lots of different materials, all thrown in there together, twisted like lazy snakes.

He stroked the back of his head, hoping his hair looked okay. He'd rinsed it with a bucket of water, because there was no running water in this miserable shack. This dump. He had to pee in the woods. He didn't mind—he'd grown up in a house with no plumbing, so he was used to that—but he didn't have a way to wash his hair.

Last week, Maddie had brought him out some water in plastic gallon jugs.

Last week. Before it happened. When Lucinda was still alive.

"Better get a move on," he said. "Starts at two, right?"

She nodded. Then she looked at him—*really* looked at him, not just turned a pair of dead-at-the-core eyes in the vague direction of his face, which was what she'd done for the past three days—and she said, "You sure about this? You don't have to go, you know."

"Yeah," he said. "I know."

"They're gonna stare. Gonna whisper."

"Know that."

"And Nick'll be there. He might take a mind to arrest you. You jumped bail on that DUI when you left in '95. He hasn't forgotten."

Eddie made a snickering sound. "You think he'd arrest me at a *funeral?* At the funeral for my own kid?"

"Yeah," Maddie said. "I think he would."

That took him aback. "Okay." Buying time. Considering it. "Okay, okay." He had an idea. "What if we just told him the truth? I mean, what if we told him why I came back here in the first place? I didn't have to. I coulda lived the rest of my life and never stepped foot back in this lousy shithole of a county. But I came back. You asked me to, Maddie. And I did."

She looked down. "No."

"Why the hell not?"

"Wouldn't work."

"He's gotta be told, Maddie. Sooner or later. Because of that night. The night she died. He's gotta know where you really were. They're asking questions, right? You can't keep lying about it. They'll know."

"I'll deal with that," she said, "when I have to. Not before."

"Maddie. Come on." With two fingers, Eddie grazed her cheek. He did it slowly and tenderly, the way he always touched her. It could drive her crazy sometimes, that tenderness. Crazy with longing. She tilted her head, and put a hand on top of his hand, not wanting him to take away his fingers. She moved his hand over to her mouth and she kissed his hard palm.

Then she slowly drew his hand down and away from her face, as if she had to limit the amount of comfort she could allow herself at any one time.

"No," she said. "You don't know Nick Fogelsong the way I do."

"*That's* for damned sure."

"He's liable to drag you off before they finish the first hymn. He doesn't look at things the way other people do. He won't care why you came back."

"Hard-ass bastard." Ordinarily Eddie would've spit, to underline his point, but it seemed disrespectful. Given the circumstances.

"Maybe." She paused. "I won't be mad if you don't come. If you want to stay here. Or if you want to just take off right now and hitch your way back to Kentucky." Another pause. "You offered to come. That's enough, Eddie. Really. It's plenty."

Eddie took a deep breath. Let it out. Running away was what he did best; it's what he knew, how he operated. Didn't surprise him one little bit that, when she'd had to guess, her guess was that he wanted to run. Because that's what he always did.

But not this time. Because he needed to be here. For all kinds of reasons—including the fact that he wanted Maddie to point out Shawn Doggett to him at the funeral.

Shawn Doggett.

The worthless sack of shit who'd gotten his baby girl pregnant. And who—Eddie was sure of it—had killed her, had strangled her, and pushed her car in the river to get rid of his problem.

It was the only explanation that made any sense.

Once Eddie knew who the punk-ass bastard was, what he looked like, he'd take care of Shawn Doggett. Oh, yeah. But he didn't want to bother Maddie about it. She had enough on her mind.

"Hell," he said. "Fogelsong wants to arrest me? Fine. She was my kid and I'm gonna go to her damned funeral. Come on. Let's hit the road. Don't want to be late."

Chapter Twenty-Three

"Looking good, boss." Hickey Leonard followed up his remark with a low two-part whistle that curled at the end, accompanied by a vigorous up-and-down motion of his bushy eyebrows. From anybody else, the motion might have looked lascivious; from Hick, however, it merely looked as if he were trying to chase away a bee from his face without using his hands.

Bell wore a simple black dress, a single strand of pearls, and black panty hose. Funeral clothes. They weren't supposed to be comfortable. But still.

"I *hate* panty hose," she hissed back at him. There oughta be a law, right? Prohibiting the manufacture and sale of panty hose? Put me in charge. I'll enforce it."

Hick, Bell, and Rhonda stood just to the left of the arched entrance to the Briney Hollow Church of the Nazarene on Monday afternoon, five days after Lucinda Trimble's body had been found in the Bitter River. Her funeral was not scheduled to start for another thirty-two minutes, and already the gravel parking lot behind the old stone church was running out of slots. People had begun to park along the side of the road leading to the church, their cars tilting precariously on the lip of the drainage ditch. Technically such parking was illegal but today, they assumed, Sheriff Fogelsong and his deputies would be inclined toward forgiveness.

The morning had started out cold, but grew progressively warmer. That was how spring announced itself in the mountains. Days were chilly at their beginnings, but by noon or thereabouts, everything changed, and temperatures could leap up with giddy abandon, like small children allowed to go barefoot again for the first time since last August. Cold and then hot: A spring day in the mountains was like two different days. It was as if—during this one magical season—your time on earth suddenly doubled.

Bell and her staff were here to work. Stationing themselves casually near the door, they would watch the mourners as they arrived and see if any behaviors indicated guilt or regret or fear or shame—anything unusual, anything upon which they could follow up later. It was a standard technique for a criminal investigation. Yet it still made Bell feel slightly shabby, as if she were exploiting the sorrow of those who had loved Lucinda Trimble, appropriating it for her own purposes.

Bell had already handed out more hellos in her first five minutes here than she'd normally dispense in a month. She knew these people. Liked a lot of them. Yet someone within the radius of her gaze—Bell was speculating, but it was based on having handled a depressing number of homicide cases in the past four years—had murdered Lucinda Trimble. As Bell had explained many times during speeches to civic groups: *Statistics tell the tale, folks. Look around. You've got a heck of a lot more to fear from that person sitting right next to you on the couch night after night than you do from a stranger hanging out in a dark alley.* But nobody really wanted to believe that, she knew. And she couldn't blame them.

Bell felt Rhonda's elbow digging into her side.

"So," Rhonda said in a conspiratorial whisper. She winked and giggled. "You behaving yourself?"

"What?"

"You know what I'm talking about, boss," Rhonda said. Her second wink had an unmistakably naughty subtext, the effect enhanced by the heaps of black mascara that turned her eyelashes into matching rows of exclamation points. "Heard from a little birdie that *some-body's* truck was parked *all night* outside a certain prosecuting attorney's house the other night." A third wink.

It was the third one that pushed Bell over the edge. "Not the time or the place, Rhonda," she snapped. "This is a *funeral,* for God's sake."

Rhonda grinned and gave Bell a thumbs-up sign.

Small towns, Bell thought. *Jesus.*

As the first mourners began to arrive, many of them gripping small personal Bibles in their work-burnished hands, Bell repeated her instructions to Hick and Rhonda in a discreetly lowered voice: "Pay close attention to who shows up. And even closer attention to who doesn't."

It was an old church, a small, squared-off heap of ancient gray river stones assembled with the aid of darker gray mortar, topped by a short wooden bell tower. The tower was painted white, and it housed a rust-ridden lump of a bell that long ago had been rendered mute, having lost its clapper as well as its structural integrity.

Before the Civil War, the church had been a stop on the Underground Railroad, one of the establishments that harbored runaway slaves during their perilous journey north. Back then, West Virginia was still Virginia—Virginia, cradle of the Confederacy, birthplace of Robert E. Lee, a proudly and implacably slaveholding state. The western part of the state—the part that in the dark days of the Civil War would officially become West Virginia, once a worried President Lincoln figured out how to finagle the split—was home to fervent abolitionists. To women and men who risked their lives to fight against slavery. The people who maintained churches like this one in Briney Hollow had done more to rid the earth of the horrific sin of slavery, Bell believed, than all the preening politicians and their noble-sounding speeches put together. She loved telling Carla about the history of West Virginia, a state specifically created on behalf of a noble cause, the cause of civil rights

Yet to Bell's dismay, the African-American population in Raythune County was negligible. There had not been a single black student in her graduating class at Acker's Gap High School. During her years in Washington, Bell had come to appreciate the casual diversity she saw every day; back here, a black face was an anomaly.

She watched the mourners as they slowly mounted the four small steps and passed under the stone archway, unconsciously matching the somber rhythm of their tread to the heavy, florid beat of the organ music that gusted up from the front of the tiny church. Many people murmured the words to the hymn as they walked: *A mighty fortress is our God, a sacred refuge is your name.* There were old women with aluminum walkers and old men with hand-carved canes. There were teenagers—Lucinda's classmates—sobbing ostentatiously. There were middle-aged women in pastel polyester dresses and suits, there were children whose hair glistened with gel and bore the wavy marks of harsh hurried combings, there were men in corduroy sport coats and Sansabelt slacks and work boots. Some of the men stopped to knock the dried mud off their boots before they entered the church; some of them didn't. Bell and Rhonda and Hick nodded to each person as she or he passed by. Sometimes they waved. Always, though, they watched.

Among the early arrivals were Alton, Wendy, and Shawn Doggett. Where was Ketchum? Bell looked around, intrigued, but then she remembered: This church had no handicap-accessible entrance. It was too old to be retrofitted.

As her eyes swept over the families who followed the Doggetts, Bell thought about Maddie Trimble. She was still amazed that Maddie had agreed to a church funeral for her daughter. Maddie was a passionate atheist, often referring to Christians as "hypocritical, weak-minded scumbags." But the way Bell heard it, the Reverend Otto Qualls—whose first cousin, Bertha Qualls, was the proprietress of the consignment shop over in Swanville from which Maddie regularly obtained the items in her sales stock that she could not make herself—was the man responsible. The Reverend Qualls, who shared Bertha's curly brown hair, spadelike chin, and oddly prominent nostrils, had put it to Maddie pragmatically: *Your child was a cherished part of this community and you have a responsibility to let her many, many friends and loved ones say good-bye to her in a dignified and traditional*

*setting. It's not about your ignorant, pigheaded prejudice against or-
ganized religion. It's about your girl and what she meant to people in
these parts. Period.* And Maddie, to the surprise of many—possibly
including herself—had agreed.

Bell nodded to Rhonda and Hick. The service would be starting
any minute now; the line of mourners had begun to tail off. It was
time for the three of them to go inside, too, and find a seat in one of
the rickety wooden pews, pews whose joints had rattled loose over
the decades due to packs of parishioners sitting and rising, sitting and
rising, at the behest of a pastor. Bell switched her phone to vibrate.
The task reminded her: The sheriff had double-checked with Maddie.
They'd still not been able to locate Lucinda's cell. Not in the car, not
in her purse. Not among the items from that purse that had been
found scattered on the riverbank: billfold, comb, lip gloss, mascara.
The cell wasn't in her room or in her locker at school.

It was, in a sense, irrelevant to their investigation; the records
from Lucinda's carrier provided a list of her incoming and outgoing
calls that night. And none of those calls yielded any insight into why
she had gone to the river—or with whom. But still it nagged at Bell.
Where the hell *was* it? No teenage girl left home without her cell. Just
didn't happen.

Had the killer taken it? Or had it been lost in the water and even
now sifted ever deeper into the muddy no-man's-land at the bottom of
the Bitter River?

The organist, Ruth Ann Munderlin—an elderly black woman with
horn-rimmed glasses, thinning hair, and a timid manner—had finished
the introductory music. She closed the hymnal, put her hands flat on
her lap, and nodded at the Reverend Qualls. He nodded back and
stepped to the lectern, at which point there was a stir in the sanctuary.
A shiver ran around the room, like the wind blowing over a field, bending the tips of the grass in a communal swoon. Slotted in their pews,
trapped and restless, people bobbed and stretched and leaned sideways
and lifted their chins, the better to see what was happening.

It was Maddie Trimble. And escorting her up the aisle, moving toward the closed white casket that had been delivered to the foot of the altar, was a tall man in a suit that didn't fit him right and a red and blue tie, his dirty-blond hair pressed flat on the back and the sides of his head. A scar twisted his upper lip into what looked like a permanent sneer. Yet there was an interesting energy about him, Bell thought. Something simmered within him. He looked like a middle-aged version of the high school bad boy. He was handsome—it was a scuffed-up, stripped-down, weather-beaten handsomeness—in a way that some women found attractive.

Hell. We all do, Bell thought. *Only some of us don't like to admit it.*

She heard the murmurings, which, in this brief interval of quiet, sounded like a thousand insect wings primping for flight. There were a few gasps, too.

She tapped Rhonda's shoulder. "What's going on?"

"Never thought I'd live to see the day—but that's *Eddie Geyer,*" Rhonda said, trying to keep her voice down. "Lucinda's daddy. Nobody's seen hide nor hair since—oh, I guess since Lucinda was two or three months old. He broke about every law there is to break around here before he left. Lord in heaven—*Eddie Geyer.*"

The swirl and drift of the whispers died down as Maddie Trimble and Eddie Geyer reached the altar. They turned around, searching for seats in the front row. It looked to Bell as if Eddie was casing the place—just as she and Hick and Rhonda had done—and that his gaze roved from face to face to face, in search of a particular one. He must've seen the face that he was looking for, because he muttered something to Maddie, and she nodded. Eddie narrowed his eyes. Thumbed the scar on his lip.

Chapter Twenty-Four

The service was too long, too windy, too sentimental, too plump with platitudes for Bell's taste, but she supposed that would always be the case when it was intended to commemorate someone young and promising. She'd been to other funerals for young people in Raythune County—too many of them—and it was always this way. Even when the death was from natural causes. Even when it wasn't a homicide.

An unsolved homicide.

Which was another reason for her impatience. She wanted to get back to work. She was vaguely aware of the closing hymn, feeling more than hearing the words as voices rose all around her: "Blessed assurance, Jesus is mine. Oh, what a foretaste of glory divine!"

As people rose and turned right and left to gather up coats and hats and children, and then began to make the slow sideways shuffle from pew to center aisle, and center aisle to front door, another disturbance erupted. This time, it originated at the front of the church. Sheriff Fogelsong approached Maddie Trimble and took her elbow. He said something to her, something clipped and sharp, and then Maddie touched the sheriff's arm and replied—Bell was squinting, trying to read Maddie's lips—*Please, Nick. Don't. Don't.* That was what it looked like, anyway. The Bad Boy scowled at the sheriff, raising his lip the way a mean dog would. Nick—to Bell's surprise—backed off.

She'd ask Nick about it later. Or maybe she wouldn't. His relationship with Maddie Trimble was not the easiest subject for them.

It was a matter now of trying to get out of this place, of moving at an excruciating pace, of pushing without seeming to be pushing. Bell accidentally bumped the people in front of her, smiled, and offered apologies. Accidentally bumped them again. And then she spotted the one person she'd been absolutely certain she wouldn't see here today.

Matt Harless.

He stood near the doorway of the old church, waiting for his turn to exit. His arms were pressed stiffly at his sides; his face was impassive. His white dress shirt bore the symmetrical creases of a garment that had been liberated from its packaging about an hour ago.

"Hey," he said as Bell came toward him.

"Hey yourself." She couldn't resist. "You here to beat somebody up?"

"Not today."

She met his eyes. "You didn't know Lucinda Trimble."

"No. I didn't."

She kept her tone light, but curiosity burned in her. "So you just like hanging out at funerals? This is fun for you or something?"

He shrugged. "Or something." People were trying to get around him, like a current diverted by a rock in the middle of the river, and when Matt realized that, he stepped to the side. A family went by, led by a grim-faced father followed by six children. The mother walked behind the children, herding them like a border collie, smoothing down the backs of their hair with a white-gloved hand.

"Seriously," Bell said. She joined him, pressing herself against the stone wall. They were shoulder to shoulder now. "What's the deal? Is this part of your research on our local customs?"

People continued to move past them, many of them crying, shaking their heads, faces swollen. Women dug in their purses for additional packets of tissues or hand-embroidered handkerchiefs. Men tightened their jaws so that their chins wouldn't quiver.

"Tell you the truth," Matt went on, "this is kind of like reparations for me."

"Pardon?"

"In a war, you don't get to be there when they lay your friends to rest. I missed a lot of funerals over in Iraq. So when I was having breakfast at Ike's this morning—been going there for most of my meals—and I heard the service was today, I decided to come. To make up for all the services I *couldn't* attend. All the times when I knew the deceased, but couldn't pay my respects. Knew them well, in fact."

Just when Bell thought she had this man figured out, thought she'd gotten a read on him, he surprised her, eluded her, slipping neatly beyond her reach, like a leaf in the wind.

Then both of them were swept up by the departing crowd, caught in the jostle and scrape and nudge, and by the time Bell was able to look back again, Matt was gone.

Chapter Twenty-Five

She had a moment before the interview was scheduled to start and so, from the seat behind her desk, Bell studied Shawn Doggett's bony wrists. They jutted from the cuffs of his dark blue cotton sweater. He had his mother's narrow face and delicate features, her slender build, and her wide, startled-looking blue eyes. A chunk of light brown hair was parked on his forehead, despite his persistent attempts to brush it back with irritated swipes by either hand. He seemed terribly young to Bell. Far too young to have lost someone he loved—if, that is, he had truly loved Lucinda.

If, that is, he hadn't killed her.

But then again, Bell reminded herself, it was entirely possible to both love *and* kill someone. Happened all the time.

"First of all, I'm so very sorry for your loss," Bell said. "I know how much you cared for Lucinda, Shawn. Why don't you tell me about her?"

It was the day after the funeral. Alton and Wendy Doggett had agreed to bring their sons to the courthouse for a meeting with the prosecutor. The appearance was not mandatory and they were entirely free to refuse; Bell had explained that carefully to Wendy Doggett on the phone, along with the salient fact that they were welcome to be accompanied by an attorney, although if they did so, such an escort might very well initiate peculiar and unsettling rumors for which Bell could not be responsible. She also asked them to agree to provide a DNA sample from each family member, just to complete the record. Their cooperation, she said, would be appreciated.

Alton sat on the couch, big thighs spread, elbows on his knees, looking around the room with amiable disdain: *So this's where my tax dollars go. Huh.* When he first came in, he'd winked at Bell and said, "How's your friend? Signed himself up for an MMA match by now?" She gave him a wince of a smile and then gestured toward the couch. Bell would've preferred talking to Shawn and Ketchum Doggett alone, but they were minors, and she was required to include their parents in any interviews.

Wendy Doggett sat next to her husband, with Shawn on her other side. She was still rigorously thin in her mid-fifties, hair dyed a creamy shade of honey-blond and arranged on both sides of her face in rhyming shoulder-length curves. Thick black eyeliner gave Wendy's eyes a slightly sinister cast. High-riding, sharp-edged cheekbones made the rest of her face look insistently geometric. She wore a long-sleeved white blouse and pleated black skirt that concluded just below her kneecaps; when she shifted her position on the couch, causing the skirt to move ever so slightly, a few light scratches on the skin of one kneecap were briefly visible.

Ketchum had maneuvered his wheelchair to a spot just to the left of Bell's desk. As he entered, she noticed that Ketchum handled himself in the chair with more grace and agility than most people did on two legs. His hair was darker than his brother's, and he had a wide, handsome face—in appearance he had taken after his father rather than his mother—and deep-set eyes that missed nothing. He occupied the wheelchair with a kind of regal ease, big hands stationed on the tops of the wheels, ready to move at a whim. His arms and his shoulders were packed with solid slabs of muscle, clearly the result of regular and intense workouts. But it was the hands that drew Bell's attention. *With those hands,* she thought, *this kid could do whatever the hell he wanted to.*

On some occasions, Bell preferred to conduct interviews in her office instead of the two small interrogation rooms that Sheriff Fogelsong maintained for such purposes; minus the harsh lights of those other locations, she could encourage a feeling of routine fact-finding, of filling in background information.

"I knew Lucinda a little bit myself," Bell said, elaborating on her question to Shawn. Hoping to prime the pump. "My daughter used to go to school here—she lives in Virginia now, with her dad—but she's a year older than you and Lucinda." That was an interviewer's trick that Nick had taught her. *Always give a little something of yourself. Can't be a one-way street.* Nothing got a person's defenses up faster, he'd explained, than the sense of being grilled.

Shawn nodded. "Yeah, okay." A pause. "Lucinda was great."

"You loved her," Bell said.

"Yeah."

"I hope you got a chance to tell her so," Bell said, lowering her voice to a sympathetic—and strategic—softness. "The last time you talked, I mean." Shawn had told the deputies that his final encounter with Lucinda was at school that day. Many hours before her death. Maybe he'd slip, though. Maybe, if he was hiding something—like the fact that he'd seen her later that night—he would forget what he'd already said.

Bell was suspicious of the *Romeo and Juliet,* star-crossed-lover scenario that so enchanted Rhonda. Rich boy, poor girl: It made a sweet story, but in Bell's experience, stories could either be sweet or they could be true. They couldn't be both.

"I don't know," Shawn said.

"You don't know?"

Wendy put a hand on Shawn's arm to keep him from responding. "Mrs. Elkins," she said, clearly annoyed. "He said he didn't know. If you're going to badger him, then maybe we should—"

"Sorry," Bell interjected. She had misread the moment. Overstepped. "My apologies, Shawn. I know it's hard to remember these things."

He frowned. Leaned away from his mother, moving his arm until her hand slid off. "What I meant to say was—yeah, sure, I told her. I said, 'Love you,' like we always did. By our lockers." He swallowed. "But she was going somewhere with Marcy after school and so she was in a hurry and so I didn't—I didn't say it like I meant it. You know? Like it mattered."

"Had you two made any plans?"

"You mean, like for the weekend?"

Gently, Bell said, "No, Shawn. I mean about the baby. About the rest of your lives."

"Oh." A blush ran up the side of his neck. "Okay. Well, here's the deal." He blew out a ribbon of air. When he resumed speaking, the pace of his sentences accelerated, as if, Bell thought, he was relieved to be saying these things out loud, happy to get them out in the world, establishing them as fact. "We were going to get married. Raise the baby. It was all planned out, okay? We talked about it all the time. I was going to go work for my dad and then—one day—take over the business. And we'd have a house and all. And maybe have more kids. Okay?"

"You didn't discuss the possibility of an abortion?"

"No." Firmly. "She'd never even consider that."

"How about you? How did you feel about it?"

"I told you. We were going to get married. We'd made *plans*. I'd given her a ring, okay?"

Until now, Alton Doggett seemed to have been paying little attention to the conversation. He leaned back on the couch, legs spread, clasped hands cupping the back of his big head, running his tongue around the inside of his closed mouth. But apparently it was time for him to jump in. He twitched, nodded, unlaced his fingers, popped forward. "That he did, Mrs. Elkins," he said in his salesman's voice, bluff and hearty. "That he did." He cocked an eyebrow, looking intently at Bell. "Family heirloom. Belonged to Wendy's grandmother. Only thing of any real value they ever had." A glance at his wife, a glance that he spiced with a smile. "Ain't that right, honey?"

"Yes." Wendy's voice was several decibels softer than her husband's, but there was nothing soft at its core. "I gave it to Shawn when he was ten years old. Explained that when the time came, he would give it to the woman he loved."

"And that was Lucinda," Bell said.

"Yes." Wendy reached over to brush a soft triangle of hair from her son's forehead. He let her do so, but didn't look happy about it. Bell felt a private sympathy for Wendy. She remembered being in the same spot with Carla; sometimes she needed to touch her, to feel that physical contact, as a way of grounding herself, but the older children grew, the less they tolerated it.

"Did Lucinda wear the ring?" she asked Shawn.

"Only time she ever took it off," he said, quiet pride lighting up his voice, "was during basketball games. Said she couldn't dribble with it on. Other than that, though—yeah. Yeah, she wore it."

Buster Crutchfield hadn't found a ring on Lucinda's body. Bell knew because she'd asked him specifically: *Any jewelry? Anything?* And he'd replied, *Darlin', didn't find a thing like that. Kinda funny for a teenage girl, you know? Usually, that age, they've got all kinda metal on 'em—rings and bracelets and necklaces and pins and those little ole things around their ankles. This gal? Nope.*

"I remember the day I gave it to her," Shawn said. "She cried. I'd never seen her cry before, but that day—well, she did." He dipped his head. When he lifted it again, his eyes had a calmness to them, a peace. The memory had consoled him, as, Bell reminded herself, memories could.

Some memories. Others could tear you apart. Send you running.

"I assume our business here is finished?" Wendy said abruptly, taking advantage of the brief lapse in Bell's concentration. "This is an upsetting time for our family, Mrs. Elkins, and I really think it would be best for everyone if we could wrap this up and—"

"Just another minute," Bell said. Polite smile, grateful smile, a smile aimed not exclusively at Wendy but meant to include all four of them, the parents and the two boys, binding them up. No promises, but still: *Your cooperation will not be forgotten,* the smile implied. *This will work in your favor. Make things easier, all the way around.*

She turned again to Shawn. "Who do you think Lucinda was

meeting that night? If it wasn't you and it wasn't Marcy Hillman—who?"

He shrugged. "Don't know."

"It was so late," Bell went on. Musing. Considering. "Leaving her house like that, without telling her mother where she was going, driving to the river—that wasn't like her, was it?"

He shook his head.

"No idea?" Bell pressed him. "It's important, Shawn. Really, really important. We need to know why Lucinda went to the Bitter River that night. If we're going to find out who did this to her—this terrible thing, unthinkable and unforgivable—then we need to know who—"

"He said he didn't know, okay?"

Ketchum's interruption came in a dangerous flash, like a jackknife rammed in a sidewall by a stranger strolling by. He bobbed forward in his chair, hands formed into blocky fists, challenging Bell with his granite stare.

"Leave him the fuck *alone,* lady," Ketchum added. "He *told* you. He doesn't fucking *know.*"

"Hey, hey," Alton said. Pointed a stubby finger at his younger son. "Language, boy. Language. You're talking to a public official. Not your buddies at school."

"Thank you, Mr. Doggett," Bell said, "but it's all right. I understand that Ketchum might be feeling protective of his brother—isn't that right, Ketchum? Shawn has been through a lot. And how about you?"

"What about me?" Ketchum sat back in his chair. He wasn't looking at her anymore, but the fury still moved in his face.

"Lucinda was your friend, too, right?" Bell asked.

"Yeah. So."

Wendy stirred on the couch, recrossing her legs. "I thought," she said, pointedly addressing Bell, "that your business here was with *Shawn.* Not Ketchum. He barely knew the Trimble girl."

"Barely *knew* her, Mom?" Ketchum said. Anger boiled anew in his voice. "Come on. That's a crock of shit."

"Thought I told you to watch that language, boy," Alton interjected again, this time more harshly. "Don't you sass your mother. You know better 'n' that."

Ketchum ignored his parents and swung his gaze back around to Bell, like a wrecking ball returning to its original target. "You know what, lady? Lucinda *listened* to me, okay? She listened a lot better than anybody else around here. She didn't make fun of me when I said I wanted to get the hell out of here. Get out and *stay* out. Go to a top college and then medical school. That's what we talked about, okay? About how I want to work with spinal cord injuries. Nerve regeneration."

"Great goal," Bell said.

"Yeah, well, tell my parents that, will you? We've been having some big-assed arguments about it." Bitter now, the bitterness spilling out of his voice. No container in the world big enough to hold it. "Because *Shawn's* the one they want to go away to school," Ketchum continued. A short, hard laugh. "*Shawn's* the one with the future, okay? Not me. They want me to stay here. Right here, okay? Until my butt grows right into this goddamned chair." He bounced a fist savagely against the armrest.

Wendy tried to interrupt again, but Bell stopped her with an upraised hand, never taking her eyes away from Ketchum's twisted-up face. Bell knew it wouldn't work forever—Wendy wouldn't be thwarted for long—but it bought her an extra minute.

"Lucinda understood you," Bell said softly. "Nobody else did—but she did."

"Yeah," Ketchum said. "Totally."

"You miss her. And you want to help us find out who killed her, right? That's pretty important, wouldn't you say?"

"Yeah."

"And on the night she died—you were all at home, isn't that right, Ketchum? Nobody left. You were all at home. All of you. Shawn, your mother and father, and—"

"For God's sake, lady—*yeah*," he declared hotly. "*Yes.* We were all there, okay? Are you deaf or *what*? Everybody was there. We had dinner and then Shawn and I watched TV and did our homework and then we played Xbox. We were all home, lady, okay? All night long. Just ask the neighbors. Bet they heard all the yelling."

"Ketchum," Wendy said. A dark warning in her voice. "That's enough. Please."

"Oh, for God's sake, Mom. Everybody knows, okay? Everybody fucking knows. It's not like this big secret." Ketchum switched to Bell. "My parents don't get along, okay? That's just one more reason I want to get the hell out of here. All the screaming and shouting. Can't even get any sleep some nights. All the arguments. All the fighting. *Jesus*." He turned to his brother, who was looking down at the floor between his shoes. "Come on, Shawn. Tell her. Tell her what it's like. Back me up on this, okay?"

Shawn didn't say a word. Never raised his face.

Ketchum stared at his brother's bowed head. In a bleak voice that barely lifted above a whisper, he said, "Fuck you, you fucking coward."

Wendy stood up. "I think," she said, snapping off the words like tiny bites from a stale cracker, "this is no longer serving any useful purpose, Mrs. Elkins, other than to shame and embarrass my family." By this time her husband and Shawn had risen as well. "I've heard about the kind of office you run down here," Wendy continued, voice icy with innuendo. "About how you bully people. About how you laugh at them behind their backs. Because you think you're superior. Because you've got your fancy office and your fancy title. And so you march around this town like you *matter*. But you know what I heard, Belfa Elkins? I heard you're not even qualified. I heard you got yourself elected because nobody else wanted the job. And you keep it because you and the sheriff are old friends. He's been covering for you, isn't that right? Hiding your mistakes?"

In the second or so before she turned to go, Wendy let her eyes say the rest: *I know you*. Bell had seen it before, in the eyes of people whose childhoods echoed her own, whose early years were stained with the same darkness, but who had perfected other strategies to live their way past it. *I know you, lady.* So *don't you* dare *judge me. Because you're not so different. Raised in a trailer. Hungry. Dirty. One pair of shoes to your name—and you only got that because they had your size at the Goodwill. Don't pretend that you don't remember. And don't think you can put one over on me, either. People like us—we're mean. Sharp and mean. We know what's behind us. We can still see it, over our shoulder. And we're never going back. Whatever we have to do, whatever we have to put up with, we're not going back. So don't you sit there and judge* me, *Belfa Elkins.*

Chapter Twenty-Six

She was supposed to get together with Clay tonight. The plan was to drive over to Blythesburg, have dinner, maybe see a movie—if they could find one that wasn't based on a comic book or an old TV show.

But Bell decided she wanted to be alone. She needed to think.

"Mind if I take a rain check?" she asked him. She sat in her kitchen, the cell on speakerphone. Clay's voice filled the small room: "No problem," he said. "You sound pretty beat, honey."

"Long interview today," she confirmed.

She hadn't turned on any lights when she arrived home; dusk was gathering in the corners and moving toward the center of the room, like a piece of paper being folded up, one tiny square at a time.

"Oh, right," he said. "I remember. The Famous Doggett Family. Hell—sounds like a country music act."

She laughed. But she didn't follow up the laugh with any details. He had to extrapolate from what he knew about her, interpreting her silence. Reading it, the way a farmer reads the sky to know the next day's weather.

"Rough one, huh?" he said.

"Yeah." A beat. "Wendy Doggett's got an attitude."

"Well, given the fact of her son's engagement, she probably knew the Trimble girl pretty well," Clay said. He was thinking, and Bell could envision him rubbing his left cheek with the back of his hand, a habit that accompanied his cogitations. "Hard to get over a sudden death," he said. "Some people don't know how to show their grief. Think it makes them look weak. So they go in the other direction. They get hard. Real hard."

"It's not that."

"It's not?"

"No. She's got a specific beef with me." Bell wanted to add, but didn't: *Certain kinds of women don't like my kind. Same goes for me and Maddie Trimble. We're natural enemies. Like owls and crows.*

"Okay, then," Clay said. "You get some rest."

She hit END and sat back in her chair. He was easy to talk to, and flexible about plans; she appreciated that. So why hadn't she told him about her little ride out to Doggett Motors with Matt Harless? And about Matt's meltdown?

She sat for a while longer. The next time she looked down at her hands, she could barely see them. Night had infiltrated the room.

Abruptly, not really sure what she was doing until she had risen from the table and returned to the Explorer and backed out of her driveway, she found herself pulling into the driveway next to Edna's house.

No lights on. The old woman was surely asleep, Bell told herself; it was late now. The only real nightlife in Acker's Gap belonged exclusively to the crickets, which were kicking up a hell of a racket in the woods next to Edna's property.

She wasn't here to see Edna. And even though there were no lights visible in the garage apartment, either, Bell could imagine Matt sitting in the dark, just as she'd been sitting in the dark a few minutes ago.

She didn't know why she was here, but she was here. She still felt guilty about having blown off Clay, but then again, they'd exchanged no promises. There'd been no pledge of exclusivity. And even if she'd made such a pledge, this little impromptu visit to Matt tonight had nothing to do with Clay in particular or her romantic life in general.

Right?

She knocked softly at the apartment door. She remembered that there'd been some liquid left in that bottle of his, so she had a line ready: *Buy me a drink?* She was willing to bet he'd smile when he heard her say it, and then he'd tilt his head, by way of inviting her in.

No answer. She knocked again.

Still nothing. He wasn't home. As she turned to go, she thought about that word—"home"—and wondered, in Matt's case, what it really meant.

Hell. She wondered what it meant in her case, too.

They came into Bell's office the next afternoon, the father and the daughter. Bert Hillman and Marcy Hillman. If you didn't already know they were related, you would have guessed it right away. His face was visible in her face, like the same note sung at a slightly different pitch. Same small eyes and tiny nose, same thin mouth, a mouth that seemed shaped with little more in mind than hosting a pout. Both had lanky bodies and hair so glossy-black that it continually reflected the light, as if they polished it with a cloth they kept handy.

"The hell you want with my girl?" snapped Bert Hillman.

Bell wasn't surprised at the lack of pleasantries. She waved at the various seating options available to visitors. Casting his face around the room with a livid scowl, suspecting some kind of trick, Bert finally sat. Marcy followed him. She hadn't said a word yet.

"So you call out to my house," Bert said, anger revving in him over and over again, like a motorcycle at a stoplight, "and you tell me you gotta talk to my girl here. First you accuse me of shootin' at the damned courthouse. Now this."

"Mr. Hillman, nobody accused you of anything. Sheriff Fogelsong simply asked you for your whereabouts during the commission of an armed assault on a public facility—a request that, given your previous written and verbal threats against this office, was entirely reasonable. You provided that alibi. We've moved on. I suggest that you do the same." While ostensibly addressing Bert, Bell took the opportunity to get a better look at Marcy. The young woman wore tight black capris and a bright pink T-shirt with NICKI MINAJ LIVE! splashed across it in pointy black letters. Marcy was nervous and blinked fiercely, as if the blinks were maintained by a hidden and inexhaustible energy source.

"Well," Bert said, slightly abashed. "We're here, ain't we? State your business with my girl so's we can get on home. It's just me and her, you know. Nobody else to do the chores."

Bell nodded. "Marcy," she said, "I didn't see you at Lucinda's funeral. She was your best friend, wasn't she?"

"I thought it would be—too hard." Marcy's voice was gentle. Not like her father's hectoring snarl.

"What do you mean?" Bell asked. She knew that Bert might jump in, answering for his daughter, but he, too, seemed to want to hear what Marcy had to say. He watched her, his mouth open so he could breathe through it, using his fist to rub at a spot on his gray work pants.

"I thought," Marcy went on, and once again her voice was hauntingly delicate, "I might lose it. Just faint or something. She was my best friend, okay? I just didn't think I could handle it. I knew what it would be like. All those people—all of them talking about her like they knew her. They didn't know her. I knew her, Mrs. Elkins. I really did. And she knew me."

"You say you knew her—but you can't say who she was meeting that night?"

"Wish I could," Marcy said. "Might be able to help you out, then. Find her killer, I mean."

"You done?" Bert muttered. He played with the flap of a scab on his left forearm. He'd rolled up the sleeve on that arm to get at it. "That all you got for my girl? If it is, then I got an official complaint to make about them state boys workin' on the road. They been comin' onto my land and if I catch 'em, I swear to you, lady, I'm gonna—"

"I've got no jurisdiction over the state highway department, Mr. Hillman." Bell kept her voice calm and even, the only way to deal with him. Matching the intensity of his agitation was, Bell knew, like the old saying about mud-wrestling with a pig: *You both get dirty—but the pig enjoys it.*

"Was Lucinda worried about something, Marcy?" Bell asked, shifting back to the young woman.

Marcy's eyes darted in another direction. "What do you mean?"

"Well," Bell continued, "she left her house pretty late that night to go talk to someone by the riverbank. It had to be important. Maybe it was important to the person she was meeting—or maybe it was important to Lucinda. Maybe she was the one who needed to talk."

"I don't know."

"Are you sure?"

Bert Hillman bolted up. Fury in his eyes. "If my girl says she don't know, then she don't." He glared down at Marcy; that was enough to cause her to rise, too, as if she were a dog and he'd blown a silent whistle. He turned back to Bell, face crumpled with anger. "You got something else to say to us, lady, you send it in a registered letter. And listen to this: I got a right to defend my property from them state road crews when they're trespassing. Constitution says so. You hear me?"

An hour later, Lee Ann called to her. "Sheriff's on line three."

Bell, who'd been reading a trial transcript and was grateful for the break, took off her reading glasses and fetched the phone. To her relief, she and Nick seemed to have finally gotten over the awkwardness at Ike's.

"Afternoon," she said.

"Bell. Glad to find out the lightning hasn't struck yet."

She didn't know what he was talking about.

Then he chuckled and added, "From you being in a church the other day, I mean."

"Hilarious," she said, trying and failing to sound irked at his little joke. She wasn't a churchgoer, a fact that had been raised more than once during her campaign for prosecutor, and that still brought some heat her way. Truth was, she was pleased that Nick was teasing her. It was one more sign that things were getting back to normal—or as normal as they could be, while Lucinda Trimble's murderer was still at large.

"Anyway," he said, "that was quite a turnout. Just like you said it'd be."

"Not a surprise, really." She picked up a pencil from the desktop, and drew tiny circles on a piece of paper while she talked. "You know how it is. A young person dies—and dies mysteriously—and it feels like it's outside the natural order of things. People are plenty curious. Pass away at sixteen—and you can expect a full house at your funeral. Pass away at ninety and you're lucky to have two people there—and one of them's likely to be the undertaker, and he's getting paid."

"Still and all, I've not seen a crowd that big in years. Good thing Deputy Greenough volunteered for traffic duty out on the highway. Otherwise, we'd have had ourselves a hell of a mess." Then he got down to the real business of his call. "Got some news about the shooting."

Bell gave a short laugh. "Yeah. Me, too. Bert Hillman was just in here, and he's hopping mad that you keep insinuating that he was responsible."

"Why the hell was he in your off—?"

"Came in with Marcy. She's a minor. I needed to talk to her about Lucinda."

"Okay," Nick said, settling down. "Well, you can tell Bert for me that I'm not insinuating anything. His alibi checks out. He's in the clear."

"Already told him. He's not much of a listener, Nick, in case you don't remember."

"I remember." The sheriff snorted his disdain. "You know as well as I do that Bert Hillman's a clown. Damned nuisance, but a clown all the same."

"So what's your news?"

"Deputy Harrison's got a friend over at the state forensics lab. They did a little legwork on their own over the weekend. Figured out where the gunshot might've come from. Based on the caliber of the bullet, we know the shooter used a high-powered rifle. Turns out we were looking in the wrong place."

"We were?"

"Yeah. That shot wasn't fired from a downtown location. It could've come from fifteen hundred feet away."

"Which means the woods. Good cover."

"Right. So Harrison and her friend extrapolated from the angle of the shot, and found a likely spot on a small rise just off Route 6. And guess what else they found there?"

Fogelsong didn't wait for her to answer. "A footprint," he went on. "Pretty damn clear one, too. Some real sharp ridges in the dirt. And guess what else?"

Bell heard a touch of excitement in his voice, one he might be trying to suppress but that revealed itself anyway. Nick Fogelsong loved the hunt, the chase. He couldn't remain aloof and nonchalant about it. He was too enthralled by his work. Too engaged. And he'd always loved talking over cases with her.

"Harrison's buddy has access to the FBI databases," he continued. "Those folks can do magic with a shoeprint. They've got prints from every kind of footgear made or sold in this country since before George Washington pulled on his muddy boots to go cross the Potomac. Or thereabouts."

"And?"

"And they didn't find a match."

"That's good news?"

"Sure it is." Nick's voice was almost bubbly now. "Don't you get it? It means the shooter wasn't wearing shoes available in this country. The shooter was from somewhere else. A foreigner."

She frowned, even though she knew the sheriff couldn't see it. She was annoyed that he'd gotten her hopes up. "Don't know if you've heard of it yet," she said, "but there's this little thing they call the Internet. People can order shoes from anywhere in the world now. Could be somebody we know real well—who happens to like a wide variety of shoes. Might not mean a thing."

"Well, it's more 'n' what we had before, which was a big fat bunch of nothing," he shot back. "You know me, Bell. Like I say when we're caught in a traffic jam—'Let's get movin', even if it's in the wrong direction.' A bad clue's better than no clue at all. And sometimes a bad clue," he added, "marks the halfway point toward getting to a good one. Doncha think?"

Chapter Twenty-Seven

A river, Bell thought, *is like a train whistle made liquid. A long sigh of discontent, draped around the mountain.*

She stood on the south bank of the Bitter River, feet spread, hands in her trouser pockets. It was just after 9 P.M. on Thursday, a week after Lucinda Trimble's body had been found here.

She'd had a full day in court, with three arraignments, two preliminary hearings, and opening statements in a major case involving the illegal sale of $100,000 worth of Lortab, a prescription drug especially prized by the addicts in the small towns of West Virginia. It infuriated Bell that when she tried to talk to outsiders about drug abuse in Appalachia, they thought she meant only methamphetamines. Meth labs, she could handle; meth labs were run by slimy bastards forced to slink around after sundown, hiding their operations in falling-down barns and basements, and whose customers were the usual run of stumbling, stinking, slack-jawed losers who were easy to spot and get rid of. Prescription drugs, though, were different; many times, people began using them for legitimate purposes—back pain from a lifetime's work in a coal mine, hip pain from years of scrubbing other people's toilets and hauling other people's loads—and found themselves addicted. Decent people. People who were deeply ashamed of themselves and their raging need for narcotics, but who were powerless to stop. And unlike meth, the pain pills were legal—at first. They were provided by physicians. Try rooting out *that* problem, Bell wanted to tell the people who chanted "meth lab, meth lab" at her when the talk turned to Appalachia's gravest challenges. *Meth lab, my ass.*

Hickey Leonard was assisting her with the Lortab case, but with the other cases, she was on her own.

Hell. She was always on her own.

Bell had a habit of visiting crime scenes. Not in the immediate aftermath; she took no pleasure from viewing the gruesome work done by guns, knives, fists, clubs, tire irons, or attack dogs. She tended to stop by a few days later, after the forensic experts had done their work, after the evidence had been collected and organized for use in a trial. She came when the echoes of the crime, the last ragged scraps, were making their final transit in the air just above the haunted ground, before moving on to another place, a place at which some heart was—even now—stirring with jealousy or hate or rage or greed or fear, a place in which the next violent act was—even now—poised and waiting to happen.

There was always another violent act, waiting to happen.

Bell looked out across the river's skin. Deep indigo color, still holding the last few filaments of the day's light. The surface shifted and trembled, as if it, too, struggled with bad dreams.

What had Lucinda's final moments been like? Was she scared? Did she know what was going to happen—or did her killer take her by surprise? Was she sitting in her car and talking to her assailant, someone she trusted, even loved? Sharing her hopes for her unborn child? Her plans for college, a career?

And *why*? Why would someone murder a young woman who had so much to look forward to? Why murder someone who—?

Bell heard a noise:

SlapSlapSlapSlapSlap.

She whirled around, her heartbeat speeding up so rapidly that she was sure it must be exploding into audibility. Her eyes had adjusted to the darkness by now.

A woman running down the road had paused—her tennis shoes rhythmically smacking the pavement were the source of the sounds—and bent over, grabbing her shorts and panting. She waved at Bell, then, one right after the other, yanked the earbuds out of her ears. Her hair was cut short. Worn in a dark curly cap.

"Hey," the woman said between gasps. "I'm—Marylou—Ferguson. I—know you—from your picture in the paper. You're—that—that lawyer lady."

"Bell Elkins."

"That's right." Finally she could breathe normally again. Started running in place, to keep loose while she chatted. "I usually run in the mornings—that's when I saw the car—but today I had to take Jefferson to the doctor. He's my seven-year-old. So I'm making up for it now."

"Must've been pretty scary, once you found out what was in that car."

"Oh, *heavens,* honey, it was *terrible*! Having little girls of my own—well, all I can say is, I hope you and the sheriff find out who killed her and you throw the book at 'em."

"Can I ask you, Mrs. Ferguson, what else you saw that day? I mean, I know you saw the top of the car in the water—"

"I sure did! It was a square of yellow, like a big old hunk of something, and I didn't realize at first that it was a car, I didn't know *what* it was, so I had to go closer. Had to go right down there on the riverbank, where you're standing."

"And did you see anything else?"

"Nope. Just those pushed-over weeds. That's all. Maybe they got like that when the killer was escaping."

"Maybe."

"But I got to admit. I wasn't really looking for clues. People're always throwing stuff in there. Like it's their own personal garbage dump."

"Yeah."

"Well," Ferguson said, "if you don't mind, I need to get back to my run. I used to be in a yoga class but we can't afford it now—my husband's been laid off for a year and a half, you know how bad things are around here—and let me tell you, six kids ain't cheap! We're barely making it. Never sure how we're gonna pay for next week's groceries, you know? And don't even talk to me about the price of gas! But I gotta get my exercise." She waved at Bell and plugged the earbuds back in.

Bell stood on the riverbank a good while longer. She didn't know why, but she wanted to stay until the moon rose; she wanted to see the moving print of the moon's reflection across the top of the Bitter River, shimmering dashes that rocked and swayed. *Like truth,* Bell thought. *Like truth, it just won't hold still. You can't make it stop long enough so you can say, "Here. Here it is. The truth." The surface is too damned unstable.* There were as many truths as there were tiny dashes of moonlight on the Bitter River, broken-up bits of radiance, a scattering of glowing scraps that rode the river like small jeweled rafts, bobbing and winking in the muted illumination.

She looked up. The moon was verging on full tonight, a bright orange ball that had ascended at speed, clearing the top of the mountain in what seemed to be a single hop. But now that moon had stalled out. It looked restless, Bell thought, and maybe frustrated, too, like something that tries to make a clean getaway, yearning for escape, but is too firmly tethered. It was as if the mountain were holding it back, determined not to let the moon out of its sight.

She drove slowly through Acker's Gap. Heading home. By now it was profoundly dark, with the kind of darkness exclusive to mountain towns. A brooding line of peaked towers of rock loomed over the streets, like the evil stranger in a fairy tale who holds open a dark cloak in hopes of sweeping unwary orphans inside.

Businesses closed up early here. The single stoplight at Main and Thornapple shut down each night at 8 P.M., switching to a yellow caution light. Bell braked at the intersection anyway. She peered up at the limestone courthouse, blunt and rooted in this block like some natural element—not like a public building for which tax funds had been collected and appropriated, not like a structure that had been designed and erected in 1867, as its cornerstone insisted, and not like a hulking clump of tired rock and worn-out mortar, but something altogether different. Something ancient and fundamental, something that preceded human presence and intent. Sheriff Fogelsong's office was in an annex off to the left. Many times, there was a light on in his office, even this late; Nick liked to do his paperwork once the courthouse cleared out and the day's crises had been dealt with, or at least evaluated and ranked and scheduled to be dealt with the next day.

No light tonight. Which made her both happy and sad. Happy that he was getting some rest, but sad that she couldn't stop in and talk to him. Talking with Nick always sharpened her thinking.

Reluctantly, she drove on by the courthouse.

Just around the corner she saw Ike's diner. Technically it was still open but nobody much patronized it at such a late hour. Bell took note of the thread of white light at the bottom edge of the blind covering the big front window. She pulled over. Joyce LeFevre, she knew, was like the sheriff; sometimes she favored tucking into her paperwork late at night, sitting in one of the booths with a cigarette on her lip and an inch of George Dickel in a short glass at her elbow. Joyce had an office in the back of the building but didn't much care for it. *Feel kinda squished and squashed back there,* she'd once told Bell. *No windows. Like a damned coffin. I like my space. Room to spread out.*

Bell walked in. Spotted Joyce in a booth.

"Hey there," Joyce called to her.

"Where's Georgette?"

"Upstairs. Already called it a day. Taking a bath, more 'n' likely. I'm telling you, Bell, that woman could soak herself for a week without battin' an eyelash. Gets herself a stack of magazines and some of that sweet-smellin' bubble bath—and that's it. Gone. Vamoosed. I've threatened to have her mail sent in."

A single white tube of fluorescent light clamped to the ceiling over the booth was all that Joyce allowed herself at this hour, leaving large pockets of the diner in darkness. She was dressed in an untucked chambray work shirt and floppy sweatpants and a pair of blue tennis shoes from which the laces were long gone. A wide red scarf was looped around her forehead and tied in the back, keeping Joyce's thick black hair out of her tired-looking eyes. She occasionally dyed her hair blond, but it never seemed right on her. Never fit. When she went back to her natural black, her customers were secretly relieved.

She smelled of cigarettes and fried potatoes. *And hard work,* Bell thought. *Can't forget that part.* Keeping this place going meant sixteen-hour workdays, no vacations, and a kind of perpetual fretting that was like a low hum. The diner vibrated with it. Some people claimed the faint buzz emanated from the fluorescent lights, but Bell knew better. It was the audible manifestation of worry. Joyce's worry.

On the table was an oversized black book with LEDGER embossed on the cover in serious gold letters. Joyce had closed it when Bell sat down across from her, and parked her two big hands on top, pudgy fingers pressed together like sausage links under cellophane.

"Don't tell me you do your accounting in that thing," Bell said.

"Okay. Won't tell you."

Bell laughed.

"You want coffee?" Joyce asked. Nodded toward her own glass. "Or maybe something stronger?"

"Just the company."

Neither seemed to mind the subsequent quietness, a quietness that accumulated around them steadily, patiently, like snowflakes piling up on a windowsill. Bell spent so much of her time every day talking—talking to her staff, talking to victims and witnesses and judges and deputies and other attorneys—that she'd grown to appreciate and even revere silence, especially accidental silence, silence that arrived mysteriously and unexpectedly, like a gift from a secret admirer.

Joyce LeFevre wasn't a close friend. Bell had had only a smattering of personal conversations with her since returning to Acker's Gap; most of their interactions were of the *Hi, how are ya?* variety, the phrase tossed back and forth when Bell came into Ike's for a meal. She wasn't exactly sure why she'd stopped by tonight. Joyce didn't seem to require an explanation.

"The Trimble girl," Joyce said. "You getting anywhere with finding out who killed her? Just an awful thing. Got a daughter of my own, you know. Grown up now, but you never stop worrying." She closed her eyes briefly. "Listen to me. Lord, Bell, you know that, too, better 'n' anybody."

Bell nodded solemnly. "Can't imagine what it's like for Madeline Trimble. And—yes, we're making some progress. But no, we're not ready to arrest anybody yet." That was her standard response when asked about a case. She hated to give Joyce LeFevre the boilerplate speech, but she had no choice.

"Makes you wonder," Joyce said.

Bell waited.

"About how people do it," Joyce continued. "When they've been hit like that. Hit in the gut." She looked down at her thick hands. "My husband walked in here one day and told me he loved somebody else. Some woman he'd met on the Internet. Said they was running off together. True love, is what it was. 'Joycie,' he told me, 'you can't fight true love.' True love. That's what he called it. Well, if there's true love, then there's got to be true hate, wouldn't you think? Well, yes. I'm here to tell you—yes, there is.

"He said I could keep this place and good luck keeping it going. Well, whoop-de-shit, is what I said back to him. Whoop-de-shit for me." Shook her big head. "Anyway, I always thought that was just about the worst thing that could happen to a person—being let go of like that, just kicked to the curb by somebody you loved and trusted and who you thought loved you right back. But you know what? It's not. It's not the worst thing. Compared to what Maddie Trimble must be feeling these days—it's nothing at all." She looked directly at Bell. "Besides, I've done all right for myself."

That might have been a subtle reference to her relationship with Georgette. Bell wasn't sure and wouldn't press for clarification; they didn't know each other that well. Maybe someday she would. But not now.

"We'll get the bastard who killed Lucinda Trimble," Bell declared. Once again, it was boilerplate; but it was boilerplate that signaled hope, so she didn't mind using it. "Don't know how long it'll take, but we'll do it."

"Sure you will." Joyce took a slow meditative sip of her George Dickel.

Bell rose. "Ought to be heading home. Enjoyed the break."

"Me, too."

"You take care of yourself."

In the dim light, the creases on Joyce's face looked as if they had deepened in the last few minutes. "You, too, Bell."

As Bell cruised past the last building on her right before leaving the city limits, she saw it.

The building was empty, like too many of the downtown storefronts. It had briefly housed a sandwich shop called Timmy's and then a discount tobacco outlet and after that, a business selling custom-made T-shirts, but now the cracked front window was coated in dust and bird shit. In the narrow strip of dirt between it and the used appliance store right next door, she glimpsed a quiver of movement. Close to the ground.

A slight wrinkle in the darkness.

A brief flash of reflected light.

After that, nothing.

At first Bell thought it was a person, crouched over, running. But it just as easily could have been a stray dog, cringing and shivering with hunger, living on the last ragged fringe before it went feral, a dog abandoned by a family that didn't have the means anymore to buy food for it, and so had left it to fend for itself. There were, she knew, a lot more dogs like that these days. Dogs dumped by people who weren't cruel, weren't bad, weren't selfish, people who loved their animals and considered them part of the family, but who did things now out of last-chance desperation. Just as Marylou Ferguson said: *Hard times all over.*

Bell grimaced, shook her head. She couldn't solve everyone's problems tonight—hell, she couldn't solve anyone's, including her own—and she drove on.

Yet she was still bothered by the odd glimmer she'd seen, that ripple in the darkness. This was her town. And she had no idea what had caught her eye. She only knew that whatever it was, it didn't belong there.

Chapter Twenty-Eight

"Can't finish," Bell said.

"You mind?" Clay was already reaching for her toast, before she'd had a chance to authorize his pilfering.

"Knock yourself out," she said. "And if you want to clean up those eggs, too, I'd be much obliged. Hate to waste food."

Clay nodded. He'd finished his own breakfast of steel-cut oatmeal with honey and now began to polish off the rest of Bell's scrambled eggs and raisin toast.

This impromptu breakfast at Ike's at 9 A.M. Friday was made possible by the fact that Clay's job site this week was in downtown Acker's Gap. Linton Albright's pizza shop needed a new floor.

All around them was the crunch and scuffle of the breakfast rush, played out amid the sounds of frying bacon, wrenched-back chairs, the occasional cell phone ringtone, and overlapping conversations that stacked up steadily in the room like fragile latticework. Georgette had to turn sideways to fit between the tables, taking new orders and answering empty coffee cups. Generally there were only seven or eight people in Ike's at any given time, but it was a different seven or eight all morning long. Turnover was quick and constant. The front door opened and closed every few minutes, and each time it did, a jingling bell offered a chipper little notification thereof.

Bell had spread out the top half of the front page of the *Acker's Gap Gazette* on the tabletop between then. It published once a week, and this was the first issue since Lucinda Trimble's body had been found in the Bitter River. Hence the headline combined two unrelated pieces of information, fastening them together with the linchpin of a semicolon: CLUES SCARCE IN TEEN'S MURDER; COUNTY UNEMPLOY-MENT RATE HITS 17.8 PERCENT.

Bell lifted her coffee mug as she studied the double-barreled bad news. Took an extended sip. Set the mug back down, then turned it around a few times on the table. She'd been in a fairly good mood to start out the morning, but that mood had shown itself to be a frail and tender thing, vanishing at its first brush with the outside world.

"Sometimes," she said, "I kind of wonder why we bother. Looking forward to anything around here, I mean."

Clay finished his bite of eggs. "Speaking of looking forward," he said. "Got a letter yesterday."

Bell let a second go by. Sometimes she could forget about the age difference between them. Other times—like now—Clay seemed very young to her. There was a radiant light in his eyes. An energy. The kind of energy, Bell thought wearily, that would burn itself off once he'd had a few more disappointments, once the world had had a chance to show him its true colors.

"Oh, yeah?"

"Yeah." He tugged a folded sheet of paper out of the breast pocket of his shirt. "Came yesterday. They sent an e-mail, too, but there's something about getting a letter. It's tangible. Seems more real some-how, you know?"

"Now you sound like you're my age. Or maybe closer to eighty."

He wasn't listening. He had spread out the paper on top of the *Gazette*. Flipped it around, so that the print was right-side up for her. "Take a look."

She saw the letterhead: MASSACHUSETTS INSTITUTE OF TECHNOL-OGY. She knew he had applied to several graduate schools in urban design, and that MIT was his first choice.

"Oh, Clay."

"Yeah. I got in. Major fellowship. Full ride." He grinned.

She wanted to kiss him, but didn't. Even if she weren't prosecuting attorney and known to most of the people who surrounded them, people who were knocking back cups of coffee and dragging toast rinds through runny egg yolks, Bell still would've held back. That was who she was.

"I'm so proud of you," she said. "I'd offer to buy you breakfast—if you hadn't eaten two of 'em already."

He laughed. Then he looked away for a moment. When he looked back, his expression had turned serious.

"I'm going to ask you something, Bell," he said. "I don't want an answer right now. Okay? Promise me that. Promise me that you won't say anything until you've thought about it."

Before she could react, they were interrupted by the teasing voice of Georgette Akers. "So how's my favorite couple doin' over here? I say to hell with Brad and Angelina. Here in Acker's Gap, we've got ourselves Clay and Belfa." She lifted the coffeepot. "You two love-birds want a refill?"

Bell was embarrassed, but knew that Georgette meant well. She used a flat hand for a makeshift lid on the top of her mug. "No thanks," Bell said. "'Bout to float away as it is."

"I'm fine, too," Clay said.

Georgette nodded. "Gotcha. Oh, and Bell, keep meaning to tell you. That friend of yours—Matt, isn't it?—is real nice. Wish you could get him to stick around longer. He's turned into our best customer. Been and gone already this morning."

"Early bird, is he?" Bell said.

"Well, he was today. Got an egg sandwich to go. Said he was going sightseeing up on the mountain. Usually he'd be sitting right here. Comes in every day at nine. Regular as clockwork. Orders his food and then stays an hour or so, reading or just looking around. Seems to have a lot on his mind."

Then Georgette abruptly left them, lured by the call of "Order up!" from Joyce LeFevre, whose domain was the busy griddle that popped and sizzled behind the long front counter. At the same time

Abner McEvoy, impatient as always in the corner booth that served as his second home, waved both arms over his head to snag Georgette's attention. He might have wanted a refill on his coffee, or he might have just wanted some company. No telling which.

Clay reached over and touched Bell's hand. "So," he said.

"So." Bell was afraid, suddenly, of what he might be about to ask her. It was impossible. She thought he understood that; she thought he understood that their relationship was casual, temporary, a thing they both enjoyed, a fling—but nothing more than that.

It couldn't be more than that. And not because of the age difference. *Well,* Bell thought, *not* only *because of the age difference.* There were additional reasons. She didn't really know where she belonged—but it was a private quest. Which meant she couldn't see herself linked up with someone, because in a marriage, you both had an equal say about your future. Bell couldn't do that. Couldn't declare to a lover: *We'll make up our minds together. Mutual decision.* Until Shirley was back in her life, Bell would live that life alone, for the most part.

She decided to be blunt with him. Meet the problem head-on. "Clay," she said, "you're not going to— I mean, I really hope this isn't—"

He looked shocked. Yanked his hand away from hers. "God no! I mean—you don't think I'm *proposing,* do you? God, Bell, I wouldn't— I mean—" He laughed. "Give me some credit, okay? If that's what I was doing, I think I'd pick a spot just slightly more romantic than Ike's, okay?"

She smiled. Relieved now. "Okay."

"No, I just wanted to ask— Well, I mean— If you could see your way clear to—"

"What is it, Clay?"

"I'd like you to visit me up there next year. When you can. As often as you can. And if you start going out with somebody else back here, maybe just—well, just tell me about it, okay? Right away. I don't want to be surprised when I come back for Christmas break."

"Not likely to happen. But—okay. It'll be really nice to visit you, Clay."

"I told you to think about it first."

"Yeah. And you know how well I follow orders."

They talked a few more minutes about Boston. Bell had been there, having accompanied Sam to a conference in Cambridge back when she was married; Clay had never seen the place. "Bloody expensive," she warned him. "And the driving? It'll make you miss these mountain roads, buddy, bad as they are. Boston's got no corners. Just these loops and circles—and crazy drivers."

He nodded, a light in his eyes. "Sure," Clay said. "I'll miss mountain roads. As if."

When Bell went up to pay the bill—it was her turn—she caught the eye of a little girl, sitting at the front counter with a man whom Bell assumed was her father. The girl, blond and chubby, spun around and around on her stool. Then she stopped herself with a satisfying jerk and smiled at Bell while her father leaned over and cut up her French toast. *That's how it's supposed to work,* Bell thought. *That's what daddies are supposed to do with their little girls. Take 'em to breakfast. Sit with 'em at diner counters. Listen to them. And love them.*

Bell waved back at Clay, who'd decided to stay a bit longer. His crew wouldn't arrive downtown for another half an hour; they first had to do the punch list for a job over in Blythesburg. He'd sit here and finish his coffee while he read the *Gazette* and its homespun litany of local news: the usual roll call of pets available for adoption at the Raythune County Animal Shelter; a description of recent car accidents with as much attention paid to the condition of the vehicles as to the condition of the occupants; an account of the latest meeting of the county commissioners.

Bell crossed the street and headed for the courthouse. She checked her watch: 9:21. She had a conference call scheduled at 9:30 with prosecutors from three other counties; they were contemplating a request to the West Virginia Legislature for yet another task force on prescription drug abuse. *Task force?* Sheriff Fogelsong had scoffed when she'd told him about this latest proposal. *You prosecutors and your damned committees. Give me ten extra deputies and the death penalty and I'll get rid of the drug dealers, right quick.*

Bell paused on the courthouse steps. Turned. Looked around Main Street. Just a brief sweep of a glance, like someone clearing a windshield before starting a car trip. It was habit, it was ritual, and it consoled her in some murky but still meaningful way. Even when she wasn't consciously thinking about Shirley, she still found herself indulging in the glimpse. One swift turn of her head. It lasted only a second or so, and then she turned back again, so that she could reach for the big double doors of the courthouse.

Which was why, when it happened, she was facing away from Ike's, toward the courthouse, and away from the explosion that suddenly ripped through the old brick building in which Ike's resided, a shattering seismic blast that pushed up a massive geyser of bricks and drywall and plaster and dirt and metal and dust, flinging it skyward, an immense and grisly fountain of wood and water and blood and smoke and bones. The earth was sucked up into a hard pocket of intensely pressurized air and then released again, dropping like an avalanche, like a bursting dam, and the force slammed Bell to the ground, although it felt as if the ground were flying at *her,* it felt as if the ground were heaving up specifically to hit her in the face, but because she was still conscious, still aware, still able to form words in her mind as Ike's was instantly vaporized, as it disappeared in a ragged maw of howling sound and spiraling dirt and whirling sticks as wide as the world itself, all at once she thought the word *Clay* and then the words *Georgette* and *Joyce* and then *Abner,* and she pictured the little girl at the counter and her daddy, as she realized—*God oh God please no*—that no one could have survived.

PART TWO

Chapter Twenty-Nine

The first voice she heard was Carla's.

When Bell pushed the cell closer to her ear—she'd fallen asleep in the plastic chair in the hospital waiting room, cell in her grip, and when it rang, she lifted it automatically and murmured, just as automatically, *Elkins*—she heard the voice she knew so well. She wanted to cry, but didn't.

"Mom, Mom—are you okay? Wait, that's stupid," Carla said. "Sorry. God, that's so stupid. I mean, *of course* you're not okay. Oh my God, Mom, I'm so, so, *so* sorry. I can't think about it. I can't think about Ike's being gone, just *disappearing* like that, and—oh *God*, Mom. Nick Fogelsong called. He said you weren't in there—but oh my God—Georgette. And Joyce. And—oh, God. Oh, God, Mom."

Carla was babbling. Bell, relieved, closed her eyes. She could listen to that babble for a long time, she decided, because it was the voice of someone she loved, and because it meant she didn't have to talk right now.

And right now, Belfa Elkins wasn't at all certain she could form a coherent sentence. A random word here or there, perhaps—but not a sentence. Not yet.

"Mom," Carla went on. "Mom, tell me. *Please*. Are you okay?

Dad saw it on CNN—he's always got it on in his office, and when they said 'Acker's Gap,' he called me and—oh, Mom—"

"Sweetie. I'm okay." Bell swallowed. Her throat was raw, as if she'd been screaming for hours. Her mouth felt as if it were stuffed with dust and sand. Her lips were sore, scaly, and cracked. She looked down at her knee. Saw a ragged hole in her slacks. Black fabric hung in shreds. *Like fringe,* she thought, *on a cowgirl's jacket. Giddyup.* She wanted to giggle. A bubble of hysteria was poised on the lip of her mind, ready to pop. *Giddyup, giddyup.* Was she dreaming? Hallucinating? The ache in her knee swept away the strangely discordant thought of a giggle.

Oh God. Ike's. The explosion.

She bent over—*Christ,* she thought as the pain shot across her abdomen, *that hurts like a sonofabitch*—for a closer look at the knee. Dried blood. Torn flesh.

She didn't know how many hours had passed or who had lived or who had died; her mind was turning too slowly to understand anything. Her mind, in fact, felt like an oscillating fan stuck on a low, low, *low* setting, so low that it was turning . . . *so* . . . *slowly* . . . as the blade made that excruciating effort time after time, each time *rising and* . . . *falling* . . . *and* . . . *rising* . . . in a torturous hiccoughing loop, a stuttering circle. The face of the fan moved from side to side—and it, too, was going so . . . *slowly* . . . that nothing came together in her head, no thoughts followed from other thoughts, nothing made sense, nothing fit.

Georgette. Joyce. Clay—oh God. *Clay.*

Clay had been inside. She felt a pain that was not physical, that had nothing to do with ripped skin. It was worse. So much worse.

Where is everybody else? Where'd they go? What—?

"Mom, talk to me." Carla was agitated. "How are you? Are you hurt? Nick said you got knocked down. He called us and told us you were at the hospital and he said—"

"Sweetie, I'm fine. Have to go now." Bell coughed. "Listen. I want you to stay right there in D.C. with your dad. I'll contact you when I can. First I have to—"

"Mom," Carla interrupted, "we're almost there. I'm calling you from the road. We're going to be there in an hour."

Bell closed her eyes. "Okay," she said. Nothing she could do to stop them, then. They were on their way. What was Sam thinking? It wasn't safe. It was a terrible idea. Why would he bring Carla here, after what had just—?

She put a fingertip on her cheek. It was wet. She was weeping. She hadn't even realized it at first, but she was weeping. Endless, endless tears.

They're coming. They're coming.

"We'll be there soon, Mom," Carla said. "And, Mom—I'm so sorry about your friends. I'm just so sorry. I love you. I love you so much, Mom. We're coming."

"Sweetie." The word came out as a low, unmelodious croak from a roughed-up throat, a sound that got tangled up in the tears and in another sudden surge of emotion. "Sweetie."

Nick Fogelsong was standing over her. Bending down. Gently, he tugged the cell from her grip. She had fallen asleep—or had she passed out again?—still clutching it in her dusty palm. Her hand was in her lap. Now she was awake once more.

"Belfa," he said. "Sorry I had to stick you out here. Figured we'd be overwhelmed. Figured we'd be running out of beds right quick. As it turned out—" He stopped. Tried again. "Seven people in Ike's. Near as we could count." A hard swallow. "We cleared out the waiting room. Cleared the families, the relatives. Took 'em to a private room. People like you, people who looked okay—we brought you here. The survivors."

She blinked, nodded. Then she lifted her head. It had been tilted sideways, propped against the back of the chair. When she sat upright, she felt a shooting pain in her neck, as if she were being jabbed meanly with a rake handle. She winced, but she didn't cry out.

"What happened, Nick? Somebody hit a gas line?"

"Don't know yet. State police're looking into it. Took out a chunk of the block. Coulda been worse, in terms of number of fatalities.

Thank God we've got those empty storefronts." A fierce frown. "Never thought I'd say that, never thought I'd be happy about a high vacancy rate downtown, but I'm saying it today." Shook his head. "You'd hardly know Ike's was ever there. Just a hole now. A hole and a hell of a mess. A hell of a lot of brick dust."

She nodded, then gritted her teeth from the pain. She'd forgotten about her sore neck. "How'd I get here? Who—?"

"Brought you over in the Blazer. Found you on the sidewalk. Conscious, but pretty much out of it. Not surprised you don't remember."

"The investigation—how far along is—?"

"You sit back," he commanded. "Not your lookout right now. Soon as some doc around here comes up for air, I'm gonna grab him and ask him to come out here and check you out." A faint flicker of a smile lived and died across his face, like lightning glimpsed at a distance. "Him or her, I mean. Him or her." He was talking, after all, to the first female prosecuting attorney in Raythune County history.

Bell looked around. She saw a man she didn't know, legs splayed, eyes closed, in a plastic chair across the room. Covered with a white-yellow dust. Bell couldn't tell if he was black or white. His face, his clothes, his hair, his hands, his shoes—all smothered by dust. He slept with his arms crossed, head thrown back, mouth open. Snores ripped irregularly from his mouth, but they were harsh, clotted, unnatural sounding.

"Nick," Bell said. "You said you brought the wounded here. To this room. Where's everybody else? Where are they?"

He put a big hand on her shoulder. It felt like a boulder. His eyes were occupied by a sadness so profound and immense that it seemed to permeate his whole body. His whole being.

"Where?" she repeated.

"This is it, Bell." He intensified his grip on her shoulder, as if he was afraid that she, too, might disappear, might fly away if he didn't forcibly prevent it. "You and that fella over there. He'd just left Ike's, too. Just before it happened. You're the survivors."

Chapter Thirty

The Raythune County Medical Center had seen only one other emergency to rival this. It happened on September 19, 1992, when an explosion in the No. 27 mine of the Brassy-Waltham Mine Company left five miners dead and another three with brain injuries from inhalation of methane gas. Coalbed gas, they call it. Sweet gas, is what the miners call it. Two of the three eventually died.

Back then, the problem for the county medical center wasn't a lack of beds but a lack of space, period. It was an otherwise slow news week, and several broadcast networks decided to set up shop in the small hospital lobby, stationing their anchors in front of the big plate glass window. Beyond that window, rising darkly in the distance and providing the anchors with a broodingly romantic backdrop, was a line of mountains. The anchors, zipped into their crinkly blue Patagonia jackets, hair carefully styled to look tousled and windswept, could furrow their brows handsomely and gesture toward the window, using phrases like, "Men with hearts as big and broad and flinty as those mountains" and "Wives and loved ones whose quiet patience and stoic endurance match those mountains out there."

And Bell, who had watched the coverage from her living room in D.C., and who knew those mountains—and the lives lived in their shadow—better than any damned TV anchor, had sneered at the

217

canned sentiment. Once the crisis was over, she knew, once the fate of the miners was ascertained and the interviews with sobbing relatives concluded, the anchors and the crews would unplug their equipment and wind the power cords around their microphones and rush out of Acker's Gap so fast that the breeze from their simultaneous exits would be powerful enough to knock over a dirty-faced toddler or two and maybe even the trailers they lived in.

She was thinking of all that, remembering, as she stumbled across the thin gray carpet of the waiting room. Nick had stayed with her only another minute or so; the radio clipped to his big black belt had spat a static-rich bulletin at him and he was gone, moving purposefully but also in a sort of daze. Bell knew him well enough to spot when he was operating on professional autopilot. Functioning, yes, but doing so by instinct. He'd been rocked, just as she'd been rocked, even though he wasn't nearly so close to the explosion.

The explosion.

What happened to Ike's? To Clay and to Joyce, to Georgette, to the little girl eating French toast at the counter? And her daddy? Nick couldn't be right about the death toll. Could he?

Bell needed answers. So she rose from the plastic chair—she wanted to scream from the pain in her hip and her knee, but she tucked in her bottom lip, forcing herself to eat the pain, the same way she'd apparently swallowed all that dirt, because she kept coughing it up—and dragged herself toward the swinging double doors that led to the hall.

The waiting room she was leaving behind was spookily subdued. No ringing phones. Except for the stranger sleeping in the corner, who didn't stir as she moved past him, there was no one else there. No one fidgeting in the seats, waiting to be called up to the counter. No one behind that counter, either, the one with the Plexiglas shield and its little half-moon, cut-out portion at the bottom, through which people were supposed to slide their insurance cards. Taped to the Plexiglas was a hand-lettered sign: PROOF OF INSURANCE *MUST* BE SHOWN *PRIOR* TO SERVICE. *NO EXCEPTIONS.*

But when Bell pushed open the double doors marked AUTHO-

RIZED PERSONNEL ONLY and peered down the long hall, she saw a different world.

People in white coats and blue coats hurried along, passing in both directions. Some had stethoscopes hastily slung around their necks like clunky jewelry. Some had clipboards wedged under their arms. One pushed a portable IV pole with just two fingers, as if he were helping along a frail elderly relative with an independent streak.

Bell heard the beeps and cheeps and chirps of medical machinery doing its work. The one thing she didn't hear—and it startled her, when she realized just what it was that was missing—was shouting. Raised voices. There was no panic. Just practiced, methodical, professional haste.

The emergency was over. This was cleanup.

"Excuse me," Bell said. She'd caught the sleeve of someone moving past her, a tall woman with black bangs and a flat closed face and a ponytail, a doctor or nurse—Bell couldn't tell for sure—wearing light blue scrubs.

"Yes?" The woman's voice was cold. Massively preoccupied.

"I need to know— I mean, I have to—" Bell struggled to speak. There was still too much dust in her mouth. And the woman wasn't helping; the woman was frowning at her. Annoyed. She'd pulled her sleeve out of Bell's grasp.

"Yes?" the woman repeated. "We're busy here, ma'am. We've had an explosion. Multiple fatalities. How did you get in here? This is a restricted area." The woman seemed to notice, for the first time, that Bell was injured. "Curtis!" she called out. "Curtis, can you help this lady? She needs assistance. Don't know how she wandered in here."

The nurse named Curtis, a large black man with a face so much kinder than the first woman's face that it made Bell want to cry, came over and put an arm under her arm. "Easy does it," he said. "Easy, now. Can you walk, miss?"

Had he not been treating her courteously, Bell would have gone to her default position—anger—and snapped, "Can I *walk*? Hey, asshole, how do you think I *got* here? On my invisible scooter?"

Instead, she looked up at him and said, "I was there. I saw it. I need to know how many people—" She paused and wet her lips with her tongue. Her tongue was dry, too, so the help was minimal, but it gave her time to get her thoughts in order. "Names. Do you know who was there? How many—?"

"Miss, all I can tell you is that it's bad. Real bad. And now—let's get you to a chair, okay? That knee of yours looks like you might need some stitches."

"Listen. I'm Belfa Elkins. Raythune County prosecutor. I have to know—"

"Belfa."

A new voice. One she thought she recognized.

Bell turned.

Yes. It was Sarah Dudek, the short, chubby, gray-haired orthopedic surgeon who'd taken care of Carla when she and Bell had first moved back to Acker's Gap. Carla's initial adventure in the big backyard of their house on Shelton Avenue had been to scale the beech tree with reckless bravado—and to promptly fall out of it, breaking her right arm in two places.

"Sarah," Bell said. "For God's sake, I have to find out—"

Dudek nodded at Curtis. "I'll take it from here."

She regarded Bell. The torn clothes. Dust in her hair. Bloody knee. "Lord," Dudek said. "You're a mess." The physician looked grim as she added, "I was over in Donnerton when I got the call." A place like Acker's Gap was too small to have its own specialists; they made rounds throughout the area, stopping at county medical centers on designated days. "Hell of a thing," Dudek went on. "My mother was a GP over in Collier County—did I ever tell you that? Practiced for over fifty years. She told me about scenes like this. Used to be a lot of multi-car pileups out on the turnpike, back when it was just two lanes and a lot of wicked curves. No matter how many signs they posted, some of those truckers would take the turns too fast. Go flying into the opposite lane. Mom would be called in to the hospital in the middle of the night and—well, when she came back home, she couldn't even talk about it." Shook her head. "I'm just glad I was close by today and could get here pronto.

"Although," Dudek added, "I haven't been all that busy, unfortunately."

Bell understood. You only need a surgeon if you have injuries. The people in Ike's had died.

"Yeah," Bell said. "The sheriff told me." The next words were difficult to say, but she said them. "I guess there was just the one guy. The one survivor. The guy I saw in the waiting room. He must've been on the street nearby, just like me."

"No," Dudek said. "They found somebody else. Under the rubble. They just brought him in. He's in pretty bad shape, but there's a chance. We've been gathering blood donations, just in case. A couple of your deputies—they've been organizing it. Bringing in people from all over the county who are eligible to give. Anybody they can find. They're doing an amazing job."

Bell swallowed hard, but this time it was from emotion, not from the dust in her throat.

"Anyway," Dudek said, "that's why I'm hanging around. The moment they get him stabilized, I'm up."

Bell was afraid to ask, but knew she had to. "A name—do you have a name, Sarah? Of the survivor?"

Dudek fished out the small memo pad she kept in the pocket of her lab coat. "Let me see. Yes—yes, it's right here. They're prepping him, so I had to pull his records." She squinted at her bad handwriting. "His name is Meckling. Clayton Meckling. Do you know him?"

Chapter Thirty-One

Eddie Geyer reached carefully across her sleeping body for the Bic lighter and the Camels. He'd set up a cardboard box on the other side of the sleeping bag. Used it as a bedside table. *Can you call it a bedside table,* he wondered idly, *if you don't have a freakin' bed?*

He was just about to light his cigarette when he heard the explosion.

"What the hell—" he exclaimed.

Maddie sat straight up as if she were hinged in the middle. She had fallen asleep after she and Eddie made love, and the explosion jolted her awake. The ground suddenly seemed as gelatinous as pudding. The walls of the cabin might have trembled slightly—she couldn't be sure, but there was a sense of quivering in every direction in which she turned her head. A golden mist of dust, shaken loose from the crumbling old walls of this place, floated on the air.

"Oh my God," Maddie said. "My God, Eddie. What was that?"

The unlit cigarette hung out of the side of his mouth. "No idea," he said. "Whatever it was, though, it sure as hell was something pretty goddamned big." He'd started to make a dirty joke about their lovemaking and about the earth moving, but thought better of it. If the heavy noise ended up being a plane crash or something, he didn't want some stupid remark of his to be the thing they both remembered about the day. Somehow, being with Maddie made him sensitive in a way he wasn't used to. Damned if it didn't.

Eddie scrambled to his feet. His nakedness made him feel ridiculous, vulnerable, but for a crazy moment he couldn't remember where he'd put his clothes. He'd been in such an all-fired rush to get rid of them—kicking off his boots, pulling out his belt with one sharp yank through the loops, tripping over his half-lowered trousers, fussing with his shirt.

Maddie had appeared at the cabin this morning with no preamble, no warning, like a shaft of sunlight suddenly shooting through the trees. She'd been doing that ever since he came back to town: showing up at odd times, in the chilly late-night hours or in the dull glaze of midafternoon or just before suppertime, whereupon she'd rush up the porch steps, wild-eyed, hungry for him, kissing him so passionately as to leave no doubt about her desires. It was just like the old days with them: They couldn't keep their hands off each other. All these years later, after the harsh words and the long separation, after almost sixteen years, here they were again: Eddie Geyer and Maddie Trimble. He was still, by her definition, a bum. And she was still, to his way of thinking, a flake. Didn't matter. They'd jumped together like two flames.

He had wondered if that would change now that their baby girl was dead, now that they had buried her in the neat little postage stamp of a cemetery next to the Briney Hollow Church of the Nazarene. Maddie's parents were buried out there, too. Eddie had been stunned at her decision—the only thing Maddie hated worse than her parents, he thought, was the Church of the Nazarene—but something had changed inside Maddie Trimble after her daughter's death. Something had softened, broken loose. When Floyd Fontaine of Fontaine's Funeral Home had approached her just before the service, asking discreetly about her plans for Lucinda's remains, Maddie had blurted, "Briney Hollow Church of the Nazarene. By a tree."

How would Maddie treat him, now that their baby girl was gone? Lucinda, after all, was the reason she'd wanted him to come back to town in the first place. To talk to the young woman. To make her understand. To use his own miserable, pathetic, screwed-up life as a cautionary tale: *Don't do what I did, sweetheart. Don't let a couple of bad choices that you make early in your life send you into a lifetime of bad choices, one piled on top of another, until the stack's too high to see around or climb over.*

He'd had that talk with Lucinda two weeks ago, when he first came back to town, much as it shamed him to do so. Had she listened to him? She'd seemed to. She was a good girl—polite, respectful. Even to him, the father who had abandoned her. She could have told him to get the hell away from her, she could have done that, but she didn't. So—yes. She'd listened to him. *You have so much going for you, baby girl. College and all the rest of it. A real life. A real one. A big life. Not the kind of small life that people around here end up having. Small and sad.*

He didn't know what she had decided to do about her baby.

Now, though, none of it mattered anymore. Didn't matter one damned bit.

Naturally, Eddie had wondered if Maddie would reject him, would send him back to *whatever craphole it is that you call home these days,* which was how she put it when she'd reached him. At that bar in Covington, where he wiped down tables for free drinks. *Come back to Acker's Gap for just a little while,* she'd said, *just a few weeks, and then you can go back to whatever craphole it is that you call home these days. Your little girl needs you, Eddie. She needs to hear about what happens when you let go of your life like it's a dirty string on a balloon. Watch it soar away from you, into the mist over the mountains. Never coming back to you. Never.*

He'd done what she asked. Like it had made any difference in the long run. Their child was dead and buried. And Maddie, Eddie assumed, might be through with him now.

Yet here she was. And if anything, her ardor had intensified. When he touched her, she was burning up. Their lovemaking this morning—they had started on the porch, standing up, and then continued on his sleeping bag, the one she'd procured for him on his first day back, apologizing for its thinness, its ripped and stained cover, to which he'd responded, *I've had worse accommodations, missy, believe you me*—had been urgent, primitive, a thing of moans and grunts and bites and tiny squeals, followed by a swampy, languorous sleep.

A sleep suddenly broken by a shattering explosion that came from the direction of Acker's Gap.

Maddie was punching a number into her cell. "Bertha," she cried. "What's going on? I heard a big noise like an earthquake or a hurricane or 9/11 and I didn't know what it—" She stopped talking. Listening now. Her eyes grew wider.

Eddie pulled on his shirt. Didn't bother buttoning it. He looked down at Maddie, her cell in one hand, rumpled blouse in the other; she held the pale blue lacy garment against her breasts in a sudden spasm of modesty. When he saw how her hair fell across her bare shoulders, he was—despite the shock of the explosion, of whatever had rocked the earth—aroused again.

"Oh God," Maddie said. "Oh, no. Bertha, I'll—I'll call you later, I'll check back to see— No, no, I'm fine." A pause. "I'm fine, Bertha. I wasn't downtown. Nowhere near."

She tossed the shut-down cell onto the sleeping bag.

"What?" Eddie said. "What's going on?"

"Some kind of explosion." She took a breath. Told him the news: "It's terrible, Eddie. You remember Ike's? Been there forever? It's gone. Bertha says—this time of day—there must've been lots of people inside. Nobody knows how many. I just can't believe it. How many bad things can happen, Eddie? How many in a row? First Lucinda—now this. It's like we're—we're *cursed* somehow. Snakebit. How much can we take?"

"Jesus." He tucked in his shirt. Feeling embarrassed now at what he'd been thinking about, only a few seconds ago. Before he knew. "Whadda we do?"

"I don't know."

He was startled, confused, like anybody would be. Wondered about fatalities. He was a selfish bastard, just like people around here had always said he was, he wouldn't argue the point, but he had his moments. Maddie had seen that in him, way back when they first got together, after she'd worked her way free of that tight-assed sheriff. She had seen the glimmer: the small part of Eddie Geyer that proved he wasn't a complete sonofabitch. The part that was decent.

The part that, he liked to think, he'd passed on to his baby girl. To Lucinda. She'd had that glimmer, too. The best of him. He could tell right away. Which was why he'd left when she was still a tiny baby: So that he'd never destroy it, never take it away from her. So that Lucinda could keep her glimmer. Her shine.

With him as a daddy—he drank too much and couldn't seem to stop doing it, he couldn't hold a job, he had a bad temper—that glimmer of hers wouldn't have lasted. Wouldn't have stood a chance.

He'd left because he loved her. Simple as that. And to hell with anybody who didn't get that, who thought it was just an excuse.

He'd show them. He'd prove how much he cared about Lucinda. He'd get that boyfriend of hers—that Shawn Doggett—because it was clear as crystal that the kid had gotten her pregnant and then killed her.

Nothing was going to stop Eddie Geyer. Not even the explosion that had just rocked the whole damned county. Not even that.

Chapter Thirty-Two

Nick Fogelsong had arrived at the scene of the explosion within four minutes—he was in his office at the courthouse, changing the ink cartridge in his printer and cursing the cost of the thing—and by the time he got there, firefighters and paramedics were already unearthing bodies from the smoking caved-in ruins and setting up perimeters and hollering at onlookers to stay back. Gus Meechum, head of Raythune-Collier Fire Rescue—the two counties had combined operations in the 1970s—showed up about fifteen minutes later. He'd been visiting his mother at the Sunbrite Nursing Home on Route 6, just outside Acker's Gap, when he got the call. Lucky thing, because otherwise the drive from Donnerton, county seat of Collier County, might have taken him twenty minutes or more.

By then a variety of emergency sirens were displacing the air, rising and dying and then rising again in a way that sounded, Nick had always thought, downright operatic. Not that he had any time to think such things right now. He had immediately pitched in with the first responders, grabbing a shovel and clearing away the sharp-peaked oceans of blasted bricks and the wildly strewn rafters and the knotted ropes of rebar, trying to bat away the huge blooms of clinging, particle-rich dust that hovered over the street. The breeze couldn't budge it. It just hung there, dark gold and dangerous to the lungs. As he pawed and dug at the rubble, Nick realized he could taste the air. Later, when describing this day, he'd say, *You could eat the air with a spoon. But you'd have to be pretty goddamned hungry to want to.*

Gus Meechum had located him right away. Gus was half-hysterical, his eyes twice their normal size, a gob of spit on his chin; he grabbed Nick's shoulder and shook it, as if Nick maybe wouldn't pay attention to him otherwise. "Gotta shut off the gas," Gus said. He was gasping, the way everybody was gasping, from the fraught air. "Right now. Right this goddamned *minute,* Nick, I'm tellin' ya—"

Nick nodded and pointed. Wally Boyd, who worked for Appalachian Consolidated Power and had the gray jumpsuit with the black cursive *ACP* stitched on the back to prove it, was running toward the alley behind Ike's—or what had once been Ike's, and which was now a sudden junkyard that seethed and smoked. The tools on the canvas belt that sagged around Wally's waist banged against his skinny hip as he ran.

That relieved Gus Meechum, and he went back to work. By that time Nick's deputies, Pam Harrison, Greg Greenough, and Charlie Mathers, had arrived, and they were the ones who supervised the removal of the bodies, although after a time Greenough and Mathers volunteered to go round up blood donors for the hospital. A crowd had gathered across the street, and Deputy Harrison arranged herself and some citizen volunteers along the sidewalk, blocking the view as the paramedics hauled out the victims, one by one, in body bags or on stretchers. Nick had phone calls to make—state police, firehouses in neighboring counties.

"Might be a secondary," Harrison had said to the sheriff, the minute she got there and reported in. "Another explosion, I mean. Could be dangerous."

He'd nodded. "Yeah," he said. "Could be. So you think we should hold back awhile and not get those bodies outta there? Maybe order a pizza while we wait?"

She didn't appreciate his sarcasm but she saw his point. Ran back to join the volunteers in making the human privacy fence.

The sirens had been going on so long now—it was only minutes, but it felt like weeks—that Nick realized that nobody had actually spoken to him at all. Not Gus Meechum. Not Deputy Harrison. Truth was, they had faced him and mouthed their respective messages, because you couldn't hear a thing with all the sirens going off, all at once.

Nick understood right away that the chance of survivors in Ike's was slim. Yet he was sure that he'd heard moans from under the heavy piles, and so he flagged down anybody close—deputy, firefighter, paramedic—and pointed wildly, and then he fell to his knees to help with the digging and the clawing. Gradually he realized that he hadn't heard any moans. It was, most likely, the sliding sounds of the many tons of brick and stone and steel, settling, sifting down. Nick felt silly but nobody chastised him. Nobody said anything about it at all.

Twenty-four minutes after the blast, a technical rescue unit from Atherton County arrived. *Thank the good Lord up above,* Nick thought, watching them swing down from the big truck, watching them unpack their gear with a snap and a practiced hustle, with rigor and efficiency. Deputy Mathers, who had sidled up next to the sheriff, muttered, *Now, those boys know what the hell they're doing. That's what we been needin' all along.*

It was true. Technical rescue units specialized in freeing people from collapsed buildings and fallen stairwells and after grievously high falls, such as those suffered by hikers and rock climbers. They were taking over the scene—they knew how loads landed and shifted, and they wouldn't do more harm than good, which was likely the case when well-meaning amateurs plunged frantically into the rubble— and the sheriff was grateful for it.

He was also grateful that the buildings on either side of Ike's had been empty. Who would've thought that a downtown on the skids— with 70 percent of the storefronts in Acker's Gap vacant for over a year—could be a blessing?

An exhausted-looking Collier County firefighter, her face wet with sweat and black from the dirt that had settled there and stuck, appeared in front of Nick. Her voice was a sawtooth-edged croak. "There's—" She coughed, spit out a black rubbery wad, coughed again. "There's people in there. Dead folks. Buried. Like in a mine."

He nodded. He didn't know exactly who'd been in Ike's at the time of the blast, except for two names: Joyce LeFevre. Georgette Akers. The owner and the sole employee.

"Buried," the firefighter repeated.

He heard the crash of breaking glass, followed by other crashes, muffled ones. The crowd had gotten big enough now to make its own sound, the humming, shuffling sound of a large group of people too aghast, at the outset, to scream or sob, but in whom the screams and sobs lay in wait, biding their time. He watched the arrival of more emergency personnel and suddenly realized he could do more good somewhere else. At the hospital, maybe. Figuring out the next of kin, for notification purposes.

Fogelsong signaled to Deputy Harrison that he was heading out. She acknowledged him with a nod. The knot of onlookers had grown bigger now, louder, more insistent. Harder to handle. Pushing forward. The sheriff was glad to have Pam Harrison on the job. She didn't take any crap from anybody.

He turned. As he headed to the Blazer he had to fight a wave of nausea, wrestle with it, beat it back down. Reasoning with himself didn't work. He had to forbid the nausea to exist. A sheriff couldn't throw up in public. That would be the end of his authority.

The street was littered with chips of brick and concrete, jagged hunks of stone. Iron bars twisted like licorice. He'd spotted part of a sink, wedged against the curb. The leg of a chair had been planted like a javelin into the spongy strip of ground next to the public library. An iron skillet rested on a roof. A box of cornflakes, weirdly intact, had landed upside down on the courthouse steps. And that terrible dust—thick as gravy, worse than any fog ever produced by the Bitter River, chewy with bits of wood and fluff and other things, unidentifiable things—wouldn't let up. It covered Acker's Gap like a snug knit cap on the head of a sickly child.

Still dizzy, now with an acid wash of vomit fouling his throat, Fogelsong saw her.

Belfa.

She was sitting on the curb on the other side of the street, over by the courthouse lawn. She was behind the crowd, which had surged into the road by now, straining against the police tape and the saw-horses, people staring and pointing and, in some cases, yelling and crying.

She looked dazed. She was holding her head; her right knee was bloody.

Belfa.

It had not occurred to him—although it surely should have—that she might be here, so close to this crisis. She sometimes had breakfast at Ike's. Or at least picked up her morning coffee in a to-go cup on her way to the courthouse. Georgette Akers liked to tease her about it: *Honey, I bet when they test your blood for somethin', it's about eighty-five percent French roast, whadda say to that?*

Georgette Akers.

Georgette.

He shook his head, to force the name to fall out of his thoughts again. He had no time right now for the luxury of grief for specific people. He could indulge that later.

When he saw Bell, the sheriff didn't call out her name, because she couldn't have heard him, anyway, over the growing thunder of the crowd, over the high-pitched racket of the sirens. Instead he hurried forward and grabbed her, pulling her up by her shoulders. Could she walk? She could.

He pushed her toward the Blazer parked three blocks away, not saying a word until they were in their seats, belts secured, windows up, momentarily cocooned, blessedly separated—just for now, just in this accidental interval—from all that was spinning around them and all that was pressing in on them, all that had occurred and all that would still have to occur in the course of this monstrous day, this disaster.

"Belfa," he said. Started the engine. Flicked on his siren, knowing he was only adding to the chaos but also knowing he needed to, so that the Blazer could weave through the multitude without running somebody down.

"Belfa," Nick said again. She hadn't opened her eyes.

He wasn't asking for a response and she didn't offer one. He'd just wanted to say her name out loud, to use it to remind himself that she was alive. It was like testing a phone. You weren't looking for a conversation. Just confirmation that there was somebody on the other end of the line.

Nick Fogelsong had a simple rule. He had maintained it for two decades: No alcohol before 7 P.M. He'd crafted that rule after observing the fate of friends in law enforcement, the ones who kept moving happy hour up and up and up, until finally they were draining highball glasses at the breakfast table. *Price of the job,* they'd explain. *Cheers.*

But if ever there was a day to break his rule, it was today. Wasn't it? And so when Louie Baumgartner, a paramedic whom Nick had known since they'd fit their skinny seven-year-old selves into adjacent wooden desks in Mrs. Rasinzky's first-grade class at Acker's Gap Elementary, offered him a swig from the bottle of Jim Beam he kept in the glove box of the ambulance, Nick said, "God yes."

He had left Bell in the waiting room, knowing—hoping, anyway—that her injuries were minor. She'd be safe, but out of the way. And then as he headed back through the corridor, he had run into Louie, who said, "Need help with the incoming. How's your back, Nicky? You up for it?" Now they stood by the ambulance entrance to the medical center. Louie screwed the cap back on the Jim Beam, watching as an ambulance driven by one of his colleagues rounded the big curve off Route 9 and headed their way, siren bawling, delivering yet another body dragged from the morass, even though, by that point, it was generally clear to all involved that the haste was unnecessary.

Chapter Thirty-Three

Bell stood at the threshold of the room. They'd let her through, which surprised her; she wasn't a family member and she hadn't lied about that. If she'd had time to think, she probably would have lied, just to make sure they let her back to see him, but she wasn't that clever. Not today. When the nurse said, "Who're you looking for?" Bell blurted, "Clay Meckling." To the nurse's next question—"Relationship?"—Bell had replied, "Friend." Simple word. But the most profound one that Bell knew. *When you grow up without friends,* she'd once explained to Clay, *you know what the word really means.* There was nothing simple about it.

She didn't go in. Not right away. She watched as Walter Meckling—faded blue denim jacket buttoned up to his chin, carpenter's pants stiff with old sweat, ancient dirty boots—leaned over his son's bed. Walter was tall and square, with a tired, hangdog face and a white beard and huge pale blocks of hands. A working man. He used one of those enormous hands to touch Clay's arm. Bell heard Walter take a hard breath, and then the old man began to sob. Great, silent sobs. His massive shoulders rose and fell with the heavy, irregular storm of his weeping. He gripped the bed rail, steadying himself against the hammer blows of sorrow that threatened to knock him down.

Clay, she saw, was unconscious. A thin plastic tube looped under his nose and up and over his ears. A white bandage had been wound expertly around the top of his head. His face was scratched and bruised in too many places.

Walter looked up. His eyes locked on to Bell's.

"He's—" The old man tightened his grip on the rail. Fought to make words. "He's my boy, Mrs. Elkins." He'd known Bell her entire life, and he'd never once called her by her first name. It was *Miss Dolan* and then it was *Mrs. Elkins.*

"Walter," she said. She had a hand on the doorframe, to steady herself. She still didn't advance into the room. "I'm so sorry, I can't imagine—but Walter, he's alive. No matter what happens from here on out, he's alive."

The old man stared at her. There was a mad abstract fury in his eyes, a fury worthy of an Old Testament prophet.

"They're getting ready to—help me, Jesus—to saw off his leg, Mrs. Elkins," he rasped. "They say it's gotta happen. My boy's gonna lose his leg. They're just waitin' to get his blood pressure down and then they're gonna do it. They're gonna cut off my boy's leg, Mrs. Elkins. *His goddamned leg.*"

Chapter Thirty-Four

They took her home.

Bell let Sam and Carla run the show. She didn't like it; she wasn't accustomed to letting other people be in charge, make decisions for her. But she was too weary, too stunned, to put up a fight.

They had tracked her down in the corridor outside Clay's room. She had retreated there when the nurse came in to check on Clay, to ready him for surgery. Walter didn't leave. He stayed right by his son's bed. But Bell felt like an outsider. Or worse—she felt like a voyeur. She had nothing to offer but pity and prayers. Both seemed very much beside the point right now; the former was insulting, and the latter— well, Bell wasn't sure if anyone would be listening at the other end.

The ride back into town was a blur. She had a jackhammer headache—pounding, driving, digging in—and every muscle in her body felt as if it had been individually stretched past any reasonable point and then pinned there for maximum agony.

She allowed Sam to help her inside the house. He kept his arm curved around her waist as she shuffled along. His other hand was cupped around her hands, hands she was clasping in front of her, knotted, fused, as if they protected a secret. His hand was so much bigger than hers that he could almost cover both of hers with one of his.

He guided her up the steps to her bedroom.

Hell, he was practically carrying her.

She was aware of falling into her bed, the one she'd bought when she and Carla first moved here. Bell had wanted it to be big enough so that Carla would always feel welcome to nestle beside her, on nights when sleep was like a faraway land to which no regular transportation was available. There was a reading lamp with a flexible neck that hung over the bed; Bell had used it to illuminate the books she loved to read aloud to her daughter, the books she'd loved as a kid, the ones that took her out of her own ragged life and all that it was lacking: *My Side of the Mountain*. *To Kill a Mockingbird*. Usually, before Bell finished a single chapter she'd look down and realize that Carla had fallen asleep, her bent head snug in the crook of Bell's arm, and Carla's small mouth would be slightly open, eyelashes trembling, knees at her chin, body curled up tight in what seemed to Bell, looking down at her little girl, like a perfect circle.

Carla was at her bedside. Small piece of paper in one hand. Bell's cell in the other.

"You had some calls," Carla said. Voice soft, tentative, studiously casual, as if the reality of her mother's survival was still too new, too overwhelming, to deal with. Shades drawn, the room was lit only by the small slice of light from the hallway, let in by the half-opened door.

"I made a list, Mom," Carla said. "I didn't want to wake you, but Dad said you'd be pissed if we didn't tell you." Even softer now. "How're you feeling?"

Bell sat up. She put a hand on her head, which throbbed with each heartbeat, as if heart and head had somehow synched up while she slept.

"I'm okay," Bell said. "And your father was right."

Carla sat down on the side of the bed. She looked at her list, trying to be efficient and businesslike, and then she looked at her mother. Her cheeks were suddenly wet.

"Mom," she said. "I was so scared, I was—"

Bell reached over and pulled her closer. She held her for several minutes. No words.

"I'm fine, sweetie," Bell finally said. "I promise. Now, tell me about the calls."

Carla nodded. "Well, Sheriff Fogelsong, of course. Just checking on you." She went back to the piece of paper. She hadn't needed to consult it to come up with Nick's name; he'd been a part of their lives for so long that his presence in it was a given. "Let's see—Hickey Leonard and Rhonda Lovejoy called. Plus a couple of TV stations. Want a comment. Oh, and Sammy Burdette." Burdette was a Raythune County commissioner. "And Dot, too, naturally." Dot Burdette, Sammy's sister, had graduated from Acker's Gap High School the same year that Bell did. Now she was manager of the town's only bank branch—and liked to think of herself as Bell's friend. "Judge Tolliver. A radio station over in Blythesburg. Somebody from the *Charleston Gazette*. Word's out, I guess. They all want a statement." Back to the list. "That Matt Harless guy. Dad ended up talking to him. Oh, and Lee Ann Frickie, too. She's called twice. Wants to know if she can bring over any food or run errands for you or anything like that."

Bell stretched her neck, checking for the sore spots. She could've saved time by looking for spots that weren't sore.

"How long have I been asleep?"

"About an hour," Carla said. "And I'm not finished with the list."

"Well, hold off on the rest of it for a little while, will you?"

Bell tried to slide off the bed. Rods of pain shot from her knee in all directions, so she changed her angle of descent.

"How're you feeling, Mom? For real, I mean?"

"I feel—" The pain caused Bell to bite her lip. "I feel okay, sweetie. Put it this way. I feel a hell of a lot better than I'd be feeling if you weren't here."

"And Dad, too, right?"

"Sure. What's he up to?"

"Fixing some stuff. The front door doesn't stick anymore. And I told him the toaster oven hasn't worked since I was in ninth grade—well, now it does. And he's balancing the washing machine. Remember how it kind of follows you all over the basement when you do a big load?"

"Yeah." Bell wasn't thrilled that her ex-husband was meddling—but hell. She could use the help. This was an old house. Filled with quirks and problems. "I remember."

Carla put out her hand. "Can I help you up?"

"No, I'm okay." Bell struggled to stand. Finally managed.

"I told everybody to stop calling," Carla said. "That you'd call them back when you could." She waited. She had more to say. It would be harder than reading off a list. "Mom, I heard about Clay Meckling." Carla hesitated again, not sure where to look. She knew about her mother's relationship with Clay. Even though Carla didn't live in this house anymore, Bell had wanted her to know.

"About his leg and all," Carla went on. "I'm so glad he's alive, but—but his *leg,* Mom. What's he going to—?" Full stop. "It sucks, Mom. That's all I can say. It really, really sucks."

Bell nodded. Couldn't have put it better herself.

As long as Carla and Sam were here to hold down the fort, Bell decided to treat herself. She'd go back to sleep for just a little while longer. Just for an hour or so. Because when she left this room, she knew what waited for her on the other side of the big oak door: the investigation of the explosion at Ike's. And the list of fatalities. The obligation to find and notify the families. To let the cold reality soak into her bones—the reality that people who'd been in her life for a long time, people she cared about, were gone forever. As long as she slept, she could pretend she didn't know.

When Bell awoke for the second time, the room was darker, with a blackness that had set in like a permanent stain. Obviously, a lot more time than an hour had passed. But how much more? Before she'd left the medical center, Sarah Dudek had given her two pills. *You need rest,* the doctor said. *Take these.* Bell hadn't asked what it was. Hadn't cared.

She rolled over. Allowed the perky red numbers on the digital clock at her bedside to register in her brain: 3:14.

She knew it couldn't be 3:14 P.M.—which meant she had slept for more than fourteen hours.

"Damn," Bell said.

Sam and Carla—and Sarah Dudek—surely meant well, but she couldn't do this anymore. She couldn't just hide here at home, door closed, shades drawn, head on a pillow. She thought about all the things that might have happened to the town while she was sleeping.

Jesus.

As Bell swung her legs over the side of the bed—slowly, gingerly, because the pain had reawakened at the same time that the rest of her did, although it had definitely lessened—she heard a brief flare of music. A jazz riff, played on a piano. It confused her, until she remembered: *My cell. The new ringtone.* Carla had left the phone on the dresser when she came in earlier.

Rising but still groggy, still a bit unsteady on her feet, Bell reached for it. Squinted. The caller ID read UNKNOWN.

"Yes?"

No reply. It wasn't a hang-up, though. She could hear what sounded like faint, regular breathing. Breathing that wanted to coalesce into words, yearned to, but couldn't.

Straining to hear, Bell also was able to make out the sound of traffic in the background: the heavy-barreled hum of eighteen-wheelers going by on the highway. The ragged *slap-slap* song of giant tires sliding across wet road.

Bell pictured a truck stop alongside the interstate. Long darkness, broken by brief islands of light cupped around the diesel pumps. *She heard about the explosion in Acker's Gap. It's all over the news,* Bell thought. *She heard about it, and she wants to check on me. She wants to find out if I'm okay. She wants to talk—but she can't. Not yet. So she's just checking to make sure that I'm here. That I'm still alive.*

Bell didn't know why she was so certain about the caller's identity, but she was. She'd left her cell number with the parole officer. So it was possible. Definitely.

The silent person on the other end of the call was Shirley.

Chapter Thirty-Five

Sam had done his best with the coffee, but good intentions didn't count. Not when it came to coffee. After her initial sip, Bell fought to keep the disappointment from showing on her face.

"Wish you'd gotten a little more rest, Belfa," he said. "You need it."

He stood against the kitchen counter, cradling his own cup in two tanned hands. Looking handsome and dapper, as always. Even in jeans and a sweatshirt.

His laptop was open on the kitchen table, bright blue screen aglow. He'd been working while she slept, Bell saw. Probably checking his e-mail. Making sure he was still connected to the world beyond Acker's Gap.

"Can't do it, Sam." She'd taken a seat at the table, thanked him for the coffee, but her restlessness was apparent. She was already dressed in black slacks, white blouse. The windows were still dark, but the first faint hints of dawn were just affecting the edges.

"Got a million things to do," she went on. "Investigate the explosion. And other cases, too. Those don't just stop, no matter what else is happening. But first—" This part was hard to talk about, and not just because it was her ex-husband she was talking to. "I have to get back to the hospital. To see Clay."

Sam took a drink of his coffee. Took another. Buying time. "I know he's important to you," he said. "I hope he's okay. They can do wonders these days with prosthetics." He set his cup down on the counter. Since their divorce five years ago, both of them had tried not to comment on the other's personal life. It was a challenge—at least it was for Bell, given her contempt for most of Sam's girlfriends. Sam, for his part, had had little to comment on, until recently; Bell rarely dated. He was surprised, Sam had told her last month, about Clay. *You and me both, buddy,* Bell wanted to reply. *You and me both.*

She took another drink from the mug. He'd put it in front of her with a flourish and a misleadingly promising "Voila!" She looked up, indicating the second floor of the house. "Carla still asleep?"

"Yeah. I had a hard time getting her to turn in last night. She's pretty worried about you, Belfa."

When she didn't reply, he spoke again. "How's the knee?"

She moved her right leg up and down. Probed it with two fingers. "Getting there. Nothing serious. Just needs some time. But speaking of physical ailments—is your back okay? That couch is pretty damned uncomfortable."

"I'll live. But don't change the subject. You sure about the knee? Nick Fogelsong called and told me I ought to make you get a follow-up check, even if I have to do it at gunpoint."

Bell laughed. "Gotta love his logic. Threaten to kill me if I don't take better care of myself. Makes a lot of sense."

Sam didn't join her in the laugh. "Time for truth, Belfa? *Nothing* makes sense in this place. Look at that big homicide case of yours. The sixteen-year-old. Way I hear it, you've got no real clues. Zero physical evidence. Too many suspects—her boyfriend, her boyfriend's mother, her boyfriend's father. Her own mother, too. And her dad. A young woman is dead, and you're nowhere close to an indictment. Not even in the ballpark. Right?"

She didn't answer, which she knew he would interpret—correctly—as another way of saying, *Yeah, okay, you're right,* with perhaps the inevitable addition of, *you bastard.*

"I want you to listen to me," Sam said. "You don't have to. You can tell me to get the hell out of your house. It's your right. I've got no claim on you at all, Belfa, and I wouldn't blame you if you—"

"Hey," she interrupted him. "I love the fact that you and Carla showed up. Really, Sam. When I heard Carla's voice on the phone yesterday, in the middle of everything, telling me you two were on your way—it was just what I needed."

He smiled. "If I hadn't agreed to drive her over, she would've sneaked out of the house and hitchhiked. She's stubborn, that daughter of ours. Mind of her own."

"Tell me about it."

She looked up at him. The smile lingered on his face longer, she guessed, than he'd meant for it to. And they were caught, ever so briefly, in that simple wash of mutual emotion that overcame all parents when they contemplated what they had created: a life independent of theirs but deeply reflective, too, of who they were and what they had once meant to each other. No matter what happened henceforth between her and Sam, no matter how many years might pass beyond the time when they had been a couple, Carla was the link, the tie—the point of it all, Bell believed, in the first place. The point of her and Sam having come together for what turned out to be only a few brief years, an interval in her life that already felt like ancient history. She had a swift inkling of what it must be like for Maddie Trimble when she thought about Lucinda—and then looked at Eddie Geyer. No matter what else he was, he was always Lucinda's father.

Bell took another swallow of coffee and fought back a shudder. How could Sam's coffee-making skills have deteriorated so far, so fast? *Probably doesn't get any practice these days,* Bell thought, remembering Carla's description of the full-time cook whom Sam employed, to make certain Glenna never had to face the heartache of a broken nail caused by routine kitchen chores.

"There's something you wanted to say to me," she reminded him. Might as well deal with it now, instead of replying to a tersely worded e-mail down the road.

"Yes. There is." He rearranged his posture against the counter. "You and I both grew up here, Bell. We know this place. The light and the dark. Right now, though, I'd say it's getting pretty damned dark. Unemployment rate is—what? Twice the national average? Three times? The median income per month has got to be way less than my car payment. Education? Fewer than ten percent of the seniors at Acker's Gap High School go on to college. The prescription drug problem? You know more about that than I do—but even I know that it's bad and getting worse."

"Okay." She knew all these things; they were the things that had brought her back here five years ago. To do what she could, regardless of the odds. What was his point?

"And now," he continued, moving in for the rhetorical kill, "you've got an explosion right in the middle of downtown Acker's Gap. Six people dead. One maimed. *Six people,* Belfa. And you were damned close to getting killed yourself. You've got a murdered sixteen-year-old and no idea who did it. Maybe—just maybe—it's time to resign and pack up and come back to civilization. I can get you a job in D.C. A good job. Practicing law with a good firm—where you'd have real colleagues. Like-minded colleagues. Not a redneck sheriff and some carpenter boyfriend. Look," he said, "I'll help you get resettled there. You know Carla would love it. Hell of a lot easier to do the joint-custody thing—a week at your place, a week at mine.

"You gave it your best shot," he concluded. "You did what you could, but it's over, Belfa. Don't you think?"

This was an ambush, plain and simple. She felt like a cowboy who'd been lured into a box canyon and who had just now spotted the rustlers massing on the ridge, rifles cocked and ready. This was a bushwhacking predicated on the fact that she was weak and hurting, stricken by grief. A stealth attack against the second most important decision she'd ever made in her life: the decision to return to Acker's Gap. The first was her decision to be a mother.

And most unforgivably, he'd woven the issue of Carla's happiness into his argument—which Bell, no matter how annoyed or disappointed or even aghast she'd ever been at Sam's actions, had never done. She'd never hinted that any of his choices meant he was a bad parent.

She stood up slowly. Her right leg quivered, almost gave way. But she stayed standing. She could feel her anger increasing by degrees, rising so fast that it skipped a few degrees along the way.

"You," she declared, "are a first-class asshole, Sam Elkins. You pretend to care about me, you act like you know me—but you don't. Or you wouldn't come into my home like this and insult me and my friends and—"

"Oh, come on," he said, cutting her off. He flapped his hand at her, as if she would magically sit down again upon his cue. In the past, perhaps she would have done just that. "Relax," he said. "Can't we discuss it?"

"No." She leaned over and gathered up her purse and her brief-case, the things she'd brought down the stairs with her this morning and stacked on a chair. "I've got work to do. Got to go see—now, what did you call him? Oh, yeah—my carpenter boyfriend. And don't forget that redneck sheriff." She turned around at the threshold. "Well, no worries about the boyfriend, Sam. He probably won't be a carpenter anymore. Doubt he'll be able to frame a house, what with having just the one leg."

"For God's sake, Bell, I didn't mean to—"

"Doesn't matter." Frowning, she added, "How'd you know about the Lucinda Trimble case? From Carla?"

"Matt Harless."

She'd forgotten about him. Where had he been yesterday morning? Up on the mountain. Away from all this. *Lucky bastard.*

Then the implication of Sam's reply hit her.

"So Matt's been *reporting* on me?" she said. "Giving you updates on our pathetic little lives here in Hooterville?"

"That's not how it is, Belfa."

"Know what? I don't give a rat's ass how it is."

She had moved to the front door and he'd remained in the kitchen, so her last remark had to be flung back over her shoulder. "Tell Carla I'll call her later. Believe it or not, Sam, we've actually got phone service up here in these gosh-darn hills. Just tin cans and little strings—but they work pretty good."

Rarely had slamming a door felt quite so satisfying.

Chapter Thirty-Six

"Hey, baby girl. How are you? You'll never guess what happened yesterday. Right here in this town. Where nothing *ever* happens—didn't we always say that?"

Maddie Trimble inched forward as she talked. She was sitting on her knees, with her rear end resting on the soles of her feet. Her corduroy jumper already had dirt and grass stains smeared across the bottom third of it, but she didn't care.

There was no headstone yet. Turned out—to Maddie's surprise—that it took a while to get the stone put up. Didn't happen right away. Even though they didn't cut the letters by hand anymore, it took time to get it delivered. Weeks, sometimes. And it was going to be pricey. She'd envisioned a long verse, something about miracles and rainbows and light, but then she was informed of the cost per line, and she'd changed her order to: LUCINDA ABIGAIL TRIMBLE, BELOVED DAUGHTER OF MADELINE TRIMBLE AND EDWARD GEYER. And the dates. Those awful numbers.

She looked around. The place was ablaze with numbers. Numbers chiseled onto all these flat-faced stones. Some of the headstones looked as thin as a sheet of paper; others were thick, almost vulgarly bulbous. Some were pink, some gray, others white and black. All of them, though, were cruelly nicked with birth and death dates. With intractable facts.

It wasn't so much the names of the deceased that Maddie noticed here at the Briney Hollow Church of the Nazarene Cemetery, but the numbers. They told the real story. The only story. Names? Names were negligible. Numbers were what mattered. The start-and-stop. The reading from the stopwatch: How long. How long they'd had.

Longer, most of them, than Lucinda had had. Hell of a lot longer.

The headstones rose around her like a dwarf forest. A few featured a carved angel or the placid, milquetoast face of Jesus—you could tell it was supposed to be Jesus, Maddie thought, by the long hair. Hippie hair, did they realize? Way past his shoulders, in most of these granite portraits.

Others just had a name. Every single one, though, had those numbers.

It was a fine, fair, blue-hued afternoon, with a sky that was clear and open-armed. A mild spring breeze bothered the treetops, causing the small early leaves to nuzzle each other, getting acquainted prior to the long summer ahead and what promised to be a constant commingling. Maddie hadn't worn a sweater. *Spring's always looking out for our signal,* she'd told Lucinda every March, from the time her daughter was a small child. *The sooner we start going without our coats, the sooner spring'll be here. Knows it's time for it to arrive. Keeps an eye out.* Lucinda had accepted that until third grade, when a science teacher set her straight. Taught her about seasons. Planetary rotations. Orbits. Said Lucinda—loyal Lucinda—every spring thereafter: *I know the science, Mom, but I like your story better.*

"Baby girl, let me tell you," Maddie went on. She was talking out loud. She was alone, but she wouldn't have cared, anyway, even if there'd been a thousand people present. She'd still have talked out loud.

"They don't know what caused it. I know you must've been in Ike's a few times—not a lot, because it's an old person's place, not like the places where you and your friends like to hang out—and maybe you remember the lady who ran it. Joyce, her name was. Big woman with a lot of hair. Well, she's got a daughter, too. All grown up. Joyce's girl lives in Manassas, Virginia. Got to town last night. They're gonna have some kind of ceremony or something one of these days. Not like yours, baby girl—there'll *never* be another one like yours." Maddie scooted forward again, centering herself on the slightly raised rectangle of freshly packed dirt. Hands gathered on her lap.

"Who was there that day when Ike's blew up? Along with Joyce? Well, let's see," she went on. "There was Georgette Akers. Worked as a waitress. You might've seen her around town sometimes. Big— bigger than Joyce. Kind of sassy. The two of them lived together, re- member? And you know the gossip. You know what people said about 'em. Well, I hope it was true. I hope they had a little bit of happiness in their lives.

"Clay Meckling. Remember him? Tall, nice-looking fellow? Well, he got trapped under a big section of the roof. It was just awful. They had to take off his leg. And let's see—there was the little Com- stock girl, Kaylie, and her daddy, Lowell Comstock. They'd stopped in for breakfast. Spur of the moment. And Abner McEvoy. Oh, Lu- cinda. Oh, baby girl."

She was silent for the next several minutes. Filled with more memories, and more emotions, than she knew what to do with or had a handy place to store. So she waited through the quiet storm. Used the quiet for stability. As something to hold, to keep from going under.

Then she heard the boxed-in roar of a big engine, heard tires bite meanly at the gravel drive. The roar stopped abruptly.

Nick Fogelsong climbed out of his Blazer. He paused to put on his hat, leveling it up. Stepped forward.

"Mornin', Maddie."

"Nick."

She didn't rise to her feet, didn't move off the shaped mound of light brown dirt.

"Kind of surprised to hear you'd picked this place for Lucinda," he said. Making conversation. "Given your feelings about organized religion and all."

She looked up at him. "You don't know a thing about my feelings, Nick Fogelsong. About anything."

It was said without rancor, but he still felt as if he'd had his face slapped. He knew she still blamed him for confronting Eddie Geyer at the service. Well, hell. He'd let him go, hadn't he? In the end? Temporarily, that is.

"Just wanted you to know," he said, "that we're not slowing down with our investigation of Lucinda's death. Not one bit. What happened yesterday at Ike's was terrible—town's never going to be the same—but we've still got our jobs to do. Nobody's forgetting about your girl."

She nodded.

"Which is why I'm here," Fogelsong went on. Firmer now. Back on point. "I need you to tell me where you were that night, Maddie. The night Lucinda died. I believe you're hiding something. I want the truth—or we're going to waste a lot of time. Time we ought to be spending in other ways. More productive ways. Were you with Eddie? If so, I need to know. Now."

She refolded her hands in her lap. "So you're wondering," she said, "why I chose this spot for my baby girl."

"Truth is, it's not my business. I really came out here to find out where you—"

"But you're curious."

"Maddie, I need to know where you were on the night of—"

"It's pretty simple, Nick," she said, cutting him off again. "I want to be able to visit her. In the fresh air. Not have her locked up in some jar that I stick on the mantel. I want her to be outside. To keep the sky in her eyes." She laughed softly. "And I know you and your law enforcement buddies sorta frown on burying people in the backyard, right? So this was my only option. Besides, I'm well acquainted with this cemetery. Used to play out here as a child while my parents were inside getting lectured at. When I come to visit my baby girl, I'll be coming to a place I know. Not a place I love or even especially like—but a place I know. Counts for something."

"It does."

Maddie rose. Stepped off the gravesite. Dusted her skirt. Shook it a second time, to shoo off a last clinging twig.

"Okay," she said. "You want to know where I was when Lucinda died? Well, you got it right. I was with Eddie. Know you don't approve."

"Not my job to pass judgment. It's my job to get the facts. Gather the evidence."

"Oh, hell, Nick. Get that stick out of your ass, will you?"

He didn't want this to become personal. He was working. "Why didn't you tell me you met up with Eddie that night? From the first?"

"I was ashamed. He's a bum, Nick. You and I both know that. And the reason I was late getting home to my girl—the reason I wasn't there for her—was because I was with Eddie. We were—" She stopped.

He nodded. He could figure out what they were doing. He'd seen them at the service. How they'd leaned in to each other. Like it was natural. Like the sixteen years of separation had been no time at all. Blink of an eye.

"When," the sheriff asked, "did Eddie get back to town?"

"Couple of weeks ago. I found him through his cousin. Sent him bus fare. Set him up in that crummy old cabin. The one where Old Man Ferris used to make his moonshine. You remember."

"Okay. But why?"

"Needed him to talk some sense into Lucinda. She was going to keep her child. Marry Shawn Doggett. She wouldn't listen to me—but I thought she might listen to her father. The poster boy for bad choices."

"Which is why you lied about where you were Thursday night."

"Yes, Nick. That's why I lied. I mean, there I was, having just lectured my baby girl about being responsible, about making smart decisions, and I'm out with this bum, this lazy—"

"With the man you were in love with, once upon a time," he said, interrupting her, but doing it gently. "And maybe still are."

She shrugged. "Don't know about that. I've been lonely, Nick. Lonely as hell. When Eddie got here, it was like—like I remembered everything. Both of us did. We remembered how it was with us. It all just came rushing back. All the good times."

"You've confirmed that you and Eddie were together on the night Lucinda died. That's all I need. All I'm here for. The rest of it—" He made a gesture with his hand, and then he turned away. Walked the five steps back to the Blazer. Her business.

"Nick," she called to him. "I really do want to know. How'd you figure I'd be out here today? I didn't tell anybody where I was going."

He had the Blazer's door handle in his grip. "You said earlier that I don't know you. Not true, Maddie. Not true at all. I knew how you felt about Lucinda. I knew where she was—and I knew you'd be here, too. Or on your way to being here."

The radio in his car crackled. Nick opened the door so he could listen.

He turned back to Maddie. The amiable expression had vanished.

"It's that goddamned Eddie Geyer," he said, his voice made livid by rage. "Took Shawn Doggett hostage over at the high school. Says he's going to cut his throat for killing Lucinda."

Chapter Thirty-Seven

Bell could still feel the anger moving roughly in her blood, a raft riding a wild current. She'd been blindsided by Sam's little speech that morning. Stunned at his gall. Hurt, if she'd ever let herself admit it, by his assumption that she didn't know what she was doing with her life, that her return to Acker's Gap had been a lark, an experiment.

She'd wanted to tell Sam about the phone call—the one that might have been from Shirley. But after his condescending little speech, she didn't bring it up. He didn't deserve to know.

When Bell felt this way, driving usually helped. Helped to get her emotions back under control. The wound on her right leg made acceleration painful—*Dammit,* she muttered each time she pressed the pedal—but she could do it. She needed to be in motion.

The shortest route from Shelton Avenue to the Raythune County Medical Center required her to pass through Acker's Gap. There was another way—longer, less convenient—and she'd waged a fierce argument with herself before she'd even backed out of her driveway. *Go the long way round. You don't need to see what's left of Ike's. Not today. Not yet.*

But the other side of her had won out, the side that said: *This is your town. Your home. You can't look away. You've got to face it, head on.* And so she drove to Main Street. The courthouse reared up on the right. The sun had risen by this time, bringing a radiance that, under the circumstances, seemed almost spiteful. She made the left turn onto Thornapple—and there it was: a blank space that once had been Ike's diner. An absence that was an appalling presence in her heart, her mind.

Clay sat up in bed. His eyes were closed; a fresh bandage had been wrapped around the top of his head. Walter Meckling—still in the faded denim jacket, still in work boots—stood beside the bed. *Has the old man moved at all since I was here last?* Bell wondered. *Surely he must've, and yet . . .*

Walter's hands gripped the bed rail as if they were now permanently attached to the plastic, fused with it by the powerful adhesive force of his sorrow.

"Mornin', Mrs. Elkins," Walter said. No matter how profound his sadness, he was never discourteous. "First time he's been up like that. Since the surgery, I mean."

"Bell?" Clay said. He spoke her name before he opened his eyes. When he did open them, he looked at her—she had advanced only a step or two into the room—and blinked furiously. "Hard to see. Kind of fuzzy. That's temporary, they say."

He lifted a hand. Waved toward the large hump beneath the white blanket, in the spot where his right leg should be. "That, I'm sorry to say, *isn't* temporary."

She had expected many different reactions from him—shock, anger, bitter bleakness, denial, resignation—but jauntiness wasn't one of them.

"They did it last night," he said. "I offered 'em my Sawzall, but they said they like to use their own tools." He laughed. Bell didn't join in. "Wasn't much left of the leg, I guess," Clay went on. "Big hunk of the roof landed on me, they say. Surgeon's name was Dudek. She was in here first thing this morning, checking on me. Says she knows you. Oh, and there's good news. You'll be glad to find out—" The jauntiness blossomed even bigger in his voice, the breezy nonchalance. "—that I'm doing fine, according to your doctor pal. Fine and dandy. Gonna live a long, long time." A sharp bark of a laugh. "Wait—was that the good news or the bad news?"

"Clay," Bell said. "I want you to know that if there's anything I can—"

"Figures, doesn't it?" he said, interrupting her curtly. "I mean, I'd just been telling myself not a month ago that I'd escaped the curse of this place. Made a clean getaway. I go off to college—a really *great* college—and I study hard, I get ready for grad school, and then I come back here to work for a year or so, just to help out my dad and—" He shook his head, a *Can you believe it?* smirk on his face. "—and I'll be damned if this sorry little shit-ass town doesn't get me in its clutches, after all. Grabs me and takes me right down."

His eyes sought Bell's. He was, she could tell, on high alert for pity. He was testing her, to see if she flinched or turned away.

"Clay. Listen," she said. "I'm sorry this happened to you. But you know what? You're alive. Six other people aren't."

He didn't speak right away, so his father did. Walter Meckling's voice was a foggy, phlegm-choked baritone—a natural consequence, Bell assumed, of his having been awake all night long, waiting for his son to be wheeled back from surgery.

"They tell me they'll be getting him up right away," Walter said. "For the physical therapy and all. They don't wait no more. They get you up and going. Give you a temporary artificial leg until you get measured for your own. Best way, they say, to get you out of here fast." He shook his big head. "Do they know yet," Walter went on, after a pause for a wet-sounding cough, "what caused it, Mrs. Elkins? Gas line, was it? That building was so damned old. Somebody was always takin' out a wall or puttin' one in. Can't believe the work was always done on the up and up."

"They're investigating," she said. She didn't know if it was relevant, but she'd told Sheriff Fogelsong about what she had seen the night before the blast. The glimmer at the edge of town. The reflection from— what? No telling. *Could it have been somebody who—?* Nick had written down what she said and then answered her: *I don't know, Bell. I'll hand it over to the state investigators. Worth a mention, for sure.*

Walter shook his head again. It was his default gesture to indicate all the things in his world he didn't understand. "Six people dead," he said. "My Lord."

"Who died, Bell?" Clay asked. No jauntiness now. "Pops here wouldn't tell me."

"Joyce and Georgette," she said. She wouldn't be coy. Wouldn't sidestep his questions. It wasn't fair. She would answer him. "Abner McEvoy. A little girl and her father. A trucker from out of town. Fella named Pauley. Drew Pauley."

Clay closed his eyes again. "Joyce," he said. "And Georgette." He'd grown up in Acker's Gap, so he knew them both. Last spring, Bell remembered, he'd helped Joyce set up Quicken software on her computer to monitor expenses at the restaurant. Until then, she'd kept all her records in a big black ledger—and sometimes she would back-slide, would return to paper and pencil, just for old times' sake. *It's the twenty-first century, Joyce,* Clay had said, gently scolding her while he typed on the Dell she'd procured against her better judgment. Her reply—*Is it? Is it, really? Land's sakes, nobody told me!*— had caused him to look up sharply; then he'd realized that she was teasing him. When she'd tried to pay him for his work, he'd said, *No thanks, wasn't a problem, Joyce,* and she'd replied, *Well, young man, you better not try to buy a meal in here ever again. It's on the house, for the rest of your life.*

He hadn't had the heart that day to tell her. To explain that he wasn't going to live his life in Acker's Gap. He had plans, dreams.

Clay looked down at the white lump, a tightly swaddled mound from which a series of tubes sprouted to catch the blood draining from the surgical wound. Then he looked up at Bell. She wondered if they were thinking the same thing. Remembering her words from a while back, when they were first courting.

In West Virginia, she'd said, *the roads bend around the mountains. So we can't see what lies ahead.* Clay had added his own coda: *And thank God for that, don't you think?*

· · ·

The lights were dimmed in the hospital room. The shade was drawn. Bell and Walter had both dozed off, slumped in their chairs on either side of Clay's bed. Clay was asleep, too, as the latest batch of painkillers had kicked in.

Bell heard a noise. Was someone calling her name? She opened her eyes. When she saw Matt Harless in the threshold, she jumped up. Too quickly: Her knee made her pay. She willed herself not to wince as she moved toward the doorway.

He held up a brown paper sack. LYMON'S was printed on the side. Dime-sized stains of grease were already congregating across the bottom.

"Had a few run-ins with hospital food myself," he said softly, trying not to wake the others, "and so I brought your friend some doughnuts. Sugar's always good for what ails you."

"Hey," she said, also in a quasi-whisper. "Nice of you to stop by."

He looked harder at Clay and Walter. Both continued to doze. "Wanted to pay my respects," Matt said. He nodded toward Clay. Toward the white mound that widened out on one side, below the young man's waist. "How's he taking it?"

Bell shrugged.

Matt motioned for her to join him in the hallway.

"It won't be easy for him," he said, as soon as Bell had pulled the door of Clay's room to a gentle latchless close. "I've seen a lot of amputees. Pretty common injury among infantry troops in Iraq and Afghanistan. Everything depends on the attitude. The will. And on getting a good prosthesis. You need to find a major medical center with a decent rehab program. As soon as possible. I mean it."

"That's up to Clay."

"It's critical, Bell. He can't just lie there and feel sorry for himself."

"I'll be sure and give him that advice."

He heard the hitch in her voice. "Something wrong?"

"Yeah," she said. "There's something wrong. We're grieving here, Matt. We need some time, okay? We lost part of our town. We lost some friends."

"I don't mean to be disrespectful, Bell, but—come on." His tone was tough now. "You lost an old building. Half a dozen people. I've seen entire *cities* destroyed. Shelled to rubble and dust. Hundreds of people dead or missing. I know people who've lost everything— parents, grandparents, children, husbands and wives, brothers and sisters. They end up with the clothes on their back. Nothing else."

"Is that supposed to make us feel better? The fact that you've seen worse?"

"No, but—"

He paused as a nurse went by, pushing an IV pole and carrying an oblong plastic bag loaded with lime green liquid. Preoccupied, she didn't look their way.

"You don't know this town," Bell declared, taking advantage of the lull, jumping in before he could finish his thought. "You don't know these people. You didn't know Joyce and Georgette—"

"No," he said, interrupting her. "Not like you did, Bell. That's true. But listen to me, okay? Just listen. I do know what it's like to lose somebody, somebody who—"

This time, he interrupted himself. He stopped. Then he seemed to get hold of himself, to snatch back his equilibrium.

There was a time when she'd admired his ability to remain calm, detached, dispassionate. She'd never known him to fake the kind of cooing sympathy that most people would automatically bring to situations such as this. He was too honest for that. Too candid. Despite what he'd started to say, she wondered if he had ever truly felt a riotous affection for another human being, ever grieved for the sudden and violent loss of a loved one. Maybe that had been trained out of him. Eliminated from his emotional repertoire, courtesy of some fiendishly speeded-up, one-man version of natural selection. Maybe the only emotions he'd been allowed to retain were the ones that had helped him survive.

"I think," she said carefully, "you ought to go. If Clay wakes up and you give him that nice little speech about how he needs to get his lazy ass out of bed, he's liable to take it the wrong way. He's liable to think you're just an insensitive bastard." She knew she was being a bit unfair to Matt, but right now, she was in an *I hate everybody* mood. Surely she could be excused for it.

"Okay," Matt said. "No sense in arguing." He held out the paper sack, hand clamped on the rolled-down top. "Got these at that little grocery store. Lady behind the counter said they're homemade."

"They are," Bell snapped. "And if you were from around here, you'd know that they've been that way for about fifty years."

She was going to refuse the gift, but it occurred to her that Walter might be hungry. He'd been here all night. So she accepted the bag.

Matt took a step down the hospital corridor before suddenly turning around again. "Meant to ask you," he said. "Was there an alley behind Ike's?"

"There was."

"Okay." His eyes took on a thoughtful cast. "Anybody spot a stranger? Anybody see a guy looking out of place in Acker's Gap?"

"Just you."

Matt laughed. "I deserve that, I guess."

"Look," she said, serious again, "if you've got a theory—any kind of suspicion—you ought to go to the sheriff right away. He's trying to get to the bottom of this."

"No theory. Just curious."

She waited. When he didn't say anything else, she said, "Now I have a question for you, Matt."

He froze.

"Forgot to ask," she said, "what kind of doughnuts you got. Betty Lymon always makes too many honey-glazed and then tries to sweet-talk out-of-towners into taking 'em. Sour cream's the best. All the locals know it."

"How about that. You're the proud owner of a half-dozen sour cream doughnuts."

"You really *are* a lucky bastard, aren't you?" She waved. She'd been tough on him. The wave was her way of asking forgiveness.

"So far, at least." He waved back. His way of granting it.

Chapter Thirty-Eight

"Eddie, come on. You got a beef with this kid? Work it out. But don't do this."

Sheriff Fogelsong was using his reasonable, *everybody calm down* voice. Slow, even, and steady. It was hard, though, to keep his temper. He'd never liked Eddie Geyer. And here was proof positive that his long-held instincts about the man—Eddie Geyer was a lazy, lying, low-life bastard, a waste of space—were correct.

"Back off, Nick. Mean it." Eddie's voice was agitated, raspy. It was the kind of voice that put the sheriff on high alert. More danger-ous than anger, it had an itch embedded in it, a rabbity desperation that could cause a man to jump, to do something he'd never intended to do.

They faced each other across the blacktopped parking lot of Ack-er's Gap High School, separated by about fifteen yards. A small con-gress of nervous students and apprehensive teachers was gathered at the front door of the school. The final bell had gone off twenty-five minutes ago; the buses had already loaded up and departed. *Thank God for that,* Nick thought. *Don't need any bigger audience than we've already got.*

The sheriff stood beside the Blazer. He'd slowly opened his coat, so that Eddie Geyer could see the gun on his hip. He hoped it wouldn't be necessary to prove his seriousness to the man, but then again.

He'd do it if he had to.

Eddie pressed himself tight against Shawn Doggett's back, left arm cocked in the flat *V* of a choke hold around Shawn's neck. In his right hand, Eddie held a hunting knife, the serrated blade bumping the bottom of the young man's chin. Shawn's skinny arms dangled and twitched. His head was thrown back, in an effort to keep his throat as far as possible from the ugly gray blade, and his eyes were wide.

Kid looks terrified, Fogelsong thought. *Ought to be.*

The late-afternoon sun was taking its sweet time sinking below the mountain. Before it went, it paused to catch the metal on the sheriff's badge and his belt buckle and the thin gold braid on his hat. It skittered across the hood of Shawn's car. The spangled reflection and the setting—the school grounds were spread out at the base of the mountain, and the looming rock seemed to hold the place in its grip—gave the moment an ancient, timeless feel, as if essential forces of good and evil were massing once more under a dying sun. *Could be Omaha Beach on D-Day,* Nick thought. *Or Agincourt. Or Antietam. Hell, it could be the plains of Troy, come to that.* This was where the residue of Nick's secret reading sometimes kicked in. He didn't talk about it with anyone, fearing their ridicule: *D-Day, Sheriff? In Acker's Gap? Not unless you mean Dumb-Ass Day.* But he'd been struck before by how every conflict, no matter when it happened or what it was all about, devolved to one moment when everything—fist, sword, knife, gun, destiny itself—was poised in a clarifying light. When the world could go either way. Life or death. Progress or disaster.

"Come on, Eddie," Nick said. "This's no way to settle things."

"Sure as hell is," Eddie sent back. He rejiggered his grip on Shawn's throat. Pushed the knife even tighter against the young man's windpipe. "This sonofabitch killed my baby girl. He killed Lucinda, Nick. Only reason you ain't arrested him yet is 'cause his daddy's got money. Plain and simple. You know it and I know it."

"I don't know any such thing," Fogelsong replied. Still calm. Still reasonable. He'd give Eddie another five seconds to come to his senses. Then Mr. Reasonable would disappear and Mr. Hard-Ass Sheriff would take over.

When Nick had driven up to the front of the school, the principal, Carlton Stillwagon, flagged him down and breathlessly filled him in. Eddie had apparently hitchhiked out to the high school—that was how he'd gotten so close with nobody spotting him, he didn't come up the long access road but around the rocks on foot—and then he waited until Shawn Doggett left the building and headed out toward the parking lot. The school had closed early on the day of the explosion but had reopened today.

Must've been easy, Fogelsong figured, for Eddie to make a decent guess about which car belonged to Shawn—the car dealer's son—and then, playing his hunch, crouch down in the general vicinity. Most of the vehicles in the student lot were shabby beaters with duct-taped rear fenders and missing mufflers and mismatched tires. Shawn's was a silver Nissan 370Z Roadster.

When Shawn had approached, Eddie popped out, spun the kid around, let the knife tip do his talking. A bus driver, watching the whole thing unfold, had alerted the principal.

Fully briefed, Nick had driven the Blazer into the parking lot. Got out, still moving with non-threatening, infinitely patient slowness. Opened his coat. He'd give this troublemaking bastard one more chance before acting in accordance with established law enforcement guidelines for dealing with a hostage situation:

I'm gonna nail the sucker right behind the eyes. And then file this one under "Golden Opportunity."

He was bluffing—bluffing himself, in this case. Not the suspect. The most he'd do would be to disarm Eddie Geyer, as painlessly as possible.

The shoot-between-the-eyes part? Wishful thinking.

"He killed my little girl!" Eddie yelled. The anxiety of the moment made his voice leap into a high-pitched squeal. "He's a killer. And if you won't do your job, I'm sure as hell gonna do it for you."

"I didn't kill her!" Shawn cried out. "I loved her! I loved her. Lucinda was—" His voice fell off into a long hiccoughing sob.

"Don't say her name," Eddie growled. "Not fit to say her name." He cinched up the choke hold, like a rodeo rider shortening the strap on the saddle until he was sure it would fit snugly even through a spill. Shawn made gagging sounds. Flapped his arms.

Nick knew he had waited long enough. Maybe too long. *Kid can't breathe,* he thought. *Gotta end this now.*

"Eddie," Nick said, "you have one more second to let loose of that kid."

Eddie wasn't listening. His mouth was pushed up against Shawn's ear, his spit spray mingling with the sweat on the young man's neck. "You did it! You did it! Tell everybody—tell 'em now! Tell the truth!"

"Okay," Shawn said. "Okay, I—"

The rifle shot came from high above and slightly to the left. A sharp whip-crack. The sound seemed to smack the side of the mountain and then drop in an ever-diminishing series of cracking echoes, spinning, tumbling, losing a bit more of itself each time it bounced against the rock face as it fell.

Eddie crumpled to the ground, screaming and clutching his knee. The knife hit the blacktop with a dull clatter. Nick bolted forward and stepped on it with his big black boot, just in case Eddie had any ideas about trying to retrieve it. Shawn Doggett, suddenly free, staggered a few steps—his legs were too rubbery right now to support him—and then bumped against the side of his car, whereupon he slid down in a quivering heap.

Knife secured, the sheriff looked up. Way up.

He saw Deputy Pam Harrison, stationed on a rock plateau about two hundred feet above the parking lot. Rifle resting on her shoulder now. She saluted him.

Fogelsong waved back. She had been monitoring the radio that afternoon, and stealthily moved into position just the way she'd been trained to do. The bullet had grazed Eddie's knee, disabling him without causing serious injury. There was no better shot in Raythune County.

Hell, the sheriff corrected himself. Might not be a better shot anywhere in the whole state of West Virginia.

"Get me a damned ambulance!" Eddie yelled. "Been hit! Been hit bad!"

The sheriff looked down at him. Much as he disliked this man, much as he always had and always would, there was a part of Nick Fogelsong that could understand why Eddie had done this. Justice was a slow, uncertain thing. Waiting for it tended to require great patience and tremendous wisdom—attributes that Eddie Geyer did not, to say the least, possess in abundance. And sometimes Nick wished he could do it this way, too—just grab a weapon and go settle things. He yearned to do it to whoever was responsible for the explosion at Ike's—because he still had trouble believing it was an accident.

Trouble was, though, he had to find the person first. And when he did—if he did—he'd have to fall back on that patience-and-wisdom thing. Price of the job.

"Oh hell, Eddie," the sheriff muttered. "Stop your caterwauling." He nudged the writhing man with the toe of his boot, making the howls louder. "The bad news—for the town, I mean—is that you're gonna live."

Chapter Thirty-Nine

"Maybe Eddie Geyer was on the right track, after all," Bell said. "Maybe Shawn did do it."

She was sitting in Sheriff Fogelsong's office the following morning, having listened once again to his description of the standoff at Acker's Gap High School. Nick had played it by the book; he had called her just after the incident, and sent a line-of-duty shooting report over to her office.

This morning, however, he'd given her a more informal account, meaning that he could refer to Eddie Geyer as "that stupid sonofabitch" instead of "the alleged assailant."

It had rained just before sunrise, a heavy, steady rain that fell in harsh vertical lines. People woke to find soaked yards and swamped driveways and flooded basements. Then the rain suddenly quit, as if an invisible engine had been toggled off, giving way to bountiful sunshine that made the town look scrubbed and almost angelically earnest, like a child after her bath.

Even the black cavity on Thornapple Avenue that had once been Ike's—set off behind sawhorses and warning flags and stern signs advising caution—seemed not quite so grim and hopeless today, having been rinsed down by the predawn deluge.

"You really believe that, Bell?"

"Don't know," she admitted. "It would just make things a hell of a lot easier."

"Says he loved her, though."

"Yes. He says that."

"You doubt it?"

"Well, there's no way to check, is there? It's one side of the story. His side. Lucinda's not talking." *The skull is mute,* Bell wanted to add, but didn't. Fogelsong would like it, would ask the source of it, and might not appreciate her quoting Matt Harless. The sheriff and her old friend had been in the same vicinity only once or twice, but Bell had sensed a mutual suspicion. *Like owls and crows,* she'd decided. Natural enemies in the wild.

"By all accounts, they had plans to marry. Plus," Nick added, twisting the lid off his big silver thermos, "there's the pesky little fact that we've got no hard evidence against him. You know what, Bell? Always gets me, those people who say—'You mean you can't solve that itty-bitty crime? Why, a three-year-old could figure that one out!' I sometimes remind them of a little something I learned when I was first hired as a deputy by Sheriff Rucker, back in—oh, never mind when it was. What he told me was this: 'Nick, it don't matter what you *know.* What matters is what you can *prove.*'"

Bell nodded. She was distracted by the thermos and by the smell unleashed upon its opening. "Don't suppose you'd care to share."

"If you can find an extra mug around this office, young lady, be my guest." He peered at her. "Thought Sam would keep you well supplied in the coffee department this morning."

"Flew the coop," Bell said with a forced casualness. "He and Carla left a while ago. Nice of them to come check on me, but she can't miss any more school. Besides, I'm fine."

She had arrived at the courthouse at 6 A.M., running inside to keep from getting soaked. The only light burning at that hour—*naturally,* she thought with satisfaction—was the one in the sheriff's office. That was where she went, even before she went to her own office.

She'd found him sitting at his desk, reading. His uniform looked as if it had been pulled out of the washing machine prior to the spin cycle; clearly, he'd been caught off guard by the early-morning storm. But he was oblivious to the soaking. Nick Fogelsong was the only man Bell had ever known who could have rainwater sluicing from his hat or mud stuck to his trousers after having rescued a stray mutt from a filthy sinkhole, and not look bedraggled. The elements never fazed him. Weather seemed to slide right off his back, literally and metaphorically.

"You ever hear of an umbrella?" she'd said, walking in and sitting down.

"You ever hear of knocking?"

The crooked pleasantries were a signal to both of them that their relationship was back on track. He rustled around in a desk drawer and finally came up with a mug. Blew in it, to rearrange the dust. Poured her a slug of coffee.

Neither one said out loud what each knew the other was thinking: *Before, we'd have gotten our morning coffee at Ike's.* It was too painful to articulate. Having been through similar tragedies, they understood— again without saying it out loud—that emotional survival depended on not constantly referring to the calamity. Not making it the milepost marker against which subsequent events were slotted in time: *Forty-eight hours ago, we were saying good morning to Georgette. If only we'd known . . .*

That kind of thinking made sorrow endless. *One week ago, one month ago, a year ago, thirty years ago . . .*

She knew, from the violence in her childhood, the way pain could reverberate endlessly unless you forced it to stop. Unless you put your fist down on the table and said, *No.*

Which was not to say they couldn't discuss the explosion at Ike's as an ongoing investigation. That was different.

"Any word from the state police?" she said. Took her first drink of his coffee. Made a face.

"Coffee okay?"

"Course it is. That's why I'm wincing."

He nodded. "Nothing official yet. But they're leaning toward ruling it a gas leak. That storefront was over a hundred and fifty years old and there's been a remodel every decade or so, not all of them done with the proper permits. Now, I'm not satisfied with that assessment—and I sure as hell know that you're not, either—but they don't much care about our hunches. Lacking any evidence to support a finding of foul play, they said—"

"Let me guess," she interrupted him ruggedly. "They said, 'Sorry for your loss. Good luck with the cleanup. And we'll take our own sweet time with the investigation, because you're a small town and this was probably just negligence by some shit-for-brains local contractor who hit a gas line.' Oh, and the tip from your prosecutor? About the little glimmer of light the night before? Tell her that next time she sees a glimmer, she ought to put the stopper in the jug and go somewhere to sleep it off."

"Good guess." He moved the tall thermos to one side of his desk, so he'd be able to look at her. "I could practically hear the eye-rolling over the phone. Not fun. But I did get another call last night that was pretty interesting."

"Do tell."

"Well, I was just about to head home. I'd booked Eddie Geyer in his cell, and then I had to take a few minutes to explain to Maddie Trimble why she couldn't bail him out until today's bond hearing—and then my cell rang."

Bell waited. Took another drink of coffee, winced again, and gave him a thumbs-up sign.

"It was—believe it or not—a guy from the FBI field office in Charleston." Nick rooted through the papers on his desk, found the one he was looking for, pulled it up, and read off a name. "Robert Sanger. That was the agent who called." He returned the paper to its messy home, a tangle that included manila file folders and purchase receipts and old spiral-bound notebooks. "This Sanger fella said they'd come across the news about the explosion. And the West Virginia part jumped right out."

"Why's that?"

"Well, turns out the FBI raided a place in D.C. a couple of weeks ago that mighta been a terrorist hideout. Made some arrests, but they know they didn't get everybody. One of the guys who escaped left a laptop behind. Hard drive was erased—he musta been tipped off about the raid, Sanger says—but those FBI boys were still able to extract a little bit of data. Part of a MapQuest search. Apparently he's headed to West Virginia."

"But why would—?"

"Nobody knows. But the FBI's not too concerned. Groups like that, they say, are interested in big cities—major population areas—not small towns."

"I could ask Matt about it. My friend from D.C."

"Why's that?"

"He might have some insight. Used to be an interrogator with the CIA. In Iraq and Afghanistan. He's retired now, but that was his job."

"So what the hell's he doing here?"

"Some R and R. Needed to get out of the city." She wanted to add, but didn't: *Just like Emmett Hostettler. Remember?* She didn't add it, because she knew how the sheriff felt about his friend, the ex-Chicago cop whose return to Acker's Gap had been therapeutic. Even lifesaving, perhaps. And because there were places in Nick Fogelsong's soul that you didn't visit without prior authorization.

The sheriff put a hand flat on his desktop. He looked down at it, as if the arrangement of his knuckles was the most fascinating sight in the universe at that moment.

"Bell," he finally said, "kind of wish you had enlightened me—before today—about this man's background. Don't you think, given the places he's been and the things he's done, that maybe I should've had a notion about him? A few details?"

She didn't answer, which was her way of acknowledging that he was right. She should have told him. She should have talked a lot more about Matt Harless, should have discussed him with Nick, should have told the sheriff stories about their long morning runs back in D.C. Maybe indicated how much she liked the man, then and now. Why hadn't she?

Truth was, she'd wanted to spare Nick's feelings. The sheriff was a proud man, and what she couldn't say to him—because he was her oldest and dearest friend in the world—was that his friendship wasn't enough anymore. She had craved someone new and different. Someone who'd lived in other countries, someone who hadn't spent his entire life in Raythune County, surrounded by mountains that seemed to crowd in a little closer every day.

"Yeah," she said. "We should've talked." She looked at her coffee cup. Nobody said the words *Maddie Trimble* out loud but they were right there, anyway, inhabiting the air above the sheriff's dented metal desk. "I guess," Bell added, "you're not the only one who's ever let an old association cloud professional judgment. Sorry, Nick."

"Okay. Anyway," he continued, "the FBI just wanted us to be on our toes."

"Sanger say anything else?"

"Yeah." Fogelsong indulged in a bleak smile that was really not a smile at all. "He asked me to call and let him know if anything happened that was out of the ordinary."

"Like a building blowing up."

"Yeah. Like a building blowing up."

"Hope you told him," Bell said, annoyance slicing through her tone, "that even the feds have probably heard about locking a barn door after the horse gets out."

"Oh, I told him plenty. Most of it, I can't repeat. You might hear some words that no lady oughta hear."

"Bet this lady would've used a few of those words herself."

Chapter Forty

Back in her office, Bell looked at the list of phone calls and e-mails she needed to return. *Jesus.* Sometimes she felt as if she spent half her life on the phone and the other half on the computer. Her mood wasn't improved by the rain, which had started up again and now barreled against the tall window in fitful heavy gusts.

Bell heard the outer door open and then Lee Ann's voice: "Go right on in, Deputy."

It was Greg Greenough, sopping wet and visibly aggrieved by it. Rainwater had darkened his overcoat by at least two shades and was dripping off the edges of his hat in a nervous gray curtain. His face looked as soggy and been-through-it as his clothes.

"Sorry to be messing up your floor here, ma'am," he said, indicating the puddle his presence had created. "Eighteen-wheeler jackknifed up on the interstate. I've been dealing with the traffic backup since five A.M., helping the state boys."

"Anybody hurt?"

"Nope. Just a hell of a tangle. Driver lost control of his rig and took out a big chunk of guardrail."

Bell nodded. *State'll handle that.* Being a county employee for almost five years now had changed her way of thinking: She instantly slotted problems into categories of responsibility. If something happened outside the borders of Raythune County, she could sympathize—but it wasn't her lookout. Just ask Bert Hillman.

"So what can I do for you, Deputy?"

Instead of replying, he lifted one side of his waterlogged coat and sent a wet hand poking around in his trouser pocket. "Promised Kendra I'd drop this by to you," he said. He pulled out a thin silver chain to which a small medallion was attached, and leaned over to place it on the desk in front of her. Water ran down his coat sleeve, and he hurriedly tried to blot it up with his other sleeve.

"Don't worry about that," she said. "Needs a good scrubbing, anyway. What's this?"

She held the medallion up to the light in order to read the inscription:

From Marcy to Shawn. LUV 4-ever.

"Hold on," she said before he could answer. "Did Shawn and Marcy date?"

"That's what Kendra just told me."

"When did they go out?"

"I'm real ashamed of my girl, ma'am, for not telling me this earlier." Greenough dipped his head, sending a concentrated spray of water droplets flicking over the front rim of his hat. "But it turns out that Shawn Doggett and Marcy went steady for a little while last year. Not real long or nothing, but they did. It was right after they broke up that Shawn and the Trimble girl got together. That's what Kendra says."

"How did your daughter acquire this?" Bell said, holding up the chain.

"From Marcy. When she and Shawn called it quits, he gave it back to her. Once the trouble started—Lucinda's death and such—well, Marcy was afraid you'd find out, and that it didn't look good, so she gave the necklace to Kendra for safekeeping. Till it all blew over. Marcy knew it was proof that she'd had considerable reason to resent

276

Lucinda. Now, when it comes to my girl—well, she just thought she was helping Marcy. Helping out a friend. Not withholding evidence."

Bell closed her hand over the necklace. "Lord, Greg—these kids of ours. Always so sure that they're doing the right thing—when chances are, it's all wrong." She was recalling Carla, who had almost gotten herself killed last fall, trying to help her mother solve a triple homicide. "They don't think about the trouble they can cause. They probably don't think, period."

"I'm real sorry, ma'am. If Kendra has messed things up too bad, I can promise you that Lola and I will—"

"Not worried about that right now, Greg." Bell reached for a sheet of paper and a pen. "I'll have Deputy Mathers follow up with Kendra. Can you make sure she's available for an interview this afternoon? If Marcy Hillman was still in love with Shawn Doggett, that gives her a motive. And a pretty damned good one. I hate to think that—but we've got to check it out."

He nodded. The gesture caused more water to transfer from his hat to the floor. "Dammit," he said, adding, "Sorry, ma'am."

"Deputy, if we have to start apologizing for using curse words around here, then I'm never going to get a goddamned thing done." Her comment sparked a grin from him, a grin that lit up his gray face and seemed to strip about ten years from his features. Bell realized how rarely she'd seen Greg Greenough smile. He was a serious man who did a serious job. When he smiled, though—even a tentative, halfway kind of smile such as this one was—she could sense the man he'd been, the younger man, lighter in all kinds of ways.

"Look," she said, "you're in the courthouse the rest of the morning, right?"

"Yes, ma'am. Jail duty."

"Then hang up your coat and hat on the rack over there. That'll keep you from leaving a trail through the building."

"Much obliged, ma'am. Got another hat in my locker. I can use it till this one dries out." As he lifted his hat—he'd been wearing one for thirty years, Bell knew, give or take—she saw that sweat had darkened the inside just as thoroughly as rain had discolored the outside. Greenough had done his best for Raythune County for a long, long time, working in all weathers.

"You know what?" he mused. "Wish I'd thought a little harder, first time I asked Kendra about all of this. I mean, she's a good girl. Always has been. But one thing I know for sure, from raising a teenager. Even the good ones have their secrets."

Chapter Forty-One

After the deputy left, Bell headed to the courtroom for Eddie Geyer's arraignment on charges of felonious assault. He was released on ten-thousand-dollars' bond put up by Maddie Trimble—she'd pledged her small house as security—with a trial date set for April 17. Eddie Geyer had *flight risk* scribbled all over him, but Bell didn't argue against the granting of bail; she was relying on her instincts, and her instincts told her Eddie Geyer wouldn't leave Raythune County until he had seen Lucinda's killer brought to justice. *And if it does turn out to be Shawn Doggett,* she'd said to Eddie just before he left the courthouse, watching him lean on Maddie while he adjusted himself to his crutches, *we'll go after him and put him on trial. But that's* our *job, Mr. Geyer. Not yours. So you stay away from that boy—or you'll wait for* your *trial date in a jail cell. You got it?*

She took his sneer as assent that he had indeed gotten it.

By the time Bell left the courthouse to drive to the hospital to see Clay, the rain had let up once more, but clearly would return when it had a mind to. The sky was gray and low-hanging, like the roof of a worn-out tent glimpsed warily from the inside. She headed up Main, and when she reached the intersection with Thornapple, once again turned her head toward the empty space where Ike's used to be. Just a glance. She couldn't help it. She would be doing that, she surmised, for as long as she lived here. Her eyes and her memories would be drawn forevermore to the spot, the spot where, even on an overcast morning, a few people had gathered, staring at an area that various pieces of heavy equipment had cleaned up and then scraped flat, taking it back down to dirt. The people stood quietly, heads bowed, hands clasped, moods solemn. The First Methodist Church of Acker's Gap had driven six small white wooden crosses into the ground. Shoulder-high green plastic fencing circled the space.

Bell allowed herself the look and then drove on.

Her cell rang. When she answered—"Elkins," she said stiffly, all business, expecting to hear from Rhonda or Hick or Lee Ann or maybe even Nick again, remembering something he'd forgotten to tell her—she could hear breathing.

Just breathing. A steady, rhythmic inhalation and exhalation.

She checked the caller ID.

UNKNOWN. That fit Shirley, right down to the ground.

This time, she was ready.

"Shirley?" Bell said softly. Not wanting to spook her. "Is that you?"

The sound stopped, as if the caller had taken a breath and now held it. Listening.

"Shirley," Bell said. "I'm okay. If that's why you're calling—if you heard about the explosion on the news—I'm okay. Six people died, but I'm okay. I got knocked down, but that's all. Same as you, Shirley. I was knocked down but I got back up. Shirley, I wish you would—"

There was a sharp click. Connection severed.

Bell kept the phone to her ear, just in case. Just in case she was mistaken and it wasn't a click she'd heard but something else. Background noise, perhaps, or static, and maybe it meant that Shirley was still there, still listening, still checking on her little sister Belfa, still concerned about her, waiting to hear words—*What can I say?* Bell thought, frustrated, casting about, *What can I say to let you know it's safe, I'll come to you, I'll come right now, just tell me what to say and I'll say it, I'll say it over and over again*—the words that, if Bell could only find the right ones, would bring Shirley home.

Chapter Forty-Two

According to the name tag pinned to her stretchy scoop-necked pink shirt, the physical therapist's name was Dawn. *Physical therapists are* always *named Dawn,* Bell groused to herself, *except when they're named Tricia.*

Well, now. Apparently Clay's bitter mood had rubbed off. Here she was, a grown woman, making fun of a person's name. *Pretty damned nervy,* she scolded herself, *coming from somebody named Belfa.*

She watched as the young woman—smiling, pretty, petite, with a blond ponytail that flipped and wobbled as she gestured emphatically, tilting her head this way and that, *so* involved, *so* interested, *so* caring— squatted in front of Clay, her small butt bouncing just above the heels of her white Nikes. They were in the center of the glass-walled reha- bilitation room at the Raythune County Medical Center, an open area just off the patient floor that featured a skylight, a row of floor-to- ceiling mirrors, two large blue rubber balls wedged beneath a set of benches, a three-step wooden ladder with a wide landing at the top, and in one corner, a lane of square red plastic mats positioned end to end. Across the way, a set of handrails designated a path. The length of that path was no distance at all, really. Ten yards. But for the people who came to this room for the first time, Bell thought, it might as well have been a marathon.

Clay was slumped over in a wheelchair. Elbows on armrests, hands dangling in his lap, refusing to make eye contact with Dawn. Dark blue sweatpants gapped at his waist and bagged around his ankles, lapping over the tops of his tennis shoes. His gray T-shirt—CAVA-LIERS, it said in bright orange letters, with UNIVERSITY OF VIRGINIA in smaller blue letters beneath it—sagged from his shoulders. His skin had acquired the waxy, dead-yellow pallor that was the can't-miss-it mark of the hospital patient. His hair was as flat and greasy as if he'd combed it with a used spatula. He looked despondent and defeated.

And he was, Bell could discern from her seat on the bench, getting royally pissed off with the pretty young woman named Dawn.

"Okay, Clay—let's give it a try. Up and at 'em," Dawn said. Chirpy voice. Cheerleader's zest, the kind of zest that's willfully oblivious to the score of the game. Or in this case, the mood of the patient. "Come on, sweetie pie. Let's stand up and give it a go, okay?"

At the phrase *sweetie pie,* Clay's head jerked up. Before the *Uh-oh* could finish forming in Bell's mind, his hand shot forward and he'd grabbed Dawn's upper arm. Held it tensely.

"Don't you *ever* call me *sweetie pie*—you hear?" Clay snarled. He was ratcheting up the pressure of his grip. Dawn's face seemed to redden slightly from the pain, but she didn't complain.

"I'm not some goddamned *kid,*" he went on. "You got it? And I'm not some old fart who gets a hard-on every time you stick your boobs in front of my goddamned face. So don't you treat me that way. I'm not your fucking *sweetie pie.* Call me that again and I'll kick you right through that glass wall over there. Still got one good leg left, lady—don't you forget it." He dropped her arm and flung himself against the back of the wheelchair. Looked away. "*Sweetie pie,* my ass," he mumbled.

Dawn was not as flustered as Bell expected her to be. She moved her shoulder up and down, rolled it around in its socket a few times, as if testing to make sure it still operated properly. She was used to this, Bell realized; she was used to the anger, the sullenness, the self-pity. Dealing with it was probably part of her training. Why wouldn't it be?

"Well, Clay, I'll give you this," Dawn said. Game grin. "You've got enough power in that arm to make my job a *lot* easier. Tons of folks have to work on their upper-body strength before they can learn to walk with the prosthetic. Not you." She rubbed her shoulder and winked at him. "Whadda you say, Clay?" she went on. "Wanna try walking with the handrails over there? Give the new leg a trial run?"

"No," he said. "No, I don't."

"Oh, come on, now," Dawn said. Tease in her voice. "Big strong guy like you? Bet you'll be a whiz. Couple of months from now, you'll be moving so fast that nobody'll even know you've got a prosthetic."

Clay looked at her impassively, all rancor gone, and said, "Go to hell, lady."

His indifference was worse than his wrath. More hopeless. His earlier anger, Bell thought, at least had some life in it, some passion. The dead-eyed stare that he offered the physical therapist, his empty voice, were ominous signs.

She wanted to intervene, wanted to cheer him up, but she knew better than to step in and offer cheap platitudes. His father had already tried the inspiration route, as he'd explained to Bell when he called her the night before. *Please come by,* Walter had said. *My boy's not doing so good. They're getting him up already and trying to get him moving, get him used to how things're gonna be from now on, but—but he just ain't taking hold, Mrs. Elkins. Not getting over it. He's mad at everybody. I brought him a bunch of cards from the folks at our church, with everybody offering their best wishes and some nice poetry and such, and you know what he did, Mrs. Elkins? He tore up every last one of them cards and he threw 'em back at me. Them little pieces of paper went everywhere. All over the floor of his room. So I got down on my hands and knees and I picked up all them little pieces of paper, and the whole time I was doin' it, Clay was saying these terrible things. Just terrible. Calling God a lot of bad names. I was ashamed of him, Mrs. Elkins. I was. I love my boy, but he's falling. Falling away from all of us.*

Bell's gaze drifted to the doorway of the rehab room. There stood Walter Meckling. Watching his son. Worry in his eyes. He was hatless now, out of respect for the hospital staff, but his hair still wore the obvious mark of its long daily incarceration beneath a baseball cap, the indentation circling the top part of his head like a greasy halo. His long arms hung straight down at his sides. Walter looked as if he'd been fixed in that spot for a thousand years or so. He was a man who'd made his living from his body, from its strength and its will and its perseverance, and even though he was older now, slower—he couldn't deny it—that body still did his bidding. It still worked hard, every day. Still defined him. He had passed on that powerful body to his only child. Yes, the boy had gotten a good education, Clay had a fine mind. But it was the body, Walter knew, that really mattered. Always had. Always would. What was going to happen to his boy now?

A part of the old Clay must still have been present, Bell surmised, because finally he decided to try. He wheeled himself over to the handrails. He didn't look at Bell. He didn't look at his father. He stared at a spot on the wall, a spot where nothing was.

Bell watched him rise from the chair, a sour expression on his face, chin bunched, jaw set like a parking brake. *Super!* Dawn gushed. *Super-duper!* Clay ignored her and took his first halting, tottering steps. Between every step, he had to stop and breathe heavily. Sweat slickened his forehead. His hands gripped the rails with such ferocity that his arms quivered. Each time he wanted to move forward, he paused for a long time before he lifted one hand from the rail—the other bore down with even more intensity—and moved it half an inch. He wasn't so much walking as falling and repeatedly catching himself. He pushed his good leg out in front of him, then dragged the prosthesis with a short lurch until it caught up, time and time again. The stiffness of his movements, the awkwardness, the flailing, gave Bell a pang deep in her stomach.

She remembered how graceful and agile he'd been when he ran or biked or climbed a ladder. She had never seen him on hunting trips with his father, but he had described the ritual to her on one of their first dates, described it so vividly that she felt as if she'd witnessed it. Clay had told her about hoisting their rifles, then crackling through the woods at dawn in their camouflage pants and tan jackets and floppy hats, pulling the cold air in and out of their lungs as if they were relishing champagne instead of simply breathing, marveling silently at the fingers of frost that curled perfectly around each twig and leaf, feeling the throb and pulse of their own excited heartbeats as they marched for many hours, fanatically alert, tracking the twelve-point buck that had been spotted near Largent's Ridge. They hadn't caught up with him last fall, but *Next year, Next year* had been the shared thought, the mantra. The plan. The hope.

Chapter Forty-Three

Because the sun had gone down, you couldn't tell for sure that Edna's house was pink. Its color was lost in the dying light. The house seemed to merge with the woods that reared up behind it; those woods were a tangle of dark gray that was rapidly becoming indistinguishable from the sky reaching down to meet it.

"Matt. Hey, Matt."

Calling his name, Bell rapped on the screen door of the garage apartment. Just above the door was a lightbulb jutting out from the siding, and it offered a vaguely triangular swath of illumination.

She'd knocked on Edna's door first. No answer. Then Bell remembered: This was choir-practice night at Rising Souls Baptist Church. Edna had a frail but very pretty soprano voice. Bell had heard her sing when Lee Ann invited Bell and Carla to a Christmas program last year. Edna's brief solo in "O Holy Night" was a showstopper.

"Matt," she said, knocking harder.

She could have called him on his cell, could have checked to see if he was home, but she'd decided to take a chance. To just drop by, as she'd done the other night. This time, however, felt much different from that earlier spontaneous visit. This time, she was going to tell him to pack his things and leave.

The weather-warped door swung open with a mild complaint.

Matt, in a red flannel shirt and gray sweatpants, gave Bell a bemused smile.

"Hey," he said.

"Mind some company?"

"Course not." He opened the screen door, stepped forward, and pulled the door shut behind him. "Hang on. Edna's got a couple of extra lawn chairs at the side of the house."

"I can't come in? I was hoping you'd play bartender again."

He looked sheepish. "Ordinarily, that'd be fine. But, uh—"

"Socks on the floor? Or worse—porn on the laptop? A hooker on the foldout couch?"

He laughed. "Nothing that interesting. Place is a mess. And besides, it's nice tonight. I was thinking of coming out here to sit, anyway." He retrieved the chairs and arranged them on the small concrete pad that served as his front porch. In the breast pocket of his shirt, Bell noticed, was the small white tip of what looked to be a much-folded-over piece of paper. She'd seen it before, she realized. Same spot, in every shirt he wore.

"Town's still pretty raw, I bet," he said.

"Hanging in there."

"Tough bunch."

"Absolutely."

"And Clay? How's he doing?"

She let some time go by before replying.

"I don't know," she said, because she didn't.

Above the seamed rectangle of concrete upon which they sat, a tiny carousel of insects had clustered round the bulb. Bell looked at Matt's face. It appeared even more angular than usual in the blunt light of that bulb, the bones prominent, the cheeks hollow, the eyes flat and unreflective. He looked pensive tonight, Bell thought. Like a lot of the men she'd known in her life—hell, it was true of the women, too—Matt had a store of darkness inside him that would not be dispelled by the light from any source.

"There was this Iraqi," he said. His voice was soft, almost lilting.

"When I met Georgette and Joyce, they reminded me of him and his brother. Good men. Honorable men. Ran a little grocery store. Their pride and joy. Put everything they had into it—not just money, but time. Heart. Life. And then one day—boom. There's an explosion. Might have been shelling by American troops, but—just as likely— could've been an IED planted by the locals. Nothing left of the place. Just dust and blood."

"So they were killed in the blast?"

"Worse. They lived."

She found herself trying to visualize the vast distance between a small city in Iraq and Acker's Gap, her mind crossing deserts and continents and oceans, flying over brown land and green land and then blue water and green land again, but as hard as she tried, she couldn't do it; the arms of her imagination wouldn't stretch that far. She could not hold both places in her mind at the same time.

Was Matt, she wondered, able to do it? Could he sit here in the middle of the West Virginia mountains and see back there, as well? Was his life in Iraq still that vivid to him?

"Hey," she said. "Need to ask you about something."

"Shoot."

"The sheriff got an alert from the FBI. They raided a place in D.C. that's very likely a hideout for terrorists. And at least one of them might be headed to West Virginia. Why? I mean, why would they come here? No high-tech facilities. No nuclear secrets. Just some old coal mines."

"Look, Bell," he said, and his voice had a sternness to it that she'd not expected. "I know you think you're this isolated little town, stuck way up here in the hills, far from everywhere—but you're not. No place is isolated. Not anymore. These days, everything's connected. Every spot on the globe is linked to everywhere else."

"But isn't that why you came here in the first place? You said you wanted someplace off the beaten path, tucked off by itself and—"

"Okay, so I did." Peeved now. He didn't want to debate.

She didn't, either. "Listen, Matt—I've got to ask you. I don't want to, but I have to. We had that terrible explosion. And nobody's sure yet about the cause. I have to know—is there anything you've done that might be related to—?"

His interruption came quickly. "Let's review a few things, okay? First—I don't know about any terrorist network in D.C. If I did, I would've reported it a long time ago." A note of condescension creased his voice. "I'm one of the good guys, remember? And second—look, I'm sorry about what happened to your friends. I've told you that. But it was an old building. You said that yourself. Could've been a gas leak, yes? Isn't that the most likely scenario? An accident?"

She didn't answer his question. Instead she said, "I need to be real clear here, Matt. If anything you've done brings any trouble here, if—"

"I *told* you," he said. "I wasn't a soldier, for Christ's sake. I was an *interrogator*. Remember?"

"I remember," she said. She moved in her chair. Re-crossed her legs. She was buying just a little bit more time. He wasn't going to like what she had to say. And so this might be the last conversation she would ever have with him. It couldn't be helped, but it made her deeply sad.

"There's more," Bell said.

"What?"

His voice sounded peevish now. Nervous, testy. Not smooth. Not self-possessed. Not like the Matt Harless she'd known all those years ago, her friend and running buddy.

"The shooting at the courthouse," Bell said, "on the day you arrived."

"What about it? It was some redneck, right? Some disgruntled old coot with a shotgun and a grudge?"

"Maybe." Bell waited. "We found a boot print, Matt, that might've been made by the shooter. It was from a foreign shoe."

"So?"

"So there are just too many questions. And too many coincidences."

"Meaning what?" he said. Voice tight. Challenge in his tone.

"Meaning I want you to leave." Her own voice was firmer than she'd expected it to be. "Can I prove that you being here has anything to do with all this? No. No, I can't. But you're the only thing that's changed around here, Matt. You're the only new thing." She held up, assuming he would argue with her, plead his case. He didn't, and so she went on. "You want more, Matt? Okay, here's more. I watched you damn near take Jeff Hinerman's head off the other day. You're hiding something. I don't know what it is. Your business. But I'm not taking any chances. Best for everybody, I think, if you just clear out. Move on. Right away."

He looked at her a long time before replying. In the absence of human voices, Bell was acutely aware of the nonhuman ones; the crickets and cicadas and tree frogs in the woods behind them had revved up their racket. It sounded like an amateur orchestra perpetually tuning up.

"We talked about this before," he said. "I can stay if I want to. For as long as I want to. I'm not breaking any laws. There's not a damned thing you can do about it. "

Bell let the silence between them linger. She was using the time to think through the thesis that someone would've followed him here. Matt was a pro. A skilled veteran. Trained by the CIA. He'd survived missions in some of the most dangerous regions in the world. Would he really have been so clumsy and careless as to leave an easy trail for someone to follow? It wasn't plausible. Didn't make sense.

Still, she wanted him gone. She was weary of the distraction his presence had created. Weary of the questions.

"Yes," she said. "You could stick around. Absolutely. Long as you're not doing anything illegal—we'd have to leave you the hell alone. But I've got to ask you, Matt—why? Why stay here, anyway? Isn't there somewhere else you'd like to be? A loved one you miss— and who misses you? For Christ's sake, Matt, you've got your whole damned life ahead of you. Isn't there somebody special you want to spend it with?"

Bell was thinking about Eddie Geyer and Maddie Trimble. About Nick and Mary Sue. She was thinking about the passions that bind people to each other, passions that can defy rational explanation but that constitute the fuel for so much of human endeavor. And it wasn't just romantic passion. There were other kinds: She thought about Maddie and Lucinda. About her own passion for Carla and for Shirley. About her passion for West Virginia. About the ache that came over you, that tore through your soul, even, when you contemplated leaving it or losing it.

Had Matt Harless ever felt that? Had he ever known what it was like to want someone with a longing so intense that you'd swear you couldn't take your next breath until you'd touched a certain person's skin, until you'd inhaled the smell of that skin, until—if the person was far away, if you were separated—you'd heard that precious voice again, just one more time? A longing that made you capable of anything, any behavior, that would bring your beloved close again?

He shifted his position in the lawn chair, a chair that suddenly seemed too small for his tall body, too flimsy to accommodate the tension in his limbs. Matt's hands, Bell saw, were curved tightly around the little plastic grips, hanging on, digging in, as if he were braced for an invisible storm. She had first gotten to know this man a long time ago—but wondered, now, if she'd ever really known him at all.

Something moved in his eyes, fleeting and stark, like the shadow of a hawk passing across the side of a mountain, and then he said, "I don't want to cause you any trouble, Bell. I'll clear out first thing tomorrow."

Her cell rang while she drove home, her headlights the only illumination as she moved through the dark streets of Acker's Gap. Those headlights startled several raccoons who were making their slow, dawdling, fat-bottomed way across the street. A possum—its low, scuttling body as white as a worm in the glare of the lights, its beady red eyes staring into hers as if it had correctly guessed all her secrets—was very nearly flattened by the Explorer's front tires, even though she was going less than twenty miles per hour.

"Elkins."

"Ma'am, it's Deputy Mathers."

"Hey, Charlie."

"Just finished up with Kendra Greenough, ma'am. I'll be e-mailing you my notes in the A.M., but thought you might want a quick summary."

"I do."

Mathers had worked with Nick even longer than Greenough—the two of them had started out as deputies under the previous sheriff, Larry Rucker—but in recent years, Mathers had grown sloppy, moody, despite his devotion to self-help books. The can-do mantras, Bell theorized, had turned him bitter and resentful: To Mathers, the world had yet to take note of his positive attitude and just kept sending the same old crap his way. Since the explosion at Ike's, however, Charlie Mathers had straightened up. He was thorough and reliable again.

"Well," he said, "the girl was crying so hard that I had trouble understanding her—I guess Greg and Lola gave her a real good talking-to about withholding information from a criminal investigation—but, yeah, Marcy Hillman and Shawn Doggett did go out for a month or so last year. Kendra said there wasn't much to it, really. Once Shawn hooked up with Lucinda, he forgot about Marcy Hillman right quick."

"How did Marcy take the breakup?"

"Kendra says she was okay with it. Says Marcy moved on pretty quick, too. I went on out to the Hillman place tonight to get Marcy's side of things. Soon as I was able to persuade old Bert to lower his shotgun," Mathers said, a note of *I'm sick and tired of the man's infernal nonsense* front and center in his voice, "I had a nice chat with the girl. 'Course Marcy started crying, too, to beat the band—what is it with these teenage girls and all the tears? Anyways, she said she's been dating Judd Hensley ever since, so losing Shawn was no big deal to her. But I don't know." Mathers sighed. "These kids. I swear, they get around. You know, Mrs. Elkins, the whole time I was in high school, I had one date. Senior prom. And that was it."

"Different world today, Charlie."

"Ain't it the truth."

"Thanks for getting on this right away."

A moment passed before he replied.

"Hate to mention it," Mathers said, "but it just makes things harder, don't it? The things we're finding out? I mean, it sounds funny to say out loud, but I'm kind of hoping some crazy stranger killed the Trimble girl. Hell, I'd rather have a serial killer running around these parts instead of—instead of having to believe that somebody close to her coulda done it."

"Know what you mean," Bell conceded. "Turns out that her best friend had a damned good reason to hold a grudge against Lucinda. And lied to us about it. So now we've officially got ourselves one more suspect."

Chapter Forty-Four

It was Nick's idea.

Just go talk to her, Bell, he'd said, as they had wound up their work the day before. *She won't bite. And she might have some information you can use. Maybe tie up some loose ends.*

So here she was, first thing the next morning, walking past the rows of kitschy knickknacks and cloyingly cute ornaments—*It's like a landfill,* Bell thought, *only better organized*—that adorned Maddie Trimble's lawn.

Maddie was everything Bell Elkins despised about some of the people who lived in this area. She had raised eccentricity to an art form, and helped perpetuate the stereotype that "mountain folk" were exotic characters running around in bare feet and cutoff shorts, mixing up weeds and herbs to make nutty potions intended to heal everything from heartaches to hemorrhoids.

"Can I help you?"

Maddie had come out on the porch. Long burgundy skirt. Peach-colored T-shirt. *Heading me off,* Bell thought. *Wants me out of here just as soon as possible.*

Well, that makes two of us, lady.

"Yeah," Bell said. "Think it's time we had a talk."

No reply, so Bell continued. "We want to find out who was

responsible for your daughter's death. But it's hard. It's hard because—and I hope I can be frank with you—I don't think you've been entirely forthcoming with us."

Bell half suspected that Maddie Trimble would point a thin finger at her and utter a strange guttural chant to summon a few lightning bolts along with the devil's eternal vengeance on her immortal soul—or perhaps just fling an iron skillet at her head.

Instead, she looked at Bell with blank eyes. Thirty seconds passed. Bell was aware of how quiet it was out here. Eerily quiet. Even the birds seemed to have hesitated in mid-song, the better to observe Maddie Trimble's next move.

"Well," Maddie said. "Guess you have a point."

She gave Bell a halfhearted, waist-high wave, apparently a request that she join her on the top porch step. The two women sat down side by side.

"What I need to know," Bell said, "is why you lied about being home the night your daughter died."

Maddie shrugged. "Like I told Nick, I was ashamed. I'd asked Eddie to come back and help me talk some sense into Lucinda—and here I was, staying out late, spending time with him that had nothing to do with our child."

What you mean is: screwing him till both of you were cross-eyed, Bell thought.

"Yes," Bell said out loud. "But that's not all of it. When Eddie first came to town, you and he sat down with Lucinda and discussed her pregnancy, right?"

Maddie nodded.

"And what did she say?" Bell asked.

Maddie's head dropped. She started picking at the hem of her skirt.

"She said what she always said, every time I gave her my little speech," Maddie said. "The speech about how she might think she was in love with Shawn Doggett, but that at her age, she couldn't know what love really was. I talked. And Eddie talked. But it didn't matter. She was bound and determined to have that baby. And frankly, it didn't seem to have a lot to do with Shawn."

"You must've been disappointed."

"I was. Terribly. I mean, I felt like she was making the same mistake I'd made—settling. Compromising. Just plain old giving up. Letting this place win. Instead of fighting back."

"You wanted the best for her."

"And I had to let *her* be the judge of that, you know? Not me. Not Eddie. Not this town." Maddie shifted her feet on the porch step. Bell had noticed the Birkenstocks right away, thought *Figures,* then she'd forgotten about them; now she noticed them again. "Eddie and I," Maddie went on, "tried over and over again to talk to her about putting the baby up for adoption. She wouldn't hear of it."

"She wanted to raise the baby herself."

"Absolutely. She said that the child was her responsibility. She wouldn't walk away. Wasn't right."

Bell waited a beat, then asked, "Do you think there's any way— any way at all—that Shawn Doggett could've killed her? Accidentally, maybe? After an argument?"

"I can't see it."

"How about Wendy Doggett? She's so protective of Shawn. Or Alton Doggett. Might one or both of them have wanted to get Lucinda out of the picture? Rescue their son from what they might have seen as a trap?"

"I don't know. Maybe, but it—it just doesn't feel right to me. Doesn't feel like that's what happened."

Bell scratched the back of her neck. Felt the moisture there. It was getting hot; today's high was supposed to be 72, but it had crossed that mark before 10 A.M.

Time to go. First, though, she had to indulge herself. Satisfy her curiosity. Rhonda Lovejoy would never forgive her if she didn't.

"So," Bell said, "you and Eddie. What's going to happen now?"

The silence stretched out just a hair too long.

"We're going to give it another try," Maddie finally said, and Bell could almost hear the blush in her voice. "To be together, I mean. Lucinda's death brought us close again. Only way I can figure it. We're both grieving. And Eddie's trying so hard. Gonna stick around. He's got a lot of work to do—that little stunt he pulled the other day at the high school is pure Eddie, and he'll pay for it—but he's gonna give it his best shot. No drinking, no running around. He promised me. That's all I can ask."

Bell was tempted to repeat the old saw, the one about leopards and their spots, but she didn't. None of her lookout.

She stood up. Maddie stood up, too. Now that Bell had concluded her business here, their mutual antipathy drifted into the picture again, like a cloud crossing the sun.

"You know we'll never be friends, right?" Maddie said. "Cards on the table. I think you're an arrogant bitch."

"That's okay," Bell replied cheerfully. "Cards on the table? I think you're a lazy, self-righteous flake."

They both felt better now. The air was clear again. Bell started back down the walk. She went slowly, making sure Maddie understood that the purpose of her languid pace was to enable a thorough and pro-longed sneer at the items spread out on spindly tables on either side of that walk.

She paused when she reached the edge of the yard. Turned around. Maddie was still poised on the top step, watching her.

"You should also know," Bell said, "but just in case you don't, I'm going to say it. I'll move heaven and earth to find out who killed your girl. My word on it."

"I know that," Maddie said. "Always have."

Chapter Forty-Five

Deputy Harrison apologized repeatedly for calling and awakening her.

"No problem," Bell mumbled.

The bedroom was dark, but at the sound of the ringtone, she'd known exactly where to find her cell on the bedside table. No groping, no slapping, no knocking over the clock or the half-gone roll of Tums or the paperback copy of *The House of Mirth*—she was reading it at Nick's behest, after he'd sighed deeply one day and said she was "as self-destructively stubborn as Lily Bart" and Bell had given him an uncomprehending look—or the reading glasses or the water glass, all of which she stowed there.

"I'm just so sorry to call at this hour, Mrs. Elkins—I mean, I know it's the middle of the night—but the sheriff said—"

"It's fine, Deputy." Bell sat up. Coughed. Groggy, still half-enmeshed in some unrecoverable dream, she squinted at the digital clock and took in its sorry-about-this display: 3:17 A.M.

"I'm putting you on speakerphone," she said into her cell, "so I can finish getting dressed while we're talking. Okay?"

She left her bed and flipped the wall switch—recoiling from the sudden splash of light—and pulled on a pair of trousers. She fingered her way through the items in her closet, looking for a sweater.

"Alton and Wendy Doggett," said Deputy Harrison, her voice now filling Bell's bedroom, "are in custody. Domestic disturbance— but while we were at the Doggett home, we found the engagement ring that Shawn Doggett gave Lucinda Trimble. And the other thing you need to know is that Wendy Doggett confessed to killing Lucinda."

It was a lot to absorb, but Bell assimilated it rapidly and stayed in motion. She was looking around for her wristwatch. Nightstand? No. Top of the dresser? Yes.

"What the hell happened?" she said.

"Well, the dispatcher got a 911 call about two thirty A.M. It was the housekeeper. Big fight, she said. Deputy Greenough and I got there at about the same time. Heard a lot of shouting and breaking glass. So we decided to go in."

"Okay." The word might have sounded slightly muffled to Harrison; Bell was pulling on a white sweater over her head. And slipping into attorney mode, speaking as if she had to explain the deputies' uninvited entrance to a skeptical judge: "Suspecting that an assault was in progress, you forced your way into the premises." Now Bell was heading down the stairs. She didn't need a light; she knew these stairs well. Reaching the bottom, she paused to turn on the overhead light to illuminate the front hallway—because finding her car keys was another matter entirely.

Lucky break. They were in a small tray on the table beneath the oval mirror. She'd put them back where they belonged. What were the odds?

"When we entered," Harrison continued, "we immediately saw evidence of a violent and prolonged struggle involving multiple rooms. Furniture thrown around. Couches, chairs, tables. Some glass objects had hit the floor and broken. We heard shouting. We followed the sounds—there was a lot of screaming, too, and a lot of obscenities from both a male voice and a female voice—and we ended up back in what appeared to be the master bedroom, where we found Alton Doggett and his wife. The bedroom was in disarray." Harrison paused momentarily to breathe. Her habit was to speak quickly, and sometimes her ambition ran ahead of her air supply. "Mrs. Doggett was in pretty bad shape, ma'am. She had a black eye and a gash on her forehead, and her wrist was red and swollen. Looked like somebody'd grabbed her and slung her into a wall."

"And Mr. Doggett?"

"He was sitting on the bed. There was a strong smell of alcohol, and when we approached him, his behavior was consistent with that of an individual who has consumed copious quantities of an intoxicant."

In other words, Bell thought, *Alton Doggett was drunk off his ass.*

"Okay," she said. "What happened next, Deputy?"

Still carrying her cell, so that she could hear Harrison's report during her drive over to the courthouse, Bell paused in the kitchen for a glass of water. Her throat felt parched, sleep-gummed. When she activated the switch, the kitchen seemed to leap to life, as if the inanimate objects—stove, refrigerator, table, sink—had been startled into brightness, rousted out of a dreamy doze, just as she had.

"Well, ma'am," Harrison said, "we asked Mrs. Doggett if she wanted us to call an ambulance for her, and she said, 'No, I'm fine.' Our next priority was to restrain Mr. Doggett, and—"

"How about the boys?" Bell interrupted. "Shawn and Ketchum."

"I don't know, ma'am. I didn't see them. Deputy Greenough asked about them—he addressed his question to the housekeeper who'd made the 911 call—and she said they always slept through the altercations. Well, she didn't call them 'altercations.' She called them 'knockdown, drag-outs.' "

"Plural."

"Yes, ma'am."

Bell twisted the tap, filling her glass for the third time. "Go on, Deputy."

"As we attempted to restrain Mr. Doggett—he was quite strenuous in his objections—Mrs. Doggett's jewelry box was knocked off the dresser. Contents went all over the place. We saw the ring right away. Matched the description in the file."

Bell pulled the heavy front door closed behind her. Moved rapidly down the steps. She hadn't added a jacket and didn't miss it; the night was mild, with little wind. Only two stars were visible, pinned to separate corners of the sky, separated by a vast black curve of space that stretched over her head like a cathedral arch. In another few seconds she was driving down Shelton Avenue, cell on the seat beside her, still on speakerphone, passing the dark, quiet homes of her neighbors. Envying, if she were honest about it, the peace of their sleep.

"Minute we got to the courthouse," Harrison said, "Wendy Doggett confessed. Started talking and wouldn't stop. Claims she killed Lucinda, then took the ring off the dead girl's finger, exited the vehicle, and then let it roll into the river."

"Her rights—you'd read them to her?"

"First thing."

"Hope her attorney was present."

"Yes, ma'am. Serena Crumpler. She's been trying to get Mrs. Doggett to hush up, but it's not working."

Chapter Forty-Six

Bell slapped the case file down on the table. It was a flimsy metal one, gray top, gray legs, with two mismatched chairs on either side, and it shimmied even from the slight weight of the file.

"I'm not convinced," she said.

Wendy Doggett sat on the opposite side. Next to her was Serena Crumpler, a very thin young woman with a beaklike nose and a sharp chin and dark straight hair that switched across her shoulders when she turned her head. Despite the hour, Serena looked fresh and ready for combat, as if, even in sleep, she'd been building up her strength for just this sort of encounter. She was a defense attorney with whom Bell had tangled on several occasions. Her black eyes glittered. In two days she would be twenty-eight years old.

Bell took a seat across from them. The file slap had been pure theater. She'd hoped to rattle Wendy Doggett, to shake her out of what appeared to be a dazed complacency. Wendy looked as if she hadn't moved since her attorney escorted her to the metal chair.

Except, Bell knew, to sign the confession that she'd recited to Deputy Greenough fifteen minutes ago.

Just before entering this room, one of two small, drab, unventilated boxes that Sheriff Fogelsong maintained for interrogations, Bell had accepted the folder from a grim-faced Greenough. She skimmed the contents. Wendy's statement was decidedly light on specifics. In fact, it was downright skimpy, as skimpy and unconvincing as a tenth-grader's term paper, the kind finished two minutes before the start of class after a Pop-Tart-fueled all-nighter.

Bell gave Wendy Doggett a long, appraising look across the table. This meeting was a world away from their last one, the tense encounter in Bell's office during which Wendy had been sneering and defiant. Bell wondered if Wendy was pondering the contrast as well. The air held a faint sparkle of cologne, improbable in this dour gray place. Wendy wore a coral-colored dress and—Bell had glimpsed them under the table when she'd entered the room—white heels. Doubtless these were the clothes she'd been wearing the day before, a day that had extended into the night and now the next day.

The bruises on Wendy's neck and cheek were in full bloom: red, black, yellow, blue. They gave her face the shiny veneer of an all-day sucker, a brazen swirl of primary colors. A long diagonal cut on her forehead was outlined in dried blood. Her swollen right wrist looked hot to the touch.

How often does he do this to her? Bell wondered. She knew, as did every prosecutor, the ritual followed by all abusers, as if there were a handbook available for download from the Internet: Nobody ever did it just once.

And yet Bell's office had no record of any complaints, domestic or otherwise, against Alton Doggett. She'd had Lee Ann check it out a week ago. Not surprising, really. Wendy, like a lot of women, had never gone to the law for relief.

"Am I to understand," Serena said, faux umbrage causing her to rock back in her seat, "that you're skeptical about my client's description of events?" Hand splayed on her chest, as if checking for heart palpitations caused by the very thought. Serena had perfected a kind of wide-eyed, earnest incredulity, like a sensitive child who's just been told about the death of a pet.

"Yes," Bell said. "Tend to get that way when someone isn't truthful. Of course, there are other words you may prefer, Serena, to describe Mrs. Doggett's behavior. 'Fibbing,' maybe? Or 'prevaricating'?"

"Ms. Elkins." Serena put a protective palm on Wendy's forearm. "Let's not be sarcastic, okay? This is hard enough for Mrs. Doggett, Lord knows, without her having to endure your well-known propensity to be a little mean and rude. Fact is, I have advised Mrs. Doggett against confessing to this crime. Repeatedly and vehemently. But she insists. And it's her choice. All I can do at this point is make certain that she's treated with respect—and not badgered or insulted or manipulated."

The door of the interrogation room smacked open. Hick Leonard— thin gray hair still bearing the evidence of a too-recently-truncated sleep, complexion a greasy and waxen shade of *I haven't been up at this hour since my paper route in fourth grade,* shirttail half-tucked— entered. With a nod at Bell, he pulled out the seat beside her, causing a screechy floor scrape that made everyone wince.

"Serena," Hick said.

"Hickey."

Bell was glad to see the assistant prosecutor. All interviews in this room were videotaped, but she still liked to have a colleague present. When she'd arrived at the courthouse, she had asked Deputy Greenough to call him. Nick was answering another 911 call in the southern part of the county.

"And so," Bell said, "I was just about to get to the part where I ask Mrs. Doggett here to explain to us how she did it. How she managed to strangle Lucinda Trimble. Remove the engagement ring. Leave the vehicle. Watch it slide into the Bitter River. And then get herself home again, without anyone else in her household being aware of her absence. Or helping her in any way. And why—in the first place— Lucinda Trimble would have left her house to meet her. It's not like Wendy here was her BFF. Frankly, Mrs. Doggett," she said, returning her gaze to the woman with the damaged face who sat impassively across from her, "this doesn't make a lot of sense to me."

Wendy didn't blink. The nicely manicured hands that she'd placed flat on the tabletop were still. She looked at her attorney, and then back at Bell, without a twitch or a flinch or a flicker.

"Go ahead," Serena said.

"I did it." Wendy's voice was so empty of inflection that it might as well have been computer generated. "I told the Trimble girl that Shawn shouldn't marry her. Wasn't right. She was ruining both of their lives. But she wouldn't listen. Refused to let him go. So I killed her and took off the ring. That ring belongs in my family—it's the only thing of any real value we ever had—and I wanted it back. I put it in my jewelry box. It was me." She looked down at the file folder and frowned. "I'm telling you I did it. Do all of the picky little details really matter?"

"Yes, Mrs. Doggett, I'm afraid they do." Bell lifted the folder again, just for the fleeting pleasure of dropping it on the table once more. "We have to be persuaded that you're speaking the truth. That you're not protecting someone else. Taking the blame. Covering up for the real killer."

"It was me. I keep trying to say that."

"And I keep trying to say," Bell replied, "that I don't believe you."

Chapter Forty-Seven

At 9 A.M., when the rest of the courthouse employees were just starting their day, Bell and Hick had been questioning Wendy Doggett for some five hours. They'd taken turns—Bell was aggressive and bad tempered, while Hick's approach was sweet, gentle, and commiserating—but neither technique succeeded in budging the woman from her story:

She had acted alone. Called Lucinda Trimble and asked her to meet at the Bitter River. Left her own car along the road to go sit with Lucinda in the Subaru. Gave her an ultimatum: *Hands off my boy. Or else.*

She'd offered the girl money, Wendy said. Thousands of dollars. *Name your price,* she'd told Lucinda. *Just name it.* Money for child support, money for college, money to help Lucinda's mother—to whom Wendy referred in her official statement as "that pathetic woman with the awful hair, who lives in that horribly trashy little house."

At 9:07 A.M., Bell looked at Serena Crumpler.

"We've done all we can do here, Serena," she said.

"So you accept her confession? And we can talk about a plea deal?"

Serena now looked weary as well, even though she'd done little more than sit there, hour after hour, as first Bell and then Hickey had questioned her client, by turns hectoring or sympathetic, blackly scornful or hand-holdingly cordial, as their respective personalities had dictated.

"No," Bell said. "But now it's up to you, Serena."

"Me?"

"Yes." Bell rose. She signaled to Hick that they were leaving. "We're going to take a break. And when we return, I fully expect that you will have talked some sense into Mrs. Doggett here. Explained to her that when we find out what really happened at the river that night— and we will—her little mea culpa act will end up hurting, not helping, her son. Or sons."

Bell retrieved the file folder. Hick's hand was already on the doorknob.

"Mrs. Elkins," Wendy said.

Bell and Hick stopped.

"Yes?"

Wendy's face remained blank. Unreadable.

"My husband," she said. "Where is he now?"

Bell was disappointed—she'd hoped for a last-minute breakthrough, hoped for the truth about what had happened at the river that night—but maybe this would constitute another bargaining chip. Another bit of leverage to use against the epically stubborn Wendy Doggett. Her husband had been booked into the Raythune County Jail on assault charges shortly after Wendy's questioning began. His attorney—Barry Haines, a big, bluff, black-haired, and wide-bellied lawyer from Swanville, known for his handlebar mustache and his permanent thirst for Wild Turkey—had secured Alton's release in what seemed like minutes.

"I can give you that information," Bell said in an amiable, *let's make a deal* voice, "but only if you start cooperating. Only if you tell us who you're protecting."

Wendy laughed. It was the first natural sound she had uttered throughout the long ordeal of the night. Her laugh was so startlingly sharp that it seemed to smack the concrete-block walls of the interrogation room like a big open palm.

"Heavenly days," Wendy said. "Please don't misunderstand. I don't give a rat's ass what happens to that bastard. Just curious, is all."

Chapter Forty-Eight

Confessions, Bell reminded herself, were good for the soul—and they were pretty damned advantageous for prosecutors, too. They saved time, money, trouble. They streamlined and speeded up the sometimes slow, clumsy, and herky-jerky journey to justice. Juries loved confessions, even if the confessors subsequently recanted; the human species seemed hard-wired to believe that if you'd ever raised your hand and blurted, "I did it," then—even if you later proved that you'd been tricked or coerced into so blurting—nothing could ever quite scrape the slate clean again. Judges, too, appreciated the neatness and efficiency of a confession, particularly during hunting season, when in-and-out trials were especially cherished.

Yet Wendy Doggett's story troubled Bell. The loose ends. The niggling implausibities. A great many cases, Bell knew, turned on the counterintuitive. *If it's logic you love,* she'd once told a young attorney who had come seeking career advice, *then steer clear of criminal law.* But the idea of Wendy Doggett—small boned, not notably athletic—possessing the strength to kill a healthy young woman with her bare hands and then leap from a rolling car was hard to accept.

Bell sat in her office later that afternoon, flicking the tip of a pencil against a white sheet of paper on her desk. The random gray dashes looked like spilled pepper.

The morning had been long, tense, and busy. After a stop at home to change into a black linen suit and pale yellow cotton blouse— the day was heating up, and Bell couldn't wait to get out of her sweater—she'd come back, ready to return numerous phone messages from Barry Haines. Along with Haines, Lee Ann announced, her callers had included Shawn and Ketchum Doggett, asking about their mother.

"Ketchum," Bell said. He'd answered after only half a ring. "This is Belfa Elkins. Are you and your brother okay?"

"We're okay," he said impatiently. "Look, we need to know about Mom—"

"She's here at the courthouse. She's safe. But I have a question. Why didn't you and Shawn wake up last night? Your parents were tearing the place apart."

"We both sleep with our iPods. Been doing it since we were in middle school. Easier that way."

"Understood." Bell began flicking the pencil tip on the paper again, making marks on top of marks. "Look. I'll be honest with you. Early this morning, your mother confessed to killing Lucinda Trimble."

"What the hell—?"

"We don't believe her."

He was quiet for a moment. "You don't."

"No. We don't. She may have had something to do with it, but she didn't do it by herself."

"So who—?"

"We don't know."

While she waited for him to react, Bell realized all at once just how much she liked Ketchum Doggett. She liked him even though she sensed he was hiding something. Maybe it was related to Lucinda Trimble; maybe it wasn't. She didn't know if he was implicated in the crime or not—the Doggett family was awash in secrets and lies, and she would be sorting them out in the hours ahead—but she liked this kid, no matter what. She liked his grit. She liked the way he'd responded to his paralyzing injury—with work and drive, not self-pity. She even liked his quick-strike anger, which reminded her so much of the anger she'd had when she was younger—a cleansing, purifying anger. A righteous anger.

Hell. She still had it now.

"Look," Bell said. "I know how this feels, okay? You're upset. Confused. You don't know what to believe right now. But listen. It's not always going to be this way. Your family isn't you. You're a part of them, but you don't have to *be* them." His silence wasn't just silence, Bell sensed; it was a listening silence. "I can tell you this. You do get over it. The things your family does to you—it's not your destiny, okay? You were born and raised here, so you may have heard a little something about my father. Well, it's true. My father was a rotten low-life sonofabitch. I never even knew my mother. And my sister just got out of prison. But their lives are not my life, Ketchum. Only person I have to answer for is *me*. Only actions I have to justify are mine." She rarely talked about her past to anyone, much less a kid she barely knew. But it felt right and so she'd done it.

"Okay." There was a muffled, choked-up sound to his voice. "Will you—will you tell Mom that I'm here? That I love her?"

"I'll tell her."

The conversation with Barry Haines was shorter, curter. Lee Ann called his office and, when he came on the line, she pointed at Bell to let her know he'd picked up.

"I understand," Haines said in his buttery voice, "that Mrs. Doggett has retained separate counsel."

Bell swore she could hear the clink of the ice cubes in his glass. Then she corrected herself. *Hell. He'd drink it neat.*

"That's right. Serena Crumpler."

"And no charges will be brought against Mr. Doggett?"

"His wife says she won't press assault charges, despite our strong recommendation that she do just that. So—no. Not at this time."

"And there is—" Haines paused. Smacked his lips. Cogitating, Bell assumed. Or maybe just savoring a recent sip. "—there is, shall we say, no *other* matter about which Mr. Doggett's involuntary presence might be required?"

He's heard about Wendy's confession, Bell thought, *and he wants to find out if she implicated her husband in any way.* Gossip leaked out of a county courthouse like chicken broth through a slotted spoon.

"No," she said. "Not at this time."

"Well, then," Haines said, voice brightening, "much as I enjoy dealing with the fine law enforcement professionals of Raythune County, I believe our business is concluded, ma'am."

"Hold on. Is Mr. Doggett at all concerned about his wife? She'll remain in our custody. Surely he'd like to know about her physical and emotional state?"

A pause. Now Bell really did hear the plop and slosh of liquid added to a glass.

"Why, naturally, ma'am," Haines said. "How *is* Mrs. Doggett? I know my client would appreciate an update. He's terribly concerned about her."

"How touching."

Her sarcasm seemed to press some hidden spring in Haines, releasing a near-to-the-surface store of hatefulness that was far closer to his actual character, Bell knew, than was the cordial banter.

"You listen here, lady," he said, in a voice that bristled with menace and with cold savvy. "Alton Doggett's put up with a hell of a lot from that bitch. Without him and his money, she'd be sweeping off the front stoop of a trailer somewhere and lining up once a month for the free cheese. I told him to cut her loose *years* ago. Won't do it, he says, till his boys are raised. But as far as we're concerned, Mrs. Doggett can go screw herself, after which she can rot in hell."

Chapter Forty-Nine

Arriving at the courthouse the next morning, Bell paused in the hall outside the open door of her office for ten seconds, luxuriating in the deliciously come-hither smell of coffee. Lee Ann already had a pot going. No surprise there.

The surprise was that Lee Ann wasn't alone. Marcy Hillman sat on a small chair in the outer office, black hair falling across her face as she hunched over her cell, thumbs twitching, clearly in the midst of an intense exchange of texts. She wore black leggings and an oversized white jersey that hung off one shoulder with strategic nonchalance.

"Morning, Belfa," Lee Ann said. "Miss Hillman here says she'd like to have a word."

They talked in Bell's office. Marcy said yes to coffee, which surprised Bell; then she remembered that Carla had started drinking coffee—secretly at first—at fourteen. *Hell, Mom,* Carla had said, compounding the revelation of her caffeine habit with a curse word, *it's not like I smoke, okay? Give me a freakin' break.*

"Sorry to bother you, Mrs. Elkins," Marcy said. "But I just thought—I mean—"

She was having a hard time. Hoping to put her at ease, Bell said, "School day, isn't it?"

"We're off. Parent–teacher conferences."

Bell nodded. She felt a little jab of sadness. With her daughter no longer attending Acker's Gap High School, she didn't know the schedule anymore.

"I had to come by," Marcy said, "because I wanted to say I'm sorry." She blushed. The redness spread from her cheeks to her throat. "For the necklace and all. It was really stupid to ask Kendra to hide it. And I'm sorry for not telling you about me and Shawn. I figured that as long as he kept quiet about it, then I was safe. That's all I wanted, I think—to be safe."

"You were scared. Of how it might look."

"Yeah." Shy nod. "Yeah. But the thing is, Mrs. Elkins, I wasn't jealous of Lucinda. Swear."

Bell let her gaze drift to a thick black stack of law books on her desk, knowing that the lack of eye contact would make Marcy Hillman nervous. Nervous people, in Bell's experience, were less able to stick with prefabricated stories.

"Really, Marcy? But even if you weren't jealous, wasn't it kind of awkward to be friends with Lucinda? With her and Shawn getting so serious, so fast? I mean, why not just pick another friend? Clean slate." She let her eyes glide back in Marcy's direction.

"Mrs. Elkins," she declared hotly, "you gotta understand. There wasn't anybody else like Lucinda. She was the best. Had a way about her. She could talk to you when you were really upset and all—and make you feel like everything was going to work out. She did that for a lot of us. Like when Ketchum Doggett first came back to school after his accident. I mean, everybody was like— I mean, *nobody* knew how to act around him or what to say. Wouldn't even look at him. But Lucinda—well, she was great. She just sat right down next to him and started talking, same as always. They talked about all kinds of stuff. About what Ketchum wanted to do with his life. She'd go pick him up and they'd sit in the car and just talk. Hours and hours. She really helped him. "

"Sounds like Lucinda Trimble was some kind of saint."

"Not what I mean," Marcy said. "She wasn't perfect, for God's sake. She had her secrets."

"How do you know?"

"Because everybody does. Don't they?"

Bell slowly tapped the pencil-tip on the piece of paper. "Yes. I believe they do."

Marcy seemed mesmerized by the motion of the pencil. And she had more to say. "Anyway, something was bothering Lucinda," she said. "For sure."

"I'm not surprised," Bell replied. "She was young and pregnant. Her life was about to change dramatically. She had a lot of important decisions to make. And—"

"No." Marcy shook her head emphatically. "Not that kind of stuff."

Bell waited.

"It was something else," Marcy said. "Not just the baby. Nobody else would've noticed. Just me. That's what it means, I guess, to be somebody's best friend—you see stuff that nobody else sees. Not even her mom, I mean. It was kind of gradual. Started a while back. Lucinda was just—different. In good ways and bad. She'd be real happy and then real sad. Lately, it was all sad. I asked her what was going on, but she wouldn't talk about it."

"Any guesses? Like you say, you were her best friend. You must've speculated."

Marcy sighed. Her shoulders rose and fell with the vehemence of her catch-and-release breath. "I wish I had something I could tell you. But I don't. I don't have any idea what was going on with her. She's the one who helped out everybody else. When it came to getting help herself, I don't know—I can't—"

Abruptly, Marcy stood up. "I gotta go," she said. "And if it's okay with you, maybe my father doesn't have to know I came by here again. He'd kill me if he knew. He—he gets real mad at me. All the time. He's always sorry later, though. And tells me so." She handed Bell the coffee mug. "Kind of weird, coming into town now. With Ike's gone, I mean. Streets don't look the same anymore."

"True."

"You think we'll ever get used to it? To things being different?"

"Can't say." Bell's finger went to the roughed-up, puckered skin on her kneecap, which Marcy couldn't see, hidden as it was behind the desk. The stitches would dissolve, they'd told her. The memory? They'd offered no opinion about that, but Bell already knew the answer: Never.

Marcy's voice had a dreamy, faraway sound to it, as if she had already moved past this moment and was traveling forward into the rest of her life and whatever it might hold. "You know, it's kind of funny, Mrs. Elkins," she said. "Everybody used to feel real sorry for Lucinda, growing up without a daddy like she did. She and I talked about it a lot. And we figured it out. We figured out that you're way better off having no daddy at all than having the wrong one."

Nick Fogelsong was in his office when Bell called, preparing for his meeting with the county commissioners. He was disinclined to spend any more time talking about the Trimble case.

"You've got a confession from Wendy Doggett," he declared. "She was jealous of Lucinda's relationship with her son. Met the girl for a chat and things got ugly."

"What if that's not how it happened?"

Through the phone line Bell could hear the sad creak of the battered and broken-down desk chair that Nick refused to replace. He was reaching for something. Pencil and notebook. Cup of coffee. Or just a paper clip, maybe, to unkink while they talked, to have something to do with his hands. *You really know somebody,* she thought, *when you can identify the ambient background noise that comes through the phone. When you don't even have to be in the same room to see what they're up to.*

She heard a short muffled shriek, which meant he was leaning back in his chair now, tormenting the elderly ball bearings. Leaning that way was his default position for thinking. "Day before yesterday," he said, "we didn't have much to go on. Today we've got a full confession. Me? I call that progress. Gotta get moving here, Belfa. Got lots of other things going on in this town."

"Still doesn't sit right."

"Might never sit right."

Her silence was her way of conceding the point.

She broke it with a question: "Any more word from the FBI?"

"Not yet. But I did go by to have a chat with your buddy this morning. He was packing. Little bit of stuff he had, I'm guessing he finished in five minutes. Probably halfway back to D.C. by now."

"Good. Needed to happen."

"I'll let you explain that to Edna," Nick said, and then he chuckled. "She was counting on the rent."

Bell grunted her good-bye and rang off. Stood up, stretched. She needed something to eat. Dumping coffee on an empty stomach—which she'd just done—was akin to walking into a biker bar and calling the first guy you see a candy-ass. Just asking for trouble.

Now that Ike's was gone, courthouse employees had reluctantly begun to patronize Linton Albright's pizza shop at Main and Carter. Not ideal—especially not for breakfast, although Linton sold a biscuit-and-sausage-and-salsa concoction he called a "sunrise pizza"—but nobody had yet keeled over from his cooking. *Good sign,* Bell thought. *Definitely promising.*

"Back in twenty minutes," Bell said to Lee Ann. Her secretary waved in acknowledgment without looking up from her computer screen. The thin wires running from Lee Ann's earbuds dangled down both sides of her neck. She was transcribing the recording of a recent interview.

Bell stopped.

She looked at Lee Ann.

Her secretary, suddenly aware of the fact that the boss was staring at her, yanked out the earbuds.

"Bell, is there something you need me to—?"

"You know what? I think I just figured out where I can find Lucinda's cell phone."

Chapter Fifty

The front yard of Marylou Ferguson's house was covered with the sort of detritus that announces MULTIPLE CHILDREN LIVE HERE as clearly as if a billboard with fluorescent orange letters to that effect had been erected over the small untidy residence. Two rusty tricycles tilted on their sides. A pink plastic dollhouse had been squashed flat and split in half, its innards trickling across the lawn, from tiny toy tables and chairs and couches and chimneys to an entire plastic family—mom, dad, kids, collie. There were baseball caps, twisted and turned inside out. Balls of various shapes, sizes, and states of deflation. A child-size yellow plastic guitar, planted neck-first in the mud. Filthy tennis shoes, doubtless ripped off and tossed aloft at the first hint of spring. Cardboard juice boxes, sucked dry until their sides collapsed and then dropped like curved rinds of actual fruit. Frisbees bearing the teeth marks of pets—and perhaps children, too. *Only forensic odontology,* Bell thought, *could tell us for sure.*

The only thing this yard didn't have was grass. That had been sacrificed long ago to the constant pressure of games, races, wrestling matches, and other tumbling squabbles.

Bell banged on the thin edge of the screen door with more fervor than she'd meant to, making it rattle back and forth in its ill-fitting frame. She was in a hurry. The sight of Lee Ann's earbuds had pried something loose from her memory: meeting Marylou Ferguson, that night by the river.

Marylou Ferguson. Running with earbuds. Using them to listen to an iPhone.

An iPhone.

Yet Marylou's husband was unemployed, and they had an ever-increasing brood, the contemplation of which generally made Nick Fogelsong sigh and quote his father: *The rich get richer, and the poor get children.*

The child who opened the screen door could have been anywhere between four and eight years old, with bow legs, a dirt-slimed face, and two grubby hands, one of which was clenched around the soiled foot of a stuffed animal of indeterminate species.

He looked at Bell. Turned his head a half a degree and hollered, *"Mom!"*

Then he drifted away, dragging the stuffed animal, letting its battered head bump across each piece of junk in a living room whose messiness rivaled the front yard's. The sounds of crying, of a dog's endless agitated barking, of a TV set in some interior room disgorging its noise: Clearly, this was the soundtrack of the Ferguson household.

Marylou appeared, rubbing her hands on a dishrag. She wore the same clothes she'd been wearing on the night Bell met her by the river.

"Mrs. Elkins," she said. A come-and-go smile. Wariness in her eye.

Bell asked if she would please join her on the porch. Marylou, after a look back into the house, as if concerned about what manner and degree of mayhem would ensue during even a brief absence, nodded and complied.

Bell was brief, cold. She knew, she said, that Marylou had found Lucinda's iPhone that morning—the morning Marylou had called the sheriff's office to report seeing a car in the Bitter River.

"Where was the cell, Marylou?" Bell asked.

"In the weeds. The weeds on the riverbank." She made no attempt to deny it, speaking in a low embarrassed voice, her gaze aimed at a knothole in the porch floor. "I was running and I saw that car in the river. And when I tried to get a closer look, going down further and further on the bank and having to go through all them weeds, I saw some junk. From a purse. And there it was. The cell. I could tell right away it was a real nice one. Brought it home and my boy Cody—he's fourteen, he's real good with that kinda thing, electronics and all, he fixes everything around here—he took out the thingamabob that lets you track it. They call it jailbreaking. That's what Cody told me.

"All I wanted," Marylou said, and now she lifted her face to peer hopefully at Bell, because she was asking to be understood, and maybe even forgiven, "was some music to listen to when I run in the mornings. Never touched anything else. Just that phone. There was a billfold, too, you know, with money in it—and I didn't take it. Didn't take no other stuff, neither. Just wanted the music. See, morning's the only time I have. Time that's all mine. I didn't think it would hurt nobody. 'Specially not that poor girl, the one who died. I mean—she didn't have no more use for it, now, did she?"

Eight minutes later, Bell was back in the Explorer. Heading to the courthouse. Lucinda's iPhone was on the seat beside her. To Marylou's worried question—*Just how much trouble am I in, Mrs. Elkins?*—Bell had replied, *Deal with you later.*

Bell pulled over to the side of the road before she was halfway back to town.

She had a hunch that wouldn't leave her be, wouldn't let her rest until she had checked it out. Lucinda Trimble was a smart and resourceful young woman. If she'd sensed any threat, any danger, if someone she trusted had suddenly become belligerent, unpredictable, had turned on her, she would've tried to protect herself. Tried to leave a record, with whatever means she'd had close by—such as an iPhone. If she'd had it in her purse, and her purse was on her lap, she easily could've recorded a conversation while her car was parked by the Bitter River.

Bell pressed the icon for Voice Memo. The old-time microphone. There was only one entry in the list of recordings. It lasted, according to the numbers on the screen, three minutes and twenty-four seconds. She put her head back against the seat, closed her eyes, and listened.

She was expecting to hear an intense conversation between Lucinda and Shawn Doggett, expecting to hear the alternating voices of a young woman and a young man in an escalating argument. A passionate back-and-forth between two people who had found themselves in a difficult situation: pregnant, anxious, confused. And indeed, the first sound on the digital recording that filled the Explorer was the strong and forthright voice of a young woman. A young woman whom Bell—unable to recall if she'd ever heard Lucinda speak when she was alive, beyond a voice that may have been part of a tangle of young voices in the hallway at Acker's Gap High School—realized must be Lucinda Trimble:

Told you before. I've made up my mind.

And the second voice was . . .

Not Shawn.

It was Ketchum. His tone veering wildly from beseeching to threatening, from frustrated to forlorn, Ketchum argued with her:

Shit, Lucinda, you're too smart for this. You don't want this kind of life.

Maybe I do.

No.

I can still do all those other things. I can have the baby and still go to college, still write poetry, still play basketball and run track, still—

No. No.

Come on. This is kind of silly.

Silly? Is that what I'm being? Fuck that. I wish I hadn't said I needed to talk tonight. Wish you hadn't picked me up. Just take me back home. No, wait—forget it. I'll call my mom. Or Shawn. Somebody'll come get me.

Ketchum. Please.

You've got everything, okay? Every fucking thing. All I wanted was—was this. Just knowing you were getting out. Out of this place—this—

It's our hometown. It's where we live.

It's a fucking hole. A trap. It's worse than my fucking chair. You've got a chance, okay? You've got to get out of here.

Look. When Shawn and I have our own place, you can come visit us. You can—

Fuck that. I don't want to fucking visit you and fucking Shawn, okay?

Don't be mad at him. He's doing the right thing. Helping me.

Helping you? Is that what he's doing?

Listen to me. There are things you don't understand.

Like what?

It doesn't matter. Just know that, whatever you think, your brother is a good person. I've made some mistakes, okay? But Shawn doesn't care about that. He—

You've made mistakes? Hell, Lucinda. It's not like you got pregnant all by yourself. You think my brother is such a great guy? He sure as hell better step up or else I'll—

You don't know. You don't know.

I don't know what? Shit, Lucinda, you're not making sense.

There are things—things people do and then they have to—they need help and—

Listen to me. You've got to listen to me. Now.

What's wrong? Why are you—?

You have to leave, Lucinda. You have to get out of this fucking town.

But why—?

Because if you get out of here, then maybe I can get out, too.

Ketchum. Oh, Ketchum. I'm so sorry. I know you're hurting. I wish I could—

Don't you fucking feel sorry for me, you bitch. Don't you do that. You hear me? I don't want your pity. I don't—

That hurts, Ketchum. I know you don't mean to, but you're—

Why don't you understand? Don't you—?

The digital recording stopped.

Bell could see the rest of it, could see it clearly. It unspooled in her mind's eye, big, bright, and vivid, as if it were a movie and she was sitting in the front row, her face bathed by the light from the screen. Ketchum is angry, distraught, hopeless, his hands flying to Lucinda's neck. Those strong, strong hands. Pressure. Intense pressure. Lucinda is shocked. Too surprised to fight back. He doesn't mean to—but she won't listen to him. She just keeps talking, trying to make everything okay. And then so fast *Oh my God Oh my God what have I*—it's over. *Oh my God—look what I—I—*

Over. It's all over. He's sweating now. *What the hell have I done?* Scared out of his mind. *I swear I never meant to—*

Grab her purse. Right now. Do it. Toss it out the window. Make it look like a robbery or something. An attack. They'd take her purse, right? Robbers, that's what they'd do, right? Yeah. They'd scatter the stuff. Looking for cash. Or drugs. He doesn't know about the cell, about the recording. Stuff is stuff. He sees her hand. Her finger. *The ring.* The engagement ring. Tugs it off her finger. Starts to throw the ring out the window, too—but no. *No.* Belongs to his mother. Too precious.

He releases the brake. Puts the car in gear.

Opens the passenger door and hurls himself out, hitting the ground, clearing the car. *Just in time.* His arms, his shoulders: His upper-body strength is tremendous. He can do this. He can do it just as well—*better, dammit*—than an able-bodied person.

He watches the car go into the river, the river instantly making room for it, as if the river had been waiting for it all along, planning for it, reserving the space. *Oh my God. Lucinda.* He claws his way up the bank, tearing at the ground, hand over hand, panting, frantic. He calls home. Needs help.

Come on. Come on.

The car sinks lower into the restless water, first the tires, then the doors, then the windows, all descending in a strange one-way baptism, rocking, shifting, until finally only a small square of rooftop remains visible on the river's dark surface.

What Bell didn't know, couldn't see, couldn't sense, was the identity of the person who came to pick up Ketchum that night. The person who helped him cover up his crime. Was it Wendy or Shawn? Mother or brother—or both?

Chapter Fifty-One

Sheriff Fogelsong listened. Bell was calling from her office, and he had answered on his cell in the Blazer. He was halfway to Charleston for a parole hearing.

When she finished, he said, "I'll take care of it from here. Send the deputies to go pick up Ketchum Doggett. My money says that, once he hears the recording, he'll admit what he did that night."

"Hope so," Bell said. She couldn't resist. "We like confessions, right? Didn't you tell me that recently?"

He let that one go by.

"Always thought he was a decent kid," Nick remarked.

"Makes two of us."

"Lost his temper, you figure?"

"He lost a lot of things. One by one."

The sheriff didn't speak for a moment. Bell could hear the sturdy rumble of the Blazer's big engine.

"So how'd the ring get back in that jewelry box?" he asked. "Who put it there—Wendy, Ketchum, or Shawn?"

"Damned if I know," Bell said. "But I can tell you this. If we try to make a case against Shawn as the accomplice, Wendy'll say she was the one who helped Ketchum. Alone. She'll take the rap—no matter what really happened at the river that night. She'll protect her children however she can. If one of her sons has to go down because the evidence is just too compelling, she'll still try to save the other one."

"You think?"

"I don't think. I know. She's a mother, Nick. She can't protect Ketchum anymore—it's too late for him, because of the recording—but she can protect Shawn. And she will. The same way that Ketchum and Shawn are protecting Lucinda's memory. That's where they learned it. From their mother."

"Thought you didn't like her."

"I don't. But I don't have to like her to know where she's coming from. Who she is."

He chewed on that for a minute, and then said, "Okay. Just one more thing you have to do."

"What's that?"

"Go home," he said. "We can sort it all out when I get back from Charleston tonight. No rush. It'll keep. You're supposed to stay off the knee, right?"

Bell didn't argue. She ended the call. Gathered up files from her desk.

A few minutes later she looked out the office window, purely for the satisfaction of watching Deputy Harrison and Deputy Greenough leave the courthouse. They would drive out to the Doggett estate and arrest Ketchum. They'd gotten the call from the sheriff, and now hurried down the wide stone steps. Slid into respective sides of the county's other black Blazer. Pam Harrison drove; Greg Greenough took the passenger seat.

Bell stayed at the window until the vehicle disappeared around the corner. Something buzzed and thudded at the back of her mind, like a fly trapped in a Coke bottle, but she couldn't take the time right now to deal with it. She needed to see Wendy Doggett and, armed with this new information, try to persuade her to tell the truth—no matter how ragged and agonizing that truth might be.

Chapter Fifty-Two

Deputy Mathers opened the cell door and turned sideways, allowing Bell to go past him. "Call me if you need me," he said.

She nodded. Waited until he'd swung the big iron door closed behind her, waited until the flat crash of his boots against the wooden floor had become fainter with distance. Mathers was a heavy man, and he moved slowly. An excruciating amount of time elapsed between one step and the next. Bell had learned a lot about patience from working with Charlie Mathers.

She looked at Wendy Doggett, who sat on the metal-frame single bed, knees locked, hands arranged neatly in her lap, face a flat mask, as if she were in the waiting room of a dentist's office, a bit early for her appointment. Serena Crumpler stood close to her. Bell nodded at Serena, but didn't speak; she wanted her first words to be aimed at Wendy.

"It was Ketchum," Bell said, plunging in with no preliminaries. She didn't believe in small talk about big things. "Isn't that right? He needed help, of course, getting home that night—but Ketchum was the one who killed Lucinda."

No reply.

Bell had expected Wendy to look wildly out of place here. She was still wearing the clothes she'd had on previously—coral knit dress with a thin white belt and white heels—on the night when Lucinda's engagement ring had spilled out of the jewelry box, spilling other secrets, too. Seeing Wendy Doggett in a cell in the Raythune County Jail would be a little jarring, Bell had assumed, like finding escargot on the menu at White Castle.

But in the long hours Wendy had spent here over the past day and a half, she had merged with her circumstances. Her complexion—the portions of it visible between the bruises—was as gray as the cinder block walls. Her hair no longer looked lacquered. Her makeup had been mostly rubbed off. Even the dress seemed to have faded a shade or two.

"You're not going to tell me what really happened, are you?" Bell said.

No reply.

"We can still hold you, you know," Bell went on. "For making a false confession. For being an accessory. Even after we charge Ketchum, you're still not off the hook."

Wendy didn't blink. "Then do it," she said. "I'm already here. Save everybody some time and aggravation."

"I just need to know why. Why you helped him cover it up."

Silence.

"Right," Bell said. Testy now. "Got it. You're not going to tell me a damned thing. Fine. But let's say you *were* the one who helped Ketchum that night. Let's say he called and said he'd needed help. And let's say you drove out there to pick him up. And let's say you hunted for Lucinda's purse, the one Ketchum had tossed out of the car, and for any other evidence—that's how you got those scratches on your knees, isn't it?—but you couldn't find everything. And you were running out of time. You had to go. Let's say it *had* been you. Hypothetically. Why'd you do it?"

"Hypothetically?"

"Hypothetically."

Wendy looked at Serena, who shrugged.

"If I'd done all those things," Wendy said, "I would've done them because—because I approved. Because I didn't want Ketchum to turn into me."

"Into you."

"Right. Wanting what he can't have."

"What the hell do you mean?" Bell said. "Your son could've accomplished whatever he set his mind to. He had plans. He's smart. He's—"

"He's a *cripple*." Wendy's tone was blunt and ugly. "He's not going anywhere. He's stuck here. Just like me. And that girl—that goddamned silly little girl. Filling his head with all that nonsense. College. Medical school. I'm *glad* he killed her. I'm *glad* he did it. She deserved it, do you hear? She tried to take both of my boys away from me. Both of them. Goddamn her, anyway. Her and that trashy bitch of a mother."

"So Ketchum confessed to you?" Bell said.

"No." Wendy made an exasperated noise in the back of her throat. "In fact, when I picked him up on the road that night, he said he'd left Lucinda in the car. He wanted her to think long and hard about how she was ruining his life—lying to him, misleading him, making him think he could leave here. He didn't say a word about hurting her." Wendy shivered. "When he threw himself out of her car, she tried to call him back. Tried to make it right. That's what Ketchum said. Lucinda started to get out and come after him. But he yelled at her and she stayed put. Stayed right where she was, behind the wheel. So Ketchum pulled himself a long way up the riverbank and along that road, in the dark and the cold, inching along, dragging his legs behind him—because he had to get away from that bitch. Fast as he could. Even after we found out she'd been killed—even after that— Ketchum still told us he didn't do it. Still insisted she was alive when he left her."

"Do you believe him?"

"No," Wendy said. "I don't. That's why I told him to keep his mouth shut about being with her that night. Nobody needed to know that."

JULIA KELLER

"You think he killed her. Strangled her and got himself out and then watched the car roll into the water. And then lied to you about it."

"Yes."

"Lucinda was his friend," Bell said quietly. "He loved her. Both of your boys loved her."

"Love." Wendy practically spat the word, as if it were a kind of burning poison, and she couldn't get it out of her mouth fast enough.

Chapter Fifty-Three

Bell returned to her office. Lee Ann Frickie, according to the note she'd left, was taking a break. Probably having coffee with Tina Sheets over in the county clerk's office, Bell speculated. They were as dissimilar as two people could be—the quiet, well-organized Lee Ann and the noisy, scattered Tina, who was half Lee Ann's age and probably only three-quarters her IQ—but somehow they'd been friends for more than twenty years.

She went to the window behind Lee Ann's desk. It was good as new, the pane having been replaced once the state police forensics unit had finished its work, and the blinds were up again. That was how Lee Ann liked it.

From here, Bell could barely see the spot where Ike's had been, the ravaged, scooped-out place where people still gathered informally, especially at dusk or at sunrise, standing in small quiet circles, looking down, sometimes weeping, sometimes holding hands, sometimes visibly praying, but mostly just standing and thinking. She wondered how many times she'd have to come to this window and not see Ike's before the profound permanence of the loss finally was real to her. She thought about Joyce LeFevre, and how hard she'd worked to make Ike's a success. The restaurant business was notoriously difficult—two others had failed last year in Acker's Gap and another three over in Blythesburg—but Joyce had a dream.

Bell had always considered dreams as positive things, as things that enhanced life, but that was not how Wendy Doggett saw it. Once she had made her devil's deal to live with Alton Doggett, dreams were repugnant to her. And dangerous.

Such a close call for Lee Ann. Bell still shuddered when she thought about it. She hadn't been able to persuade her secretary to take any extra time off, however. Lee Ann said she had far too much work to do to let a little thing like a bullet keep her from doing it.

The office phone rang. Bell reached for it but continued to stare out the window.

"Elkins."

"Thought I told you to go home," Nick said. "Don't you know how to take orders?"

"Well, I don't answer to you," Bell replied, teasing him right back. "Separation of powers, remember?"

"Point taken. Hey, I'm on the road, but I just stopped for coffee. Got a call from that FBI agent," he said, warming up to the real purpose of his call. "They think they know who the guy was—the guy in that terrorist cell who got away. They want us to be on the lookout for him. Hang on." Rustle of papers. "Here it is. Name's Yusef. Rashid Yusef."

Bell had that fly-in-the-Coke-bottle sensation again. Something moved in the back of her thoughts.

"Anything else?" she said. "Physical description? Information about why the hell he might be headed here?"

"That's all they had."

"So in the meantime—"

"We're supposed to stay alert," he said.

"Nice of them to care so much." She tried and failed to keep the bitterness out of her voice.

"This is West Virginia, Bell. Not New York or L.A. You know how it goes. We don't matter. They're not going to send any manpower here unless they absolutely have to. Besides, we take care of ourselves, right? Always have, always will. Don't need any damned FBI."

Bell hung up. She was thinking. *Yusef. Yusef. Isn't that—?*

She looked out the window but she was no longer seeing the street. She was seeing into the dark heart of the world, and the sight made her realize that Acker's Gap was still in grave danger; no matter how high the mountains, they couldn't protect it anymore. There were no safe places. Hurriedly, ominous dread overwhelming her thoughts like the river in flood stage, she left the office.

Chapter Fifty-Four

Edna wasn't sitting on her front porch. But maybe that didn't matter; this wasn't an ideal afternoon for porch-sitting. The day had turned hot, with the kind of out-of-season humidity that made people cranky. Even the sporadic breeze felt heavy. Edna's pink house looked raw and tender in the relentless sunshine, like skin on its way to a bad burn.

Bell didn't hesitate. She reached for the front door, stepped in, called out, "Edna? Edna, it's Bell Elkins." Moved a few feet into the living room. She'd been in Edna's house once before. Three years ago, Edna, along with half a dozen others, had witnessed a hit-and-run on Main. After Deputy Mathers had tracked down the cowardly bastard over in Collier County, Bell came by Edna's house to interview her as part of the trial preparation. She remembered the cookies Edna had served her—small drops of shortbread rolled in confectioner's sugar—and the hot tea. Edna, as it happened, didn't have to testify, after all; the man confessed. Edna, Bell had sensed, was a bit disappointed at missing her big moment in court.

It was hot in here. Edna didn't believe in air-conditioning. A lot of older people in Acker's Gap felt that way, Bell knew. *Open a dang window,* she'd heard Edna tell people, when they bellyached about their electric bills, *and give the AC a break.*

Still, the heat in the small house was oppressive. And there were,

Bell noted with irritation, a substantial number of flies. Odd, this early in the year.

"Edna?"

She moved toward the kitchen, still talking. "Sorry to just bust in like this, but I was worried about—"

Her eyes dropped to the floor. *No. Oh, no, no.*
No.

Edna was lying on her back, legs twisted up under her at a terrible angle as if she'd first dropped to her knees and then fallen straight back. Open-eyed, mouth agape, she stared at the ceiling. The blood from a wound at the base of her skull had drained away, creating two irregularly shaped stains that flared out across the floor. She'd been struck from behind while standing at the stove, Bell surmised, but she hadn't gone down easy. She must have staggered, grabbing the edge of the tablecloth. Yanked it off, like a magician in the big finish, sending a coffee cup and a vase of daffodils crashing onto the linoleum. She still clutched a corner of the tablecloth she'd dragged off, and in the other hand, a copy of *The Mill on the Floss*. The plastic wrapper on the book was stamped PROPERTY OF RAYTHUNE COUNTY PUBLIC LIBRARY.

Bell kneeled down, just to be sure. But she'd been sure before she kneeled. She had seen enough violent death in her life. She knew.

She didn't want to disturb the crime scene any more than she'd already done, destroying clues with every motion, every gesture, every breath. So she stood up, backing slowly out of the room, touching nothing. Pushing the door with her elbow, instead of using the knob. Her shock, her sorrow for Edna, was crowded out for the time being by anger and by questions.

Standing on the porch, she pulled out her cell and hit the sheriff's number on her speed dial. Her hand, Bell noted with an almost scientific detachment, was shaking. The call went straight to voice mail. *Dammit. He's got a parole hearing in Charleston.* She'd forgotten. And the parole board, she knew, required cell phones to be turned off.

Wait. What if Matt hadn't gotten away? The sheriff only saw him packing, not leaving. Whoever killed Edna might have started—or finished—with him.

Bell headed to the garage apartment. The small door was unlocked. She pushed it open.

"Matt?"

The room was bare. No backpack. No laptop. He was gone.

Her cell rang. A check of the caller ID made her feel almost sick with relief: FOGELSONG, NICK.

Nick'll know what to do. He'll send the ambulance for Edna and figure out what the hell—

But it wasn't Nick on the line.

"Belfa?"

Bell realized her mistake. The call was coming from Nick's home phone. It was Mary Sue.

"Listen, Mary Sue, I'm a little busy right now, so maybe—"

"Belfa. I need you. Please. I can't reach Nick—he's in Charleston, his cell's turned off—and there's a man here. He's injured. He's been shot. He says his name is Harless. Matt Harless. Hurry, Belfa. Please. I think he's dying."

Chapter Fifty-Five

Twelve minutes before making that call to Bell, Mary Sue Fogelsong had heard the knock. She didn't react. She was sitting in a rocking chair in her living room. Not rocking. Sitting.

It was well past noon but she was still in her nightgown, a long white one with a frilly lace collar and rhyming lace across the bottom hem. She tried to get dressed each morning—it was an important goal, one that she'd carefully written down in the journal her therapist advised her to keep—but she'd had a few setbacks lately. Nick was gone for long periods these days. She knew he had to work. There was a big murder case. She'd read about it. A young girl. So sad.

The knock came again. Could she just ignore it? Yes. That's what she would do. Ignore it.

A third time. Well, it was daylight, so maybe it was okay.

Mary Sue opened the door.

The man who stood on the front porch had very short pale hair—it was almost as short as Nick's, which was saying something—and a stare so intense and penetrating that it made her want to button the top button of her nightgown. Made her want to go back under the covers. Disappear.

"Fogelsong," the man said. He gasped it, really, as if the three syllables were two syllables too many. "Sheriff Fogelsong. Is he here? Is he—?"

"No."

"Do you know where he is? He's not at the courthouse. His vehicle's gone. Thought maybe he'd stopped by here." The man grimaced, but he'd found a new store of strength in order to form sentences. He held one hand tight against his stomach. The other hand hung down at his side, twitching. Despite the effort that the words were costing him, he didn't seem desperate. Simply resolute.

"No," she said. "He's not here." Something about the man made her nervous, made her keep talking. Babbling, really. "He's in Charleston today. A parole hearing. He has to testify." *Shut up, Mary Sue!* she screamed at herself, an internal scream, but still. *Shut up Shut* up. Why was she telling this man that Nick wasn't home? Why hadn't she just said he was up in the shower or out back or—or something, anything?

And then she saw the man's stomach. A red stain was spreading across it, blooming out past the edges of his fingers. He took his hand away, looked at it, then put it back.

"I've been shot," he said unnecessarily. There was a calmness to him, a calmness that—despite the content of his words—calmed her. "Name's Matt Harless. I would appreciate, ma'am, if it's not too much trouble, a glass of wa—"

He started to collapse. Mary Sue opened the screen door wider to try to catch him, but as she did so, a crackling flurry of automatic gunfire hit the porch swing. The swing bounced, jumped, and danced as the wood splintered and flew apart.

Mary Sue shrieked. Her instinct was to duck back inside and lock the door, but she'd gotten a hand under the slumping man's arm. Heard him moan. She propped the door open with her bare foot for another few seconds, pulling him past the threshold by the shoulders—he was helping her, grabbing at the doorframe and hauling himself across, grunting and moaning—as another terrifying flutter of gunfire raked the porch railing. The mailbox—it was black, with the name FOGELSONG streaming across the side in swirling green letters painted by Mary Sue when they first moved in, before she'd gotten sick—instantly disintegrated.

"Oh my God," Mary Sue said. "Oh my God."

She crouched down just inside the door. The man was heaped beside her, hand on his belly, breathing hard and fast, his breaths coming in hard rattles. Now she saw a second source of blood: his left thigh. He'd been hit again during the last assault.

Crawling on her hands and knees, afraid to rise and make herself a target, Mary Sue slowly inched over to the end table. Grabbed the phone. Dialed Bell's number. Delivered her message.

Bell was on her way. After that call, Mary Sue tried another: 911. But the line was dead. Between her first and second calls—just that fast—the line had been cut.

She reached for her cell on the coffee table. No bars.

What the—?

Cell phone jammer. She remembered Nick telling her about the devices. That had to be it.

With each discovery, Mary Sue became increasingly aware of the sleek and ominous premeditation of this attack—the use of automatic weapons, the cutting of phone lines, the disabling of cells. Her visitor wasn't some unlucky bastard caught in a random crossfire. And the assailant wasn't some liquored-up Sawyer Fork redneck toting his grandfather's Winchester, pissed off at the sheriff and sworn to vengeance. This was somebody who knew what he was doing.

And what he was doing was trying to kill them. Not scare them, not warn them or toy with them, but kill them.

The man on her floor moaned again. After an interval of perhaps ten minutes—she didn't really know how long it was, she'd lost all sense of time, of anything but a perpetual and scary *now*—there was a third round of automatic gunfire, smashing across the living room windows and sending shattered glass and bits of blue curtain flying through the room in a nicked-up frenzy, and only then did the piercing hopelessness of the situation strike Mary Sue Fogelsong: She was under assault with no way to fight back, she was watching a man die with no way to summon more help—or to warn Bell Elkins that she was heading into a trap.

Chapter Fifty-Six

Even from a distance, Bell knew what she was hearing: gunfire from
an automatic weapon. She was driving with her windows down, and
the noise—from afar, it was a benign-sounding *pop-pop-pop-pop,* a
linked chain of small tidy explosions—was instantly familiar to her.
Nothing benign about it. She'd grown up with guns. In one of the better foster families she'd lived with, the father was a man named Hank
Sherber, and he was a hunter. He'd taught her all about guns: pistols,
rifles, semiautomatics. Nowadays, every chance she got, she liked to
join the sheriff or one of his deputies over at the shooting range. Best
way in the world to work off the residual anger that always seemed to
be building up inside her.

She knew what an automatic weapon sounded like. And she knew
that Nick and Mary Sue Fogelsong lived too far out in the rural part of
Raythune County for the noise to attract attention from neighbors.

Her next thought: *Matt.*

Somehow, it all must come back to him. Edna's death. Mary Sue's
panic. Bell was responsible for bringing him here—and so she would
take care of it. She'd handle it. But she wouldn't go straight in. The
fact that she'd grown up in Raythune County gave her a distinct advantage; she knew at least a half-dozen alternative routes to get anywhere.

She turned off the main road and bumped down a nameless dirt path; it was trafficked more often by cows than by cars. The rugged lane tunneled through heavy brush, forcing her to make sudden detours around sharp-edged conglomerations of boulders—many higher and wider than the Explorer—that had broken off from the mountain, year by year. The road finally stopped for good at the boarded-up entrance to a coal mine that hadn't been in operation since the early 1950s. From here, it was about a half-mile excursion through a staircase-climb of tight woods to get to the back of Nick's property.

She found them in the living room. Mary Sue was crouched in a ball, nestled next to the wall. Nightgown drawn over her knees, head down, breathing in and out with a slow, deliberate rhythm. Matt was lying on his right side by the front door, body curved in a sharp arch that testified to an exquisite and unfathomably intense pain. Blood was leaking steadily from his stomach and his leg. He wasn't moving.

"Mary Sue?" Bell whispered. Didn't want to startle them.

No worries there. Matt was past the point of being able to respond to stimuli, and Mary Sue didn't flinch or scream, but only lifted her head and blinked at Bell, once, twice, three times, then dropped her face again into the spot between her raised kneecaps, as if she'd willed herself away from this place, and didn't believe Bell was really here. Just another hallucination.

"Mary Sue," Bell repeated. She was crawling carefully along the floor, focused on keeping low. The windows, she saw, were destroyed, the panes shattered by gunfire. Millions of bits of glass were flung across the floor, enough to constitute a glittering new carpet.

"Are you okay?" Bell said. "What the hell's going on? Who's out there?"

Mary Sue didn't respond.

"Call somebody. For God's sake, Mary Sue—"

Mary Sue looked up. "Tried. Can't. Cells don't work."

Bell made a quick visual assessment of Matt's wounds. She grabbed the small orange rag rug just to the left of the front door. The one, she recalled from her visits here, that Mary Sue was always hectoring Nick to wipe his boots on when he came home at night.

"Look, Mary Sue, I need you to hold this rug right here. On his leg. To stop the bleeding. Just hold it as tight as you can while I go get help and—"

"No. Can't."

"What—"

"Can't touch him, Belfa. I'm afraid to touch him. All that blood." She began to cry. Great, shoulder-bobbing sobs.

"Okay, okay, Mary Sue. Hold on," Bell said, trying to soothe her. She wasn't very good at soothing people. "Tell you what. I'll hold the rug. I'll do it. You go for help, okay?"

Mary Sue's face clouded over. The sobs had tailed off into sniffles. "Been hearing voices again, Belfa. Loud ones."

"We're all going to die unless you—"

"The voices."

"You can do this. I know you can."

"The voices. The ones in my head. They're so loud, Belfa. They're drowning out everything else. I could barely hear what you just said to me right now. They're loud. They're telling me—"

Bell grabbed Mary Sue's arm. She didn't do it gently. She looked into Mary Sue's eyes. There was no time for kindness.

"Voices?" Bell said.

"Yeah. Loud."

"Okay, well—tell 'em to shut the hell up."

Mary Sue laughed. Then she caught herself, slapping a hand over her mouth as if she'd said something naughty. No one had ever talked to her like that about her illness. Her husband, her psychiatrist, her counselor, the disability administrator—they were always patient and kind, treating her the way she used to treat her third-graders at Acker's Gap Elementary School back when she was still teaching, before this disease got its hands around her brain. They treated her with that faint singsong lilt of condescension in their tone, with the soft pat of *there, there* in their voices. With everything that indicated they never really believed she would ever recover.

Not Bell. Not now.

"Mary Sue," she said. "We need to get some help. So you have to go. And you can do this."

"The voices—"

"Screw the voices, Mary Sue. Focus. *Focus,* okay? I need you. I need your help. Right now."

"It's hard." Mary Sue said it with a catch in her voice.

"I didn't say it wouldn't be hard. I just said I knew you could do it."

Mary Sue closed her eyes. She held up her fists to either side of her face. Gritted her teeth. Made a grunting sound.

"They tell me," Bell said, "that mental illness is the same as a physical illness, right? That's why there shouldn't be any stigma about it. No shame. Well, if you had a broken leg, Mary Sue, I'd be saying the same thing. You have to push through. Overcome the pain. Just tell it to go to hell."

Mary Sue, eyes still closed, nodded. It was a hard, emphatic nod. Not a soft, ambiguous, *maybe I will and maybe I won't* nod.

She was ready.

She was going to try.

"I knew it," Bell said. "I knew you'd do this. Nick always told me you're the bravest person he's ever met."

Matt moaned but didn't move. Bell increased pressure on the wound in his thigh. The rug was already soaked through, Matt's blood darkening the orange.

Mary Sue nodded again. She rose. Gathered the bottom of her white nightgown and brought it up close to her waist, twisting two hunks of it into a knot so that it wouldn't interfere with her running. In the bright sunlight suffusing the room, her slender legs looked, Bell thought, as if they belonged to a twelve-year-old girl. To a girl who could run for days, leaping over creeks and dodging fallen trees, and she wouldn't even be breathing hard.

"Go to the nearest neighbor," Bell said. "Tell them to call Nick. Call Sheriff Fogelsong."

"But his cell is—"

"Call five or six times in a row. Over and over. When it goes to voice mail, hang up and call again. He'll see. He'll see the missed calls and know something's up."

Mary Sue reached down and put a hand on Bell's shoulder. Bell looked up at her. No farewells. Farewells didn't suit either one of them.

"Listen," Bell said, "if the gunman tries to stop you, then—"

"He won't stop me, Belfa."

And then, with a flap of white nightgown and a deft rise and fall of small pale bare feet, she was gone.

Bell had to stay crouched down, close to Matt, so she couldn't watch. She could only listen. A few seconds later, she heard the *pop-pop-pop-pop* as the sniper drew a bead on the flying white figure crossing the field. Mary Sue, Bell imagined, must've looked like a small fluttering bird when she first sprang into view. And maybe that moment of slight discombobulation—what bird would fly so low?— had given Mary Sue what she needed. A head start.

An edge.

A decent chance.

Maybe the shots were landing just behind her, or in front of her, or beside her, as she ran for her life.

For all their lives.

Chapter Fifty-Seven

Nick Fogelsong had just finished his presentation to the parole board. He slid the papers back into the brown file folder, one of three he'd brought, then lined up the edges of all the folders before sliding them back into his satchel. He didn't much care for briefcases, but at times he needed one, and so he chose an object that seemed least like a briefcase while still being in the briefcase family: an old mail satchel that had belonged to his father, Big Jim Fogelsong. Big Jim had used the battered leather bag—scuffed and gouged and worn to a beautifully tender texture, butter-colored, with streaks of rusty red—to pick up the mail out at the box when he was a kid, and bring it back to the house. The mailbox was on Route 12, a mile and a half down a dusty road from the farmhouse in which Big Jim was raised and, after he grew up and inherited the farm, in which Nick and his brother, Winston, were raised.

Now the farm was gone and with it, so many other things were gone, too, including Big Jim and Winston. But Nick still had the satchel. Sometimes—usually after he'd had an extra drink or two, on a rare off-duty night—he'd pick up the satchel and rub it, and he'd imagine he could fit his fingers onto the very spot where his father had once rubbed it, after having slung it over his little-boy shoulder, straining at the welcome weight of the mail.

He'd just buttoned the front of the satchel and turned on his cell when it rang.

Two other sheriffs, also there to testify, frowned at him. Nick frowned right back. None of their damned business. The hearing was over, wasn't it?

"Fogelsong."

"Nick! *NickNickNick—oh my God*—"

It was Mary Sue. When he heard her voice he felt, in three perfectly equal measures, weariness and concern and irritation.

"Slow down, honey. Get hold of yourself. Tell me what's going on."

"Nick, it's Bell, she told me to call you—"

He was instantly alert. If Bell had instructed Mary Sue to call him, the matter was serious; Bell knew where he was, knew he shouldn't be disturbed except for an emergency.

"Honey, what is it?" Nick said, trying to keep his voice calm. Badgering Mary Sue, hurrying her, never paid off. She just became angry and flustered. You had to let her tell you things in her own way, at her own pace.

His calmness seemed to travel through the phone lines and engulf her spirit. "Nick," she said, and he could hear the hysteria ebbing away now. She was matter-of-fact. "We need you right away. I'm calling from Mrs. McClatchy's trailer. Bell's back at our house with somebody named Harless. He's hurt—hurt very badly—and Bell can't leave him. We're under fire, Nick. There's a sniper—"

"A *sniper*? My God, what—?"

"Just listen," she interrupted. All at once he was the agitated one, the out-of-control one, and she was the voice of reason. They had switched roles, just like that. "Calm down. We need you back here, but you'll have to be careful. He's got the house covered. He's got automatic weapons. If you come straight in—"

"I won't come straight in." He was already crossing the parking lot, having swung on his coat with his free hand, the satchel's fraying strap looped over his shoulder. He had the Blazer in sight. He was thinking about the layout of his property, about entrances and angles and trajectories. About what instructions to give Deputy Harrison.

He'd started up his vehicle and was getting ready to flip on the siren. "Do you need me to stay on the line with you?" he asked Mary Sue. "Are you okay?"

"For heaven's sake, Nick," she said, and he could hear, clear as the air on a cold morning in early spring, the return of the third-grade teacher's voice, the one that had been subsumed by mental illness, by the imaginary voices, by the panic attacks. The voice he heard now was brusque and focused. No nonsense allowed. No lollygagging. "Hang up," she said, "and concentrate on your driving."

Chapter Fifty-Eight

"I screwed up, Bell." Matt's voice was faint, faltering. "I was leaving town. I was. Swear it. But I had to—to do what I came for. One last chance. Lure him into my trap. Thought I finally had him." A bitter laugh, instigating a spasm of coughing. "Other way around."

"How did he find you?"

"I let him. I *wanted* him to find me. Led him right here. That was—that was the whole idea. From the beginning." He groaned from the effort of speaking.

He had passed out at least twice. Maybe a third time. Bell couldn't tell. He was moving in and out of consciousness, moving from darkness to light to darkness again, like a time-lapse movie of a landscape in which centuries of change are crammed into scant minutes.

She looked down at him. He seemed smaller now, blurred and diminished by his suffering. The reality of his presence was more a thing of smell, more a matter of how he felt in her grip, than of what he looked like. He smelled of sweat, a rank and unruly smell, and he smelled, too, of blood, that sharp metallic odor that cuts cleanly through other smells, rising above them, asserting its elemental primacy.

She'd tried to tie off the leg wound, knowing that the femoral artery was relentlessly pumping life-robbing amounts of blood all over the floor, like a nicked hose that continues its business until someone turns off the water main.

"I'm cold," Matt said, stuttering the *D* sound at the end of the word: *Cold-d-d-d*. As if he didn't have the energy to stop the word where it needed to be stopped. The word got the better of him.

She unfolded the rug and tucked it around his torso. She did it with no tenderness. She was prepared to watch the life drain out of him.

Because of this man, Clay Meckling had lost his leg. Because of him, Joyce and Georgette were dead. And Abner McEvoy. And the little girl and her father, too. Because of him, Ike's was gone.

Matt clutched at the rug, at the blood-soaked fringe along its edge. "Thanks," he said. His shivering intensified.

"Why did you come to the sheriff's house?" she said.

"He's—he's got guns. Figured he'd help me." He gasped the words. "In over my head this time."

"So who the hell's out there, Matt? Who is it?"

He didn't answer. Had he passed out again? She shook him to keep him focused, not caring if it caused him more pain. She didn't give a damn about his pain.

"Needed—," he said, the word coming after a groan.

"Needed what?"

"Needed a place—a place where I could kill Yusef. With nobody interfering. Nobody trying to stop me."

"Why?"

He coughed. It was a dry, dusty cough that concluded in a spasm of choking. She didn't offer him any water.

"I knew—" He closed his eyes. Tried to wet his lips, but there was no spittle left in his mouth. As his parched lips came unstuck once more so that he could continue speaking, she heard a faint crackle. "I knew he was coming," Matt said, "and I knew he'd always be coming. No end to it. Only way to stop him was to kill him. Had to find a place where nobody'd be around. So I could do it. My way."

"You brought him here." Bell wanted to kick him. Make him suffer even more. "Here. To a town filled with innocent people."

His dry lips tried to curve into a smile, but got only halfway there.

356

"Nobody's innocent," he said. His voice had grown so raspy now that she had trouble discerning his words. "Nobody."

You fucker, Bell thought, but didn't say out loud. She didn't want to give him the satisfaction of her anger. *You miserable fucking sonofabitch. This is my town. My town. You bring all this to my town. All this sorrow. All this pain. As if we didn't have enough already. As if we weren't already burdened—we have to deal with you and your fucking revenge, too.*

"Why?" she pressed him.

"I loved her." He said it smoothly, easily, as if he weren't lying in a bullet-torn living room with a mortal wound in his thigh. As if he were telling a simple story. A child's bedtime story. "I loved her, Bell."

"Who? What the hell are you talking about?"

He'd opened his eyes but now he closed them again, as if he wanted to savor the vivid private memory that bloomed in the wake of the words. "Amatullah Yusef. Abdu's sister." He coughed heavily. The result—blood mingled with phlegm—dripped from his chin and landed on his shirt. Bell made no move to wipe it off. "She was a translator at the base in Arbil," Matt said. "We fell in love and—and—oh, God, it was like nothing I'd ever felt before. Nothing I could—nothing I'd ever known. She was beautiful. And brilliant. And I just—" He suddenly cried out, body bucking and thrashing, grabbing his bloody thigh. *"Fuck,"* he cried out fiercely. "Fuck, fuck, *fuck*—it hurts."

"Yeah." She had no sympathy for him. Sarcasm flattened her voice. "That'll happen with gunshot wounds. Go on. Tell me the rest."

"Her family—" He tried to scoot his leg an inch or so in any direction, searching for a less painful angle. Couldn't find it. "Muslim. Muslim family. Very strict. So our love affair—it couldn't be. They wouldn't allow it. They found out, and—" He stopped, but not to cry out in pain. He'd just stopped.

Bell waited. When she looked down at his face, she was startled to see tears there. A comma of snot curled out of one nostril.

"They killed her, Bell," he said. "Her brothers. Abdu and Rashid. They killed Amatullah because of—because of her love for me. She'd dishonored them. The whole family. So they stabbed her. Watched her die. They stabbed her in the place where she had betrayed them—in her heart."

Bell had heard of that tradition. Honor killings, they were called. Hell of it was, she'd known similar stories from back in the hollows and deep in the mountain valleys. Families who didn't cotton to outsiders, who wouldn't let daughters marry outside the clan. And who enforced their prejudices with violence.

"So when you had Abdu in custody," she said, "it was time for payback."

At first he didn't answer. Then he closed his eyes and grunted his assent.

"You killed him," Bell went on. "Deliberately."

Another grunt.

"And so," she said, grim certainty giving her words a snap and a bite as she uttered them, like tumblers clicking into place just before a vault door springs open, "knowing that Rashid will be coming after you, you make sure he follows you to Acker's Gap. You know he'll show himself—because you make it easy for him. The day you get here, he takes a shot at you in the courthouse. Almost hits Lee Ann." She paused, biting her lip to keep her emotions in check. "He watches you. Learns your routine. You *want* him to. You *want* him to try. He sets off the bomb in Ike's, thinking you'll be sitting there with your goddamned scrambled eggs, just like always. Oh, but you got lucky with that one, right? You were up on the mountain that morning. He missed you. So you have to set up your own little O.K. Corral—but he turns out to be the better shot, right? The better fighter? Smarter, too. And so your luck runs out. Right?"

This time, there was not even a grunt. Bell peered at him, feeling nothing that was soft. No pity. No regret. Nothing. Only anger. Only rage. Matt's eyes were glassy. His breaths had gone from shallow to nonexistent. He was either dead or so close to dead that the difference didn't matter anymore.

"Lovesick bastard," she muttered. It was the only kind of good-bye she could muster at a moment's notice for a man she now despised.

His eyes fluttered open. "Can you—?" He tried again. "You never—"

She waited.

He tried again. "You never told me. The name. Acker's Gap. Who was—?"

"Jesus, Matt."

"Please."

"Jesus. Of all the fucking stupid—okay." She spoke harshly. "It's not a person's name, okay? They used to grow a lot of tobacco in these parts. Called it 'backer.' The 'backer crop. So this was Tobacco Gap. Backer's Gap. Over the years, it got kind of slurred. Lost its edge. Like everything else around here. Acker's Gap. There. That's it, you fucker. Just like I promised. There you go."

Did he smile? She couldn't tell. In death, she knew, a spasm of the facial muscles could mimic a grin. His mouth was twisted, frozen in its final expression.

A tiny triangle of white crested the breast pocket of his shirt. The note. The one she'd seen in that spot on multiple occasions and wondered about. Bell tugged it out.

The faded blue ink on the oft-folded page was smeared at the edges, but the drowsy, beautiful, languid-looking handwriting was still legible:

My dear darling Matthew, My heart is full tonight, as full as the moon I see above the dark sands, and if I had words to tell you my love, those words would burn this page the way my love for you burns my heart, and you could touch the page and feel it, you could

The writing went on for several more lines. Pledges of love, promises of eternal devotion. Bell let her eyes drop to the end.

Forever yours, Amatullah

With the fold lines as her guide, she made the paper small again, small enough to fit back in Matt's shirt pocket. He had carried it thousands of miles, he had kept it next to his heart, and now, she supposed, it ought to accompany him on the longest journey of all.

He was gone, but his face still had not relaxed. It was taut, the skin stretched tightly over the bones. Everything about him was hard. It had always been hard. Hard and honed.

Except for one thing: his love for the woman named Amatullah. That was the only weakness he had ever allowed himself. Love. And it had brought joy and ruin. Happiness and destruction.

An explosion of disintegrating glass ripped the air over her head. Another round of automatic gunfire. *It's coming,* she told herself, whole body flinching, crossing her arms over her head. Yusef was on the move again.

Closing in on his prey.

Chapter Fifty-Nine

Pam Harrison nodded. And nodded again.

To each instruction from Sheriff Fogelsong—terse sentences that he repeated twice to make sure she understood—she responded with a separate curt nod. She could have waited until the end of his address and just nodded once, but she knew how nervous he was. Seeing her nods—*Yep. Yep. Got it, boss*—would, she knew, help settle him down. Show him she was focused and ready.

The deputy had met him at the intersection of Rathmell Road and Route 12, behind Smithson's Rock. During her call from the McClatchy trailer, Mary Sue had given him a sense of where the gunfire might be coming from; the assailant had moved in close to cut the phone lines and set the cell jammer, but then he'd apparently moved out again, climbing back up on Smithson's Rock, firing from different angles, keeping an eye on whoever might approach the house.

"And Pam," Fogelsong said. "Don't take any chances, okay? I need you in one piece."

Never before had he called her Pam. It was always "Deputy Harrison." And never before had he expressed concern for her physical safety. That wasn't how Nick Fogelsong operated. Risk was a given. Price of the job.

She reached into the open trunk of her car and retrieved her

JULIA KELLER

equipment: the Heckler & Koch HK13E assault rifle that she'd inherited from her father, Homer Harrison, a munitions specialist in the first Gulf War. With Nick's backing, Deputy Harrison had received special permission from the West Virginia State Police and from the ATF to keep the weapon. It was a handful, measuring almost four feet long and weighing about eighteen pounds, and it was, she liked to say, *a real mean sonofabitch when you're on the wrong side of it,* with a 30-round magazine that hammered out 750 rounds per minute. Deputy Harrison kept herself sharp on the HK just in case. It was, like the panic button in the courthouse, one of the things that helped people in Acker's Gap sleep better at night, amid all the news about terrorism.

"What's your range?" Fogelsong asked.

"Six thousand feet," she said. "Maybe more."

He watched as she moved into position, her gestures crisp, smooth, efficient. She'd set up a spot next to the road on a short shelf of rock. Somewhere below here, in the midst of the high trees that clung to the side of the mountain, was the shooter. And below the shooter, visible to Harrison and the sheriff when they peered over the edge of the cliff into the valley stretching out in the mountain's craggy shadow, was the house belonging to Nick and Mary Sue Fogelsong.

The house that contained, as Mary Sue had matter-of-factly informed them during the phone call, a dying man. And Bell Elkins, whose physical condition at present was unknown.

"Ready?" Fogelsong said.

"Ready." Harrison flopped onto her belly. Adjusted her grip on the gun.

The sheriff pulled his service revolver out of the holster. Held it straight up in the air. Fired four shots. Then he, too, hit the deck.

Just as Harrison had predicted, an answering burst of machine gun fire came smashing out of a gap in the trees below them. *He'll figure we've got rifles and pistols,* she had said, *and he'll give away his position right quick. Cocky bastard won't be able to resist. Thinks he's got the only assault weapon in a thousand-mile radius.*

She aimed, fired. The systematic spray of bullets carved up the

362

trees with ravenous speed, butchering leaves and bark in a headlong horizontal swath.

They waited.

Silence.

"Now?" Nick said.

She nodded.

He rose to his knees, lifted his pistol. This time, he fired only twice. No sense wasting ammunition.

Silence.

A different kind of silence this time. A silence that seemed to guarantee that when they climbed down closer and checked the approximate spot where the shooter had been hiding, they'd find a bloody corpse.

"Think you got him," the sheriff said.

Harrison didn't reply. She was already on her feet, securing her weapon, switching out the magazine. Just in case.

The sheriff watched her. He'd not intended to say anything else right now, but couldn't help himself. "Partly my fault," he said.

"Your fault."

"Yeah."

"How do you figure?"

"Mary Sue saw him. A few nights ago. Swore she saw a face at the window. I'll bet every last dollar I have that it was the same son-ofabitch who just tried to blow our heads off. Probably casing the place. Found out where I lived—me, the guy in town with the most firepower—and did some reconnaissance. If I'd paid more attention to her—"

"Hey," Harrison said, interrupting him. "Look at it this way. I needed some practice with the HK. You did me a favor. Can't beat a live target."

Chapter Sixty

Bell was riding in Nick's big Blazer. She was exhausted, she was brittle with fatigue and utterly spent, but she needed to make a call to Sam. She had to do it.

Bell was hopping mad—she'd never understood the phrase *hopping mad,* but now she did, because she felt a crazy urge to run; she felt as if only physical activity could purge the anger that was throbbing in her body like a second and far fiercer heartbeat—and she had to talk to him. *Now.*

Deputies Greenough and Mathers were handling the crime scene in and around the Fogelsong house, assisting the paramedics who dealt with the bodies of Matt Harless and Rashid Yusef, and taking Harrison's statement about the line-of-duty shooting. An FBI team had already been dispatched to Edna's house.

"Hate to do this in front of you, Nick," Bell said. "No choice. Has to be done right away."

He nodded. Not sure what she meant, but trusting her judgment.

She hit a number in her cell's contact list. Listened.

Then she pounced.

"Sam," Bell said. Her voice quivered with rage. "You *knew.* You knew why Matt wanted to come to Acker's Gap, didn't you? And you set it up."

"Belfa, hey, I—"

"Shut up. Shut up. Just shut the hell up. Don't try to justify it. You put an entire town at risk. All these people. You *bastard,* you—"

"Just listen to me, okay? I didn't know everything," Sam said, "but yeah—yeah, I knew the basics. I didn't have a choice. I owed him. And he's not the kind of guy you just walk away from. You know that now. I had to do what he said. He'd sent some government business my way, pulled some strings, cut some corners, and if he told anybody, I could've been indicted, I might have gone to prison or—"

Interrupting him, her voice dropped to a snarl. "It's your home-town, too, Sam. Your friends and neighbors. These are people you grew up with. Who trust you. Who think the world of you, in fact. Who're so proud of you. So damned proud. And this is how you pay them back? You let him do this. Here. *Here.* You bring this *here.* You offer us up. Like goddamned sacrificial lambs."

"Look, Bell, I knew Carla was safe. She was with me. And I tried to get you out of there, too." His voice was hasty, wheedling. A sales-man's voice. "Remember? After the explosion at Ike's? I tried to get you to move back to D.C. I tried to—"

"*Move back?*" Shouting now. Hoping the volume hurt Sam's ears. Hoping it didn't hurt Nick's. Either way, though, she wouldn't stop. "This is where I *live.* This is my *home,* Sam. Acker's Gap. Don't you understand that? Don't you get it? Nobody's ever going to run me out of my home again. Nobody. *Ever.*"

The funny thing was, Bell later reflected, she didn't really know she felt that way until she'd said it out loud. Until she articulated it in the heat of the moment. Until she answered Sam's remark about mov-ing somewhere else, moving to a place, perhaps, where the mountain didn't watch her every move, where the past didn't wait around every bend in the road.

"To hell with you, Sam Elkins," she declared. "To hell with you." She used her thumb to mash the END button with such force that she was half-afraid the cell might melt from the heat of her fury.

The inside of the Blazer was silent now, except for the woolly thrum of the big engine. They'd reached the courthouse. Nick had wanted to take her straight to the big stone house on Shelton Avenue, but she declined the offer. "Work to do," was her only elaboration. He had work to do, too. He'd already called Homeland Security; they were on their way. Nick had not yet released the news about Edna Hankins to the public and dreaded the moment when he had to. Bell had put it best: *In a small town, everybody is next of kin to everybody else.*

Making the first right turn in the courthouse corridor, Bell saw them: Serena Crumpler and Hickey Leonard were standing in front of the prosecutor's office. Serena, briefcase in hand, a worried frown pulling at her thin face like a drawstring, making it look even thinner, had tied back her hair into a limp ponytail. Hickey was holding a sheaf of papers. His face, too, was dark with concern.

"Boss," he said. "We've got a problem."

Bell moved past them and opened her office door. Maybe if she ignored them, they'd go away. Worth a shot, anyway.

They followed right behind her. First Hick, then Serena. Bell turned and gave her assistant a glare she was sure he'd recognize. If he was paying attention, he'd know it was time to back off and go home.

"Not a good time right now, guys," she said. She didn't want to go into any of it—the gun battle and deaths of Edna and Matt Harless—because she'd be reciting the story again and again in the hours and days and weeks ahead, she knew, as the official investigations commenced. She wanted another five minutes of peace. "Really swamped."

"This can't wait, Bell. We have to talk to you," Hick said.

"Fine." No cordiality in her tone. She moved into her own office, yanked out the chair from under her desk, and sat down in a heap, making no attempt to be graceful or ladylike. If Hick and Serena wanted to sit down, they could suit themselves; she didn't offer them chairs. They damned well knew where the chairs were.

They remained standing. Serena spoke first, but only because Hick had paused to take a breath.

"It's Ketchum Doggett," the young woman declared. "He didn't do it. He didn't kill Lucinda."

Bell rubbed her eyes with her index fingers. "Look, Serena, save it for the arraignment, okay?"

Now Hick spoke. "You've got to listen to this."

"Really."

"Yeah. You do." There was a flicker of anger in Hick's voice. Over the years Bell had heard a variety of things in that voice of his—amusement, cynicism, sarcasm, disillusionment—but anger was rarely on the list. It surprised her. She stopped rubbing her eyes.

"What's going on, Hick?"

"New information has come to light," he said. "And just like Serena said, it could mean that Ketchum Doggett didn't kill Lucinda."

"Hard to believe," Bell said dubiously. "We've got the recording of Ketchum arguing with her in the car. We know Ketchum was with her that night at the river."

"Not saying he wasn't," Hick replied.

"Then what *are* you saying?"

Serena beat him to the punch.

"We're saying," she declared, "that he wasn't the *last* person with her."

Chapter Sixty-One

Hick sat down on the couch for the rest of the conversation. Serena tried to, but couldn't manage it; she needed to be in motion, and so she paced. Pacing caused her ponytail to tick-tock earnestly back and forth. Bell had to resist a powerful urge to lean over from her desk chair and grab the twitchy dribble of black hair and hold it still.

"Got a call this afternoon from Buster Crutchfield," Hick said. "He'd been trying to reach you, but when he couldn't, he tracked me down instead. Told me he'd just received some more extensive results from the state lab." Hick paused, then plunged: "Shawn Doggett was not the father of Lucinda's baby."

"Is he—?" Bell had started to say, *Is he sure?* but realized how silly that sounded. Of course he was sure. Buster Crutchfield might have been a thousand years old or thereabouts, but he knew his business.

Hick waited for her to go on. When she didn't, he did. "I called Serena. As the attorney of record for Wendy and her sons, I thought she might be able to shed some light on things."

Serena had stopped marching. "Wendy Doggett was absolutely stunned at the news," she said. "So was Ketchum. But not Shawn. Turns out that Shawn knew all along that the baby wasn't his. He'd agreed to marry Lucinda so that the baby would have a father. And he promised her that he'd never reveal it wasn't his child—no matter what. He kept his promise. Even if it meant he might be prosecuted for her murder."

"So who *is* the father?"

"Shawn doesn't know," Serena said. "Lucinda never told him. He asked her, of course, but she wouldn't tell."

"So how do we—?"

"*Shawn* doesn't know," Hick said, interrupting her, "but *I* do. And I'd bet my house and everything in it that Lucinda's killer was the father of her unborn child."

After breaking the news to Serena, Hick said, going on with his story in a dogged, headlong voice, a voice that revealed no glee about its revelations, he had called Madeline Trimble. "That was the key," he explained to Bell. Leaning forward from his spot on the couch, elbows perched on knees, he was barely able to hold his agitation in check. "I'd read the sheriff's notes about his initial interviews with Lucinda's mother. It was all part of the trial preparation," he continued. "Remember how Maddie said she'd been home by midnight the night of the murder? But then Nick found out she'd actually spent the night with Eddie Geyer?"

"Yeah," Bell said. She didn't bother to hide her disgust. "Which made Maddie spectacularly useless in the investigation, as most lowlife liars turn out to be." Her animosity toward Maddie Trimble would surely outlast the mountains and all the rivers, too. Bell knew it was unbecoming of her to hold such a ferocious grudge—but didn't really care.

"Right," Hick said, ignoring her umbrage. "But Nick also asked her if she'd seen anything before she left that night. Any strange cars in the area."

"And she said no."

"Exactly. No *strange* cars. He didn't ask her about cars, period. He didn't ask her about familiar cars—cars she recognized because they were there almost every night, night after night. A deputy sheriff's car, for instance. Which was there because Nick had asked him to stop by now and again, to keep an eye on the house after her mail-box was vandalized last year."

"Holy shit." Bell stared at Hickey, hoping she was misunderstand-ing him. She pictured a big, aging face, a face usually lost in shadow beneath the broad brim of a regulation hat. Burly body. The strong hands of a law enforcement officer. "You don't mean Greenough. Greg Greenough?"

"Yes. I kept pushing at Maddie, asking her what she'd seen before she left that night to go be with Eddie Geyer—and finally, finally, *finally,* after she'd thought long and hard about it, she said, 'Well, there was Deputy Greenough's squad car, of course, but he's always out there. He's been coming by for months now. On account of him, we can relax. Hardly even notice him anymore, truth be told.'"

Instantly, Bell was profoundly angry with herself. Why hadn't she figured this out on her own? If it were possible, she would've fired her-self on the spot. Why hadn't she seen it? Then she recalled that she hadn't read Maddie Trimble's statement with the kind of thoroughness and meticulousness that she usually brought to her work. Her contempt for Maddie Trimble had gotten in the way of her professionalism—just as Nick's affection for Maddie Trimble had gotten in the way of his.

"I bet Greenough followed Lucinda that night," Hick said, voice speeding up with grim confidence. "I think he'd been following her on a regular basis, ever since their affair started. Keeping tabs on her. That night, he tracked her to the Doggett house, where she picked up Ketchum, and then to the Bitter River. Greenough had to wait—he had to wait far enough back so he wouldn't be spotted. But he was used to spying on her that way. Used to keeping his distance. After Lucinda and Ketchum had their argument, and Ketchum was picked up along the road, Greenough must've made his move. It was Gree-nough and Lucinda, alone in the car. He tried again to persuade her to give up the baby. If she had that baby, he might be exposed. Lose his job, his family. Everything."

"So he strangled her," Bell said solemnly. "And he dumped out her purse on the riverbank and he let the car roll in the water. Because knowing forensics, he was afraid he might've left some evidence in there."

"Yes." Hick's face looked peeved, not triumphant. "Hell of it is, though, we can't prove a damned thing. We can't even prove that Greenough was the father of Lucinda's baby. We don't have a DNA sample to give Buster Crutchfield. And until we have more evidence— more, anyway, than my fancy theories—no judge is going to force Greenough to give us one."

Slowly, Bell rose. From the desktop she picked up a piece of note-book paper, the one she'd been doodling on for days now. As she folded the paper in half she had an odd and fleeting notion, unusual for her because she so prized rationality: The gray flecks from the pencil tip could have been a code, arranged in a seemingly random pattern that, viewed from the right angle, might reveal everything, every secret hidden in every human heart from the beginning of time right up to this fraught and haunted moment.

She moved toward the coat rack in the corner, upon which dan-gled Deputy Greenough's coat and hat, now dry, the coat hanging in stiff black folds, the brown hat permanently discolored from so many years of sheltering the man's perspiring head. Since that rainy morn-ing the sky had been a clear, innocent-looking blue. Greenough had yet to return to pick up his foul-weather gear. Hadn't needed it.

"Hate to contradict you, Hick," Bell said, "but we *do* have his DNA."

When they arrived at the coroner's office with their cargo, Buster Crutchfield was not as elated as they'd hoped he would be. He met them in the reception area, hands punched disconsolately into the frayed pockets of his white lab coat.

"We're way down on the priority list at the state lab," he said. "Could take quite a while to get the results back. Days, maybe. Even weeks. By that time—well, you can't build your case until we know for sure. And I don't know when that'll be. Might leave too much time for the man to get wind of your suspicions and concoct a story to explain himself. Or destroy other evidence. Or, hell—maybe even to leave the state. I'll send it over to 'em right now, but all I can tell you," he said, winding up his lament with a sad little shake of his crusty bald head, "is that I'll call you when I know something."

Bell sat down in an orange plastic chair, one of the chairs bolted in a solemn row in which grief-dazed family members were obliged to hold their makeshift vigils, numb with dread until the coroner summoned them back to identify a body. Hick took the seat on her left. Serena, on her right.

"We'll wait," Bell said.

Nick Fogelsong was standing over her, hand on her shoulder, shaking her awake. Once alert, Bell realized that his gesture reminded her of the previous time he'd awakened her like that—the terrible morning at the medical center, right after the explosion at Ike's. This time, though, she didn't ache all over. And this time, when she looked up into Nick's face, he was smiling. A grim smile, but a smile nonetheless.

"Got him," he said.

Bell, confused, looked around for Hickey and Serena.

"Hick's making some calls," the sheriff explained. "Serena had a meeting with another client. She's a go-getter, that one." He looked around, too. "Can't believe you guys spent the night." He couldn't resist teasing her, even at such a tense time. "Appreciate the dedication, but you better not put in for overtime, Belfa. County can't afford it."

Bell squinted at her wristwatch: It was 6:12 on the morning after she, Hick, and Serena had hustled over here with Greg Greenough's hat, hoping that Buster Crutchfield could extract DNA from its sweat-soaked interior and prove that the deputy had fathered Lucinda's child. Sometime in the middle of the night she had fallen asleep in the chair, arms crossed, legs thrust out in front of her and crossed at the ankle, head tilted back against the cinder block wall.

"And Greenough?" Bell said.

By this time the sheriff had sat down next to her. He didn't look as if he'd indulged in a sleep any more restful than hers.

"I confronted him with the evidence," Fogelsong said, "and he capitulated so fast, I had to get him to stop talking long enough for me to get out my notebook and read him his rights. Told me the whole story. They always do, have you noticed? Always have to explain themselves. Every pathetic bastard I've ever arrested has got to make sure I understand why they did what they did." The sheriff shifted his bottom in the chair, searching for a comfort that wasn't going to come. "You'd think I would feel betrayed, knowing him all these years like I did, working side by side with the man, but it wasn't like that at all. I'm pissed off, mainly. Damned disgusted." Shook his head, as if to get rid of the excess emotions and the leftover memories. Work to do. "Greenough started up the affair with Lucinda about six months ago. Night after night, he'd be there checking on the house. Maddie'd go on to bed—or be out late herself, more recently—and Lucinda would come out on the back porch and she and Greenough would strike up a conversation. And pretty soon—well." Nick dipped his head. He lifted it again a second or so later, but he still couldn't look at Bell when he told this part of the story. He'd known her when she was ten years old, and sometimes had trouble remembering that she was all grown up now.

"He was a father figure to her," the sheriff went on. "Something she'd never had. He was protecting her—or so she thought—and she admired him. Wanted to make him happy. Way I hear it, Lucinda was the kind of young lady who wanted everybody to be happy. Wanted to make things right. Was she in love with Greg Greenough? Doubt it. Hell, she had the Doggett brothers chasing after her. Good-looking young men. But she could see that Greenough was sad and depressed—and she wanted to help him. Wanted to save him. Wanted to save the whole damned world, seems like. Which makes her sound a lot like another young lady I knew once upon a time, another one just burnin' up with a sense of justice."

Bell gave him a sideways scowl. Not the time.

"Okay," she said, before he could elaborate on his thought, "I get all that, but Greenough has a family. A reputation. He'd risk all that for—for an affair with a sixteen-year-old?"

"When I talked to him a few hours ago, the whole story came out like a hot wash of vomit," Nick said. "Greg was feeling old and useless. Knew he'd never make sheriff. He looks around and he sees Pam Harrison. Half his age—and it's clear that she's headed for the sheriff's job one day, if she wants it. Not him. Never him. He lacks the skills and the temperament—and he knows it." Fogelsong looked down at his big hands. Blew out a spurt of air. "Can't imagine how hard this'll be for Greg's wife and his daughter to deal with," he said quietly. "You'd like to believe he might've thought of that, somewhere along the way. But you know what, Bell? Seeing yourself in the eyes of somebody who thinks you hung the moon—it can turn your head, I guess, pretty damned quick. It's a powerful lure. At least it was for Greg Greenough. And the fact that Lucinda was such a wonderful young woman—so smart, with such a bright future—well, it just made it all the sweeter for him. Human heart's a funny thing, Belfa. No accounting for it.

"When she told Greenough she was pregnant, he hit the roof," Fogelsong went on. "Begged her to get rid of it. She wouldn't. And then her boyfriend, Shawn, instead of being mad, instead of rejecting her, was there to help her out—'cause he loved her, Bell. Imagine that. He loved her enough to help her raise another man's child. Not even knowing who the real father was. Marcy didn't know, either. Lucinda didn't tell a soul. These kids—they're loyal, loyal to a fault. And then came that night at the Bitter River. Greenough follows her there. Waits for her to finish with Ketchum. Waits for his chance. Not his chance to kill her—that part just happened, he says, and I suppose I believe him—but his chance to talk some sense into her. If he can just get Lucinda to *listen*. To stop caring so much about that baby and to *listen*. Greenough gets in her car and he begs Lucinda one more time to have an abortion. One more time, she says no. He loses his temper. He's scared out of his mind. Desperate."

"And he chokes her to death."

"Yes." He let a moment go by. There had been no triumph in his recapitulation of Greenough's confession. The peace that usually descended on the sheriff at the conclusion of a case—order restored, the town tucked in safe and tight like a child at bedtime—was missing. Fogelsong leaned forward in his chair and squinted, as if he dearly wished for another angle from which to regard human nature. A more obstructed view, perhaps. One not quite so clear and vivid.

"And Shawn?" Bell said. "And Wendy and Ketchum?"

"Released this morning. Rhonda took care of the paperwork. They got home a while ago and found out that Alton Doggett's packed his bags and gone. Got himself a real nice place over in Drummond. Ten bucks says he won't be spending his nights alone, you know what I mean?"

Bell frowned. She was remembering the scenario that had unspooled in her head, the motion picture that starred Ketchum Doggett as the murderer. Some parts of it *had* happened—Ketchum had indeed left the car, crawled up the riverbank, called his family to come get him—but the crucial part of it hadn't. Her intuition about crime scenes? Total crap. She'd never be able to trust it again.

She was still thinking, still going over the events as she knew them. "Ketchum didn't kill her—which means he didn't take the ring off her finger after she died," Bell said. "She was alive when he left her. So how'd the ring get back in Wendy's jewelry box?"

"Thought that question might occur to you. I talked to Ketchum this morning and asked him. Turns out he got the ring from Lucinda during their conversation that night. Put it back in the box himself."

Bell was still puzzled. "But why would she give him the ring?"

"It's what you *didn't* hear," the sheriff said. "You didn't hear it, because it wasn't on the recording. Lucinda had shut the dang thing off. Realized she didn't need to be afraid of Ketchum." He rubbed a thumb across his bottom lip. Thinking. "Turns out she wasn't going to marry Shawn after all. Her talk with Ketchum by the river that night had helped her sort it all out. She was going to have that baby—but she wasn't going to marry Shawn. She didn't love him. And no matter how rough her life was going to be, no matter how much she'd have to struggle and fight, her intention was to take her child and go away. Start a new life. Handing over the ring to Ketchum was her way of making that promise to him. And—even more important—to herself."

"But he left her there in an angry huff. If everything was okay between them, then why—?"

"Everything *wasn't* okay between them. You've got to remember one thing," the sheriff said, his face briefly unclenching into a rueful smile. "Ketchum was in love with her. He was still upset. True, she wasn't going to be with Shawn—but she wasn't going to be with *him,* either. She wasn't going to be with anybody. It would be her and her baby, out in the world. Just the two of them. She'd made up her mind."

The realization came to Bell: *Maddie was absolutely right to ask Eddie to return to Acker's Gap. Their conversations with Lucinda had mattered. The young woman had listened to them. Her decision wasn't the one they wanted—but it was hers. All hers. They had given her the strength and the confidence to follow her heart.*

"Greenough couldn't let Lucinda have that baby," Bell said somberly, taking over the story. "He couldn't take the chance. He'd always be vulnerable. And so he killed her. Tossed her purse out the window to make it look like a robbery—the cover-up we'd attributed to Ketchum." She stretched out her legs and winced. "Jesus, Nick. Guess I'll have to sleep late more often. You all did my whole damned job for me."

He snorted. "Not quite. You've got about six different federal agencies wanting to talk to you about Matt Harless and Rashid Yusef. They're itching for the details. There'll be a thorough debriefing. If I know the feds, you'll be tied up from now till next Christmas."

"God help me." She groaned.

Hick came around the corner, sliding his cell in the rumpled pocket of his trousers. Between the spiky white stubble on his chin and the dirty circles under his eyes, he looked like ten miles of bad road. "Hey, boss," he said. "You're up."

"Well," Bell said, rising and patting the plastic chair, "the accommodations in this joint leave a little something to be desired, but yeah, I'm up." She waved toward the interior of the coroner's office, the area beyond the padded double doors. "I guess Buster got them to do a rush job on that DNA, huh? And good thing, since it made Greenough come clean."

"Actually," Nick said, "the results aren't back yet. State boys said it'll be at least two weeks. Lucky for us, though, Greenough didn't know that. I told him we had the DNA results in hand. He bought it." The sheriff stood up, too. Put both hands on the small of his back, preparatory to an epic stretch. "I first met Greg Greenough almost fifty years ago. Knew his folks. Hunted with his brother. Sat with him on the night his daddy died. Gave a toast at his wedding. Went to Kendra's baptism. You think you know a person, but—"

"You don't," Bell said, not so much interrupting him as finishing his thought. "Hell, it's tough enough to know your own damned self. How can you ever expect to know somebody else?"

Chapter Sixty-Two

The wind at this height raked their faces like a Brillo pad, harsh and artless. Bell's hair kept whipping into her eyes. She had to peel it off strand by strand as if it were a spider web, picking assiduously at the threads and defusing the tangles.

They were up on the mountain. It was seconds before sunrise on the day after Greg Greenough's arraignment for the murder of Lucinda Trimble, the first chance they'd had to do what needed to be done. Sheriff Fogelsong was here. Hick and Rhonda. Maddie Trimble, too. Maddie was having an even harder time with the wind than Bell; her hair was like a thick gray flag that reached across her features and showed every indication of wanting to stay put. Nature's blindfold.

Also present was a woman they didn't know very well: Joyce LeFevre's daughter, Jackie. She was thirty-four years old and, like her mother, large and dark and quiet. Yet the quietness, Bell noted, had a power inside it. It was not a meek quiet. When Joyce and her husband had divorced, Jackie was away at college in Tennessee, and she'd never come back to Acker's Gap. Until now.

They were here to spread the ashes of Joyce and Georgette, and of Edna Hankins, too. Edna had no living relatives.

Except that she did.

In a small town, Bell reminded herself, *everybody is next of kin to everybody else.*

Bell had hitched a ride here with the sheriff. They had parked along the road—the one that zigged and squiggled up the mountain—and hiked the last few hundred feet to the overlook.

Clay wanted to come, but couldn't yet make the climb and had reluctantly admitted that to Bell. He was gradually adapting himself to his prosthetic leg; still, he faced a great many months of grueling physical therapy. Conversations about the future of their relationship seemed as daunting as this steep ascent. Bell didn't know what they would end up being to each other, how they would relate given this new reality—the reality not of Clay's injury, but of how he saw himself in the wake of it. Two days ago she had leaned over the rail of his hospital bed and tried to kiss him, and he'd turned his face away from her. *Okay,* she'd told herself. *Okay.* Grad school had been put on hold. Clay planned to live with his parents as he went through rehab; private time would be hard to come by. When it did occur, it would surely be stilted and formal. *I'm fine. And you?*

Maddie was climbing the rocky path just ahead of Bell, holding up her long skirt so that she wouldn't trip. The reconciliation with Eddie Geyer hadn't worked out, after all. Despite his promises, he'd gone right back to his old ways. Picked up for drunk driving over in Grantham County, he was being extradited back to Kentucky on an outstanding warrant for an aggravated assault charge. In the single conversation Bell had had with Maddie Trimble about it—they'd run into each other at Lymon's Market—Maddie had muttered, *Once a bum, always a bum, is what my daddy used to say. Sure wish I'd listened.*

The night before this gathering on the mountain, Bell had driven out to the Applebee's on the turnpike. Melvin Stump, the second-shift manager who also tended bar, had called and asked her to come by if she could. Two years ago Bell had prosecuted his stepson for grand theft auto—it was Melvin who'd ratted the kid out, referring to him as "that worthless sumbitch," adding, "Prison's too good for his bony ass"—and he and Bell had stayed in touch.

"Funny thing happened the other night," Melvin had told her, once she'd taken a seat on a red-topped barstool and let him serve her a Diet Coke in a curvy glass with a striped straw. "Eddie Geyer come in here and he was acting kind of peculiar."

"Peculiar how?"

She'd had her choice of seats. Weeknights, Applebee's cleared out early. Waitresses stood in the corners, admiring their manicures and fending off clumsy advances from the busboys.

"Well," said Melvin, an obese man with a frizzy fringe of strawberry blond hair that shaded his forehead like an awning, "he orders hisself a drink and then when I brung him the glass he says, 'Go ahead and get the whole damned bottle on over here, Mel, and do it right quick.' That wasn't like him—not like him these days, that is, 'cause ever since he's been back this time, Eddie ain't touched a drop, and I know that for a fact—but he was pretty riled up about it, you know? So I brung him the bottle.

"And then he done the strangest thing," Melvin went on. He was polishing a glass with a yellow dishrag and as his tale went along, he polished harder. "Eddie done poured that dadburned bottle all over hisself. Made a mess of the floor, the bar—everywhere. He was gettin' pretty loud and gettin' pretty sloppy and botherin' the other customers and so finally I had to ask him to leave. You'd think, from lookin' at him and smellin' him, that he was drunk as a skunk. Truth was, though, he never touched a drop. Not one drop."

Melvin flipped the dishrag over his shoulder so he'd have a free hand. He held that hand straight up, as if he were taking a solemn oath in court. "Believe me, Mrs. Elkins—if he'd been as shit-faced as he looked, I'd-a-never let him go out and get in a car, which is what he did. I heard they picked him up over in Grantham County, drivin' Maddie Trimble's car and weavin' and speedin' like a crazy man. Wouldn't take a Breathalyzer, neither—which is kinda funny when you think about it. Most folks refuse it 'cause they know it'll hang 'em, even though it means they take you to jail right then, no questions asked. And old Eddie refuses it, too—but he was dry as a bone. Whadda you think about that?"

She moved the straw around in her Diet Coke, watching the ice cubes shift and bob.

"I don't know, Melvin," she said, although she was fairly certain that she did. Sometimes it was better to leave people with a clean bright dream of what might have been—than to get involved in the ragtag mess of reality. Maybe Eddie realized he couldn't change, and he didn't want Maddie to put all that hope and heart into a future that was never to be.

"You know what, Mrs. Elkins?" Melvin said. "You just never can tell about folks, can you?" He shrugged. Plucked the dishrag off his shoulder, ready to resume his polishing chores. "You want some of them spicy peanuts? Got a little bowl of 'em right over here."

"My mother loved these mountains," said Jackie LeFevre.

Once they'd arrived at the spot that Sheriff Fogelsong had scouted out the day before, Jackie broke the news: She planned to use the insurance settlement from her mother's death to purchase an empty storefront in Acker's Gap. Open a restaurant there. She would call it Joyce's Place.

Now it was time. The wind had settled down, as if it, too, recognized the gravity of the occasion and didn't want to steal the show with its orneriness.

Jackie held out a small ceramic vase. Pink and cream-colored, with a fluted lip that struck Bell as a bit too delicate to contain the mortal remains of those two admirably strong and enviably self-sufficient women, Joyce LeFevre and Georgette Akers. *Mountain women,* Bell thought. Highest praise she knew.

Jackie removed the lid. With three heaves of the vase, she flung the ashes in three different directions. Then it was time to repeat the gesture with the vase containing Edna's ashes; they surrendered themselves just as readily to the dance of the air currents and disappeared in the light of the coming day.

Bell let everyone else leave ahead of her. She'd catch up.

She looked out across the foothills, across the creamy folds and delicate undulations. The morning mist had yet to dissipate. It rode low on the ground, a benign fog that spread democratically in every direction. She knew these mountains. She had played here as a child and she always relished the mountains on spring mornings, when the mist caused things to appear both strange and familiar. The landscape seemed, at this moment, a place fit only for the newly dead, for those who had crossed the invisible line and now made their way—after one last look back, a look filled with love and yearning—toward the mountains in the next world.

Chapter Sixty-Three

The sheriff drove her home after the ceremony. They didn't speak; they didn't need to. As the Blazer reached the edge of Bell's neighborhood, she looked with simple gratitude at the sturdy old houses. With their roots clenched deep in the dark soil, their redbrick chimneys slotted against the blue sky, their backyards melting into the woods that had been pushed back to make room for them, they were like natural facts of the landscape.

Fogelsong executed the slow right turn onto Shelton Avenue. Bell had closed her eyes for just a moment—not only because the morning sun was intense but also because she was dog-tired. She knew the trip was over when she heard the engine stop.

"You're home now," he said.

She opened her eyes. Looked first at him, and then over at the big two-story stone house with the cinnamon-colored slate roof and the wide front porch.

Standing at the top of the porch steps was a tall, alarmingly thin woman in black Wranglers, baggy gray sweatshirt, dirty white tennis shoes. Her long, yellow-gray hair ended in a scraggly patch of split ends that spread across her hunched shoulders.

No.

Yes.

It was Shirley Dolan. Her sister.

"Nick," Bell said. Voice a husky whisper, from all the backed-up emotion that was trying to escape along with the words. "Did you—? Is it—?"

"Yeah." He touched Bell's arm. "It's Shirley. She got hold of me last week. Said she'd called you from the road a few times, tried to talk, but couldn't work up the nerve. So she just hung up. I was afraid she might not show. That's why I didn't tell you, Bell. Didn't want you to be disappointed all over again. But I think she figured it was time. High time for her to come home."

Bell nodded. She began to open the car door.

Abruptly she closed it again, pulling her hand back from the handle as if it were scalding hot. Panic on her face, in her voice.

"Nick—oh my God, it's been so long—I don't know if I can—I don't know what to say or what to—"

He reached across her lap and opened the door.

"You'll think of something."

Turn the page for a sneak peek at
Julia Keller's next novel

Summer of the Dead

Available August 2014

Chapter One

The flat-roofed shack was situated along a country road sunk deep in summer darkness, the kind of darkness that comes after a day of brash sunlight and thus seems more intense and deliberate than ordinary nightfall. The lights in the small tavern made it look, by odd contrast with that shadow-blackened road, like a living thing, shimmying and caterwauling and ready to leap up and lurch away, leaving behind a shallow hole and the sullen stink of piss.

Bell Elkins knew it was an illusion. She knew the only real motion came from the quivering lights in four porthole windows across the building's front and from the ugly thuds of the live band's bass beat, a percussion that hit like a fist on the heart. Yet she hesitated anyway, remaining for a few more minutes in her vehicle at the edge of the dirt-ridged parking lot. Other cars were stuck at crazy random angles, abandoned by their drivers with don't-give-a-damn nonchalance.

It was 3:42 A.M. on a sticky-hot Saturday night—no, Sunday morning—in the middle of June, and Bell was angry. The anger moved across her mind like a wire being threaded slowly through her veins, millimeter by millimeter. It didn't flare, the way her anger usually behaved; this time, it was gradual. A steady, ominous rise. As she reminded herself of each galling fact, the anger ticked up a notch, and then a notch past that.

Fact: Her sister Shirley hadn't been home in three days. Shirley was a grown woman, and the house rules were loose—but still. Three days. And no call, no text.

Fact: The cell on Bell's bedside table had played its perversely chipper tune just before 3 A.M. On the other end of the line was Amanda Sturm, a deputy sheriff in Collier County. "Got a call 'bout a ruckus over at Tommy's," Sturm said after identifying herself. She didn't have to identify Tommy's. It was a bar—this bar—out along Burnt Ridge Road, a place notorious for fights and drugs and trouble. "Looked in on things," the deputy went on, "and got the lay of the land and then figured I oughta give you a call. Sorry 'bout the time."

She hadn't awakened her; Bell hardly slept these days, and spent many of her nights sitting up in the battered old easy chair in her living room, reading or trying to. Tonight, she'd actually made it upstairs to bed, but sleep was a non-starter. Still, though, the call had startled her. "What do you mean?" Bell had asked. Her cell was as light and sleek as a Hershey's bar, yet she used both hands to wrangle it, one to secure it against her ear, the other to keep the bottom half tilted against her chin.

There was a pause, and then the deputy said, "Well, ma'am, one of 'em says her sister is the Raythune County prosecutor and I better lay off. Checked her wallet and sure nuff—you're listed as contact person. Shirley Dolan's her name."

Fact: Commingling with the clientele in a place like Tommy's could put Shirley in real danger of violating her parole.

Fact: Shirley was well aware of that. She also knew Bell was grappling with a terrible case, the brutal and apparently unprovoked murder of a retired coal miner two nights ago, right in the man's own driveway on the west side of Acker's Gap. The town was still reeling from the shock of it, from a crime that had injected a paralyzing chill into the warm, loose-limbed languor of summer in the mountains.

Fact: Shirley didn't give a rat's ass. She didn't care what sort of extra hassle she caused for Bell, what kind of shame or embarrassment or inconvenience.

Fact: Shirley was not only selfish; she was reckless, too. Dropping Bell's name to a deputy sheriff to garner special treatment was bad enough, but when you added the risk this posed to Shirley's fledgling status as a free woman—well, the whole thing made Bell so incensed that she wrapped her hands even tighter around the steering wheel of her Ford Explorer, glad to have a way to channel her rage, a place to direct it temporarily.

She'd done everything she could do for Shirley. In the three months since her sister's return, Bell had given her a place to stay, bought her clothes, tolerated her smoking. And she'd stayed out of her hair, letting Shirley make her own decisions—and by "decisions," Bell meant "mistakes." The two words had become synonymous in her mind, when it came to Shirley.

There'd been trouble from the start. One night, Shirley fell asleep in a kitchen chair with a burning cigarette notched between two fingers, jerking awake just in time to avert disaster, and another, she came home drunk and surly, and when Bell tried to guide the weaving woman to a bed, Shirley shook off the helping hand, and the foul word that fell out of her mouth made Bell shudder in shock, as if Shirley had coughed up a toad or a spider.

Such behavior confirmed her sister's lack of judgment, of manners, of respect, of—well, maybe Sheriff Fogelsong had nailed it. "Lack of gratitude," he'd said to Bell when she confided her frustration about Shirley. "That's what's really eating at you. You expect her to be grateful. Even humble. For sticking by her, for waiting, for taking her in. Plus—ever held a cork underwater? And then let it go? Shoots up like a geyser. Way the hell up in the air."

The sheriff, Bell quickly decided, had a point. "Ever get tired," she had countered, "of being right all the damned time?"

His reply: "Oh, I'm wrong on purpose every now and again, just to keep things interesting."

The recollection of that encounter reminded Bell of how much she missed him—and not just because she was staring straight in the face of an unsolved homicide that had left the town edgy and restive. Fogelsong had taken a month's leave of absence. He was scheduled to return in the coming week, at which point Pam Harrison would hand back over the top spot and resume her job as chief deputy—but still. Even a short spell without him was too long for Bell. Nick Fogelsong knew her better than anyone else; he understood her right down to the ground, and she appreciated his perspective. Needed it, more to the point.

Shirley, he'd gently remind Bell when her irritation got in the way of sound thinking, was a forty-six-year-old woman who'd never had a chance to be young. She'd been in prison for three decades, and in that bleak and tightly regulated place, every step was monitored, every spontaneous impulse blocked.

So Bell had cut her some slack. Backed off. Held her tongue.

But tonight an entirely new threshold had been crossed. This was the first time Shirley had stayed away for several days running. Or used Bell's name in a scrape with the law. This was disturbingly fresh territory. And it came at a time when Bell ought to be focusing on public safety in general, not a misbehaving sister in particular. If Shirley was caught up in a sweep at Tommy's—the bar's proprietor, Tommy LeSeur, was himself a convicted felon, having served four and a half years on a narcotics charge—her parole could be revoked.

"Hey, pretty lady."

At the same moment Bell heard the words, she smelled the hot oniony stink of the man who had suddenly thrust his face in the Explorer's open window. He'd taken her by surprise, so intent was she on her thoughts as she stared at the run-down bar. But she wasn't frightened. She was pissed off. The man had a fat face, swollen to the point of resembling an allergic reaction. Bristles of beard stuck out from his round cheeks and from the undulating rolls of blubber that propped up his tiny chin. Booze, sweat, and the heavy fug of a recent bout of vomiting invaded her space.

Before Bell could react, he was talking again. He'd hooked his hands across the bottom of the window and hung on as if it were an upper-story sill.

"Lookin' for somethun?" he slurred. "Or some*body*? Wanna party?" A wicked leer seized his mouth, making both ends of it pointy. A pearl of sweat—or maybe another liquid, although who'd really want a positive ID?—was poised on the bottom rim of a nostril. His eyes were bleary. "How 'bout it, baby?"

First Bell wanted to laugh—*Oh, yeah, here I come, you're freakin' irresistible, mister*—and then the anger roared back, this time mixed with revulsion.

"Get the hell away from me," she said. Low voice. Words measured and calm, but laced with threat. Only a fool would miss her meaning.

"C'mon, baby. Don't be doin' me like that," the intruder said. His oily wheedle—delivered on the back of a gust of smelly breath—was enough to make Bell's stomach turn.

With a gesture so quick that it caught him in the middle of a wink, she flung open the car door. Knocked back, he teetered for a tenth of a second and then landed flat on his ample butt.

Behind him, starkly visible in the glare of the crude spotlight rigged to a corner of the building, was a stumpy ring of three men— his buddies, Bell assumed, because these types always traveled in packs. The men pointed at Fat Ass and stomped their work boots and laughed, a hard-edged, mirthless laughter that sounded like another variety of assault. They wore baseball caps and long-sleeved plaid flannel shirts with the cuffs buttoned and the shirttails flapping out behind them, even though this was the middle of summer; such, Bell knew, was the year-round uniform of the good ole boys, the kind you could find lining the back roads around here like lint on a comb.

"Bitch!" Fat Ass yelled at her. He'd yet to rise from his seat on the ground, thwarted by, in equal measures, obesity and drunkenness. "Goddamned bitch."

That only made his friends laugh harder. "Looks like she up and tole you what she thinksa you," one of them opined, nudging Fat Ass with the toe of his boot, as if his buddy were a clump of dirt that needed relocating. The others re-upped their laughter, hooting like fools, slapping at their knees when they weren't using their fingers to point at Fat Ass. A gray scab of moon regarded the scene indifferently from above.

Bell pondered her next move. Her mission was simple: Go in the bar, find Shirley, and somehow persuade her to come home. She wasn't looking for a fight. If these creeps kept it up, though, and interfered with her, she would handle it. Fat Ass didn't know what trouble was until he'd tangled with the likes of her. Her seventeen-year-old daughter, Carla—currently living with Bell's ex-husband, Sam, but due back in Acker's Gap for summer vacation in a week—had put it best: "Mom," Carla said, "when you get mad, I think I'd sorta rather deal with the guy in the *Texas Chain Saw Massacre* movies, you know?"

The bar's double doors flapped open. During the few seconds that the interior of the establishment was exposed—the hot wild noise, the undulating red lights framed by the solid black night—it looked, to Bell's eye, like a peephole into hell.

A female deputy sheriff—short, hatless, and heavyset—came striding out of Tommy's, turning this way and that to cut a path between the parked cars. Her long gray hair was funneled into a twisty braid that perched on her shoulder like a pet. Black boots chopped at

SUMMER OF THE DEAD

the gravel with each forceful step. Her gun was holstered on her wide hip, but she kept her big right hand in contact with the grip, a *Don't make me use this* set to her meaty jaw.

The three men scattered like scrap paper swept off a desktop by a sudden draft. Fat Ass, also highly motivated, flopped over on his hands and knees and crawled a short distance and then hoisted himself up, courtesy of the rusty back bumper of a Dodge Ram 1500.

As he and his buddies hustled away, the deputy nodded in approval. "Evening, ma'am," she said to Bell. "Deputy Sturm. Thought you might be arriving right about now."

"Met the welcoming committee." Bell stepped out of the Explorer and gestured toward the severe darkness that bordered the lot, a bottomless pit into which the four men had disappeared. The darkness seemed all the more menacing because of its adjacency to the garishly lit space. There was no middle ground. If you left the illuminated area, it was as if you'd fallen off the edge of the world. *No dark like summer dark,* Bell thought. *No end to it. Goes on forever.*

She shuddered. She'd had a sudden unwanted memory of the crime-scene photo still on her desk back at the courthouse: Freddie Arnett's lanky body facedown on the oil-stained concrete of his driveway, blood and brain matter shining wetly in the velvety glow of the front porch light.

"Those boys tried to get friendly with me, too." Sturm chuckled. With two fingers, she tapped the badge pinned to the left breast pocket of her gray polyester shirt. "Then they saw this."

Bell nodded. Enough with the small talk. "Where's Shirley Dolan?"

"Right where I left her—rounded up in the back of the bar with a bunch of troublemakers, waiting to see if I'm going to give 'em even more of a hassle than I already have. Maybe haul 'em in for drunk and disorderly. They've been calling me every name in the book and then some."

"What started it?"

"Don't know. I mean, Bobo Bolland's here with his band, and it seems like he brings trouble wherever he goes. Somebody calls somebody else a low-down sumbitch or a man-stealing whore or something similar, and before you know it, the whole place goes crazy." Two more cars fishtailed into the lot, one right behind the other. The drivers must have caught the glint of the badge on Deputy Sturm's broad chest—or, the more likely scenario, simply sniffed out the presence of the law after long experience with dodging same— because their hasty U-turns back onto the road were executed with a panic-fed zeal.

Sturm barely noticed. She and Bell had begun walking toward the door of Tommy's, and something else was on her mind. "Listen," Sturm said. "Before we go in, I wanted to say—well, I heard about that poor old man. Hell of a thing. Bet folks in Acker's Gap are plenty shook up."

Bell nodded. Freddie Arnett had suffered multiple blows to his head from a sledgehammer—that was the coroner's preliminary analysis, given the shape of the wounds and the fact that the probable murder weapon was lying in the grass next to the driveway—in an astonishingly vicious assault. No prints, no motive, no suspects, no leads; it was, Bell had reflected, almost as if the summer night itself had reared up and come after Arnett, as if the darkness had taken shape just long enough to grab a handy weapon and use it to crush an old man's skull, then spread itself out again in a soft black ooze.

"Makes you wonder," Sturm said.

"Yeah."

They had reached the entrance to Tommy's. Bell heard muffled thuds from the other side of the wall, along with wicked guitar licks and fuzzy throbs from a cheap amplifier and the ominous insect hum of packed bodies rubbing up against one another.

Sturm's big right hand reached for the dirty wooden handle. The upper half of one of the doors was smothered by a thumbtacked white poster that showed off the wobbly work of a black Sharpie:

TONITE! BOBO BOLLAND AND HIS ROCKIN'
BAND!!! 11 pm to ????

Bell followed her into the bar—and into the kind of frantic, sweaty bedlam that Bell had spent a good portion of her adult life trying to avoid, because it reminded her too much of her childhood, when the world was big and bad and loud and out of control, and she was the weakest, frailest thing in it. The prey.

There she was.

Shirley Dolan stood at the far end of the bar, her back to the nicked brown counter that featured what looked to be at least a century's worth of interlocking rings from wet-bottomed glasses of beer. Long gray hair frizzled down her narrow back. Bell had anticipated that it might take a few minutes to locate her sister in the raucous crowd; she'd thought her eyes might have to rove over at least a dozen or so sweat-shined faces with sloppy grins and pinprick eyeballs—but no. She picked her out right away, even though Shirley was dressed in an echo of what everybody else wore: cowboy boots, tight jeans, T-shirt, untucked flannel shirt.

Shot glass pressed to her lip, Shirley took a long soulful slug. Then she shook herself with gusto, like a dog after a deluge, as the fiery liquid pitchforked its way through her insides. She twisted her torso to thump the glass back down on the bar. It was then—with Shirley in a half-turn, licking her bottom lip—that her eyes met up with Bell's. The three-man band in the opposite corner had just commenced another number, and the blistering bass beats seemed to make the small building shimmy and throb.

Before Bell had a chance to speak, another commotion erupted.

Several chairs tipped and crashed, the top rails of their wooden backs clattering against the red concrete floor as people jumped and scattered. Three round tables were upended; glasses slid off and shattered. First one woman screamed, then two more. The band stopped playing—not gradually but abruptly, as if someone had kicked out a power cord.

Jesus, somebody muttered. *What the hell*, came from somebody else, followed by yet another opinion: *Drunk as a goddamned skunk, just like always. Leave him be, why doncha.* There was a sudden batch of ear-ripping static from the electric guitar, until the skinny, big-nosed guitar player—having brushed the strings with his sleeve—silenced it again with a hand clamped over the fret.

The crowd parted clumsily, opening up a Z-shaped lane to the source of the tumult. Sprawled facedown on the greasy floor was a wiry, black-haired man in a pale yellow flannel shirt and dirty white carpenter's pants. Sturm and Bell moved simultaneously to the spot. The deputy, reaching it first, called out sharply, "Hey, mister—you okay?" and then lowered herself to his side with the velocity of a dropped rock. Sturm's movements, Bell saw, were surprisingly nimble and efficient for a woman her size. She groped under his chin for a pulse. Nothing. With two hands, she turned him over.

An orange-handled screwdriver had been punched into the man's chest, after which the force of his fall pushed it sideways, ripping the wound wider. A dark stain fled rapidly across the front of his shirt, as ominous as a storm system filling out a digital weather map. His acne-chipped face was white, his jaw slack. Eyes open. Pupils fixed and dilated.

Sturm's big head swung up to look at Bell. There was a stunned, uncertain quality to the deputy's stare. *When you do this for a living,* Bell reminded herself, *you always think you're prepared, but you're never prepared. Never.* Bell felt a swell of nausea cresting in her belly. She fought it, clenching her jaw. And she was aware as well of a cold

sense of dread throwing a shadow over her thoughts like a cloud crossing an open field. *First the old man back in Acker's Gap. Now this.*
Jesus.

The deputy quickly recovered her composure. Still on one knee,
she unclipped the radio from her belt and thumbed it on. The bar had
grown eerily quiet—no one so much as coughed or shuffled a foot or
bumped a table—and that fact gave the few simple words of Sturm's
summons for an ambulance the chiseled mien of a haiku.

Call completed, she barked at the stunned onlookers: "Anybody
know this guy? Anybody see what happened? Anybody?"

More silence.

The deputy reached in the dead man's pocket, hunting for ID. Bell
was just about to tell her to back away to preserve the integrity of the
crime scene when Sturm pulled out a small white business card. She
scanned it, then passed it up to Bell. *Can't matter much at this point,*
Bell thought, accepting it. There had already been enough contami-
nation of the scene to piss off the state forensic folks, the ones who
would be showing up in their fancy van just as soon as the techs back
in Charleston finished their argument about whose turn it was to make
the drive over crummy roads in the tricky dark. Communities as small
as this one didn't have their own crime-scene units. They had to wait
their turn, just as Bell and the deputies had had to wait two nights ago,
when they stood, helpless and appalled, alongside Freddie Arnett's
shattered body. And they would have to wait now.

Bell scanned the black embossed letters on the card:

SAMPSON J. VOORHEES. ATTORNEY-AT-LAW. NYC.

No phone number, no fax, no e-mail address. *Strange way of doing*
business for a law firm, Bell mused. *Usually they're throwing their*
contact info at you so fast, you have to duck. Her ex-husband worked
for that kind of firm. *Hell,* she'd often thought, *given half a chance,*

he'd probably slap the company logo on the toilet seats in the men's room. She turned over the card. Along the bottom edge, another name had been hand-scrawled with a blue pen:

Odell Crabtree

Sturm was reaching up now to retrieve the card, because it was evidence. Part of the official record. Bell wanted a longer look, but complied; this was Deputy Sturm's turf, Deputy Sturm's investigation. Collier County would be calling the shots. Which was good news: Raythune County had all it could handle right now.

Still, Bell was curious. She wondered what link there could possibly be between a publicity-shy New York City lawyer and a body on the floor of Tommy's bar in the middle of West Virginia on a sweat-oiled summer night, the life in that body having recently seeped away amid a sour backwash of sloshed beer, bad jokes, loud cackles, high-hanging gray webs of cigarette smoke, and the foot-stompin', good-time tunes of Bobo Bolland and His Rockin' Band.

READ THE ENTIRE
Bell Elkins Series

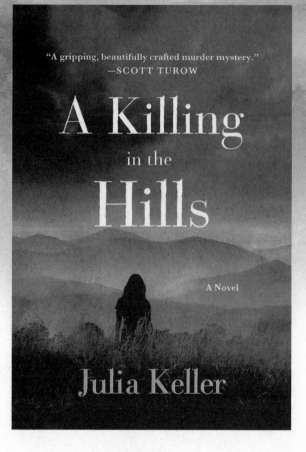

"A gripping, beautifully crafted murder mystery."
—SCOTT TUROW

A Killing
in the
Hills

A Novel

Julia Keller

Don't Miss:
A Killing in the Hills
Bitter River
Summer of the Dead